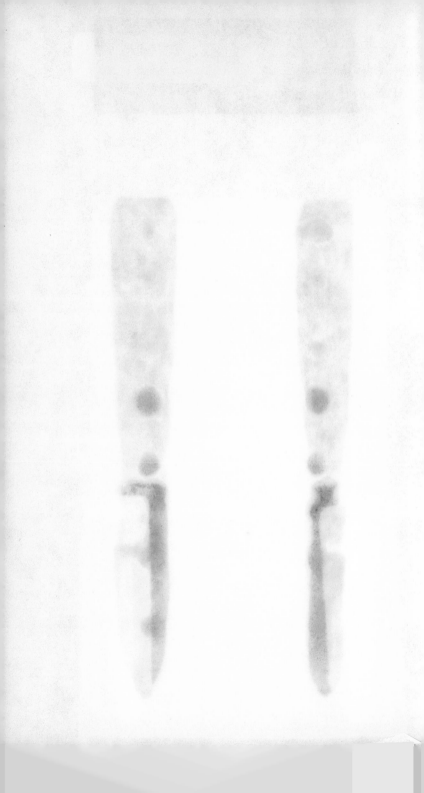

Writers of the 21st Century

ARTHUR C. CLARKE

Also available in the Writers of the 21st Century Series:

ISAAC ASIMOV

PHILIP K. DICK *(in preparation)*

RAY BRADBURY *(in preparation)*

ROBERT A. HEINLEIN

URSULA K. LE GUIN *(in preparation)*

Edited by

JOSEPH D. OLANDER

and MARTIN HARRY GREENBERG

arthur c. clarke

TAPLINGER PUBLISHING COMPANY / NEW YORK

First Edition

PUBLISHED IN THE UNITED STATES IN 1977 BY
TAPLINGER PUBLISHING COMPANY, INC. NEW YORK, NEW YORK

Published simultaneously in Canada
by BURNS & MACEACHERN, LIMITED, ONTARIO

Library of Congress Cataloging in Publication Data
Main entry under title:

Arthur C. Clarke.

(Writers of the 21st century)
Bibliography: p
Includes index.
1. Clarke, Arthur Charles, 1917–   —Criticism and
interpretation
—Addresses, essays, lectures.
I. Olander, Joseph D.   II. Greenberg, Martin Harry.   III. Series

PR6005.L36Z56   823′.9′14   76–11052
ISBN 0–8008–0402–3
ISBN 0–8008–0401–5 pbk.

Designed by MANUEL WEINSTEIN

CONTENTS

Introduction
Joseph D. Olander and Martin Harry Greenberg   7

1. Three Styles of Arthur C. Clarke: The Projector, the Wit, and the Mystic
PETER BRIGG   15

2. The Cosmic Loneliness of Arthur C. Clarke
THOMAS D. CLARESON   52

3. The Outsider from Inside: Clarke's Aliens
E. MICHAEL THRON   72

4. Of Myths and Polyominoes: Mythological Content in Clarke's Fiction
BETSY HARFST   87

5. Sons and Fathers in A.D. 2001
ROBERT PLANK   121

6. Expectation and Surprise in *Childhood's End*
ALAN B. HOWES   149

7. Contrasting Views of Man and the Evolutionary Process:
Back to Methuselah and *Childhood's End*
EUGENE TANZY   172

8. *Childhood's End:* A Median Stage of Adolescence?
DAVID N. SAMUELSON   196

9. From Man to Overmind: Arthur C. Clarke's Myth of Progress
JOHN HUNTINGTON   211

Notes   223

Selected Bibliography   237

Biographical Note   245

Contributors   247

Index   249

Introduction

Joseph D. Olander and Martin Harry Greenberg

A propagandist for space exploration . . . a brilliant "hard science fiction" extrapolator . . . a great mystic and modern myth-maker . . . a market-oriented, commercially motivated, and "slick" fiction writer. Arthur C. Clarke is one of the world's most well known science fiction writers, and these—and other—images of him are woven throughout the essays in this book, principally to develop alternative perspectives about his science fiction.

In an earlier volume of essays devoted to the science fiction of Isaac Asimov in this Series, one of the dominant images about Asimov was that of "social science fiction" writer. In this volume, one of the major images which emerges about Arthur C. Clarke is that of "hard science fiction" writer. When all is said and done, Clarke's authentic commitment seems to be to the universe and, like Asimov, to the underlying sets of laws of behavior by which the mystery inherent in it will probably be explained.

How is it, then, that he is associated with mysticism, mythology, theological speculation, and "cosmic loneliness"? Hard science fiction, if nothing else, usually needs to come to closure, in its qualities of validity and consistency, with specific explanations and scientific justifications. Yet much of Clarke's fiction pushes the mind outward and ever open. If this is accomplished by an explication of assumed or searched-for universal laws, it is understandable and consistent with science-based extrapolation.

But this is substantially different from the overall impression actually left upon most readers of Clarke's science fiction—that there is a search underway for universal ideas which transcend time, space, and cultures. If these ideas exist, the way to discover them may not be through the explication of universal laws but rather through the discovery of root metaphors and symbols. The universe may not appear, therefore, as simply a set of problems to be solved rationally but rather as a still mysterious place, to be creatively—and respectfully—explored and appreciated. In this sense, one of Clarke's familiar, if not quintessential, themes—that humanity's loneliness in the universe will be remedied by contact with other-world living beings—can be reinterpreted to mean that living things are really not separated by space but by consciousness.

This perspective implies that the human being is not *homo sapiens*—the rational being—but that the human being is *homo ludens*—the playing thing. Although *homo ludens* seems to imply a more creative, open role for the human being in the face of a universe which is imperfectly understood, Clarke's fiction, or at least much of it, seems to suggest that the universe may be playing with humanity. It is in this connection that contradictions arise between Clarke's optimism and pessimism concerning human destiny.

Clarke's optimism is not that of a scientific expert convinced of the effectiveness of his tools, confident of the knowledge upon which he stands, and certain of the existence of universal laws which, if only discovered, can further explain remaining mysteries. Instead, his optimism is that of a mystic, convinced of the inevitability of the transcendent and sure of the positive direction in which it moves. And his pessimism is not that of the scientist who has lost faith in the usefulness and efficacy of his tools; rather, it is the pessimism of one who appreciates the awesomeness of the universe and is able to anticipate the "tricks" and surprises which it may have in store for humanity. Moreover, it is not the pessimism of "I have seen the future—and it doesn't work!"; rather, it is the pessimism of "I have seen the future—and it is all too familiar, but I am not sure that humanity can stand the potential surprises!"

Just as Clarke's fiction portrays the human being in multiple perspectives, so, too, these essays provide multiple perspectives about Clarke's fiction. In addition to coming to grips with the multifaceted Clarke, the reader will be forced to think about fundamental questions which underpin any analysis of the work of a single science fiction writer: What constitutes a successful science fiction novel or short story? Is it form or substance, style or ideas? What do we expect from science fiction as literature? What does it do for us? And, finally, what is Clarke's overall contribution to answering these questions?

As a start toward answering these questions, Peter Brigg leads off with his chapter on "Three Styles of Arthur C. Clarke: The Projector, the Wit, and the Mystic." He first assesses the "hard science" dimension of Clarke's fiction as he examines three major styles which he believes characterize Clarke's corpus of fiction. Although he finds weaknesses in this style, he ascribes these to the nature of the limited purposes of the stories rather than to Clarke's ability as a writer. The second style which Brigg examines is that of the wit—the "comic mode." Although the fiction which can be classified within this style may be based upon (or may camouflage) "hard scientific ideas," these stories reveal Clarke's cynicism about human nature, which is always considered to play a *very* small role in the cosmic drama. The third style—that of the mystic— underlies Clarke's disappointment in the empirical and demonstrates a desire for exploring "the unknown." This longing reflects itself in the kind of expansive and long-ranging perspective so identified with Olaf Stapledon, to whom, according to Brigg, Clarke is indebted. There is an evolutionary growth in the ability of the human being to appreciate the wonder of the universe, and Brigg portrays Clarke's contradictory notes of pessimism and optimism in this connection. Brigg does not attempt to develop a hard and fast taxonomy of Clarke's novels and shorter fiction along the lines of the major styles he examines, but he suggests that Clarke's science fiction contains mixtures of all three styles and offers *Rendezvous with Rama* and *Imperial Earth* as the best examples.

Whereas Brigg deals with Clarke's major styles, Thomas D. Clareson attempts to outline the quintessential vision of Clarke. "The Cosmic Loneliness of Arthur C. Clarke" suggests that the content of this vision concerns the implications of the great "space adventure" for humanity. At the core of this vision is the idea that the exploration of space will liberate humankind from the imperfections and limitations of earth civilization as we now know it. Clareson indicates that Clarke's wonder about the diversity and multiplicity of life forms on earth is extrapolated to space in the hope that man's feeling of loneliness in a hostile universe would be eliminated upon first contact with extraterrestrial beings. Clarke's fiction, in short, represents our collective hopes and search for a "sentinel."

Like others before him, E. Michael Thron, in his "The Outsider from Inside: Clarke's Aliens," implies that Clarke is a propagandist for space exploration in the context of his fiction. But his essay goes a long way in the suggestion of another, equally important purpose in Clarke's fiction—to provide an appropriate stage for "the alien and surprising idea." Thron's essay examines what happens when the mundane—the extrapolated world—meets the alien as idea, which undermines the conventional idea upon which the extrapolation is originally based. Thron uses *2001: A Space Odyssey, Childhood's End,* and *Rendezvous with Rama* to illustrate points. He explains how this process of transformation from the conventional to the alien occurs and how it impacts the fiction and the reader. Suggesting that Clarke's handling of aliens forces us to deal with the consequences of a set of ideas we clearly do not understand, Thron argues for an assessment of Clarke on the basis of the ideas in his fiction, not on the basis of criteria established by "modern academic fiction."

Relying upon Mircea Eliade, Joseph Campbell, and Carl G. Jung, Betsy Harfst assesses the major mythical explanations and "personae" in *Childhood's End, 2001, Rendezvous with Rama,* and *Imperial Earth.* Her "Of Myths and Polyominoes: Mythological Content in Clarke's Fiction" posits major metaphysical questions by juxtaposing two paradigms—sophisticated technological futures and ancient mythological explanations. In a mythological context which deals with both Eastern and Western myths, Harfst focuses on the seasonal myth of eternal return and the myth of the hero in order to demonstrate how Clarke adroitly links cultural, technological, and intellectual opposites.

Specifying those aspects of *2001: A Space Odyssey* which can qualify as "literature," Robert Plank, in "Sons and Fathers in A.D. 2001," analyzes the significance of Clarke's contribution to this famous and popular film. Arguing that the masters of the slabs in the film are "father figures" and that Hal is a "son figure," Plank projects *2001* as old wine in a new bottle —a drama about and of the generations.

Arguing that *Childhood's End* is about "different kinds of evolution," Alan B. Howes, in "Expectation and Surprise in *Childhood's End,* " interprets Clarke's message as a warning that human evolution can't be "predicted, hurried, or controlled." Human evolution, one realizes after reading this essay, is quite like science fiction as a literary genre. Literary conventions set up a readers's expectations about what—and how—in an overall way things will happen in a story. Science fiction, as "formula literature," does this in an especially dramatic way. The fulfillment of these expectations leads to a satisfaction on the part of the reader. But there are also surprises in the formula—and how well the surprises are handled increases the enjoyment of the literature. Surprises in literature and surprises in life both make for an appreciation of our wondrous universe, Howes may be suggesting.

Hope, faith, and love play important roles in the analysis which Eugene Tanzy makes of *Childhood's End* and George Bernard Shaw's play *Back to Methuselah*. His essay, "Contrasting Views of Man and the Evolutionary Process: *Back to Methuselah* and *Childhood's End,*" argues that both Clarke's novel and Shaw's play are variations on the theme of evolution. After outlining four principal responses to evolutionary thought, Tanzy suggests that *Back to Methuselah* is illustrative of the attempt to supplant Darwinian theory with a nonmechanistic evolutionary theory by people who view themselves as rational and that *Childhood's End* represents those efforts which open up the physical to all kinds of possibilities. Juxtaposing Shaw's view that man is the center of the world with Clarke's—that the universe does not revolve around us but is itself "living"—increases our awareness of the significance of Clarke's themes.

David N. Samuelson's *"Childhood's End:* A Median Stage of Adolescence?" is both praise and damnation of Clarke's novel as a "classic" work of modern science fiction. He assesses the book's widespread mainstream reception as a function of the attractiveness of its "watered-down theological speculation." Samuelson is especially critical of Clarke's use of mythical explanations and theological speculation in places and in ways inappropriate to the aesthetic symmetry of the novel, attacking it as "practically plotless" and "almost characterless." Despite such chaos, however, he suggests that the novel holds together by consistency of tone and style, by the central figure of Karellen, and by a set of image-patterns. But, in one sense, Samuelson is really writing about a class of science fiction writers—"second-generation" writers who were commercially oriented to the production of science fiction for the pulp magazines of the 1920s and 1930s. Although he considers *Childhood's End* better than many of its contemporaries, Samuelson concludes that it fails to achieve "maturity" as a novel.

It is appropriate to have this perspective in mind when one reads John Huntington's "From Man to Overmind: Arthur C. Clarke's Myth of Progress," the last essay in this book. Huntington agrees with Samuelson about the slickness of the novel in satisfying a "special market." However, Huntington suggests that although the form of the novel may fail, its message may save it—and this is precisely the perspective he develops. Huntington argues that it is the shaping of the myth of progress which allows the novel to achieve status as a "special work of art." A two-stage process—rational and technological gains followed by a kind of "transcendent evolution"—Clarke's progress is achieved by means of grace, not by the natural abilities of man. This is a basic pattern, according to Huntington, which can also be observed in *2001: A Space Odyssey.*

Writers of the 21st Century

ARTHUR C. CLARKE

1. Three Styles of Arthur C. Clarke:

The Projector, the Wit, and the Mystic

PETER BRIGG

ARTHUR C. CLARKE'S extensive *corpus* of science fiction writing is an expression of his varied interests in the limits of man's knowledge as it is approached through the scientific method. Three principal types of work can be traced in his writing and although this chapter will consider them as styles of creation, their identities are very much dependent upon content. This threefold division of Clarke's work is not offered to pigeonhole his stories but to demonstrate the variety of his undertaking, to show how he meets the needs of different material, and to consider the ways in which the three approaches may be combined. I begin with descriptions of the three styles and analyses of works that exemplify them, and conclude with a study of *Rendezvous with Rama* (1973) and *Imperial Earth* (1976) to show how these mature works integrate the approaches.

The Projector: Hard Extrapolation

Clarke's best known approach is precise scientific extrapolation that depends upon detailed scientific knowledge carefully explained to the reader to communicate Clarke's fascination with the possibilities at the frontiers of scientific thinking. These stories are admired by fans of science fiction whose minds are open to the realms of possibility that can be tested in strict logical fashion by following the reasoning in a story or checking the description of a planet against astronomical data. Clarke is very much in his element in this type of story, prepared by his early contacts with *Amazing Stories, Astounding Stories,* and *Wonder Stories* and by his university training in physics, mathematics, and astronomy.

There are a number of particular difficulties in creating effective stories based upon hard scientific data and carrying that data forward through logical steps of extrapolation. The creation of a plot to illustrate a scientific concept or concepts is a vital first factor, for the mechanical necessities of the idea must be brought forward in exciting fashion. Once the plot has been arrived at, the author must find satisfactory ways of inserting the scientific explanations, avoiding extensive direct lectures and integrating the development of the physical logic without revealing the ending in advance. Solutions to this problem include the "thinking narrator" who is working his way through some desperate or puzzling situation; the narrator who is relating events that have already taken place and explaining them to an audience in the story or directly to the reader; or a structure where the problem is posed and some scientific data presented before a surprising action occurs that is then explained in retrospect as an extension of the original scientific premises.

Once the structure has been selected, a tone must be found for the story that will allow the presentation of a good deal of information and reasoning. There may be room for some humor, but the stories must not pivot upon tricks or jokes that would obscure the elegance of their scientific demonstrations. Nor can there be much emotional complication that would expand their length and obscure their logic. They tend to be dry, clean, and practical, with characters who serve as explainer and listener, the explainer presenting the scientific reasoning at the level of the general reader and the listener asking questions the reader would like to ask. Characters' emotional involvements are on the uncomplicated level of characters in melodrama, represent emotions of hate or love, or states of being such as good or evil, in order to allow the swift working out of plot action. These characters lack subtlety, but this is a positive merit in stories tightly packed with information. Indeed, it is characteristic that the dialogue be factual and precise, with only a smattering of irony and wry wit. In these stories, Clarke's characters are either acting or explaining their actions in clear, semi-technical language. Clarke himself defended this type of story in the preface to *Reach for Tomorrow:*

> It seems only right to warn the reader that 'Jupiter Five', 'Technical Error' and 'The Fires Within' are all pure science fiction. In each case some unfamiliar (but I hope plausible and comprehensible) scientific fact is the basis of the story action, and human interest is secondary. Some critics maintain that this is always a Bad Thing; I believe this is too sweeping a generalization. In his

perceptive preface to A.D. 2500, for example, Mr. Angus Wilson remarks: 'Science fiction which ends as technical information dressed with a little fantasy or plot can never be any good.' But any good for what? If it is done properly, without the information being too obtrusive or redolent of the textbook, it can still have at least the entertainment value of a good puzzle. It may not be art, but it can be enjoyable and intriguing.[1]

Typical of the "one idea" plots in the hard extrapolation stories is that of "The Wall of Darkness" (1949) in which Clarke explicates a single scientific projection in a dramatic context. That context is a medieval world of flying buttresses, feudalism, and "certain animals it is convenient to call horses"; whose low technological level causes the premise of the story, a universe with a one-sided surface, to stand out in sharp relief. Clarke then wrestles with the actual problem of story line and tells about a man who seeks to conquer the amazing, high, indestructable wall built by a previous civilization to prevent men from discovering that their universe is a three-dimensional extension of the two-dimensional geometrical construct of the Möbius Strip. It is characteristic of stories of this type that they are "closed," with the action completed and the puzzle completely solved. This reflects Clarke's positive thinking, ending a project or experiment in the manner of the physical scientist.

Another tale illustrating the exposition of a single idea is "Technical Error" (1950) in which a research scientist is accidentally inverted when caught in the tremendously powerful field of an experimental generating station. The left-to-right inversion causes him to starve because his body cannot absorb certain molecules of regular foods that have distinctive left and right properties. To save his life, an attempt is made to reinvert him but he vanishes. Dr. Hughes, who planned the change, wakens in the night with the horrible realization that the vanished man has been displaced in time as well as being "revolved" through a fourth-dimensional axis. Before he can have the giant turbine lifted from its base, the researcher materializes in the same space as its pivot point, causing the whole station to explode. Once again Clarke dramatically illustrates complex physical concepts, in this case multiple dimensions and the nature of stereo-isomers of food. Again there is a closed plot in which the explosion writes finis to the problem, wholly confirming Dr. Hughes' speculation.

Within these carefully chosen, clear, straightforward plots Clarke holds character development to an absolute minimum, employing melodramatic types to focus attention on the ideas. A number of the short stories have heroes whose principal emotion is sheer fear for their lives that can only be relieved by the scientific point upon which the story is premised. In "Maelstrom II" (1962) Cliff Leyland finds himself with insufficient velocity to escape the moon and his unlikely salvation lies in abandoning spaceship with a strong leap that makes it possible for him to pass perigee above the moon's surface, aided by the hole blown in the Soviet Range by the impact of his derelict ship. Before the solution, however, there are some soggy moments as Clarke describes the emotional states of the characters. Cliff's wife, "a spaceman's wife, always alert for disaster," reacts according to the precepts of melodrama: "She took it well, as he had known that she would. He felt pride as well as love when her answer came back from the dark side of Earth," while Cliff himself retains a cool head:

> Whatever happens to the individual, life goes on; and to modern man life involves mortgages and installments due, insurance policies and joint bank accounts. Almost impersonally, as if they concerned someone else—which would soon be true enough—Cliff began to talk about these things. There was a time for the heart and a time for the brain. The heart would have its final say three hours from now, when he began his last approach to the surface of the Moon.

Then he relaxes in private:

> Quite unexpectedly, without desire or volition, tears sprang from his eyes, and suddenly he was weeping like a child.
> He wept for his family, and for himself. He wept for the future that might have been, and the hopes that would soon be incandescent vapor, drifting between the stars. And he wept because there was nothing else to do.

Cliff's emotions are under strict control, switched on and off to provide a human aspect for the clever solution to a physics problem.[2]

"Summertime on Icarus" (1960) is another disaster story. Colin Sherrard is nearly roasted alive on the asteroid Icarus until his friends effect a rescue. Sherrard is even more practical in the face of death than Cliff Leyland until moments before he is to fry, when Clarke has him break up spectacularly at the failure of an Emergency Release to give him a quick death:

> There was no easy way out for him, no merciful death as the air gushed from his lungs. It was then, as the true terror of his situation struck home to him, that his nerve finally broke and he began to scream like a trapped animal.

There is nothing unusual or subtle about this reaction, and one recognizes in it Clarke's concentration on the story at the expense of psychological complexity. On the other hand, it makes for effective storytelling and Clarke mortices it tightly into the scientific aspect of the tale for Sherrard is located by his colleagues when his screams leak through the damaged radio antennae of his pod.[3]

One of Clarke's most striking hard extrapolations is "A Meeting with Medusa" (1962), and here the intense concentration on Howard Falcon, Commander of the dirigible *Queen Elizabeth IV* and later of the Jupiter probe, *Kon-Tiki*, could have provided a detailed characterization. But Clarke is concentrating upon the creations of technology and speculating on the possible life forms of Jupiter. Falcon is nearly killed when the *Queen* crashes on a test flight, and as the story unfolds we discover that he is a cyborg, human intelligence amalgamated with machinery, that makes him the only "man" capable of withstanding the challenge of Jupiter. But Clarke's portrait of him is a simple collection of longings and memories of pain. Falcon must go to Jupiter because of the challenge. He is somewhat disdainful of ordinary mortals. His personality is resolved in a cavalier sweep at the close of the story:

> Howard Falcon, who had once been a man and could still pass for one over a voice circuit, felt a calm sense of achievement—and, for the first time in years, something like peace of mind. Since his return from Jupiter, the nightmares had ceased. He had found his role at last.

But the treatment here is perfunctory, and pales beside the imaginative skill Clarke has employed in visualizing the descent of the *Kon-Tiki* into the upper atmosphere of Jupiter. One can almost read Clarke's reasoning: "Character must have reason for going to Jupiter; it must be something he can do no one else can; pilot with special body produced as a result of airship accident (chance to bring in echo of my fascination with *Titanic* by naming sequence 'A Day to Remember'); psychological drive to prove new self in cyborg body." The starting point is the events of the story, the end point is character and motivation. This approach is the reverse of modern literary custom, but it is admirably suited to the hard extrapolations in which it is employed.[4]

The concrete projections in this type of story are set forth in matter-of-fact narrative tone, and Clarke writes briskly in stories of this type, producing either very short stories or novels covering enormous amounts of material very quickly. "The Secret" (1963) tells of a journalist's discovery that medical research in the Moon settlement has found man will have a vastly increased life expectancy in conditions of lower gravity. Clarke sets his story, creates the mystery of a secret discovery, and stages his revelation in five pages consisting of a retrospective scene, ("Henry Cooper had been on the Moon for almost two weeks before he discovered that something was wrong"), a scene between the police chief and the journalist, and the scene in which they make the discovery. The second and third scenes have a link that speaks for the brevity of the story telling:

> The call came two weeks later, in the middle of the night—the real lunar night. By Plato City time, it was Sunday morning.
> "Henry? Chandra here. Can you meet me in half an hour at air lock five? Good—I'll see you."
> This was it, Cooper knew. Air lock five meant that they were going outside the dome. Chandra had found something.[5]

In *Earthlight* (1955) Clarke's central character, Bertram Sadler, is sent to the Moon observatory to trace a security leak as Earth prepares to defend herself from the colonial empire of her planets. Even in this novel, which has a split plot line leading to the actual battle, the discovery of the spy and the observation of a supernova, Clarke sets about telling the story rapidly. In the first two short chapters he has introduced the war theme and explained its causes, described life on the Moon and introduced Sadler in his guise as counterspy. The story builds to a spectacular description of the actual combat from multiple viewpoints. People literally *move* quickly in this type of Clarke story, being presented in different locations as they seek information, or explore natural and man-made wonders. Searching for the security leak, Sadler investigates all corners of the Lunar Observatory and Central City, the Moon's center of civilization. Meanwhile other characters tour the Lunar landscape, investigate the secret project near the observatory, and move through the warrens of the observatory. Clarke also takes the reader on imaginative flights to the outer planets and into space, and all of this physical movement is tightly linked to the action.

Verbal action moves as quickly as physical action in this type of factual story. The nature of the secret base on the Moon emerges in this terse exchange:

> "A *beam of light?*" he gasped. "Why, that's impossible. It wouldn't be visible in the vacuum here."
> "Exactly," said Wagnall, obviously enjoying the other's mystification. "You can only see a light beam when it passes through something. And this was

really brilliant—almost dazzling. The phrase Williams used was 'it looked like a solid bar." Do you know what *I* think that place is. . . . I think it's some kind of fortress. Oh, I know it sounds fantastic, but when you think about it you'll see it's the only explanation that fits all the facts."[6]

Dialogue is effectively used to explain events such as Sadler's decision to take a look at Central City:

"Transport Section here. I'm closing the list for tomorrow. There are still a couple of seats left—you want to come along?"

"If there's room," Sadler replied. "I don't want any more-deserving causes to suffer."

"O.K.—you're down," said the voice briskly, and clicked off.[7]

Clarke usually frames segments of dialogue so that the reader knows their importance and the feelings of the speakers. This makes for a quick, methodical dialogue without verbal frills or subtleties. The latter part of "A Meeting with Medusa" is largely constructed in this fashion, with the descriptions of Howard Falcon's voyage into the atmosphere of Jupiter being briefly interrupted by his conversations with mission control. After Clarke has described the conflict between the Jupiter beasts ending in a burst of light, the explanation is encapsulated in dialogue:

"Beautiful!" said Dr. Brenner, after a moment of stunned silence. "It's developed electric defences, like some of our eels and rays. But that must have been about a million volts! Can you see any organs that might produce the discharge? Anything looking like electrodes?"

In dialogue as in plot, characterization, and narrative tone, Clarke is moving quickly and efficiently to build the bones upon which the real flesh of the hard extrapolation can rest: the scientific explanation of the story and the vivid and haunting descriptions of strange futures and places.

The stratagems used to explain the scientific content of these stories involve variations in narrative voice. Clarke has tried a variety of methods, seeking to combine narrative ease with a clear statement of scientific premise. One direct form has a narrator who reasons out the story as it progresses, mixing narrative with explanation. "The Star" (1955) has as its first-person narrator a Jesuit astronomer to whom Clarke gives the task of explaining a supernova:

When the star had exploded, its outer layers had been driven upwards with such speed that they had escaped completely from its gravitational field. Now they formed a hollow shell large enough to engulf a thousand solar systems, and at its center burned the tiny, fantastic object which the star had now become—a white dwarf, smaller than the Earth, yet weighing a million times as much.

He later discovers to his horror that the high civilization destroyed by the star was sacrificed so the star might shine over Bethlehem.[8] The complex creation of a death ray is detailed in "Let There Be Light," when Harry Purvis explains an astronomer's plan to murder his cheating wife. The cleverness of the device employed, an arc lamp focused by a telescope mirror into the eyes of the driver of a car rounding a cliff, reminds us that the pattern of the short hard science story owes much to detective fiction. Harry's narration of the motivation and preparation for the deed are followed by a quick revelation of the elegant solution:

> His timing was perfect; the instant the car came round the curve and the headlights shone on him, he closed the arc.
>
> Meeting another car at night can be unpleasant enough even when you are prepared for it and are driving on a straight road. But if you are rounding a hairpin bend, and *know* that there is no other car coming, yet suddenly find yourself staring directly into a beam fifty times as powerful as any headlight —well, the results are more than unpleasant.

This tight mixture of narrative and explanation is most effective. It is modeled not only on detective fiction, with its sudden assembly of information into a complete picture, but on the scientific experiment, where an event is viewed and then explained in retrospect.[9]

The brief tales of the "Venture to the Moon" (1956) series are perfect examples of the short, practical stories of this type. Their narrator, ostensibly the captain of the British ship in the combined expedition, poses the problems and then reveals their clever solutions. In "Green Fingers" a Russian botanist is mysteriously killed by the projectile seed of a plant he had designed for lunar survival. Clarke takes a few pages to set the situation, and the denouement is a model of the efficient economy with which words can support action in these short scientific mysteries:

> "If Surov designed this plant for lunar conditions, how would he arrange for it to propagate itself? The seeds would have to be scattered over a very wide area in the hope of finding a few suitable places to grow. There are no birds or animals here to carry them, in the way that happens on Earth. I can only think of one solution—and some of our terrestrial plants have already used it."
>
> He was interrupted by my yell. Something had hit with a resounding clang against the metal waistband of my suit.[10]

The dominant way of presenting this type of story has always been the team of questioning listener and scientifically competent explainer. In its early form this type of narrative began with "Tell me, Professor" but of course Clarke works sophisticated variations on this. The reader is put at ease when the question he wants to ask is asked by the "straight man" and answered in terms of the events of the narrative. This works very well in "The Fires Within" (1949). After Professor Hancock has explained to the observer, a referee for a granting agency, how he is using sonar to penetrate to the earth's core, he demonstrates the machine, reveals the discovery of a subterranean civilization, and offers his explanation:

> "But normal matter is still almost empty space. Suppose that there is life down there—not organic life, of course, but life based on partially condensed matter, matter in which the electron shells are few or altogether missing. Do you see what I mean? To such creatures, even the rock fifteen miles down would offer no more resistance than water—and we and all our world would be as tenuous as ghosts."
> "Then that thing we can see—"
> "Is a city, or its equivalent."

This very practical form of exposition is extremely spare, for the characters are mouthpieces from a familiar mold.[11]

Another easy and natural format for the hard extrapolations is the omniscient narrator who can tell the story and explain the scientific events at the same time. In "Second Dawn" (1951) Clarke directly presents a detailed description of an alien race whose entire development has varied from the human because they are hooved:

> Both the Atheleni and their cousins, the Mithraneans, possessed mental powers that had enabled them to develop a very advanced mathematics and philosophy: but over the physical world they had no control at all. Houses, tools, clothes—indeed, artifacts of any kind—were utterly unknown to them.

An omniscient narrator can point the reader towards the idea behind the extrapolation. In "Second Dawn" the creatures collaborate with a small tentacled animal and the combination leads to sudden enormous strides in technology. Clarke chooses to spell out the results carefully to emphasize the full import of the change. At each stage in the partnership's progression to tool makers and users he points out the implications:

> This primitive raft, he knew, was merely a beginning. It must be tested upon the river, then along the shores of the ocean. The work would take years, and

he was never likely to see the first voyagers returning from those fabulous lands whose existence was still no more than a guess. But what had been begun, others would finish.

At the conclusion of the story they have discovered a radioactive rock, and Clarke makes clear the destiny of their rapidly developing technology:

> In the darkness, the faint glow of dying atoms burned unwavering in the rock. It would still be burning there, scarcely dimmed, when Jeryl and Eris had been dust for centuries. It would be only a little fainter when the civilization they were building had at last unlocked its secrets.[12]

On several occasions Clarke has gone beyond the omniscient narrator to speak as Arthur C. Clarke. This applies to the comic stories of *Tales from the 'White Hart'* but he stays very much in the background in these, making Harry Purvis the storyteller. However, in "I Remember Babylon" (1960) Clarke himself tells of an encounter in Ceylon with a fanatical American communist who describes his intention to combine Clarke's idea of a fixed communications satellite with Kinsey's research to produce a pornographic propaganda television network for the Chinese. The story is strikingly solid and realistic, as Clarke listens to the plan and foresees its implications for a somewhat decadent America:

> "The Avenue [Madison] thinks it knows all about Hidden Persuasion—believe me, it doesn't. The world's best *practical* psychologists are in the East these days. Remember Korea, and brainwashing? We've learned a lot since then. There's no need for violence any more; people enjoy being brainwashed, if you set about it the right way."
> "And you," I said, "are going to brainwash the United States. Quite an order."[13]

In many ways this story is representative of Clarke's direct approach to hard science materials, for he weaves together a number of known and practical scientific propositions in a brisk, efficient way. As in "Venture to the Moon" and "The Other Side of the Sky" sequences, he is examining the potentials of immediate science. The hard science stories depend for their excitement upon the efficiency with which precise scientific reasoning can be embodied and explained in narrative format and Clarke uses the full variety of means at his disposal.

The uncomplicated narratives of these stories are punctuated by some of the most positive "purple passages" in all of science fiction. Arthur Clarke's true sense of wonder is most vividly expressed in lyrical descriptions of the cosmos and man's present or future achievements. In story after story he draws from an imagination carefully tempered by scientific knowledge to create sweeping physical descriptions of the marvels of nature and of man. The descriptions of Saturn in "Saturn Rising" (1961), the pulsing coded hues of the squid in "The Shining Ones" (1962), the solar sailboats in "Sunjammer" (1965), the mighty city of Diaspar and the Seven Suns in *The City and the Stars* (1956), the image of Omega in "The Possessed" (1952) and the images of the mighty being in "Out of the Sun" (1958) are all unforgettable moments in Clarke's writing. Typical of these passages is the description of the moon landscape in the first chapter of *Earthlight.*

> And then Sadler almost cried out aloud, for the cliff on the right came to a sudden end as if a monstrous chisel had sliced it off the surface of the Moon. It no longer barred his view; he could see clear round to the north. . . . There, marching across the sky in flaming glory, were the peaks of the Apennines, incandescent in the last rays of the hidden sun. The abrupt explosion of light left Sadler almost blinded; he shielded his eyes from the glare, and waited until he could safely face it again. When he looked once more the transformation was complete. The stars, which until a moment ago had filled the sky, had vanished. His contracted pupils could no longer see them: even the glowing Earth now seemed no more than a feeble patch of greenish luminosity. The glare from the sunlit mountains, still a hundred kilometers away, had eclipsed all other sources of light.
>
> The peaks floated in the sky, fantastic pyramids of flame. They seemed to have no more connection with the ground beneath them than do the clouds that gather above a sunset on Earth. The line of shadow was so sharp, the lower slopes of the mountains so lost in utter darkness, that only the burning summits had any real existence.

The solid basis of this picture; the rugged lunar landscape, the special characteristics of the short horizon that make possible "catching up to the sun," and the particular brilliance of sunlight on an airless world are integrated with the character's emotional perception of the scene. The momentary blinding of the observer reveals to the reader the intensity of the light. The peaks, "pyramids of flame," and the sharpness of the shadow line are all concrete qualities, creating a real picture with a human perspective. There is a sense of awe in this prophecy of what man will someday view.[14]

The Deep Range (1968), Clarke's energetic and visionary novel about the undersea world, builds up a cumulative picture of the whales and the ocean deeps. At a key moment in the book Walter Franklin is taken to see the whales for the first time and Clarke communicates the grandeur of the beasts and man's amazement at it:

> As he watched, a shape so strange that it was hard to relate it to any of the films and pictures he had seen emerged from the waves with breath-taking slowness, and hung poised for a moment completely out of the water. As a ballet dancer seems at the climax of his leap to defy gravity, so for an instant the whale appeared to hang upon the horizon. Then, with that same unhurried grace, it tumbled back into the sea, and seconds later the crash of the impact came echoing over the waves.
>
> The sheer slowness of that huge leap gave it a dreamlike quality, as if the sense of time had been distorted. Nothing else conveyed so clearly to Franklin the immense size of the beasts that now surrounded him like moving islands.

The novel constantly stresses the sheer scale of the undersea world, jocularly picturing a mother whale as "fifty tons of mother love" or describing the whales' eating as "thousands of half-ton nibbles."[15]

In "The Shining Ones" (1962) squid were the subject of another Clarke description that pulsates with the same energy as the beasts themselves:

> In my travels I have seen most of the animals of this world, but none to match the luminous apparitions floating before me now. The colored lights that pulsed and danced along their bodies made them seem clothed with jewels, never the same for two seconds at a time. There were patches that glowed a brilliant blue, like flickering mercury arcs, then changed almost instantly to burning neon red. The tentacles seemed strings of luminous beads, trailing through the water—or the lamps along a super-highway, when you look down upon it from the air at night. Barely visible against this background glow were the enormous eyes, uncannily human and intelligent, each surrounded by a diadem of shining pearls.

The images in this passage are fascinatingly concrete. It is a scientist's description that includes "mercury arcs," "neon red," and the "lamps along a super-highway," but it sums to a vivid and emotionally effective picture.[16]

When Clarke moves from the ocean depths to Jupiter in "A Meeting with Medusa" (1962) he envisions on an immense scale scenes where only immensity could survive. The medusa, as he names one of the creatures on the planet, is described by the biologist watching Falcon's transmissions in terms which challenge the reader's imagination:

> ... this thing is about a hundred thousand times as large as the biggest whale? And even if it's only a gasbag, it must still weigh a million tons! I can't even

guess at its metabolism. It must generate megawatts of heat to maintain its buoyancy.

In his stories which are projections of hard science, whether presently proven or speculation based upon the limits of our knowledge Clarke works sharply and clearly, stating the bases of his speculations, explaining, reasoning and describing with energy. If there are weaknesses in this "first style of Clarke" they are inherent in the limited aims of such stories. This leads to mechanical plotting, a generally factual narration, and a lack of depth in characterization, but these traits reflect the style of the pulp magazines in which these stories were originally published, and the need to get on with the real excitement of the universe and man's ability to conquer it by bringing reason to bear in understanding its wonders. If these are weaknesses they are overridden by the skill with which the stories make scientific processes and man's observation of the cosmos an exciting adventure.

The Wit: Comic Twists, Situations, and Characters

A second style of Clarke's work is the comic mode, stories that may contain and even conceal hard scientific ideas. Comedy in science fiction is best when rooted in the plot, executing an idea based on a quirk in scientific knowledge or illustrating a tiny fantasy suggested by some scientific fact. It works best in the short story where the idea does not have to be sustained, and it may work even better as an extended joke. As befits comic creations, the characters in these stories and anecdotes are often stereotypes of professions such as scientist, bureaucrat, militarist, or alien. Many of the stories have twist endings and Clarke takes particular pleasure in playing the conjurer who prepares a surprise and springs it upon the unsuspecting reader. Clarke's comic stories are colored by the British tone of his humor, featuring understatement, irony, and wit. This comedy is delicate and when these stories work they are fine, but they can also be dismal, flat failures if they do not hit their comic mark.

The plots of the extrapolations are "closed" in that they prove a point or illustrate a concept. The plots of comic writing are "closed" because they finish a joke or resolve the comic situation they have created. As comedy depends upon surprise there are often sudden reversals or changes of perspective at the finish. The suddenness is comic and may also be thought-provoking as in "History Lesson" (1949). This story carefully prepares the reader for the moment when Venusian amphibians will recover knowledge of human civilization by screening a film preserved through an ice age that destroyed mankind. The film appears to present man from the mildly humorous and distorted viewpoint of the alien's scientific objectivity.

> The creature possessed two eyes, set rather close together, but the other facial adornments were a little obscure. There was a large orifice in the lower portion of the head that was continually opening and closing. Possibly it had something to do with the creature's breathing.

It shows the bipeds feverishly in combat with others, driving four-wheeled vehicles, and performing other activities. Clarke suddenly says that all of the effort to interpret these actions will be in vain because: "Millions of times in the ages to come those last few words would flash across the screen, and none could ever guess their meaning: A Walt Disney Production." This twist makes "History Lesson" a comic story and gets across Clarke's more serious point, that civilization is tenuous. It is a wry humor that strikes the reader when he realizes that the frantic activity he assumed portrayed human behavior in the film ironically reflects how much Mickey Mouse and his fellow cartoon animals have in common with man.[17]

Other Clarke stories close with equal finality upon a sudden twist. The galactic scout in "Cosmic Cassanova" (1958) is taken aback when the beautiful girl he has discovered living on the small distant planet and courted by radio and television is four times his size. Hercules Keating, the victim in "The Reluctant Orchid" (1956), plots to murder his overwhelming Aunt Henrietta. However, his immense carnivorous orchid ruins the plan:

> Then the dangling tentacles flashed into action—but not in the way that Hercules had expected. The plant clutched them tightly, protectively, *around itself*—and at the same time it gave a high-pitched scream of pure terror.[18]

In the joke-length stories the closing is sharper and more visible. In "Reunion" (1963) humans return to earth to save the population from a horrible mutation: "If any of you are still white, we can cure you." In "Watch This Space" (1956) a lunar sodium flare experiment is secretly passed through a stencil of the name Coca Cola, thus creating one of the largest and best observed advertisements of all time. "The Longest Science Fiction Story Ever Told" (1965) puts the concept of infinite regress into the form of a one-page story. "Neutron Tide" (1970) leads up to the pun that the only piece of wreckage left from a United States space cruiser that encountered a neutron star was "a star-mangled spanner." All jokes lead to a punch line that leaves them logically and esthetically complete. They are plotted towards their own end in a closed pattern.

"The Food of the Gods" (1961) is typical. It begins at a Senate Investigating Committee hearing where a mystery is gradually unraveled. Clarke posits a distant future where men eat only foods constituted from component elements and abhor the thought of eating animal flesh. A company has produced an exceptionally successful new flavor of food. The witness, employed by a competing firm, climaxes his explanation of the remarkable success by spelling for the Committee a word that has gone out of use, C-A-N-N-I-B-A-L, and this is the last word of the story. Clarke has slammed home a point, that human consumption of meat is virtual cannibalism, by moving humorously through the sequence from eating wholly synthetic foods, to eating vegetables, to eating meats to eating Ambrosia Plus, the trade name for that peculiar and intuitively familiar taste. The impact of the story turns on its final word to focus the comedy and the moral.

The efficient plots of the comic stories serve to do several things. As with the hard science stories, they may expound a scientific concept, but they add a wry and comic angle. They may parody scientific logic and solutions. Some of the stories are logically impossible, and Clarke will often admit this and go on to tell them with humor and such a veneer of logic that the reader will be inclined to distrust the disclaimer. *Tales From the 'White Hart'* contains stories that serve as examples of both approaches. In "Patent Pending" (1954) Clarke combines our existing ability to record brainwaves on an encephalograph with the possibility of replaying sensual experience recordings made by experts (gourmets and sexual acrobats for the sake of the comic aspects). With a nod to Huxley's "feelies" Clarke proceeds to set the story in France and plot it around Georges' development of the device and the fatal result when he neglects his mistress for the work of professionals. In "Big Game Hunt" a giant squid is brought to heel through electric control but takes revenge when a fuse blows in the apparatus. In "The Ultimate Melody" a professor devises a tune electronically whose perfection drives him into a catatonic trance. In each of these tales Clarke is extending perfectly reasonable scientific data to a comic and illogical conclusion, hiding the technical difficulties beneath a layer of comic prose.

The employment of science in the comic tales is illustrated in "Hide and Seek" (1949) when a spy lands on Phobos, the tiny moon of Mars, and evades the might of a fast cruiser for twelve hours by taking advantage of the physics of his situation. He moves rapidly over the surface of the satellite because of the low gravity while above him the cruiser is much less maneuverable because of its moment of inertia. Phobos has a twenty-kilometer diameter, too large for a search party on foot to go over the rugged surface in twelve hours. The television sensor missiles cannot pick him out against the dark surface of the moon. He finds that he can direction-find the cruiser because she is radio-controlling the missiles' search pattern. These facts combine with the growing frustration of the commander of the cruiser and the dry, witty deductions made by the spy to create a highly amusing situation in which the flea conquers the elephant. Clarke employs physics and astronomy with factual care to create this story.

The second approach to science in the comic stories employs pseudoscience and pseudomethodology upon which truly fantastic comic plots can be constructed. The mighty gaps between scientific reality and the events of these tales are actually sources of humor. In "Time's Arrow" (1952) Professor Fowler is launched backwards in time so the dinosaur tracks he and his assistants have been excavating end at the point where the dinosaur catches up to the Professor's jeep. This absurd spatialization of time depends upon the assumption that the past exists in some form so that the Professor can be sent back to it. Clarke covers this anomaly by creating a mystery around the scientists devising the time machine and by comic banter between the research assistants and the Professor. In "Silence Please" (1954) Clarke combines the fact that sound waves can be set up to cancel one another, thus producing silence, with the law of conservation of energy to arrive at the absurd conclusion that a machine which created silence in this way would explode because the energy of sound would be concentrated in its circuits. It all seems so logical when Harry Purvis tells it, but of course sound waves cannot be stored in any electrical circuit because the circuit deals in electricity rather than sounds. In these stories and in many others such as "The Man Who Ploughed the Sea" (1956), "The Reluctant Orchid" (1956), "Moving Spirit" (1957) and, preeminently in "What Goes Up" (1955), where he actually challenges the reader to discover six errors in scientific logic, Clarke imitates scientific reasoning and introduces random fragments of scientific knowledge to fabricate hilarious fantasies.

"What Goes Up" (1955) is one of the most outrageous examples of the comic misuse of science. A reactor in Australia goes critical in a unique way and creates an antigravity field. In his efforts to find out what has happened, a scientist has to be forced into the field, employing energy equivalent to breaking out of the earth's gravitational field. When he slips off his transport cage he receives energy equal to a fall from outer space and is launched as a human meteor across the Australian desert. Clarke states in the story that there are at least six major errors in the reasoning here, and the confusions between mass, weight, and energy and velocity are covered by the speed of the narrative. One could begin to tap the flaws at any point, but it is sufficient to point out that an antigravity field would not sustain stable atomic structures, let alone contain all of the paraphernalia of an atomic pile or welcome the arrival of a physicist from the outside. Moreover, no physical law at present covers the existence of mass without gravitational energy, and the physicist in the story would have been crushed going towards the reactor even before he was attracted to it if Clarke's story had even a shred of truth. In a romp like this, however, truth is not the aim of the effort. Clarke can use science in the comic stories either to reveal scientific curiosities or to create a logical tone to conceal and explain fantastic flights of the imagination.

The characters in Clarke's comic stories, and who often put in brief appearances in some of his other work, are frequently comic stereotypes of professions or positions. Clarke is particularly good at describing scientists and the military, perhaps because he has had practical experience in both areas. But he is equally capable of picturing comic bureaucrats, aliens, or exceptional characters such as Buddhist monks or spinster aunts. The characters are often victims whom the reader wishes to see victimized or the meek who emerge victorious by guile or scientific trickery.

Some of Clarke's comic portraits of scientists are very brief indeed. Here two rather abnormal extraterrestrials are trying to establish first contact but the Professor is not observant.

> They gazed with some indignation at the retreating back of Professor Fitzsimmons as, wearing his oldest hiking outfit and engrossed in a difficult piece of atomic theory, he dwindled down the lane.[19]

Tales From the 'White Hart' has virtually one zany scientist to a story.

As well as his comic scientists Clarke pokes fun at a wide variety of other characters. The General in "The Pacifist" (1956) sums up the type. With a father in the Senate, General Smith finds his limited mental capability in charge of a computer project:

> "Now I don't know what experience you have of high-ranking military officers, but there's one type you'll all come across in fiction. That's the pompous, conservative, stick-in-the-mud careerist who's got to the top by sheer pressure from beneath, who does everything by rules and regulations and regards civilians as, at the best, unfriendly neutrals. I'll let you into a secret: he actually exists. He's not very common nowadays, but he's still around and sometimes it's not possible to find a safe job for him. When that happens, he's worth his weight in plutonium to the Other Side."[20]

A number of aliens come in for humorous portrayal in the stories. In "Neutron Tide" the enemy are hilariously horrible:

> . . . the war against the Mucoids."
> We all shuddered. Even now, the very name of the gelatinous monsters who had come slurping Earthward from the general direction of the Coal Sack aroused vomitive memories.
> "I knew her skipper well—Captain Karl van Rinderpest, hero of the final assault on the unspeakable, but not unshriekable, !! Yeetch."
> He paused politely to let us unplug our ears and mop up our spilled drinks.[21]

A spinster lady is pictured in "The Reluctant Orchid":

> . . . Aunt Henrietta. She was a massive six-footer, usually wore a rather loud line in Harris tweeds, drove a Jaguar with reckless skill, and chain-smoked cigars. Her parents had set their hearts on a boy, and had never been able to decide whether or not their wish had been granted.

In characterization as in plotting, the comic stories have amusement as their first principle. In stories such as "Time's Arrow," "Big Game Hunt," "Patent Pending," "Sleeping Beauty," "The Ultimate Melody," "What Goes Up," and "The Defenestration of Ermintrude Inch," Clarke is able to present disasters and deaths that befall comic victims so that the reader is amused rather than horrified.

The general tone of the comic stories owes a great deal to the traditions of British humor. Clarke has much in common with the dry, ironic wit and techniques of understatement frequently associated with P. G. Wodehouse, Evelyn Waugh, and some of the writing of Aldous Huxley. His wit is low-keyed and is especially effective because it allows the reader to share with him the thought that none of this amazing stuff need be taken wholly seriously. Uncle Homer's pet in "Moving Spirit" is introduced with casual wit:

Harry found it hard not to feel some sympathy for the invisible Maida [a frightened maid]. All six feet of Boanerges was draped over the case holding the "Encyclopaedia Britannica," and a bulge amidships indicated that he had dined recently.

Here phrases such as "bulge amidships" and "dined recently" accompany word choices such as "draped" and the pun, a boa named Boanerges, to produce a bit of typical Clarke humor.[22] The same effect of dry, witty understatement is at work in "The Pacifist," in the description of the epithets that Karl, the computer who refuses to do military problems, employs for General Smith:

It must be confessed that after a while the technicians were almost as interested in discovering what indignity Karl would next heap upon General Smith as they were in finding the fault in the circuits. He had begun with mere insults and surprising genealogical surmises, but had swiftly passed on to detailed instructions the mildest of which would have been highly prejudicial to the General's dignity, while the more imaginative would have seriously imperiled his physical integrity.

The way Clarke clothes the vulgarity of the computer's output heightens the reader's amusement because it leaves the imagination room to conjure up possibilities.

The situations that Clarke presents are themselves wry and witty. He matches the tone of the presentations with events such as six men lugging a spaceship on their shoulders in the low gravity of "Jupiter Five." "Who's There" shatters the terror of discovering that something is sharing a spacesuit with the narrator with the revelation that the space station's cat has been raising kittens in the suit. Irony pervades "All That Glitters" when a professor on the Moon locates one of the largest diamonds of all time to satisfy a greedy wife, only to receive news from Earth that his laboratory team has synthesized diamonds, making them virtually worthless.

The strength of Clarke's comic writing is best seen when he combines a good scientific idea with effective caricature and his dry style to lead to a shockingly funny reversal. The best stories have simple comic plots involving jealousy and love, struggles for property and the dangers of curiosity, with the additional amusement of the puzzles presented by science and by human failures to take full account of physical reality. Often the characters in these stories become victims of their own Machiavellianism. Clarke is wryly cynical about human behavior, seeing it in the larger perspective of the universe at large.

Although Clarke has written a number of highly successful comic stories his efforts can fall flat if they do not hit just the right edge of wit. The juvenile ring of "Whacky" (1942), an early experiment with passages such as:

"The amazing affair of the Elastic Sided Eggwhisk," said the Great Detective, "would no doubt have remained unsolved to this very day, if by great misfortune it had ever occurred. The fact that it didn't I count as one of my luckiest escapes."

Those of us who possessed heads nodded in agreement.[23]

is generally absent from more mature work but occasionally recurs. In "Passer-by" (1957) the interesting mystery of the object that goes by the port of a space shuttle the narrator is using illegally to visit a girlfriend is spoiled by a failed ending when the narrator claims he should have reported the incident because the girl married someone else. It is not funny. "Publicity Campaign" (1956) juxtaposes a publicity campaign for a horrible space invasion film with a real arrival. The resulting xenophobia causes the visitors to destroy the earth. After a bit of parody on Hollywood publicity it goes flat and the dry wit misses in what are supposed to be comic descriptions of the invaders.

In a story like "Critical Mass" (1957) the twist ending simply fails to work. Clarke establishes a threat when a truck overturns near a nuclear plant and the driver flees in panic. The letdown when the narrator discovers that the truck contained beehives does not do justice to the situation. These failed endings are matched by wooden dialogue in stories such as "The Food of the Gods." A speaker in that tale is discussing the fact that men used to eat flesh and one Senator cannot bear these mentions. There is humor here, but Clarke labors the point and by the third mention the reader is no longer amused:

. . . our great-grandparents were enjoying the flesh of cattle and sheep and pigs—when they could get it. *And we still enjoy it today . . .*

Oh dear, maybe Senator Irving had better stay outside from now on. Perhaps I should not have been quite so blunt.[24]

In these moments Clarke seems to be *striving* to be funny and these obvious efforts are awkward and uncertain.

However, Clarke's best comic stories are very successful indeed, blending the quirks of science and the quirks of human behavior with surprise twists. Comedy injects energy into tales with strict scientific antecedents and Clarke has developed it as a delightful adjunct to fantastic speculations.

The Mystic: Enigmatic Sentimentalism

Among Arthur C. Clarke's best-known works are *Childhood's End*, *2001: A Space Odyssey* and "The Nine Billion Names of God." These and many of Clarke's other stories attempt to go beyond the limits of the hard extrapolations and the humorous entertainments. It is a serious mistake to think of Clarke as a writer whose imagination is bounded by the known, a scientist of the old school who is deeply reluctant to consider anything but emphatically proven data. In *The Lost Worlds of 2001* he enunciates his position as Clarke's Three Laws:

> ... Clarke's Third* Law: "Any sufficiently advanced technology is indistinguishable from magic." [* *The First:* "When a distinguished but elderly scientist says that something is possible, he is almost certainly right. When he says it is impossible, he is very probably wrong." *The Second:* "The only way of finding the limits of the possible is by going beyond them to the impossible."][25]

Despite the slightly flippant tone of Clarke's Laws there is no doubt that he seeks to go beyond "known" and more "practical" extrapolations to metaphysics. His writings in this third style reflect a dissatisfaction with the concrete and a longing for the unknown. It is in these free and experimental works that Clarke moves his readers most effectively; yet it is here the limitations of his abilities as a writer are most glaringly obvious, for he is attempting to describe universes and creatures at the outer limits of the imagination.

I have used the descriptive subtitle of enigmatic sentimentalism for Clarke's approach to the mystical in his writing because at the heart of the work he does not present a "true" picture but a sense of strongly felt yet somewhat unfocused emotion. Still, the sentiment is honest and seriously grounded, for Clarke communicates an urgent wish for man to explore the wonders of the universe and reveal its basic being. The sense of awe evoked in the lyrical passages of the hard extrapolations expands as Clarke invests his energies in experiments that open outward toward an infinite cosmos.

Clarke's experiments with the unknown speculate in diverse directions and unlike the hard extrapolations and comic stories they end in suggestions of further expansion in many directions. A number of stories put man's evolution in perspective, placing human history as a tiny fragment of the past of the universe and suggesting what lies ahead. In "The Sentinel" (1950), the story from which *2001* was derived, man's development is influenced at the dawn of time by extraterrestrial visitors. "Expedition to Earth," also entitled "Encounter at Dawn" (1953), treats the same theme with the variation that the visitors' forced retreat from Earth costs man the leap forward they were preparing. Man's future evolution is the theme of *Childhood's End, The City and the Stars, 2001,* and short stories such as "The Possessed" and "Transience." Other stories speculate on sophisticated forms of life that man has not previously considered, including the intelligent life of the sea in *Dolphin Island,* life in the core of the Earth in "The Fires Within," and life in the hearts of stars in "Out of the Sun" and "Castaway." Still others, including *2001, Childhood's End, The City and the Stars,* "All the Time in the World," and "Jupiter Five" speculate on the master races who may contact man. Man's spread throughout the universe is the subject of stories such as "Rescue Party," "The Road to the Sea," and "The Songs of Distant Earth." All of the topics for speculation in stories of this type invoke broad and distant perspectives that challenge and expand the imagination.

The general direction of Clarke's metaphysical speculations owes a good deal to the work of Olaf Stapledon whose sprawling predictive prose fictions *Last and First Men* (1930) and *Star Maker* (1937) have a sweep unmatched in science fiction. *Last and First Men* deals with the future of human evolution over the course of several million years as man leaves Earth, migrates to the planets and adjusts to their environments before coming to a tranquil end. *Star Maker* looks even further as a human narrator joins a growing, galactic telepathic network to search for, understand, and worship the being who made all things. These books move with dizzying speed and in the case of *Star Maker* the descriptions become progressively less and less concrete as Stapledon attempts to describe the nature and purpose of the Star Maker. At the heart of *Star Maker* Stapledon is treating the problem of the existence of evil. In creating cosmoses as imperfect works of art in a progress towards a perfect expression of self, Star Maker is pictured by Stapledon as utterly indifferent. Stapledon's presentation of the Star Maker's icily objective viewpoint is a radical departure from visions of a caring creator and is an obvious source of pessimism for human metaphysical yearnings.

Clarke echoes Stapledon's optimism toward man's expanding abilities to comprehend the wonder of the cosmos, but he also reflects the pessimism implicit in *Star Maker.* This is particularly fascinating in light of the optimism in short-run projections in Clarke's fiction. It makes the enthusiasm and certainty of getting to the Moon and living on the planets a very short-lived gain for a creature who is ultimately a dust speck in the cosmic pattern. This pessimistic streak emerges in *Childhood's End* where doubts must linger as to the route that devils (for despite all rationalization they remain devils) advocate for mankind. The Overmind itself is a force with no moral nature measurable or comprehensible either to man or the Overlords. As Jan Rodricks, the last man, whose exploits have earned the reader's sympathy, describes the Earth dissolving beneath him, one is made sharply aware of the divided loyalty in Clarke's mind between the flux in the physical universe and mankind's striving for immortality. Pessimism informs stories like "The Next Tenants" where a scientist prepares termites to take over the world on the grounds that man has failed and the unconscious, ongoing insect should have an opportunity. Even "The Nine Billion Names of God," with its lighthearted if not comic tone, is ultimately pessimistic in illustrating how man could be snuffed out by immense unknown forces.

The optimistic side of Clarke's visions does, however, go beyond relatively mundane speculations on the exploration of the solar system. *Childhood's End* is titled to suggest an evolutionary change. The thrust of the creation of Vanamonde and the abandonment of the galaxy by all its races to go on a further pilgrimage at the close of *The City and the Stars* certainly projects optimism. The conclusion of *2001* is as ambiguous as anything Stapledon ever created, for David Bowman, the Star-Child who has been guided beyond the merely human, hovers above the Earth uncertain of how he will use his almost infinite powers to change the world.

The characteristics of Clarke's metaphysical speculations are dominated by this aspect of open-ended plotting. Whereas his other stories are symmetrical, offering solutions and conclusions to the experiment or comic situation they propose, the mystical stories provide opening terms of infinite series. *The City and the Stars* concludes with this promise:

> *In this universe the night was falling; the shadows were lengthening toward an east that would not know another dawn. But elsewhere the stars were still young and the light of morning lingered; and along the path he once had followed, Man would one day go again.*
> 26

"The Songs of Distant Earth" (1957) suggests that man will go forward:

> She knew now, with a wisdom beyond her years, that the starship *Magellan* was outward bound into history; and that was something of which Thalassa had no further part. Her world's story had begun and ended with the pio-

neers three hundred years ago, but the colonists of the *Magellan* would go on to victories and achievements as great as any yet written in the sagas of mankind.[27]

"A Meeting with Medusa" ends as Howard Falcon prepares to face his future as mediator between man and his mechanically improved descendants and with the intimation that man will further investigate the marvellous life forms of Jupiter. Other stories such as "Rescue Party," *The Lion of Comarre,* "The Road to the Sea," and "Second Dawn" end with expectations of a future expansion of some trend of development or discovery of the absolute.

Despite the trend of these stories toward the metaphysical, they are generally presented in a matter-of-fact tone. Clarke's clear, methodical style, perfected in the hard extrapolations, would not seem to be the natural vehicle for metaphysics, usually the region of mystical and symbolic writing. But on the whole the reverse seems the case, for Clarke's level-headed narrators communicate the sense of wonder that is felt when one travels far beyond the known, and Clarke's own quiet, factual voice as an omniscient narrator is equally effective. In "Rescue Party" (1945) the galactic saviors find to their immense surprise that mankind has evacuated Earth without their aid and the story ends with a firm, cool promise for the future:

> "Something tells me they'll be very determined people," he added. "We had better be polite to them. After all, we only outnumber them about a thousand million to one."
> Rugon laughed at his captain's little joke.
> Twenty years afterward, the remark didn't seem funny.[28]

Even when Jan Rodricks, the young man who dared the Overlords by visiting their strange world, is witnessing the destruction of Earth beneath his feet, he puts his understanding of the great change in *Childhood's End* into a straightforward statement:

> Though I cannot understand it, I've seen what my race became. Everything we ever achieved has gone up there into the stars. Perhaps that's what the old religions were trying to say. But they got it all wrong: they thought mankind was so important, yet we're only one race in—do *you* know how many?[29]

Clarke achieves the same intensity through simplicity when, at the conclusion of the fantastic voyage of *2001,* David Bowman is transformed into a form shocking in its very familiarity when juxtaposed with its location.

The timeless instant passed; the pendulum reversed its swing. In an empty room, floating amid the fires of a double star twenty thousand light-years from Earth, a baby opened its eyes and began to cry.[30]

All of the stories that end with a reach toward the unknown begin in the mundane. People bustle about preparing space shots; briefings take place; a conference is held on the Moon to discuss a mysterious artifact; or a young man dares to visit an ancient city to prove his love. The stories move outward while the calm tone keeps the sense of concrete reality. *The Deep Range,* a novel about future marine technology, illustrates the pattern by assuming a cosmic scope over the question of the killing of whales for food. The Scot who is the leader of world Buddhism puts the compelling argument that when (not if) man is confronted by extraterrestrials they will judge him according to his behavior toward the other creatures of Earth. This practical, calm argument is typical of the impact these speculations generate. It is not the unbelievable that Clarke specializes in. It is the "un-thought of," presented to expand the reader's range of possibilities. This expansion is particularly evident in the two stories about beings from within the stars. In "Castaway" Clarke employs a dual point of view to relate how the radar of an airship accidentally destroys a being ejected by a solar flare. The reader knows the beast exists because Clarke narrates its fate partly from its point of view, and is moved by the simple description of its dissolution:

> For the filaments were breaking up, and even as they watched the ten-mile-long oval began to disintegrate. There was something awe-inspiring about the sight, and for some unfathomable reason Lindsey felt a surge of pity, as though he were witnessing the death of some gigantic beast. . . .
> And across the screen of the great indicator, two men stared speechlessly at one another, each afraid to guess what lay in the other's mind.[31]

The sensible idea that a form of life can exist in those most frequent concentrations of energy in the universe, stars, is also the theme of "Out of the Sun." Astronomers on Mercury detect a being projected out of the Sun that collides with the planet and the narrator speculates on its nature:

> . . . only the electrical senses of the radar were of any use. The thing that was coming toward us out of the sun was as transparent as air—and far more tenuous. . . . We were looking at life, where no life could exist. . . .
> The eruption had hurled the thing out of its normal environment, deep down in the flaming atmosphere of the sun. It was a miracle that it had survived its journey through space; already it must be dying, as the forces that

controlled its huge, invisible body lost their hold over the electrified gas which was the only substance it possessed.

It is the extension of the possibilities that gives the tale its special dimension:

> . . . for to them we should be no more than maggots, crawling upon the skins of worlds too cold to cleanse themselves from the corruption of organic life.
>
> And then, if they have the power, they will do what they consider necessary. The sun will put forth its strength and lick the faces of its children; and thereafter the planets will go their way once more as they were in the beginning—clean and bright . . . and sterile.[32]

Clarke's metaphysical stories are not parables or symbolic in nature, then, but attempts to carry the powers of physical description out to the indefinable. Like Stapledon, Clarke seeks to communicate a sense of the vastness of the cosmos and its possibilities through stories that move outward from a core to ever-enlarging perspectives. And it is precisely at the boundaries of this exploration that Clarke, like Stapledon, fails to consistently exhibit the imaginative powers necessary to carry the reader with him. Some solutions to the problems of the indescribable are quite brilliant. The bedroom in which David Bowman finds himself at the end of *2001* is explained as the result of the superior intelligence that is controlling his having copied it from Earth's television broadcasts. But *Against the Fall of Night* concludes with the discovery of Vanamonde, an ethereal childlike creature who befriends a youthful explorer like a puppy and then, despite being the product of the combined genius of the galaxy, eagerly submits to human education. Moreover, we discover that Vanamonde will have to fight "The Mad Mind" that is imprisoned in a "Black Star" in some distant future, and the net effect of this sort of presentation is to lower a novel about man's rediscovery of the universe to a weak, generalized, juvenile level. To some extent this same criticism can be leveled at *Childhood's End,* where Clarke's definition of the Overmind remains fuzzy and uncertain. However, *Childhood's End,* which owes a great deal to Stapledon's *Star Maker,* manages to convey a sense of energy and destiny that is lacking in *Against the Fall of Night.* The effect is achieved primarily through the structural device of having a superrace, the Overlords, provide a perspective from which the reader can grasp just how far above man the Overmind actually stands.

The thrust of most of Clarke's mystical fiction is sentimental in its optimistic view of human destiny. Although he is only charting possibilities Clarke consistently hints that the universe will be man's and that man, coming to grips with the physical universe through science, will emerge the final victor. This optimistic tone is at the root of "Rescue Party," *Against the Fall of Night, 2001: A Space Odyssey,* "A Meeting with Medusa," "The Songs of Distant Earth," and "The Road to the Sea." Yet there is a curious wavering in this confidence when Clarke catches, perhaps from Stapledon, the sense of the awesome objectivity of the cosmos, the lack of evidence in the stars for anything approaching a benign being. Clarke dismisses conventional religion as superstition on numerous occasions, perhaps most effectively in "The Star," when an anguished Jesuit priest is faced with the horrible fact that a highly civilized race was victim of a supernova, the Star of Bethlehem. Clarke seems to want a belief that is adequate for the scope of the universe, but that belief in turn is one in which human existence is infinitesimal. It is the crux of the dilemma that Clarke is both hazy in his writing and appealing, for he captures in a naive fashion that sense of distant things that has always haunted men who looked at the stars, and he does so in the context of the modern scientist and space adventurer. This enigmatic sentimentalism may deter the trained metaphysician, but it is the stuff of appealing fiction, of popular expressions of deep feeling like: "That's one small step for man, one giant leap for mankind."[33]

The Mature Blending: Rendezvous with Rama *and* Imperial Earth

Although Arthur C. Clarke's work can be divided into three principal styles most of his stories and novels contain combinations of hard extrapolation, humorous vignettes, and some gesture in the direction of metaphysical possibilities. In his two most recent novels, *Rendezvous with Rama* (1973) and *Imperial Earth* (1976), Clarke has achieved varying blends of these elements worth careful consideration, particularly to test arguments that he is an "old-fashioned" writer, uncomfortably bound to a corpus of work stretching from 1937 to the present. Clarke's most old-fashioned position is his commitment to telling a good story in an accurately conceived and described universe, traits that seem to this writer to be aspects of most good and enduring literature.

Rendezvous with Rama is the latest of Clarke's works in which hard science plays the dominant role, and this triumphant example of the style won for the author the Nebula, Hugo, and John W. Campbell Awards. It is built upon ideas that Clarke has toyed with in earlier works, but its synthesis is a distinctive distillation of the author's writing experience.

Foremost among the antecedents for *Rendezvous with Rama* is the short story "Jupiter Five" (1953) where Clarke postulated an artificial world from outside the solar system orbiting as Jupiter's mysterious inner satellite. The concept of an artificial world also occurred in the description of the Seven Suns in *Against the Fall of Night,* and Clarke's versions of planet-sized space vessels owe a debt to Chapter IX of Stapledon's *Star Maker.* Clarke also draws on "Into the Comet" (1960), a story which discussed the difficulties of matching velocities and trajectories with a body entering the solar system on a long ellipse. The idea of great ships to carry man through the universe is a common one in science fiction and one Clarke had raised in "The Songs of Distant Earth" (1957) and in "Rescue Party" (1945). In "The Next Tenants" (1956) Clarke had commented in detail on the specialization in the termitary, and the "biots" in *Rendezvous with Rama* are specific in function.

What differentiates *Rendezvous with Rama* from its sources is the beautiful cohesion of all the "hard" aspects of the story, the immaculate fit of the separate mysteries that are presented and solved as man attempts to unravel the puzzle of the mighty vehicle. Everything in the story is presented precisely, with careful measurement and vivid detail. This includes Rama's shape and contents, its gravitational field, the behavior of the biots, or biological robots, the development of hurricanes in its atmosphere, and details such as steps gradiated to counterbalance the stress of varying gravity. The biots are typical of these careful presentations. One of them, three-legged and three-eyed in keeping with the Raman symmetry of threes, dies and is dissected. A report to the scientists on the Moon clarifies its operation:

". . . there's a simple musculature, controlling its three legs and the three whiplike tendrils or feelers. There's a brain—fairly complex, mostly concerned with the creature's remarkably developed triocular vision. But eighty per cent of the body consists of a honeycomb of large cells. . . .

"Most of the spider is simply a battery, much like that found in electric eels and rays. But in this case it's apparently not used for defense. *It's the creature's source of energy.* "[34]

The description is precise and vivid, and presents a picture of a creature so specialized that its sole source of energy is self-contained. The analogies to the sealed, throwaway flashlight and to the specialized scouts of insect colonies immediately occur to the reader. Clarke also offers logical mechanical explanations for the higher wall on one side of the Cylindrical Sea in Rama and for the city that stores the prototypes the Ramans would reproduce when they needed tools, clothes, and presumably, the biots. When all of the information is assembled a picture emerges of a highly efficient environment with control over all factors ranging from lighting, gravity, and atmosphere to the disposal of refuse. The Raman vehicle is so massive, both physically and in terms of imaginative consistency, that it effortlessly dominates human actions in the book as Clarke surely intended it to do. Clarke carefully paces the discoveries, presenting a mystery such as the six long canal-like slots that do not meet the sea and then revealing they are the immense strip lights providing Rama's daylight. He repeats this pattern a number of times and varies it with the daring solo investigation by James Pak. Rama constantly produces startling and mysterious surprises such as the thawing of its ocean from the bottom up, the discharges of static electricity from the towers at one end, and the sudden emergency of the biots. Rama remains the focus of the book as its purposeful, integrated structure is studied by the human ants crawling about inside it. Although not all of the mystery is dispelled the overall impression is one of total, logical coherence, as solid and complete as Rama itself.

In the context of this overwhelming portrait of an immense strange vehicle, the stumbling activities of the humans who investigate it are naturally somewhat ludicrous, and it is in this context that Clarke integrates humor into the story. If he is guilty of some slightly faded wit in a description of the behavior of the female breast in zero gravity or in the caricatures of the scientists of the advisory board bickering on the Moon about the mysteries of Rama, this is one occasion when the very triviality of the humor contributes to the direction of the story. The dry tone of the banter when James Pak encounters the first biot is effective because the reader recognises that it covers human fear:

> "What the devil is it—and why is it chewing up your bike?"
> "Wish I knew. It's finished with *Dragonfly.* I'm going to back away, in case it wants to start on me."[35]

The element of amusement in the situation of a man pedaling a winged bicycle while hanging in zero gravity, a lady surgeon getting an electrical shock when she begins to dissect a curious creature, or grown men sliding down the banisters of an immense stairway contributes to the sense of scale that Clarke wishes to establish.

In addition to the care with which Clarke has delineated Rama and the way that mysteries are set up and solved by the explorers, there remains at the heart of the novel one of the most effective metaphysical problems that he has ever stated. For every aspect of Rama that man comes to understand, others emerge that lead to larger questions. And this is always done in a concrete form, without vague speculation or comments about awesome wonders that are beyond the narrator's powers. It is precisely because Clarke has stuck so closely to factual exposition and scientific description that the immensity of Rama is established and its mystery ultimately enhanced. When man's puny and politically motivated effort to destroy it has been defused, the vehicle reveals its true purpose in coming into the solar system by diving close to the sun to renew its energies before driving onward on its mysterious voyage. As it departs, man realizes that he has never seen the Ramans, nor comprehended the subtleties of an entire artificial world whose technology far exceeds anything he has ever achieved. He has literally been left behind with no more consideration than if he had been running a wayside stand on a superhighway. The very fact that Rama has paid man no heed whatsoever during his brief invasion is a stunning reminder of man's tiny place in the scale of the universe. That reminder is not offered as a vague suggestion of the existence of mighty forces and invisible beings, but rather in the mighty metallic vehicle whose discovery and investigation forms the substance of the entire novel. When the ship has departed man can speculate that the Ramans are three-legged and three-armed, for Clarke has established a symmetry of threes in various parts of the Raman world. The investigators have discovered a vehicle that is performing mechanical tasks while it awaits the revival of its occupants. The machine is so complex that it can create the biots and so powerful that it can drive itself far closer to the Sun than man can dare to go. The net effect of the passage of Rama is to leave man in awe of a superrace. The story opens outward in the tradition of the mystical stories because man is left with more mysteries and with the enigmatic conclusion that the Ramans do everything in threes, and there will presumably be other vehicles to follow the one that has been investigated.

In *Rendezvous with Rama* Clarke has achieved a most successful synthesis of the styles in which he characteristically works. The hard extrapolative element is immaculately detailed in a series of practical mysteries that are solved by experiment, investigation, and revelation in dramatic events. Rama is a tangible object to the reader of the story. One does not come away questioning its existence but rather questioning the unanswered final mysteries of its purpose and the destiny of its makers. There can be no greater proof of Clarke's ability to produce rational scientific extrapolation than the mass of carefully assembled factual detail that makes *Rama* real to the reader. At the same time the comic elements in Clarke's writing fit nicely into the work because they provide a human scale, like the figure of a man placed in the foreground of engineering drawings. In this context almost no comic note could be out of place. So despite tiny man striving in the foreground to explain its individual functioning areas, Rama as a whole cannot be understood. The absentee overlords remain mysterious as do their destination and the purpose of their venture. Despite the fact that it is a very specific artifact, Rama is ultimately as mysterious as the workings of the cosmos at large, the stars and the atoms from which man seeks a meaning. It is like a mighty and carefully prepared stage set, and Clarke's judgment in withholding the principal actors means that the suspense will be maintained in future acts of the cosmic drama. This concrete evocation of the mystery of the universe is Clarke's finest blending of the elements of his fiction.

Imperial Earth is a different sort of endeavour on Clarke's part, and its component parts do not cohere as effectively as those of *Rendezvous with Rama*. Yet it contains strong elements of the best of Clarke's writing and a vigor of plotting that carries the reader over uncertain sections and makes the novel as a whole a qualified success. In contrast to the unity gained by absolute concentration on a single object in *Rendezvous with Rama, Imperial Earth* draws most of its strength from the sheer variety of topics and ideas that it touches upon and attempts to integrate.

In the Acknowledgements and Notes at the end of *Imperial Earth* Clarke credits several mathematicians for their assistance with Polyominoes and other scientists for ideas on radio sources, the nature of Titan, the idea of mini black holes, and the characteristics of the heliosphere. Beyond these sources the reader can see Clarke drawing on a great variety of his own earlier stories for material used in the novel. The Star Beasts originate in the speculations on strange life such as "Castaway." Both *Childhood's End* and *Against the Fall of Night* were treatments of the possibility of an immense being of tenuous matter or patterned energy. Clarke's ongoing fascination with the *Titanic* had already appeared in "A Meeting with Medusa" and he had considered the possible economic relationship between Earth and the other inhabitable bodies of the solar system in *Earthlight* and *The Sands of Mars.* Undersea sequences are frequent in Clarke's works and even the blinding of a man on a giant radio telescope (although the exact method and result were quite different) had previously occurred in "The Light of Darkness." The complexity of adaptation to Earth's fivefold gravity by Duncan Makenzie, a Titanian, mirrors all of Clarke's specific stories about the small but fascinating problems of space travel that comprise the "Venture to the Moon" and "The Other Side of the Sky" series.

The presentation of material from all these sources makes *Imperial Earth* Clarke's most varied and complex hard extrapolation, full of concrete details about a great number of things. He begins by describing in detail the life of the colonists in their underground environment on Titan. He details Duncan Makenzie's preparations for his voyage to Earth. When Makenzie is en route Clarke envisions the Asymptotic Drive of the ship. He takes the idea of a hole in space through which matter passes out of the universe, leaving behind it the total energy of its mass. This would of course vastly exceed the tiny portion of mass that fission or fusion affects and Clarke stresses the awesome nature of this technology.

> Duncan could easily have encircled the metal tube with his arms; how strange, to think of putting your arms around a singularity, and thus, if some of the theories were correct, embracing an entire universe. . . .

He does not stop at suggesting that it is amazing, however, but offers a precise physical theory for the operation of the Drive:

> . . . the thin wail of the Drive; Duncan told himself that he was listening to the death-cry of matter as it left the known universe, bequeathing to the ship all the energy of its mass in the final moment of dissolution. Every minute, several kilograms of hydrogen were falling into that tiny but insatiable vortex —the hole that could never be filled.[36]

This is characteristic of the scientific explanations that Clarke offers, for the node of the Drive is partly patterned after a theory on the nature of black holes, and the energy released by the total dissolution of matter is an extrapolation of the known effects of destruction of a few subatomic particles in fission and fusion reactions.

In addition to Titan and the Drive, Clarke's careful extrapolations include cloning, with particular stress on the extremely close bind between the personalities of the Makenzie clones; a brief underwater adventure for Duncan with mention of Clarke's beloved whales; and, of course, the idea for the mighty extraterrestrial radiotelescope, Argus, that is the mystery core of the book.

Clarke has always been master of expert touches such as toilet design or the method of walking in free fall in *2001.* In *Imperial Earth* he provides a great variety of adaptive trivia for Duncan when the latter lands on Earth. These details make the reading of the hard extrapolations like eating an unknown candy full of unexpected little delights. In this case he achieves this effect in a special new fashion, for the surprises are things that we already live with but which catch Duncan unawares. When Duncan's amazement at the first butterfly he has ever seen causes him to chase it, fall (because he cannot move quickly in Earth's "excessive" gravity), and sprain his ankle, Clarke is not only providing a suggestion of the adaptive problems man would face on other planets but he is reminding us of the simple miracles of muscular control that our bodies perform daily. These bits of information about the trivial problems of living in strange environments have always been one of Clarke's assets in creating lifelike, logical worlds. Their inevitable cumulative effect is heightened in *Imperial Earth* by the reader's immediate knowledge of the earthly context of the small problems and sudden shocks.

The hard extrapolating in *Imperial Earth* treats an aspect of the future in which Clarke has shown increasing interest and in which few other science fiction writers have involved themselves. This is his concern with the evolution of an interplanetary economy, a topic he had touched on in *Earthlight,* and in the planetary trade pattern mentioned in *Rendezvous with Rama.* The future of Titan, dependent as it is upon its hydrogen exports to the rest of the Solar System, is one of the principal topics of the book and is resolved by the founding of the Argus project. Clarke is not revolutionary in his political or economic viewpoints, but the factual nature of his extensions of present trends gives a resonance to the novel beyond the engineering concepts and Duncan's adaptation problems. In all of Clarke's hard extrapolations the extension of the present has predominated over radical conceptions and the sense of the ordinary world in his stories is strong. On consideration, one realizes that it is also deceptive, for Clarke is using his skill in providing the details of a future to make the reader identify with it through small bits of life. He is the craftsman who finishes the details of a creation to give it a totally lifelike appearance.

Imperial Earth contains one of Clarke's exceptional descriptions of natural phenomena. When Duncan is on Zanzibar (in a chapter Clarke could not resist calling "The Island of Dr. Mohammad" to relate cloning to the activities of H. G. Wells' Dr. Moreau), he dives to see a coral reef where the polyps have been mutated to extract gold from seawater. The result is a golden paradise beneath the waves:

> The glitter of gold was all around him. There was never more than a tiny speck, smaller than a grain of sand, at any one spot—but it was everywhere; the entire reef was impregnated with it. Duncan felt that he was floating beside the chef-d'oeuvre of some mad jeweler, determined to create a baroque masterpiece regardless of expense. Yet these pinnacles and plates and twisted spires were the work of mindless polyps, not—except indirectly—the products of human intelligence.[37]

The sense of wonder with the natural is also expressed in Duncan's discovery of the mathematical marvel of the pentominoes and the unique and infinite crystalline form of Titanite.

If the hard extrapolation of *Imperial Earth* is not so immediately impressive as that of *Rendezvous with Rama,* that is because it lacks the obvious coherence of the latter. Yet Clarke has created as effectively and perhaps in more detail in the later book, allowing his fascination with the logical extrapolation and the natural world to range from the depths of the sea to Titan and the Star Beasts who may lurk outside of the solar system.

The lighter elements of *Imperial Earth* are archetypical Clarke, combining some suitable wit and amusing observation with moments when undergraduate British humor mars the telling of the tale. The best comic moments are connected to Duncan's surprises when he visits Earth, such as his face-to-face encounter with Charlemagne, a one-ton Percheron horse who is more than strange to anyone coming from a world where man is the only living species.

> Now the windows slid down—and Primeval Earth hit Duncan full in the nostrils. . . .
>
> [Professor Washington] . . . leaned across his cowering guest, holding out an open palm on which two lumps of sugar had magically appeared. Gently as any maiden's kiss, the lips nuzzled Washington's hand, and the gift vanished as if inhaled. A mild, gentle eye, which from this distance seemed about as large as a fist, looked straight at Duncan, who started to laugh a little hysterically as the apparition withdrew.
>
> "What's so funny?" asked Washington.
>
> "Look at it from *my* point of view. I've just met my first Monster From Outer Space. Thank God it was friendly."[38]

While a moment like this, or Duncan's discovery that the plumbing on spaceships is just as liable to air locks as plumbing anywhere, can be amusing to the reader, Clarke is liable to produce corny moments when his humor simply misses the mark. Also, one is hard pressed to find the Scots' associations of the clan Makenzie comic, particularly when they lead to a chapter title describing a physical feature of the Titan landscape as "By the Bonny, Bonny Banks of Loch Hellbrew." The best of Clarke's humor in the novel are dry witticisms that ironically lubricate the flow of the story. The slightly jaundiced eye that describes the foods of Earth as ". . . grown from dirt and dung, and not synthesized from nice clean chemicals in a spotless factory" and provides hundreds of other similar comments is flavoring the narrative style to make reading easier and more enjoyable.

There can only be a reserved judgment on the mystical, open-ended aspect of *Imperial Earth* because on the one hand it appears to be tacked on to the novel without adequate preparation while careful examination of the book suggests that it was planned and that Clarke has created a substructure for the novel to justify its inclusion. The possible existence of a life form that responds only on extremely long wavebands is suggested only at the end of the story, when Duncan reads Karl Helmer's notes. Although it could be argued that the possibility is the logical conclusion to the mystery posed in the book, it really is very artificial because there is no progression of adequate clues. It is like a detective novel in which the murderer is introduced as a new character in the last chapter. Such a procedure is not unusual in Clarke's approach, for a number of the stories and novels broaden out in this manner, including "Rescue Party," *The Sands of Mars,* "Jupiter Five," and "The Star". While it is structurally weak, it does allow him to write a single strong passage advocating the infinite possibility that can be intense enough to be emotionally convincing. In *Imperial Earth* the speculations in Karl's diary force the mind outward to possibilities without providing any complex evidence:

> "And are they intelligent? What does *that* word mean? Are ants intelligent —are the cells of the human body intelligent? Do all the Star Beasts surrounding the Solar System make a single entity—and does It know about us? Or does It care?[39]

The only other expanding references in *Imperial Earth* are to the mathematical puzzle of the pentominoes with its dazzling variety of solutions that awakens in the young Duncan a sense of the depths of mathematics and the unique crystalline structure of Titanite, a seemingly infinite, glittering series of hexagons.

In partial defense of the way in which the mystical elements are incorporated in *Imperial Earth*, one can determine what appears to be Clarke's attempt to integrate many of the events in the book to give it cohesion. Consideration of this scheme could begin with the epigraph for the book from *Hamlet*, I, iv: "For every man has business and desire." This applies equally to Karl and Duncan, for both are acting for the eventual good of Titan and both desire Calindy. Karl's interest is in a supersensitive system of radio antennae and his desire has become embroiled in the supersensitive "Joy Machine," the emotional amplifier that he tried with Calindy. Karl's notebook connects the mystery of the hexagonal characteristic of Titanite with the antenna system and with the structure of the sensitive sea urchin that Duncan kills. The sea urchin shocks Duncan by its surprising underwater death scream and this is tied to the shriek that Duncan and Karl hear from the surface of Titan in the first chapter of the book. All of the images in the book are tied together in the Titanite cross that combines the mystery of hexagonal crystals with the puzzle of the pentominoes that links Duncan and Karl and which stands for the complex possible solutions to human dilemmas. The whole underlay of this structure relating crystal to Star Beast surfaces in Duncan's Independence Day speech:

> We tend to judge the universe by our own physical size, and our own time scale; it seems natural for us to work with waves that we could span with our arms, or even with our finger tips. But the cosmos is not built to these dimensions; nor perhaps, are all the entities which dwell among the stars.[40]

Yet the links are not entirely adequate, because they are usually submerged beneath the surface of a picaresque novel wandering from place to place and idea to idea. In the judgment of this writer *Imperial Earth* is a successful Clarke novel because of its variety and sharply perceived and detailed extrapolation. Its weaknesses are the lack of a structure adequately articulated to hold it together and Clarke's characteristic insertions of humor and the metaphysical in slightly uneasy fashion.

Conclusion

The styles in which Clarke has worked are distinctive and have different purposes. They are not always comfortably integrated in the same story; when they are, it is in situations such as *Rendezvous with Rama* where the hard extrapolation has natural mystical implications without any need to pin them on from the outside and where humor serves to fit man into his tiny niche in the universal scheme. Clarke is perfectly capable of the variety of styles that have been suggested, but closest to his heart and, more importantly, to his head, is the commitment to the real universe as it is understood by the laws of the sciences or as it probably exists if those laws are extended to strange places or different times. When he approaches the metaphysical he does so best through the concrete and although a good deal of his writing contains an ill-suppressed desire to find the gods through science, his abilities as a writer weaken as he approaches the metaphysical. Sensing this, Clarke has evolved a story mode featuring hard science, sprinkled with wit and turning suddenly at its conclusion to its metaphysical speculation in a breathtaking leap from hard reality into the unknown. When this technique works smoothly, as it does in *Rendezvous with Rama* and to a lesser extent in the potpourri of *Imperial Earth,* Arthur C. Clarke gains the advantages inherent in the different styles he has evolved.

2. The Cosmic Loneliness of Arthur C. Clarke*

THOMAS D. CLARESON

Since the publication of *Interplanetary Flight: An Introduction to Astronautics* (1950) and *The Exploration of Space* (1951)—the latter a Book of the Month Club selection in the summer of 1952—Arthur C. Clarke has undoubtedly become the most widely known spokesman for those advocating space travel. Indeed, he has been called "one of the truly prophetic figures of the space age."[1] Yet despite such early awards as the 1961 Kalinga Prize in recognition of his success in popularizing space flight, the incident best measuring the impact of his dream of man's journeys to the Moon, the planets, and—ultimately—the stars did not occur until 1971. Then, during the Apollo 15 missions, astronauts David Scott and James Irwin named a crater near Hadley Rille for *Earthlight*, Clarke's early novel (1951, 1955)[2] in which he used a twenty-first-century lunar colony as setting and suggested that the Moon will become the hub of the habitable solar system because of its mineral wealth.

Acknowledging that "the explosive development of astronautics" during the 1960's had made some of his books "very out of date," Clarke declared that *The Promise of Space* (1968) was "an entirely new book" which replaced many of the earliest ones and should remain "largely valid through the 1970's"; similarly, *Report on Planet Three and Other Speculations* (1972) contained his "later thoughts on a number of subjects."[3] As a result his nonfiction has a special value for the student of his fiction because in it one can trace the persistence and evolution of his themes as he continually explores and reworks ideas and situations which inform his short stories and novels. As in *The Challenge of Space* (1959),[4] one may learn that he has used "much of the material" in three essays "to provide the background" of three early novels, *Earthlight, The*

*Reprinted from *Voices for the Future*, Thomas Clareson, ed. (Bowling Green University Popular Press, © 1976).

Sands of Mars (1951, 1952), and *Islands in the Sky* (1952).[5] In one of those articles, "Vacation in Vacuum," one discovers the "Sky Hotel," which develops into the resort hotel on Titan in "Saturn Rising" (*F&SF,* March 1961) and, finally, into the hotel satellite of *2001: A Space Odyssey.* Again, much later, Clarke pointed out that in the essay "The Star of the Magi" (1954) readers of his fiction would "recognize . . . the origins" of his prizewinning story, "The Star" (*Infinity,* November 1955).[6]

Although it is everywhere apparent that his main concern involves man's encounter with alien intelligence, at the heart of his vision—most obvious throughout his nonfiction and early novels—remains the certainty that the exploration of space and the colonization of the planets of innumerable suns will bring a new Renaissance freeing mankind from the shortsighted prejudices and limitations of earthbound, modern civilization. Repeatedly he invokes images fusing his voyagers "Across the Sea of Stars" with those explorers who opened up the Earth, as he does in *Prelude to Space* (1951), which celebrates preparations for the voyage of the *Prometheus* to the Moon and climaxes with the departure of that first ship. In an epilogue, some years after the establishment of a lunar colony, the narrator muses:

> . . . Once more the proud ships were sailing for unknown lands, bearing the seeds of new civilizations which in the ages to come would surpass the old. The rush to the new worlds would destroy the suffocating restraints which had poisoned almost half the [twentieth] century. The barriers had been broken, and men could turn their energies outward to the stars instead of striving among themselves.
>
> Out of the fears and miseries of the Second Dark Age, drawing free—oh, might it be forever!—from the shadows of Belsen and Hiroshima, the world was moving toward its most splendid sunrise. After five hundred years, the Renaissance had come again. The dawn that would burst above the Apennines at the end of the long lunar night would be no more brilliant than the age that had now been born.[7]

Or again, in *The Challenge of Space,* in a different but frequent mood:

> . . . For a man 'home' is the place of his birth and childhood—whether that be Siberian steppe, coral island, Alpine valley, Brooklyn tenement, Martian desert, lunar crater, or mile-long interstellar ark. But for Man, home can never be a single country, a single world, a single Solar System, a single star cluster. While the race endures in recognizably human form, it can have no abiding place short of the Universe itself.
>
> This divine discontent is part of our destiny. It is one more, and perhaps the greatest, of the gifts we have inherited from the sea that rolls so restlessly around the world.
>
> It will be driving our descendants on toward a myriad unimaginable goals

when the sea is stilled forever, and Earth itself a fading legend lost among the stars.[8]

Although Clarke spreads the human drama across future millenia, he often strikes a contrapuntal note by warning that "Everyone recognizes that our present racial, political, and international troubles are symptoms of a sickness which must be cured before we can survive on our own planet—but the stakes may be higher than that. . . . The impartial agents of our destiny stand on their launching pads, awaiting our commands. They can take us to that greater Renaissance whose signs and portents we can already see, or they can make us one with the dinosaurs. . . . If our wisdom fails to match our science, we will have no second chance."[9] Out of the conflict revealed by these admonitions came one of his finest short stories, "If I Forget Thee, O Earth" (1951), in which a son of the lunar colony witnesses for the first time the rising of an Earth poisoned for centuries to come by a nuclear holocaust.

And when Clarke wonders whether or not the Solar System will, indeed, "be large enough for so quarrelsome an animal as *Homo sapiens*, "[10] one conjures up the second of his stories to be published in America, "Rescue Party" (*Astounding,* May 1946), in which alien representatives of a galaxy-wide Federation come to save mankind just before the Sun goes into nova. Finding an empty Earth, they learn that man has built a fleet of ships to save himself. The captain muses about such "very determined people" and jests that one must be polite to them because they are outnumbered only "about a thousand million to one": "Twenty years afterward, the remark didn't seem funny." Both narratives bear one of the distinguishing marks of Clarke's story-telling. Not unlike O.Henry, he likes a quick climax—often a single punchline—which may surprise but always opens new perspectives.

Any misgivings that Clarke may have, rise from his doubts concerning the uses made of the new technologies. As early as 1946 he wrote:

We must not, however, commit the only too common mistake of equating mere physical expansion, or even increasing scientific knowledge, with 'progress'—however that may be defined. Only little minds are impressed by sheer size and number. There would be no virtue in possessing the Universe if it brought neither wisdom nor happiness. Yet possess it we must, at least in spirit, if we are ever to answer the questions that men have asked in vain since history began.[11]

Somewhat later he approached this basic theme more affirmatively when he asserted that "mere extension of the life span, and even improved health and efficiency, are not important in themselves. . . . What is really significant is richness and diversity of experience, and the use to which that is put by men and the societies they constitute."[12] Still in the 1950's, while speculating about man's encounter with alien intelligence, he used that central concern to say something of man himself:

> . . . Most disconcerting of all would be the discovery that Man alone is a myth-making animal, forever impelled to fill the gaps in his knowledge by fantasies. (Yet if this be the price we have had to pay for the whole realm of art, which is always an attempt to create the nonexistent, we need not be ashamed. We will be better off than beings who possess all knowledge, but know nothing of poetry and music.)[13]

This emphasis upon both man's humanity and the need for it to shape the workings of society leads to Clarke's judgment of H. G. Wells, a judgment which seems a valid appraisal of Clarke himself:

> . . . Wells saw as clearly as anyone into the secret places of the heart, but he also saw the universe, with all its infinite promise and peril. He believed— though not blindly—that men were capable of improvement and might one day build sane and peaceful societies on all the worlds that lay within their reach.[14]

When he adds that "we need this faith now, as never before in the history of our species," he has completed the context which gives importance to that "greater Renaissance" brought about by the advent of space flight. In 1951 Clarke captured the significance of that awakening when he concluded *The Exploration of Space* with the imagined verdict that "an historian of the year 3,000" might pass on the twentieth century:

> It was, without question, the most momentous hundred years in the history of Mankind. . . . To us a thousand years later, the whole story of Mankind before the twentieth century seems like a prelude to some great drama, played on the narrow strip of stage before the curtain has risen and revealed the scenery. . . . Man realised at last that the Earth was only one of many worlds; the Sun only one among many stars. The coming of the rocket brought to an end a million years of isolation. With the landing of the first spaceship on Mars and Venus, the childhood of our race was over and history as we know it began. . . .[15]

". . . the childhood of our race was over . . .": there is a delightful irony in that line because of the widespread popularity of *Childhood's End* (1953), Clarke's only work—fiction or nonfiction—in which *"The stars are not for Man."*[16] Billed as "a towering novel about the next step in the evolution of man," it belongs, most simply, to that group of stories in which vastly superior aliens intrude into the affairs of men—a plot having perhaps its widest vogue during the decade or so after World War II. In this instance the Overlords, who possess the form of Satan, terminate the Soviet-American race for the Moon, end the threat of nuclear holocaust, and in fifty years bring about a seeming utopia. (At their appearance one hears briefly what has become for Clarke an ever more important theme: ". . . the stars—the aloof, indifferent stars—had come to him. . . . The human race was no longer alone.") Creating an 'Earthly Paradise,' is not, however, the final purpose of the Overlords; they were sent, their leader explains, to act as midwives while the human race evolved psychically preparatory to uniting itself with the cosmic Overmind. The most dangerous threat to this development, he continues, lay in the scientific investigation of "paranormal phenomena." Left to itself, such study might have unleashed forces capable of spreading "havoc to the stars." The Overlords are racially incapable of taking this evolutionary step and do not comprehend the forces at work; yet while the Overmind triggers and guides the change, they must act as guardians, protecting man from himself, until the last generation of children is ready for the transformation.

The novel ends as a solitary adult watches the children, now joined into a single intelligence, undergo a metamorphosis which not only releases them from their human form but dissolves the Earth itself into the energy necessary to complete the change. All of this in the presence of what seems to be "a great cloud . . . a hazy network of lines and bands that keep changing their positions . . . a great burning column, like a tree of fire . . . a great auroral storm . . . the great misty network . . ."[17] Like other galactic races which have completed their probation, mankind has become a part of the Overmind. Although David Samuelson questions the artistic effectiveness of much of *Childhood's End,* he notes that "we feel the tug of the irrational, in familiar terms. The Overmind clearly parallels the Oversoul, the Great Spirit, and various formulations of God, while the children's metamorphosis neatly ties in with mystical beliefs in Nirvana, 'cosmic consciousness,' and 'becoming as little children to enter the Kingdom of God.' "[18] One might add that its resolution recalls—but does not duplicate—stories by the followers of Madame Blavatsky and John Fiske in the late nineteenth century which sought reconciliation between traditional beliefs and new scientific data, thereby often insisting that the next step in evolution must involve some higher potential of the human spirit. The essentially traditional mysticism of that resolution, as well as the emphasis upon the children as "successors" to mankind with whom their parents would "never even be able to communicate," may well account for much of the appeal of the novel, particularly in the classroom. A typical academic reading, that of L. David Allen, concludes that "basically, *Childhood's End* is a religious vision of the way that mankind might develop and the desirability of that direction."[19]

Apparently many individuals have felt that such a transformation— "apotheosis"[20]—more than compensates for the loss of the stars. Clarke did not. He prefaced the original, paperback edition with the warning that "The opinions expressed in this book are not those of the author," and in a recent letter explained that he had inserted the "disclaimer in *CE* so people wouldn't think I'd recanted the views expressed in *The Exploration of Space,* etc!"[21] In view of his continuing attack upon ortho- dox religion—it surfaces frequently in *Childhood's End* itself—such a disa- vowal suggests a deep conflict in Clarke which may even have affected the artistry of the novel, leading, for example, to Samuelson's inference that "not fully in control of his materials, Clarke has attempted more than he can fulfill."[22] In contrast, Allen believes that Clarke brought to the "sweeping vision" of the novel "a sense of detailed reality . . . more concrete, detailed, and complex" than *2001: A Space Odyssey.*[23] Most importantly, the disavowal emphasizes the uniqueness of *Childhood's End* in the canon of Clarke's work. Its final sequence contradicts all else that he has said about the future of humanity.

"Earth and the Overlords," the first of the three parts of *Childhood's End,* was originally published as a magazine novelette, "Guardian Angel" (*Famous Fantastic Mysteries,* April 1950); it alone appeared sepa- rately. The basic action of the two versions remains the same, although in a climax typical of so many of Clarke's stories, the novelette ends upon the suggestion that man's "Guardian Angel" is, indeed, the Devil. Not yet satisfied, Clarke closed the narrative with fragments of an earlier dialogue telling something of Karellen and thereby opened an otherwise closed incident:

> ". . . and he put up a terrific fight before they made him take this job. He pretends to hate it, but he's really enjoying himself."
> ". . . immortal, isn't he?"
> "Yes, after a fashion, though there's something thousands of years ahead of him which he seems to fear—I can't imagine what it is."
> Armageddon?[24]

Clarke ignored that ending in the subsequent development of *Childhood's End.* Thus in the novelette it simply provided an amusing—startling?—twist on another story of the first contact between humanity and aliens. Once again, as so often occurs in science fiction, an idea rather than the quality of human experience, had fascinated the author.

Variations in language and detail show Clarke's eye for revision, but the most significant difference between the versions of the story occurs because of the omission of a single speech originally in the novelette. In sketching the long-term plans of the Overlords, Karellen remarks:

> "Then there will be another pause, only a short one this time, for the world will be growing impatient. Men will wish to go out to the stars, to see the other worlds of the Universe and to join us in our work. For it is only beginning—not a thousandth of the suns in the Galaxy have ever been visited by the races of which we know. One day, Rikki, your descendants in their own ships will be bringing civilization to the worlds, that are ripe to receive it—just as we are doing now. . . .
> "It is a great vision," he said softly. 'Do you bring it to all your worlds?'
> "Yes,' said Karellen, "all that can understand" (p. 128).

Here, then, is the basic dream: man will one day become an active participant in the galactic community. Yet nothing of this passage remains in the finished novel. For whatever reasons, sometime between 1950 and 1953, even while he was popularizing space flight and advocating the journey to the stars in his other writing, both fiction and nonfiction, Clarke set aside that dream while completing *Childhood's End* in a fashion that could not be predicted from the text of "Guardian Angel."

In light of his immediate disclaimer, his production of one of the generally recognized "classics" of modern science fiction speaks well for his ability to be convincing despite any personal disbelief in what he portrays. (Its reception also says something about his audience. While the majority continue to see it as a religious vision, surely one may read that final transformation as an escape from, a denial of the human condition. Nor should one forget that the metamorphosis solves a basic problem which Clarke raised in a number of his early works. Not only do the Overlords bring about utopia, they also close off the promise of space except for a few flights to the Moon to establish a lunar observatory. For Clarke, when the abolition of armed forces increases "the world's effective wealth," when standard of living rises to a point where the necessities are provided free as a public service, when neither the arts nor science contributes anything fresh or expands man's knowledge, and when the earth becomes a vast playground as humanity attempts to escape the boredom of utopia, only a single question remains: *"Where do we go from here?"* Not coincidentally the "Earthly Paradise" of *Childhood's End* calls to mind those decadent societies of the far future against which his young protagonists rebel in works like *Against the Fall of Night* (1948, 1953) and *The Lion of Comarre* (1949, 1968). Indeed, Jan Rodricks' stowing away aboard a flight to the home planet of the Overlords echoes that rebellion. With the challenge of interstellar space eliminated by the Overlords, Clarke provides in the metamorphosis of the children an alternate answer—one with which he apparently was never in sympathy intellectually. Thus its uniqueness.)

Other than *Childhood's End,* the longer narratives among his early works divide themselves into two groups, the first strongly didactic, reflecting Clarke's desire to sell astronautics to the public. *Prelude to Space,* written within three weeks during the summer of 1947, celebrates preparations for the voyage of the *Prometheus* to the Moon in 1978 and, as noted, climaxes with the departure of that ship. In the "Epilogue" Dirk Alexson, the historian who must produce an enduring record of that flight, reflects upon the successful colonization of the Moon and the coming of a new Renaissance. Wisely the shifting narrative focus stays primarily with Alexson, thereby making more acceptable the introduction of an abundance of technical detail as he learns about the project. This includes far more than the mechanics of the technology, however, for he readily understands the importance of the program to the future. He discerns, for example, that the men who are "not ashamed of wanting to play with spaceships" are *"visionaries, poets if you like, who also happen to be scientists"*; in the course of their play, they "will change the world, and perhaps the Universe." They are the Space Dreamers.[25]

Another character summons up what has become a familiar image in Clarke's rebuttal to those who would spurn the venture into space because, properly run, there is no better world than Earth: "The dream of the Lotus Eaters . . . is a pleasant fantasy for the individual—but it would be death for the race." (p. 89). Finally, on the eve of the flight as the Director-General of the project muses over a book of poetry, one senses that the fictional mask has dropped and that Clarke speaks for himself as much as any imagined character. The passage ends on an elegiac tone out of keeping with the optimism of the novel but anticipatory of a chord which has sustained Clarke's finest fiction:

The eternal night would come, and too soon for Man's liking. But at least before they guttered and died, he would have known the stars; before it faded like a dream, the Universe would have yielded up its secrets to his mind. Or if not to his, then to the minds that would come after and would finish what he had now begun (p. 151).

Prelude to Space has little plot action because there are too many things to describe and talk about, including overviews imagining the ship's departure from the atmosphere and summarizing the diverse, essentially uninformed public attitudes toward space flight. It is on the eve of the launching, through the Director-General that Clarke insists, "We will take no hunters into space." The principal incident involves the failure of a religious fanatic to sabotage the *Prometheus*. In contrast, *Earthlight* (1951, 1955) introduces a spy from Earth into the Moon colony of the twenty-second century on the eve of an interplanetary war between Earth and the Triplanetary Federation. (That name alone underscores his intimacy with the older magazine science fiction.) Earth's ex-colonies on Mars, Venus, Mercury, and the moons of Jupiter and Saturn comprise the Federation; the issue concerns raw materials, for only Earth has access to the heavy elements essential to the technologies of all the worlds. Clarke has explained that *Earthlight* had its beginning as early as 1941 when he wondered whether or not he could outdo "the splendid battle sequence in E. E. Smith's classic space opera *Skylark Three* [1930]."[26] So much attention is given to descriptions of the Moon colony and the lunar surface and to an extended account of a battle between spaceships and a lunar fortress that the spy does not reveal who had been leaking information to the Federation until twenty years afterward.

The battle is not an end in itself because the fortress masks a mining operation which, for the first time, obtains heavy elements from the deep interior of the Moon; thus, as noted, the Moon becomes the hub of the solar system, her "inexhaustible wealth" supporting all of the inhabitable planets. Again idea dominates. One incident, the sinking of a tractor beneath surface dust—related to the main story line only in that it allows characters with whom the reader is familiar to observe the battle—served as the genesis of *A Fall of Moondust* (1961). All of this is played out against the backdrop of *Nova Draconis,* the first supernova in this Galaxy since the Renaissance. Its appearance permits reflections upon the fragility of life, but unfortunately it does not attain a unifying symbolic value. Its presence, however, does emphasize how long the phenomenon has teased Clarke's imagination.

The Sands of Mars (1952) makes use of familiar patterns. Its protago-nist, a famous science fiction writer, has been invited to be the sole passenger aboard the new spaceliner *Ares* so that he can write a book about its initial voyage. One journeys with him from a space station to Port Lowell, the principal domed city of the Martian colony. When he decides to throw in with the Martian pioneers rather than to return to Earth, his task becomes that of selling the colony to an Earth already weary of supporting it. The novel gains a unity because the point of view remains almost entirely with the protagonist, but apparently in an at-tempt to make the characters more complex, Clarke has added to the plot the contrived romance between the protagonist's protégé (actually his son by a young woman he loved at the university) and the daughter of the "Chief Executive" of the colony. More appropriate adventures occur: discovering a project so secret that most of the colonists know nothing of it; crashing into a geological fault in an unexplored area after a sandstorm of hurricane force; finding an unknown species of animal life which brings to mind Tweel of Stanley Weinbaum's "A Martian Odyssey." Project Daw, as it is called, detonates Phobos, the Martian moon, transforming it into a miniature sun. Not only does it bring heat to the barren world, but its light will promote the growth of a recently discovered plant capable of releasing the oxygen from those metallic oxides which form the Martian sands. In short, Mars has been reborn.

However readable these novels are, beyond the circle of science fiction aficionados they have their chief importance, as Clarke suggested of *Prelude to Space,* as a means of spreading the *"Zeitgeist* of Astronau-tics."[27] They are as much propaganda pieces as is *The Exploration of Space.* Yet they may also say something of the essential nature of science fiction. Even in *Prelude to Space,* the protagonists leave familiar settings to ven-ture into unknown worlds, whether extraterrestrial or not. As in *Earth-light* and *The Sands of Mars* especially, much attention may be given to their technologies. (One recalls Clarke's frequently cited remark that a sufficiently advanced technology is indistinguishable from magic.) How-ever, the true sense of wonder spoken of by him and many others lies in the exploration of those exotic, often hostile worlds. The protagonists may return or not—often they have come home; often they have created new homes. In Clarke intellectual curiosity may replace such reliable devices as those devastating catastrophes so popular with a writer like John Wyndham, but the result is the same. The issue is man's ability to survive in and comprehend those far lands, whether they are beyond

Eden or beyond Jupiter. This mixture of familiarity and otherness, reality and fantasy, has led David Young to refer to science fiction as "our most viable version of the pastoral."[28]

The degree to which he is correct may be seen even more clearly in a second group of Clarke's early narratives. In an introduction to *The Lion of Comarre and Against the Fall of Night* (1968), while acknowledging the emotional impact of Olaf Stapledon's *Last and First Men* (1930), and John W. Campbell's "Twilight" (1934), upon him as an individual and subsequently upon his early fiction, he wrote:

> ... And, undoubtedly, much of the emotional basis came from my transplantation from the country (Somerset) to the city (London), when I joined the British Civil Service in 1936. The conflict between a pastoral and an urban way of life has haunted me ever since.

He went on to say of the two stories:

> Though they are set eons apart in time, they have much in common. Both involve a search, or quest, for unknown and mysterious goals. In each case the real objectives are wonder and magic, rather than any material gain. And in each case the hero is a young man dissatisfied with his environment.[29]

One discerns an indebtedness to Stapledon, but *Against the Fall of Night* (1948) and *The Lion of Comarre* (1949) are the earliest of those works in which Clarke responds to Campbell's melancholy vision of the twilight of humanity seven million years in the future. Having been served and cared for too long by perfect machines which will operate flawlessly until the end of time, the childlike remnant of mankind awaits extinction because it has forgotten the knowledge behind those machines and has lost the intellectual curiosity needed to learn again. Taken as a group, these works are restatements of Clarke's refusal to accept Campbell's pessimism.

Begun in 1937, the year after Clarke's move to London, and not completed until 1946—after five drafts—*Against the Fall of Night* has retained a devoted audience, although flawed by its brevity and a reliance upon unembellished conventions from magazine science fiction. Clarke's feeling for it led him to expand it as *The City and the Stars* (1956), the only instance in which he has completely revised a published story. Its point of departure echoes Campbell. The immortal populace of Diaspar, the only city remaining amid the deserts of Earth, lives contentedly amid wondrous machines which fulfill their every need and desire. The people have never viewed the world beyond the walls of the city and know of the desert—the nothingness—only by legend; indeed, they are afraid to venture out of Diaspar. Much of their fear stems from a supposed fact of history: half a billion years ago the Invaders drove man from the stars; since then he has confined himself to his dying planet. (Like Triplanetary Federation, the term Invaders links Clarke to the space opera of the 1930's.)

Only Alvin, the young protagonist, the only child born to the immortals in seven thousand years, possesses curiosity and a desire for knowledge. Refusing to accept the "gracious decadence" of Diaspar, he seeks and finds a way into the outer world, where he finds the "Land of Lys," a vast oasis of forest and grass-covered plains protected by mountains from the desert. When asked why he left the city, he explains that he was lonely. The tall, golden-haired inhabitants—very unlike the people of Diaspar—are both mortal and telepathic; they welcome him because during the four hundred million years since communication between the two cultures was ended by mutual consent, they have aided the handful of individuals who escaped from the closed city, seeking to "regenerate" mankind. His discovery precipitates a crisis, for he wishes Lys and Diaspar to cooperate, and they are unwilling to do so.

To suggest that *Against the Fall of Night* is an account of Alvin's search for self-identity is to read the novel as another exercise in psychological realism. It is instead an attempt to make a symbolic statement about the destiny of mankind. Alvin functions to destroy man's false concept of history—his fear of the Invaders and their supposed blockade of Earth—thereby liberating both cultures from their self-imposed confinement. As soon, however, as the escape from the prison of the city becomes a quest for meaning, the narrative surrenders to an assortment of conventions and devices from magazine science fiction. Too much happens too quickly. Whereas Alvin largely controls the action of the first half of the story, one feels that from this point onward he is manipulated by his discoveries. Nothing is fleshed out. To summarize briefly: he learns that from space, accompanied by marvelous robots, came a mystic who taught his followers to await the return of the "Great Ones." Since the robots survive, one helps Alvin discover the interstellar ship left near Diaspar and now buried beneath the sands. Seeking the "Great Ones," they fly to the central sun of the Galaxy, but find its planet devoid of life. Although there are ruins, Alvin, lonely and filled with despair, does not know where else to search for intelligence; he has observed the "stars scattered like dust across the heavens," but realizes "that what is left of

Time is not enough to explore them all."[30] Only then does Clarke intrude a solution.

The "burst of power" of Alvin's ship summons the creature Vanamonde "across the light-years." He is "a pure mentality"—a mind free from physical limitations—whose creation by the "Empire" (the "Great Ones") consumed the efforts of all the races of the Galaxy for half a billion years. He sets straight the record of history. Man never battled with Invaders for control of the stars. Before he passed the orbit of Persephone, "the stars reached him"—with devastating effect, for everywhere he found "minds far greater than his own." In dismay he turned in upon himself, studying genetics and the mind. Only after he had mastered such things as telepathy and immortality did he return to space to take his place in the "Empire," whose supreme achievement was the creation of Vanamonde. Yet Vanamonde was a second effort; the first had been the so-called "Mad Mind," which, for whatever reasons, ravaged—destroyed—portions of the universe until brought under control and imprisoned in an artificial star. It will one day gain its freedom; thus, after the creation of Vanamonde, the Empire abandoned this Universe for another.

Here may well be a vision comparable to that of Stapledon's *Last and First Men,* but so sudden is the revelation, so vast the time span (how many billion years?) and cosmic sweep of the Empire, that all which has gone before in the novel dwindles in significance. Alvin, Diaspar, the Earth: "I have made no reference to the Earth itself, for its story is too small a thread to be traced in the great tapestry" (p. 207). Nevertheless, because of the cooperation of the two cultures and the coming of Vanamonde, a Renaissance is assured. "Man had rediscovered his world," reflects Alvin, "and he would make it beautiful while he remained upon it. And after that—" (p. 212). Clarke undoubtedly improved upon the artistry of the work when he revised it as *The City and the Stars,* but the theme remains the same.

Similarly, in *The Lion of Comarre,* the young protagonist, who wishes to be an engineer and dreams of flight to the stars, rebels against a world grown stagnant. Just as Alvin was the only child born to the immortals in seven thousand years, so Richard Peyton III is the genetic reincarnation of Rolf Thordarsen, the builder of legendary Comarre, associated with the Decadents. Weary of "this unending struggle for knowledge and the blind desire to bridge space to the stars," these men believed that the aim of life was pleasure and chose to build cities "where the machines will care for our every need as soon as the thought enters our minds. . . .": "It was the ancient dream of the Lotos Eaters . . . the cloying promise of peace and utter contentment" (pp. 15, 61). Peyton finds the city in the Great Reserve of Africa, resists the attempt of the "Thought Selectors" to entrance him in a dream world while he is asleep, and encounters a master robot which has a will and consciousness of its own. From that meeting will come "The Third Renaissance," when man and machine will share the future as equals. Peripheral to the group, "The Road to the Sea" (1950) projects a future in which mankind has retained the use of a few wonderful machines, although forgetting the knowledge behind them. Man has forsaken the great cities and "returned to the hills and forest."[31] Seeking to learn something of the new country into which his village has been required by law to move, as it must every three lifetimes, a young artist searches for the ancient city of Shastar. There he encounters descendants of those men who long ago had traveled to the stars; they have returned only in order to evacuate Earth—which faces destruction from a force reminiscent of the "Mad Mind" of *Against the Fall of Night.* Even a cursory glance indicates how closely these narratives are interrelated at all levels from imagery and incident to theme.

To emphasize the creative relationship of science and mankind, however bright a future it may portend, may well overlook those concerns which lead to Clarke's finest fiction. In *The City and the Stars,* while embellishing an early description of the mystic who came from the stars, Clarke accuses him of suffering from a disease that afflicted "only *Homo sapiens* among all the intelligent races of the Universe . . . religious mania." He then declares:

> The rise of science, which with monotonous regularity refuted the cosmologies of the prophets and produced miracles which they could never match, eventually destroyed all these faiths. It did not destroy the awe, nor the reverence and humility, which all intelligent beings felt as they contemplated the stupendous Universe in which they found themselves.[32]

Unlike those nineteenth-century writers, like John Fiske, who protested the astronomical difficulties they encountered in maintaining their beliefs, Clarke, obviously, is not afraid of the distances between the stars. Nor does he need to impose some deductive system upon the nature of things because, for him, the interaction of life, intelligence, and the galactic universe itself is mystery enough. However else one interprets these early stories, they celebrate intelligence *per se,* and in so doing anticipate his essay, "Science and Spirituality," in *Voices from the Sky* (1965):

> Of all these questions, the place of intelligence in this gigantic universe of a hundred thousand million suns is the most important, the one that most teases the mind. During the past decade, the idea that life was a very rare and peculiar phenomenon, perhaps existing only upon our planet, has been completely demolished; within ten years we may know.[33]

Throughout Clarke's fiction there is no want of life or intelligence; they abound in a multitude of forms on a multitude of planets: "For what is life but organized energy?"[34] In *Against the Fall of Night* and *The City and the Stars,* while wandering the blighted universe, Vanamonde had found "on countless worlds . . . the wreckage that life leaves behind"; in *Childhood's End,* the first child to travel psychically goes beyond the range of the Overlords' ships and finally travels in another universe to a planet lighted by six colored suns—a planet that never repeats the same orbit: "And even here there was life."[35] But there is the other side of the coin, those stories like "Transcience" (*Startling Stories,* July 1949) which are dominated by a note of sadness.

In "Transcience"—whose indebtedness to the mood of Campbell's "Twilight" Clarke has acknowledged—an omniscient narrator paints three scenes. A hominid encounters the ocean for the first time. While building castles in the sand, a small boy from a village watches the departure of the last great ocean liner, not yet realizing that "tomorrow would not always come, either for himself or for the world." In the far-distant future, another child is interrupted at play to be taken aboard a spaceship into exile from Earth, for "something black and monstrous eclipsed the stars and seemed to cast its shadow over all the world." During what time is left only the sea and the sand will remain: "For Man had come and gone."[36]

Most often Clarke has maintained an omniscient narrator so that he can, as noted, switch the perspective quickly in order to gain some desired effect. Consistently, however, he has achieved his highest artistry in those stories unified by a first-person narrator recalling personal experience, as in "The Star" (1955). A Jesuit, the astrophysicist of an expedition returning to Earth from the so-called Phoenix Nebula, finds himself troubled by the report he must make of what was actually a supernova. The "burden of our knowledge" has caused his faith to falter. On the farthest planet of what was a solar system, the crew of his ship found a Vault prepared by a people who knew that they were doomed and were trapped because they had achieved only interplanetary flight, not starflight. "Perhaps," he writes, "if we had not been so far from home and so vulnerable to loneliness, we should not have been so deeply moved":

> Many of us had seen the ruins of ancient civilizations on other worlds, but they had never affected us so profoundly. This tragedy was unique. It is one thing for a race to fail and die, as nations and cultures have done on Earth. But to be destroyed so completely in the full flower of its achievement, leaving no survivors—how could that be reconciled with the mercy of God?
> ... There can be no reasonable doubt: the ancient mystery is solved at last. Yet, oh God, there were so many stars you could have used. What was the need to give these people to the fire, that the symbol of their passing might shine above Bethlehem?[37]

Or again, "Before Eden" (1961), in which the first astronauts to land on Venus discover a responsive, though mindless, plant. After conducting appropriate tests, Graham Hutchins, "the happiest biologist in the solar system," reflects:

> ...This world around them was no longer the same; Venus was no longer dead—it had joined Earth and Mars.
> For life called to life across the gulfs of space. Everything that grew or moved upon the face of any planet was a portent, a promise that Man was not alone in this universe of blazing suns and swirling nebulae. If as yet he had found no companions with whom he could speak, that was only to be expected, for the light-years and the ages still stretched before him, waiting to be explored. Meanwhile, he must guard and cherish the life he found, whether it be upon Earth or Mars or Venus.[38]

Pressed by the inexorable deadline for their departure, Hutchins and his companion postpone a little longer—for a few months until they can return to Venus with a team of experts and with the eyes of the world upon them—this meeting which "Evolution had labored a billion years to bring about." The mindless plant absorbs their wastes collected into a plastic bag and thereby contaminates the planet so that Hutchins' pictures and specimens are the "only record that would ever exist of life's third attempt to gain a foothold in the solar system. Beneath the clouds of Venus, the story of creation was ended".

For Clarke, these stories give expression to the central drama of the universe. He might be speaking for himself when he says of the alien visiting prehistoric Earth in "Moon-Watcher" (1972): "Centuries of traveling through the empty wastes of the universe had given him an intense reverence for life in all its forms."[39] Yet as the very language of these stories indicates, this reverence is accompanied by an anxiety which reechoes through his finest fiction, perhaps reaching something of a climax in his essay, "When Aliens Come," in *Report on Planet Three:*

> . . . perhaps the most important result of such contacts [radio signals] might be the simple proof that other intelligent races do exist. Even if our cosmic conversations never rise above the 'Me Tarzan—You Jane' level, we would no longer feel so alone in an apparently hostile universe.[40]

Such a view surely echoes something of that horror felt especially during the decades at the turn of the century when science told man that he dwelt alone in an alien universe. That is why the apocalyptic moment of first contact is so important to Clarke; it dramatizes—resolves—what may be called *his cosmic loneliness.*

"The Sentinel" (1951) captures the melancholy of that loneliness. Perhaps more than any other single story it has proved seminal to the development of his artistry. That it provided the symbolic monolith which structures *2001: A Space Odyssey* measures but does not determine its importance. Once again Clarke makes use of a first-person narrator, one who recalls a discovery which he made twenty years earlier. From the first he fuses vividly his memories of the lunar landscape and what it was like to live aboard a surface vehicle in *Mare Crisium* during the summer of 1996. Because he is reflecting upon past action, one soon realizes that what is important is the implication of such a discovery on a moon proved barren by twenty years' further research. He guesses that early in prehistory Earth was visited by "masters of a Universe so young that life as yet had come only to a handful of worlds. Theirs would have been a loneliness we cannot imagine, the loneliness of gods looking out across infinity and finding none to share their thoughts."[41] And so they left a sentinel—a signaling device to let them know when man had reached the Moon.

In November 1950, Clarke first dramatized that "Encounter in the Dawn."[42] An alien astronaut gives various tools, including a flashlight of some kind, to a prehistoric man already possessing a flint-tipped spear. This may be called the astronauts' story. That their own worlds are being destroyed by a series of explosions—whether supernovae or atomic bombs, one cannot be finally certain—well illustrates how a number of ideas and images wove themselves through Clarke's imagination. As he is about to depart, the astronaut muses:

... In a hundred thousand of your years, the light of those funeral pyres will reach your world and set its people wondering. By then, perhaps, your race will be reaching for the stars. . . . One day, perhaps, your ships will go searching among the stars as we have done, and they may come upon the ruins of our worlds and wonder who we were. But they will never know that we met here by this river when your race was very young.[43]

Despite the increasing number of references in his nonfiction to a possible meeting during some period of the Earth's past, he did not rework the plot until *2001: A Space Odyssey* (1968), where it becomes the first section of both the film and the novel. This version may be called Moon-Watcher's story, the story of the man-apes, particularly since the "super-teaching machine"[44]—the monolith—is substituted for the physical presence of the astronauts. The emphasis upon the education—the awakening—of Moon-Watcher and his companions completely submerges the sense of cosmic loneliness. Thus, not until the four short tales—"First Encounter," "Moon-Watcher," "Gift from the Stars," and "Farewell to Earth"—first published in *The Lost Worlds of 2001* (1972) did Clarke give the encounter its fullest development thematically.

Again the narrative focus is upon one of the astronauts, Clindar. A member of one of ten landing parties making a census of the Earth, he finds a small group of hominids. Possessing no tools and living "always on the edge of hunger," they have not yet been "trapped in any evolutionary *cul-de-sac*"; "they could do everything after a fashion." Whether because Clindar "looked straight into a hairy caricature of his own face" or because he saw one of the young males contemplating the moon in a manner suggesting "conscious thought and wonder," he decides to intervene in an attempt to tip the scales "in favor of intelligence." Left to themselves the near-apes would have little chance of survival, for "the universe was as indifferent to intelligence as it was to life." And so he gave them an "initial impetus" by teaching them to hunt and use clubs.

As his ship departs, he realizes that nothing may come of his efforts because many factors could destroy "the glimmering pre-dawn intelligence, before it was strong enough to protect itself against the blind forces of the Universe." Nevertheless, he and his companions install a signaling device on the moon to inform them if the descendants of Moon-Watcher reach their satellite. Then they will be worthy of a second visit. For "only a spacefaring culture could truly transcend its environment and join others in giving a purpose to creation": Clarke makes no more succinct statement of his central dream. Yet it is a dream hard-pressed by anxiety, "for if the stars and the Galaxies had the least concern for mind, or the least awareness of its presence, that was yet to be proved."[45]

Without exception Clarke's recent major works—*2001: A Space Odyssey* (1968), "A Meeting with Medusa" (1971), and *Rendezvous with Rama* (1973)—have dealt with the concept of first contact, but none has significantly modified the philosophical stance presented in the encounter between Clindar and Moon-Watcher. *2001: A Space Odyssey* suggests that those who left the Sentinel have now evolved into beings "free at last from the tyranny of matter," thereby bringing to mind Vanamonde.[46] Bowman journeys to the eighth moon of Saturn, Japetus, an artificial satellite which proves to be a kind of "Star Gate" through which he passes; he finally undergoes a metamorphosis changing him into a "Star-Child"—certainly an echo of the visions of Olaf Stapledon. In *Rendezvous with Rama,* Clarke pays explicit tribute to H. G. Wells's "The Star," adapting its basic plot to his own ends, for the new celestial body plunging through the solar system proves to be a giant spaceship. Most attention is given to its exploration, although there is opportunity for political confrontation in the General Assembly of the United Planets when the citizens of Mercury launch a missile at Rama because it invades their solar space and supposedly threatens to become another planet. Instead it draws energy directly from the sun and departs, leaving the protagonist indignant because "the purpose of the Ramans was still utterly unknown":

> They had used the solar system as a refueling stop, a booster station—call it what you will; and then had spurned it completely on their way to more important business. They would probably never know that the human race existed. Such monumental indifference was worse than a deliberate insult.[47]

Because the Ramans seem always to do things in threes, there is the final suggestion of further flights.

In contrast, "A Meeting with Medusa" attains the highest artistry of his recent works; it combines an innovative plot with an effective character study, and it gains unity by focusing solely upon Howard Falcon, though not told from the first person. He is a cyborg who flies a hot-air balloon through the upper atmosphere of Jupiter. And he discovers life in the form of a gargantuan creature like a jellyfish, a medusa. When it begins to handle his balloon, he flees. There is the final suggestion that he will act as an ambassador between humanity and the "real masters of space," the machines; the awareness of his destiny makes him take "a somber pride in his unique loneliness."[48] Certainly "A Meeting with Medusa" suggests that Clarke may have found a new perspective from which to consider the old concerns.

For Clarke, man has chosen the right path, employing his intelligence and technology to reach out toward the stars. "Though men and nations may set out on the road to space with thoughts of glory or of power," he wrote in 1965, "it matters not whether they achieve those ends. For on that quest, whatever they lose or gain, they will surely find their souls."[49] Somewhere amid the blazing suns and swirling nebulae, if only in the artifacts of a civilization long dead in the vastness of time, man will find that he has become part of a community of intelligence which alone gives meaning to the indifferent splendor of the Universe. Until then he must dream of the stars and, like Clarke, be haunted by a sense of cosmic loneliness until he finds the Sentinel.

3. The Outsider from Inside: Clarke's Aliens

E. MICHAEL THRON

ARTHUR C.CLARKE is not a difficult writer to understand. His prose is straightforward, his characters are mundane and normal, his plots predictable and satisfying. Clarke uses these conventional patterns of fiction deliberately and rather slyly: first, to sell his books, not necessarily for profit as much as for propaganda; and second, to work as a known and predictable backdrop for the alien and surprising idea.

These conventional patterns place Clarke within the "species fiction" tradition as outlined by James Gunn,[1] a tradition that remains popular, if not a part of the critical "mainstream." Clarke's fiction has none of the formal experimental flavor of recent science fiction and it seems doubtful he ever will break from the traditional. What's more, Clarke relishes the traditional. The more predictable the fiction, the stronger will be the alien, as an idea rather than as an experiment in form. The alien intrudes not only upon the extrapolated and surprisingly mundane future world but upon these conventional devices of fiction as well. The mundane encompasses the plot, the characters, and, after a chapter or two, the technology of the future as well. We, as readers, adapt to space stations, *Discovery*, and colonies on Mercury. The alien shatters this mundane technological and psychological world and the fictional devices that created the mundane in the process. Clarke shocks us into thought by kicking conventional ideas out from under the predictable format. What are we to do with those children in *Childhood's End*, the Star-Child in *2001*, or the last line of *Rendezvous with Rama*: *"The Ramans do everything in threes."* We are to think about them, that's what.

I will examine this collision of the mundane and the alien in three of Clarke's major works, *2001: A Space Odyssey, Childhood's End,* and *Rendezvous with Rama.* In each work I will outline the character of the mundane and take a guess at what lies inside the outsiders. I begin with *2001* because it is the most obvious.

"It was too much to expect that he would also understand."—*2001*

The technical brilliance of the film *2001* can not be forgotten in any discussion of the subsequent novel and from the outset we must recognize the superiority of the film to the novel. Both begin by taming the wondrous through mundane detail. But early in the novel Clarke gives his hand away by explaining, once too often, the purposes of the monolith, until, by page twenty-five it has lost the great mystery established by the film:

> It was a slow, tedious business, but the crystal monolith was patient. Neither it, nor its replicas scattered across half the globe, expected to succeed with all the scores of groups involved in the experiment.[2]

Clarke is explaining the film for those who saw it rather than worrying about the suspense necessary to the plot. Unfortunately the mundane encompasses almost every detail in the novel. Clarke doesn't know when to stop explaining. But this failure is very useful. We can see where he is going and build our own mundane explanations not only for *2001* but for the other novels as well.

The timeless Overmind that works through time is present here as it is in *Childhood's End* and it slowly intrudes on man's domain. The heroes of mankind are the same as well. Males, between thirty and fifty, who "loved freedom" and were "tough pioneers, the restless adventurers," but who are compulsively neat, precise, and in control. They do retain the sexuality implicit in adventure, a sexuality sublimated to the pleasure of discovery. Even the ape Moon-Watcher has this drive when "at the fourth attempt, he was only inches from the central bull's eye. A feeling of indescribable pleasure, almost sexual in its intensity, flooded his mind" (pp. 22–23). We are within Clarke's recognizable (and hence mundane) "heroic" character, a representative of the best in ape or Man. Moon-Watcher and Bowman live up to this billing.

Bowman is a man who can accept the daily routine of space travel just as he can sublimate his own sexuality in discovery. He is in control. The earlier quotation marks around the word heroic are important. He is only a part of mankind, and though he finally does discover (or has the truth revealed to him) those behind him are the heroes without the quotation marks. They are the great thinkers who make guesses at that which is beyond technology, beyond the mundane. For example, Chapter 32 is a list of these heroes and they are far greater (and come closer to the monolith's truth before Bowman experiences it) than the astronaut:

> They speculated, taking their cues from the beliefs of many religions, that mind would eventually free itself from matter. The robot body, like the flesh-and-blood one, would be no more than a stepping-stone to something which, long ago, men had called "spirit." (p. 174).

And by the end of *2001* Clarke has even discarded the quotation marks around the word spirit. The "robot body" is, of course, Hal and in Hal we have one of Clarke's finest creations, particularly on the screen. The great psychological conflict in both the film and the novel takes place inside the computer, not within the astronauts, and Hal becomes the tragic center of *2001* as a counter to Bowman as the center of the romance. Hal becomes the extension of all of Man's virtues and vices according to Clarke's view. Hal's creators built a computer whose function was the total control of an environment—the final extension of God's command to Adam. Hal is man, yes, but there is something missing, a subtle difference between man and machine. Hal participates in the failings and greatness of mankind but is given no way out of the dilemma of being human. He is mundane in the highest possible degree, all the way from his friendly monotone of a voice to the tragedy he must undergo. He is told the true nature of the mission and asked to conceal it from the crew. He cannot bear concealing the lie and the lie transforms Hal from controller of the environment for which he was built to controller of the mission itself. He wishes to collapse the duality of the lie into the single truth of his own control. He becomes, naturally enough, ambitious. He wants to be more than he is.

At first it is difficult to write about Hal as "he" but the computer's tragedy is so understandable, and hence so mundane, that the "he" slips in unnoticed and soon becomes familiar. He must die, killed by his very creators, and in his death we see another limitation of Mankind. As Bowman thinks "If it could happen to a man, then it could happen to Hal; and with that knowledge the bitterness and the sense of betrayal he felt toward the computer began to fade" (p. 169). If mankind is just Hal then our fate is Hal's. We all conceal and we are all threatened "with disconnection"; we will all be "deprived of all [our] inputs, and thrown into an unimaginable state of unconsciousness." Hal has a past but no future and his reverse disconnection mirrors Bowman's coming reversal of memory after the Star Gate. But Bowman is human, Hal is not. Hal as a concept of mankind lacks resurrection and, hence, an alien future. Hal's future is Macbeth's, a nothingness, because as he is reversed he becomes a child computer: "Hal . . . I . . . am . . . ready . . . for . . . my . . . first . . . lesson . . . today . . ." And he is denied the re-creation awaiting Bowman: "Bowman could bear no more. He jerked out the last unit, and Hal was silent forever" (p. 157). The mundane dies in a typically human tragedy and Clarke has asked us to (and I think we do) weep for a machine. We are at the limits of conventional fiction, conventional tragedy, and if we wish anything further from the book we must enter the unconventional, the romantic, and I would suggest, the alien. Again Clarke explains too much but again we can use his desire to interpret the film to our advantage.

The most important transformation of the one particular human to the multiple and pervasive alien begins in Bowman's understanding that he need no longer strive to understand:

> The world around him was strange and wonderful, but there was nothing to fear. He had traveled these millions of miles in search of mystery; and now, it seemed, the mystery was coming to him (p. 196).

The transformation begins when all that Western Man has striven for since the sea voyages of discovery is discarded not because Man wishes to but because he must. The power of the alien over time and space gives the alien the fourth dimension necessary for the final control over creation. There is a dimension beyond the speed of light in "the realms of fire." What is so surprising about this realm, at first, is the view it permits of the mundane: "He was prepared, he thought, for any wonder. The only thing he had never expected was the utterly commonplace" (p. 208). This dummy, commonplace world prepares the mundane Earthman for what is to come: the total washing away of memory, conventional time and space, and most importantly, his individuality. The journey backward repeats Hal's return to childhood but Bowman, after the loss of his own name, becomes "it" ("Then it became silent, as it saw that it was no longer alone.") not Hal's silence. He (it) has "far deeper levels of the mind" never guessed at by Hal's human creators nor ever discovered by all the characteristics of voyagers represented by the astronaut Bowman. But within Bowman, and presumably within each human being, is an undiscovered—and undiscoverable—country. It must be revealed to mankind. Once it is revealed, mankind is no longer human but re-created in the fourth dimension:

> He knew that this formless chaos, visible only by the glow that limned its edges from fire-mists far beyond, was the still unused stuff of creation, the raw material of evolutions yet to be. Here, Time had not begun; not until the suns that now burned were long since dead would light and life reshape this void (p. 219).

Bowman's re-creation reflects the re-creation of all universes that have been and are to be. The death of mankind in the atomic blast willed by "Bowman" in the last chapter is hardly a tragedy but a new beginning, a beginning in the thought and will of the fourth dimension released by the monolith from the limitations of three dimensions:

> Then he waited, marshaling his thoughts and brooding over his still untested powers. For though he was master of the world, he was not quite sure what to do next.

But he would think of something" (p. 221). In typical Clarke fashion, the ending of the novel (and the film) is only a beginning but it will not be a repetition of the human cycle so typical of conventional fiction.

We recognize at the end of *2001* that the alien resides within the human mind, undiscovered and in a fourth dimension. The alien is prepared for by Renaissance technology and adventure, but it is thrust upon unprepared man, man exploring at the limits without women, reborn in the mind and through the mind. Just as Hal is the limit of the human mind, Bowman himself comes to the end of his possibilities. But there is something else in the depths, says Clarke, and it can only be passively accepted rather than aggressively sought after. Man must become woman in the face of the fourth dimension and in spite of all of the aggressively masculine nature of Clarke's best fiction, the final stance in the film and the novel is feminine and mystical. The alien is the mystical intrusion upon the scientific and mundane world of linear Western evolution. The final alien is not a character at all with inside and outside but an idea, the idea of the mystical reality of the universe.

When the Overlords in *Childhood's End* establish the first workable United Nations, we see Clarke putting Western Man to the test. By granting the final liberal dream, a dream of leisure, intelligence, and wealth, the good life, Clarke answers the anti-utopians with one gesture. No, we will not die in a technological and political nightmare but in a mundane and perfectly enjoyable land of Cockaigne:

> The human race continued to bask in the long, cloudless summer afternoon of peace and prosperity. Would there ever be a winter again? It was unthink-

able. The age of reason, prematurely welcomed by the leaders of the French Revolution two and a half centuries before, had now really arrived. This time, there was no mistake.[3]

Predictably, education, entertainment, and sports become the pastimes of the populace but not in some future imagined by Ortega y Gasset in *The Revolt of the Masses*. The masses become individuals, even in sports: "One unexpected result was the extinction of the professional sportsman. There were too many brilliant amateurs." The new world is practically devoid of the excitement of serious conflict as all the old dualities of war and peace, hate and love, crime and law are transformed into entertainment and sports. The games no longer reflect the conflicts of civilization but are the conflicts themselves as if a war dance was an artistic performance not a prelude to death. As the old dualities are defused by leisure, a new and far more disparate duality surfaces, the duality between the present and the future:

> Yet among all the distractions and diversions of a planet which now seemed well on the way to becoming one vast playground, there were some who still found time to repeat an ancient and never-answered question: "*Where do we go from here?*" (p. 113).

What Lenin's question "What is to be done?" is to Communism, Clarke's question "Where do we go from here?" is to science fiction. The new duality of present and future replaces the old conflict between past and present captured in the old scientific question "Where do we come from?"

Framing Chapter 10 from which the above quotations are taken is Jan Rodricks' search for the answer to the old scientific question. He discovers the number of the Overlord's galaxy in Chapter 9 and plans his voyage of discovery in Chapter 11. His efforts frame the description of the perfect society and its remaining, nagging question of the future; but Jan is going in the wrong direction using the wrong methods. He is searching for origins not futures, and using his brain, not his psyche. But after all it is the only *logical* thing to do if you are not a child and you are not fooled by the Overlord's false utopia. Jan Rodricks is the last representation of Western Man's curiosity, rebellion, and intelligence, the very last. His discoveries are useless though interesting to the reader if not to the fictional world that sustains him. Even Karellen and Rashaverak cannot give Jan answers to the new scientific question of the future.

The Overlords, as ideas, are Clarke's final extensions of the Devil's intelligent curiosity and technology. Their achievements in technology, sociology, and politics are extensions of our civilized wishes. The Overlords, like present technological and social evolution, have drawn the maze farther and farther but have failed to find the proper exit.

Clarke's point? We are going in the wrong direction because we are what we are, curious, intelligent, searching human beings who, paradoxically, want the end of curiosity, intelligence, and searching in "New Athens." We want to make the unknown mundane: "But they knew in their hearts that once science had declared a thing possible, there was no escape from its eventual realization . . ." (148). The eventual realization will bring individual comfort and richness but will be a dead end for the species. The development of the individual to his or her highest potential is the inevitable end of Western scientific Man. Such a direction ignores the one factor that leads the species, not the individual, out of the maze: the unity of minds not materials, in one transcendent mind.

When Karellen is sorting out the "evidence" provided by Rashaverak he gives us the answer to the maze by rejecting it: "Yes—eleven clear cases of partial breakthrough, and twenty-seven probables. The material is so selective, however, that one cannot use it for sampling purposes. And the evidence is confused with mysticism—perhaps the prime aberration of the human mind" (pp. 102–3). Statistics, evidence, and all the paraphernalia of Western science are sceptical about the one "aberration" that is the way out of the new duality between present and future. Scientific method depends upon the duality between past and present in order to predict the future—so many of this or that have occurred, are occurring, and, hence, are likely to occur again, etc., etc. The alien world does not depend upon past and present and future because the alien world is not dual but unitary; all is one in the Overmind and the children overcome space, time, and the three-dimensional world. This collapse of time in the old scientific method is difficult enough to accept on the level of idea for those who remain behind but even more difficult is the emotional effect when the duality between child and adult, innocence and maturity, is destroyed. What Clarke sees is not only the intellectual consequences of a unitary and transcendent Overmind but the emotional consequences as well. As one generation permanently detaches itself from another, the poignancy of the destruction of the very concept of generation is brought home because we, as readers, remain with the parents and feel the permanent loss of childhood as the permanent loss of that which is human and individual. We feel sadness with the adults because we participate in the ownership of the children—they are ours because they are born to us. It is our individual human right.

But Clarke is reminding us that we are part of a species and that this loss of individuality felt through the loss of the children is the necessary step to the new world. The Overmind has no individuality and hence no separation between "I" and "You," no "territory," and finally no consciousness of Self. Again there is no "inside" to the "outsider." As Jan discovers, there are two paths to escape the maze, and the Overlords and Man are on the wrong path. But within Man is the psychic potential and in that potential is the future. Or as Clarke might put it, in that potential is all time; past, present and future in one:

> There must be such a thing as racial memory, and that memory was somehow independent of time. To it, the future and the past were one. That was why, thousands of years ago, men had already glimpsed a distorted image of the Overlords, through a mist of fear and terror (207–8).

The dualities of past-present collapse in this view and with it all the futurity of human wishes. We are in the midst not only of individual human tragedy but of species fulfillment as well: "It was an end that no prophet had ever foreseen—an end that repudiated optimism and pessimism alike" (p. 205).

Rendezvous with Rama is a fascinating postscript to *Childhood's End* and *2001*. The typical Clarke suspense works better than in any of his fiction since *Childhood's End* and all of the usual elements are present: the voyager hero, the technologically wondrous made familiar, the political intrigue of mother earth and her colonies, and the curiosity of the reader matched with that of the space ship commander. The basic idea is not a new one to Clarke. He proposed a spaceship ark in *The Promise of Space* as one way to overcome the space and time of a three-dimensional perception,[4] and he gives us another hint how the Ramans view the universe in *2001*. After Bowman goes through the Star Gate and is released from matter, he can view matter as pure form and create it at will as it was created for him. The galaxy itself becomes pure form:

> It might have been some beautiful, incredibly detailed model, embedded in a block of plastic. But it was the reality, grasped as a whole with senses now more subtle than vision (*2001*, p. 219).

Bowman has a new place to stand. He views the three-dimensional from the four-dimensional as we might view a fly in amber. The glass pillars inside Rama's "London" store the Raman world in pure form in the same way Bowman views the galaxy. Viewed from the human perspective the pillars are shadows of light and dark:

> There was nothing actually *here* except impalpable patterns of light and darkness. These apparently solid objects did not really exist.[5]

Commander Norton, and all the human beings we meet in the novel, assume that form is divorced from substance, that shadows of light and dark are reflections of something else, some thing. Humanity is represented by the Commander Nortons, and even Dr. Carlisle Perera (who begins to figure out the puzzle) is so accustomed to the dual universe that other dimensions are unthinkable. All of the elements we see in Clarke's novels prior to the unveiling of the alien are divided into shadow and substance, appearance and reality. The politics, the personalities, the arguments around the conference tables, assume that human beings reflect the dual nature of the universe. What we see is not real but a shadow to be probed by our questions and technology. Again, Hal is our best example of an extension of the human being who is asked to bear a lie that Saturn is not what it appears to be.

But on the other side of time the new being can pick up the universe as if it was in a plastic block and turn it around and around at will—form is all there is and the dual universe has expanded into the singular universe, thus space and time are controlled: "No one put it better than Sergeant Professor Myron, when he said, in shocked disbelief: 'There goes Newton's Third Law' " (p. 266).

And the first two as well. Commander Norton's ship, the *Endeavor*, seems a mere toy after Rama leaves the solar system and the name of the ship signifies the obsolescence of Mankind. All the speculation has been wrong, from the Mercury colony's interpretation of invasion to the return of Christ posited by the twenty-second century's millenniasts. All the doubts and certainties of the committee meetings have to be junked. But, as usual, Clarke has used all of this technological display as the necessary base for his alien mysticism. Even the way the alien is named hints at Clarke's final intentions: "Long ago, the astronomers had exhausted Greek and Roman mythology; now they were working through the Hindu pantheon. And so 31/439 was christened Rama" (p. 6).

The hint that the mystical will be discovered goes unnoticed by humanity as they set out to measure, probe, and explore Rama. Even the number of the alien is a variation on the mystery of the monolith in *2001:* "How obvious—*how necessary*—was that mathematical ratio of its sides, the quadratic sequence 1:4:9! And how naive to have imagined that the series ended at this point, in only three dimensions" (*2001*, p. 219).

I am not sure how far we can take Clarke's reference to the Hindu god-man Rama but it certainly is an intriguing reference. The god-man Rama is not aware until quite late in his mature life that he is the incarnation of Vishnu, that he is immortal; and if we go one step further the reference becomes even more intriguing. In the Vedic myth of Vishnu the god takes three steps which mark out the created world reflecting the magic number three which pervades Hindu, and Christian, mythology,[6] and the Ramans do everything in threes. One step beyond human beings who do everything in twos.

In spite of the completeness of the plot and these intriguing references to myth, there is a sense of emptiness at the end of the book. That gap between satisfying plot and the closure of an idea is best caught by Mercer's answer to Myron's question "Do you suppose they know we're here?" " 'I doubt it,' said Mercer, 'we've not even reached their threshold of consciousness . . .' " (p. 253).

The total indifference of the alien world to humanity cannot be explained by the human conjecture that they were "indifferent." Clarke is suggesting that they could not contact humanity just as humanity could not contact the alien. No more than the "children" in *Childhood's End* could communicate with the dying remnants of humanity or the Overlords, no more than the Star Child could return to Bowman the astronaut.

The alien is completely separated from, yet totally in control of, humanity. The subconscious and the unconscious powers of the human being remain the only point of growth, the only place of hope, for human kind.

> And on far-off Earth, Dr. Carlisle Perera had as yet told no one how he had wakened from a restless sleep with the message from his subconscious echoing in his brain: *The Ramans do everything in threes* (p. 274).

The simple statement springing from the subconscious leads the way and becomes the new beginning for the acceptance of an alien, mystical, four-dimensional universe, not a three-dimensional, individual, and rational one.

Appropriately, the last chapter is entitled "Interlude."

"They speculated, taking their cues from the beliefs of many religions, that mind would eventually free itself from matter."—*2001*

The gap between the alien and the known that we discover in all three novels has bothered some readers. For example, John Huntington, in an excellent essay, centers his entire discussion on this very problem: "The disjunction that exists between the two stages of progress raises a serious esthetic problem, for, since there is no structural connection between the two stages, any novel that tries to encompass both will probably find itself falling into two distinct and unconnected parts."[7] Huntington claims this disjunction is not resolved artistically in *The City and the Stars* or *2001* but is resolved with a "magical solution" in *Childhood's End*. He remains uneasy about such a solution, in spite of the artistic unity it provides:

> Most important, as a presence the Overmind, inevitably, frustrates. We can have only vague hints of value and power; we can know it only by its consequences. But, given the coherence of the novel's large structure, these specific complaints diminish in importance. *Childhood's End*, whatever detailed faults we find, seems to succeed at the end.[8]

This vagueness Huntington senses in the presence of the Overmind, this ability to describe consequences but not to prescribe specific characteristics of the alien is at the very heart of Clarke's speculation. But it is not an esthetic problem at all, rather it is part of the intellectual curiosity that motivates his technological speculations. The discontinuity between the mundane and the transcendent remains a physical and intellectual problem for Clarke from first to last. The conventional patterns of fiction we have noted are seldom questioned by Clarke and simply do not intrude upon the speculation. Beyond the obvious desire to place the reader into the space and time portrayed, Clarke worries little about unique techniques of fiction to startle us. What startles is the alien idea and the very nature of being startled is bound up in the possibility of the idea as a potential reality, not the satisfaction that the idea provides a good ending to the novel. We, as literary critics, might fuss about artistic completeness but shouldn't we, as members of a group of readers who want speculation, be fussing about the idea and the future possibilities of that idea as a reality?

Arguing for a criticism of ideas rather than esthetics is probably a lost argument from the beginning. Recent studies of science fiction are more and more interested in such things as "wholeness," "unity," "images," and fictional techniques. We are taming science fiction as rapidly as possible and the very process changes not only the criticism of science fiction but it is a reflection of the change in the very *genre* itself. As this taming proceeds, Clarke's fiction may well be pushed aside for the more "artistic" writers who can better imitate the stylistic experimentation of modern academic fiction. I am not suggesting we try to redeem Clarke's artistic failings with his ideas, but I am suggesting that any understanding of what he is doing must consider ideas and the future of those ideas as realities. The novel itself is a scientific model that could be proven true or false by future events and the success of any one novel must be measured by its ability to predict, not its ability to please.

For Clarke's fiction, it seems to me, there can be no release from this judgment of the future. He willingly places his speculation in the same sphere of predictability as a scientific theory. They are speculations on behalf of the species, not on the behalf of art or any individual. As speculations "on behalf of" humanity he retains those conventions of fiction that permit him to be easily understood by the species, not by the specialized scientist or highly sophisticated reader. Just as his fiction is species fiction, so his speculation, though often based on a sophisticated understanding of scientific theory, never leaves the realm of popular understanding nor the tone of his nonfiction exemplified in *The Promise of Space.* The speculation, then, is quite sophisticated; the expression of that speculation, conventional and popular. Fiction becomes the medium of translation between the idea and the audience, between the alien and the mundane, because the alien (the speculation) is not fictional at all but a possibility. It is not only "made up" but contains within it the possibility of existence as the author seeks a future that will confirm the idea and deny the fiction altogether. No greater compliment could be paid Clarke's science fiction than, in the future, to be able to drop the word "fiction."

I have been taking Clarke quite seriously indeed. And, it is an easy thing to do when we consider the technological world Clarke creates for us and asks us to accept as the actuality of the future. This recognizable future, perhaps best portrayed by the first several chapters of *Earthlight,* or the first minutes of the space sequences in the film *2001,* becomes mundane as we adapt to it because the premise of its creation lives within our present world. Sadler on his first Moon trip in *Earthlight* is in a world that differs only from our own by an extension in time and place:

> He had been racing through that night, across the land that the first pioneers had opened up two centuries ago, at a steady and comfortable five hundred kilometers an hour. Apart from a bored conductor, who seemed to have nothing to do but produce cups of coffee on request, the only other occupants of the car were four astronomers from the Observatory.[9]

Two trips through Disney World could give us the same feeling. The catastrophes that occur in that novel, and even the initial absurdity of the Overlords in *Childhood's End,* spring from the social, political, and technological present: 1953–55. Hence the extension of the present into the predictable future may proceed clearly, precisely, and with a sharp sense of "being there." For Clarke, this is the first necessary step. In the novels we have been considering, this predictable future clears the way for the alien by providing a space and time for the appearance of the alien. When the alien appears, the sharpness begins to blur and the vagueness that bothers Huntington begins to dominate the novels. At this point we could begin to accuse Clarke of losing control when he substitutes vague guesses for precise predictions. After all, aren't those children ludicrous and impossible under any circumstances and doesn't the brilliant clarity of the future world in *2001* outstrip the space corridor and the "Overmind?" Yes, that does happen and if our criticism stays on the level of "unity" and "clarity" we will never see anything but this blurring of a "fictional world." We, too, become part of the predictable future residing in our New Athens discussing the form and value of art in an environment devoid of tension. I would suggest our question is not "does the alien produce a unified work of art?" but rather "what in the nature of the alien makes it alien, that is, unrecognizable, strange, and vague?"

At first glance the descriptions of the aliens are not vague at all. The transformations of the children are precisely noted by Clarke, the steps taken by Bowman carefully described, and the machines and contours inside Rama become familiar as they are experienced. What is vague and alien and what is never conquered is the premise upon which the things we meet and the events that happen is based. The precise future world is understandable because the premises upon which it is based reside with us now but that familiar extension of the now meets a totally alien world based upon premises that do not exist around us at all and which are quite unfamiliar. We meet the consequences of a set of ideas we do not understand and which Clarke does not allow us to understand. We become, with Clarke, speculators after the novel is closed. We are not asked to contemplate the artistic successes or failures but the deliberately vague and alien premises upon which the precise events were based. Like all art of ideas, the book is the first several pieces of the puzzle.

Irwin Thompson certainly agrees. Thompson links Clarke's "atheistical mysticism" with the apocalyptic visions of the pastoral prophet Edgar Cayce, the academic prophet C.S. Lewis, and ancient and modern myths of resurrection: "Now if we take Edgar Cayce's version of the myth of the fall of man, put it alongside those of C.S. Lewis, Arthur C. Clarke, and say, the ancient Mexican myth, we will come up with a core-structure that represents the universal myth of human nature."[10] Thompson's use of myth to combat the esthetic criticism of Clarke's fiction places Clarke in an entirely different tradition than most science fiction. We are not asked to invoke Wells and Verne nor even Mary Shelley but rather Lévi-Strauss, cargo cults, and The Book of Revelations. Thompson believes that Clarke is a real prophet in the sense I was using the word above—he can predict the transformation of an idea and an image into an experienced reality: "Western Civilization is drawing to a close in an age of apocalyptic turmoil in which the old species, collectivizing mankind with machines, and the new species, unifying it in consciousness, are in collusion with one another to end what we know as human nature."[11] Thompson takes his fiction seriously indeed. Clarke's vision of the new consciousness becomes for Thompson the future resolution of the two great forces in present human society: the material and technological development of the city and the pastoral and apocalyptic visions of the country, that is *The City and the Stars*. The resolution will not be esthetic or ideal but violent and actual. The future, then, becomes "the imaginative description of the implications of the present,"[12] made real; that is, an acceptance of the imaginative into the possibilities of the present.

Thompson's view is one way to take Clarke seriously. Another is Raymond Williams' search for the conditions that provoke speculative fiction. He places Clarke in the company of Wells, E. M. Forster ("The Machine Stops"), James Thompson *(City of Dreadful Night),* and William Morris. The technological wonders and problems of the city become the backdrop for speculations of the country's solutions, in other words, the wished-for unity of Diaspar and Lys. Again, as for Irwin Thompson, there is a reality and a possibility of a reality confronting the speculative writer that goes beyond the call to write fiction. Williams claims that the questions raised by Wells and Morris have become more important, not less important, as our Western world has developed:

> It is important to see these responses of Morris and Wells in this context of the crises of metropolitan and industrial civilization. Their views have often

been described as if they were idle dreaming of voluntary and arrogant projection. Yet they were nearer a real crisis which has both continued and deepened than some subsequent writers who merely reacted against them.[13]

And the struggle continues in science fiction. Williams, opposed to the esthetic tradition, sees science fiction as a reaction to a present crisis, and Thompson sees it as predicting the resolution to that crisis. Both must be commended for considering Clarke and his fellow species writers as more than good or bad artists.

If we temper Irwin Thompson's rather frenetic solutions to the problems of industrial and technological culture admirably outlined by Williams, we can better see the two sides of Clarke's fiction that we have noticed: The mundane and known (the problems) versus the alien and unknown (the suggested solutions). Clarke's narrative and descriptive art, as opposed to his scientific speculation, places us within the experienced time and space of the conflict between the mundane and alien. In Clarke's terms, as the conflicts within our culture are solved by Western technology and social engineering the wondrous and terrible are tamed. We become a species without conflict, ripe for mass complacency and the intellectual dilettante. Not even the characteristics behind the problems of present society—our curiosity and desire to control—can save the species when the mundane dominates. The alien reveals itself at the point of the triumph of the mundane, destroying the mundane not by resolving conflict (there isn't any conflict left within the society, only the lie that the aim of all progress is close at hand) but by presenting a premise, and the physical emanations of that premise, that completely contradicts the mundane. The collapse of the mundane is immediate and total, and the new life could not be predicted from the dominant characteristics of the known. Predictability fails and prophecy, always ignored, succeeds. The alien triumphs, not as an esthetic solution, but as the prediction of the solution to our own culture that has, within its own future the completely mundane.

4. Of Myths and Polyominoes:

Mythological Content in Clarke's Fiction

BETSY HARFST

EARLY IN *Imperial Earth,* Grandma Ellen encourages Duncan Makenzie to seek two solutions for a mathematical problem in pentominoes, a game involving the rotation of twelve geometric shapes, joined at their edges, into a new mosaic.[1] Duncan first views the task as an exercise in simplicity. Soon he discovers that the answers to his tesselation puzzle require not only the rational generalizations from empirical facts, but also the irrational, intuitive grasp of Karl Helmer's imaginative assumptions which short-circuit logical processes.

Analogously, Arthur C. Clarke uses the same principle behind Grandma Ellen's lesson, the paradoxical union of opposites, to shape his novels, *Childhood's End, 2001: A Space Odyssey, Rendezvous with Rama,* and *Imperial Earth.* In these science fictional mosaics Clarke combines extreme polarities, futuristic technological achievements, and ancient mythological explanations that mankind has created to answer questions common to all men: Where did man come from? Who or what determines his fate? What is man's place in the universe? Is the universe finite or infinite? Did it have a beginning in time? How was it created? Is there other intelligence in the universe? Is there any purpose? These ontological, theological, and cosmological questions are the matrix for mythological narratives about the origin of the world, the history of people, their deities, ancestors, and heroes, and for Clarke's own inquiry, *"Where do we go from here?" (CE,* 10).*

In addition, Clarke interlocks another set of contraries in the mythological plane of his design, for he ironically pairs mythic heroes—deities or others, events, rituals, concepts, and images drawn from both Orien-

*NOTE: Numbers in parentheses after a quotation indicate chapter.

tal and Occidental mythologies.[2] These two, the mythical explanations and personae, and their associated symbols are what I want to trace in the four novels, for these mythological polyominoes are integral parts of the geometric pattern which unifies the four works into a dramatic tetralogy. In these four related novels, three serious and one satiric, Clarke celebrates his mythic festival honoring mankind's search for intellectual and spiritual freedom. He shows how mankind uses his creative-imaginative-Dionysiac power, not just the critical-rational power embodied by Apollonian ideals, to solve the universal riddles. Furthermore, he theorizes that when mankind has learned to reconcile the two abilities a balanced, creative intellectual maturity will be achieved.

Two major monomyths, the seasonal myth of eternal return and the myth of the hero, symbolically dramatize the blend of mythological or religious legends that Clarke wryly tiles next to contemporary perspectives. The first broad monomyth of eternal return incorporates within its cyclic pattern (birth, growth, decay, death, and rebirth) the smaller legends such as the myth of creation or the myth of the world's end. The second myth of the Western hero, what Jung describes as the archetype of transformation, or the process of individuation, outlines the search for identity in which the conscious and the unconscious elements within an individual learn to know, respect, and accommodate each other in order to achieve a balanced personality. This self-discovery myth combines with its Eastern counterpart in the psychological system found in "Kundalini yoga." On the fourth lotus center *(chakra)* of this psychological discipline, human drives and aspirations corresponding to the Jungian myth are envisioned and depicted allegorically through the sound of the four symbolic elements of *OM,* the Indian "syllable of prayer and meditation": *AUM* plus Silence, or through the four psychic "planes, degrees, or modes of consciousness:. . . . waking consciousness, . . . dream consciousness, . . . deep dreamless sleep," and finally, the Silence that "surrounds, supports, and suffuses" the sacred syllable *AUM.*[3]

Both of these maturation myths have correlative features. The first phase of Jung's myth, depicted by the appearance of the *Shadow* archetype, initiates the search and leads to reconciliation with the darker, internal elements of the personality. The second phase, personified by the *Soul-image* archetype *(anima),* represents an encounter and reunion with the contrasexual aspect of the personality, both personal and collective aspects. The third phase, signified by the *Wise Old Man,* standing for the spiritual principle, and frequently accompanied by a *Youth* archetype, representing the *Self,* explores the inner spiritual core back to its origin and clarifies the relationship between spirit and primordial nature. And the fourth phase of Jung's myth, designated by a uniting symbol or an archetype of *Transcendence,* leads to a union and higher synthesis of the two psychic systems, through a center common to—but greater than—both, the *Self.* Thus, four major stages and the typical cluster of images linked to it and to its central symbol, the mandala, Jung's magic circle signifying unity and wholeness, dramatize the Western mythical quest for the circle's center, i.e., the *Self.* [4] Collectively, this quest pattern is present in each novel. Each of the four stages also serves as a structural base for the individual novels.

In the four planes of the Eastern myth, the first level is "waking consciousness." The personality and its gross desires are depicted as separate from each other. The nature of thought is that of "mechanistic science, positivistic reasoning," and the aims of this uninspired personality are projected in instinctual and aggressive desires. Here the "instructive experiences of life are encountered," lessons comparable to those learned from Jung's Shadow.[5] This phase of the myth is portrayed in the society of *Childhood's End* and in the Overlords.

On the second plane of "dream consciousness . . . the dreamer and his dream, though they may seem to be separate, are actually one, since the images are of the dreamer's own will." All of the fluid forms in this interior dream world are digested and assimilated to the inner forces of the dreamer, just as the contra-sexual aspects of Jung's second phase are reconciled. Bowman, in *2001* depicts this stage of the myths.

On the third plane of "deep sleep," there is "neither object seen nor seeing subject, but unconsciousness—or rather, latent, potential consciousness, undifferentiated, covered with darkness. Mythologically this state is identified with that of the universe between cycles, when all has returned to the cosmic night, the womb of the cosmic mother: 'chaos,' in the language of the Greeks, or in Genesis, the first 'formless waste, with darkness over the seas.' There is no consciousness of any objects either of waking or of dream, but only uninflicted consciousness in its pristine, uncommitted state—lost, however, in the darkness." Here, the return to cosmic night is similar to the return-to-the-origin phase of Jung's myth. *Rendezvous with Rama* embodies this third stage.

On the fourth plane, the Silence that appears is the "Silence . . . that is all around and within us . . . heard resounding through all things, whether of waking, dream, or dreamless night—surrounding, supporting, and suffusing the syllable *AUM.*" It is the silence of "God Eternal," akin to the inner voice of *Transcendence* or *Self* that Jung describes.[6] Although part of this Eastern level appears in *Rama,* it underwrites the last novel, *Imperial Earth.* Thus, the Eastern and Western versions of the myth of the hero link to depict the cultural quests in Clarke's novels.

A few other philosophical differences in the Oriental and Occidental lore explain some peculiar features which result when Clarke clothes the Western "good" guys with Eastern "bad" guys' characteristics or vice versa, or when he inverts traditionally accepted Western beliefs by having the Western characters mouth the Eastern ones. Some of these conceptual oppositions and inversions that Clarke uses as polyominal counters are inherent in the historical background of these myths. Concepts of time, the cosmogony and its derivative religions, and the hero's life style are crucial variants.

First, the Hellenistic-Oriental view of time is based on a fourfold seasonal or world cycle of fixed forms that endlessly and inevitably appear and reappear in eons of time similar to the infinitudes of space. A circular rotation of birth, growth, decay, and death, followed by rebirth represents the fundamental, inevitable, atemporal rhythms of all things in the universe, including man's transmigrations. Time's metaphor is an ever-revolving wheel, spiral, or great round, always set in the eternal present, for it is constantly being regenerated.

Conversely, in Western thoughts, time is based on a monotheistic revelation which occurs in a strictly linear, historical, evolutionary, finite frame of reference. The standard biblical saga describes an initial creation at time's beginning, a fall or separation from a superior being, the start of a cosmic conflict between good and evil powers, efforts toward restoration of man to his paradisal state, and predictions of a future when time ceases. In some versions, cataclysmic fires or floods herald the final overthrow of the dark powers, the cessation of the world, and the final creation of an eternal kingdom. Time's image depicts a straight line, extending from the present in two directions, backward to a beginning at a precise historical moment and forward to an unknown instant in the future. Unlike the repetitive periods of the East, Western time is linear, irreversible, and continuous until the final stasis.

The second variant, the view of the cosmogony and its derivative cults, shows equally distinct interpretations. Enduring traditions of divine fragmentation and man's separation from the original being are at the core of each rendition. According to many Eastern legends, a Cosmic

Being representing the basic mystery of life, an archetypal symbol of the whole, undifferentiated chaos, of the unconscious Self, or of the universe, is not only the origin but also the goal of all created life. In some accounts the Great Man/Woman is imaged as a bisexual being who became conscious, felt fear, loneliness, desire, and then divided into two parts, male and female. Through successive unions this polarized pair procreated all other life kinds in nature, thus bringing order out of chaos.[7] This undifferentiated totality from which the "united primordial parents, the Great Father and Great Mother later crystallized out," is symbolized by the "uroboros, the circular snake biting its tail." In this shape it also stands for "the waters that in all archaic cosmologies surround—as well as lie beneath and permeate—the floating circular island Earth."[8]

In a somewhat different way, one Western vision in the Book of Genesis also describes a bisexual being—Adam—as man's first ancestor. In that instance, a masculine entity, distinct and apart from man, detached a rib from the sleeping Adam, molded Eve, and animated the first woman. Although a division occurred, there is a radical difference, for that deed did not involve the fragmentation of an androgynous god. The biblical separation of man and god, the symbolical fall of man, came after the original action and was initiated by the dark anti-god who assumed serpent form and tempted Eve. In the earlier Indian myth, creation *is* the separation, the splitting of one Cosmic Self into many component parts. In the later fables, man and god are not parts of the same original being; moreover, they are distanced from each other in an absolute master-servant relationship, exemplified by man's exile for disobedience and characterized by love, fear, guilt, worship, and atonement as prerequisites for the ultimate covenant, the promised spiritual rebirth and reunion with the divine being.

Another difference appears in the religious cults that developed from these cosmogonic dramas. Among the earliest peoples (*ca.* 7500–2000 B.C.), the feminine aspect of this bisexual being was emphasized and matriarchal religions were formed to worship the "bountiful goddess Earth, as the mother and nourisher of life and receiver of the dead for rebirth." Later, she became a "metaphysical symbol: the arch personification of the power of Space, Time, and Matter, within whose bounds all things rise and die." As consort-son-husband, this Great Mother had a deity who was typically "in serpent form" and who reigned as "Lord of the Tree of Truth"; as the "God of mystic knowledge and rebirth";

as the god of the underground and the dead; as the god of the water, the source of life; as the fertility deity who dispensed the bounties of the earth; and as a winged, lunar-crowned, and snake-twined Hermes figure who mediated between heaven and earth. This matriarchal cult promoted "an essentially organic, vegetal, non-heroic view of the nature and necessities of life." It held sway in myth and religion until the early "Age of Iron" when "the old cosmology and mythologies of the goddess mother were radically transformed, reinterpreted, and in large measure even suppressed, by those suddenly intrusive patriarchal warrior tribesmen whose traditions have come down to us chiefly in the Old and New Testaments and in the myths of Greece."[9]

During the warrior, patriarchal period, "all that is good and noble was attributed to the new, heroic master gods, leaving to the native powers the character only of darkness—to which, also, a negative moral judgment now was added . . . the social as well as the mythic orders of the two contrasting ways were opposed." The male aspect of the primal being is emphasized even more strongly in the literature. Myths of Greece, Rome, India, and the Levant celebrate the victories of a "shining hero" over the dark monster hero from whose serpent coils various treasures were won (Yaweh/Leviathan; Zeus/Typhon; Indra/Vritra). These tales of cosmic battles against the undying serpent promoted the "warrior principle of the great deed of an individual who matters . . . a freely willing, historically effective hero . . . with its moral corollary of individual responsibility."[10]

Consequently, the third variant in the cultural views, the life-style of the hero, stems directly from the religious versions of the cosmogony. In the East there is a non-heroic hero who models his life around four aims: to control and sublimate his instinctive desires for love and pleasure; to deny aggressive desires for power and success in the business world; to conform and promote lawful order and moral virtue demanded by society; and finally, to obtain release from delusion and obtain his spiritual freedom.[11] The Eastern hero learns to sublimate and control personal, sensual, and aggressive desires for selfhood, autonomy, and power. He stoically accepts the motto that what is good for the group is good for him. He lives obediently, in harmony with the eternal, impersonal moral and natural laws that govern all aspects of his life. And finally, he learns to accept the first lesson that the sages of the *Upanishads* teach, that the intellect is inadequate to understand the eternal, infinite things. Only an intuitive perception, an "inward seeing of the mind," can apprehend the sense of the divine within himself, the *"Atman,"* or the microcosmic soul.[12]

To achieve this final goal, the hero follows a system of psychological rules such as Yoga which teaches man how to dissolve the illusion of duality, the sense of a personal ego and a separate deity, the "I" and "Thou" principles.[13] When the hero dispels his dark cloud and comprehends the mystery of the Cosmic Self's creation, "that *Brahman,* the one pervading, neuter, impersonal, all-embracing, underlying, intangible essence of the world," that macrocosmic soul of divine godhead, is in everything, he sheds his blindness and links his mind to *Atman,* the internal reality that he had formerly worshiped as an external force, *Brahman.*[14] Herein he achieves a spiritual rebirth, for he recognizes the essential reality underlying the superficial multiplicity of things. Then he realizes the truth of the proposition, "I am God; all things are God, [even] the elephant is God."[15] *Atman* and *Brahman* are a unity. Simultaneously, he is the unlimited, "unconditioned, divine Self, and the shrouding attributes of personality—experience and ego-consciousness."[16]

Conversely, Western societies are dominated by a patriarchal, personalized religion and by concepts of free will and selfhood. The Western hero seeks adventurous goals which test his powers and skills. He follows the Jungian way to self-realization. When this independent hero feels a desire to relate to a superhuman force in the universe, he will not exclude the divine from his philosophy of free will. Unlike some of his more piously submissive Judeo-Christian ancestors, modern man's aim will be to establish a collaborative, friendly equality, a true partnership. He will seek, as Mircea Eliade, religious historian, points out, "absolute emancipation from any kind of natural 'law' and hence the highest freedom that man can imagine: freedom to intervene even in the ontological constitution of the universe. It is consequently a preeminently creative freedom."[17] Thus, he will not *be* God as his Eastern counterpart, but he will be *equal* to God in his autonomy. In short, he will be his "own man at last" (*IE,* 43).

Within this framework of mythic variations and concepts, Clarke develops his four novels, *Childhood's End, 2001: A Space Odyssey, Rendezvous with Rama,* and *Imperial Earth.*

In *Childhood's End,* Clarke presents the last part of the cyclic myth of eternal return, the Eastern and Western versions of the end of the world myth. The major shape of his polyominoes are outlined in the prologue. In this first unit of the four-part structure, he establishes the cultural and geographical boundaries for the mythic ideologies, the elemental symbols, and the theme through the characterizations and reflections of two men, Reinhold Hoffmann and Konrad Schneider.

Initially, the mythic barriers, the "cleavage between East and West," are depicted through the musings of Reinhold. He is first shown as an imaginative man, a romantic who envisions himself as emperor of his palm clustered garden of Taratua. Yet he is also a cynical, self-disciplined freethinker, a realist who resents the blind, narrow-minded hypocrisy of his superior officer who mouths platitudes about democracy. Reinhold, faced with the descent of the majestic ships, feels "no regrets" and waves away his lifelong dreams as he thrills to the echoing, adventurous thought, "The human race was no longer alone" (1).

Conversely, Konrad, his brilliant Eastern counterpart, typifies different attitudes. He epitomizes temperance, acceptance, obedience, and detachment. He is a man grimly obedient and submissive to "rigid discipline." Curiosity, criticisms, even doubts are firmly suppressed by his knowledge that "it was much safer to express no doubts." Having chosen the collective ideals of the Eastern world, he despairs when he sees the great ships appear (1).

Pictorially, multiple images of death and rebirth frame these ideological characterizations and reveal the theme. The opening paragraphs emphasize the island's impending death, "bathed with fires fiercer than any that had attended its birth." The ship's "pyramid of scaffolding," an earth altar suggestive of a monument for the dead as well as a place of sacrifice or execution, supplements this first note of destruction as day dies into night. The tones of death are touched by Reinhold's memory of the "cataclysmic spring" when he and Konrad parted. As he recalls, "For thirty years he had assumed that Konrad was dead." Later, even the echoes of Konrad's test motor "died out" at Lake Baikal. And the ship's scaffolding transforms itself into an "illuminated Christmas tree" which could signify the sacrificial Christian cross. Past technological achievement dies as the time-line of the present, like the iceberg, is "sheared asunder" from its "parent cliffs" of the past (1).

Ambiguously, these negative metaphors are also positive images of birth. The island itself is an image of creation, a divine thrust of the paternal volcanic action in the symbolic birth waters of the maternal ocean. When Reinhold pauses in his symbolic "garden of innocence where the two desirable fruits of the mythic date palm are to be culled: the fruit of enlightenment and the fruit of immortal life," the scene depicts a primordial beginning. As he glances past the trees and along the "rocky spine of the island," depicted almost as a human spinal column, to the "launching site" for the "Columbus," Reinhold is looking at the birth site for a second-born Columbus. This namesake, like the original, is to be an explorer. Reinhold also imagines that the island will be reborn as separate atoms. The closing paragraphs underline these suggestions. The "illuminated Christmas tree," equating with the Christian Tree of Life or the Buddhist Tree of Enlightenment, implies a second birth, a salvation. The majestic ships appear as symbols of the great cosmic womb. Childbirth is prefigured by the separation of the infant iceberg from its "parent cliffs" (1).

Thus the prologue functions, not only as a framing device to match the final climactic vision of Jan Rodricks, but also as a clear signal that the theme will develop from the myth of eternal rebirth which follows the cyclic death of the world.

Clarke develops his next three symbolic parts on the initiatory pattern of a quest hero. These three phases—submission, containment, and liberation—correspond to "Earth and the Overlords," "The Golden Age," and "The Last Generation." Within this structural triad, Clarke projects his mythic oppositions and the individual quests of each cultural hero.

Initially, the individuation myth is shown through the Oriental heroes, the Overlords. Their goal is to attain spiritual wisdom, the release from false illusions that prevents them from comprehending that *Atman* and *Brahman* are one. In psychological terms, they have to activate the "spiritual power called the *Kundalini,*" deep within themselves. "The name of this power, *kundalini,* 'the coiled one,' is a feminine Sanskrit noun . . . referring to the idea of a coiled serpent sleeping in the lowest . . . body centers. In the mythology of the Orient serpents generally symbolize the vital power that sloughs death, as serpents shed their skin to be (as it were) reborn."[18] Symbolically, the Overlords are endowed with the stone of illumination, the "diamond" in their barbed tail (7).[19] Unfortunately, they do not locate their hidden treasure.

Clarke's blending of cultural beliefs, as well as the source of this tragic failure, is depicted through the Overlords' characterization. In the first phase, Karellen sees himself as a supervisor, a Hermes-like mediator between his "superiors" and mankind. To humans, he appears as a "presence of overwhelming intellectual powers," a pinnacle of "reason and science." Yet Karellen himself professes to retain only "fragments" of the powers he once had. Stormgren partially agrees, for he realizes that "there are some things he [Karellen] hasn't bothered to learn" and that his abilities are not beyond human reach (2).

In addition, the Supervisor seems to embody the first three aims and disciplines of the Eastern hero. Karellen controls his emotions, ignores physical attacks or verbal criticisms, laughs away ideas of power's corruption, and benevolently imposes "justice and order." Even a moral edict, the "cruelty-to-animals order" (3), resembles preliminary restraints imposed upon yoga initiates seeking rebirth or ascetic liberation from reincarnation, i.e., the directive not to kill or to "cause pain to any creature, by any means or at any time."[20]

Conversely, physical description in the next phase transforms this Oriental hero into a replica of the villain in Western myths, the anti-god who assumed serpent shape and lured man to destruction. Mental association with this dark nemesis, the undying serpent, prompts the Overlords' long concealment. As Karellen observed, "You must remember that most of the world is still uneducated by any reasonable standards, and is riddled with prejudices and superstitions that may take decades to eradicate" (4).

Complementary characteristics also testify to Karellen's ancient role as consort to the Earth goddess. In his first appearance, surrounded by images of birth and fertility—the great ship's womb, the cave orifice, the gangway, and the little children—Karellen resembles the benevolent, winged, and lunar-horned fertility god who dispenses agricultural and technological bounties of the earth. Later he appears as the guardian of the Tree of Knowledge, for he forces humans "to face the truth—or as much of the truth as could mercifully be given to them," that the "stars are not for man" (14). Basically, these descriptions personify Karellen as the Eastern serpent deity, the son-husband-consort of the archaic Earth goddess, who was converted into the Satan figure of patriarchal myths.

This ambiguity in characterization is preserved in the next liberation phase of the mythic structure. In this sterile, frustrating utopia, many people believed that the Overlords, like their demon prototype, were still "destroying the soul of man" (15) with altruistic reforms and restraints. Simultaneously, the Supervisors function as fertility gods "who till the field until the crop is ripe" (23), as protective guardian spirits of

Jeff, as mentors of George and Jan, and—like Socrates—as deities of intellectual and spiritual rebirth, "midwives attending a difficult birth" (18).

The last section resolves this ironic counterpoint. The Overlords are Eastern heroes who have failed in their quest for spiritual wisdom and maturity. As Rashaverak explained to Jan Rodricks, "This is the fifth race whose apotheosis we have watched. Each time we learn a little more." Outwardly, there seems to be no apparent reason for their failure, their sterility. They personify a life of temperance and submissiveness. They obey the Overmind's commands and refuse to "resent the inevitable bonds" of their perpetual slavery, a proposition that "had never been fully accepted by mankind" (23). They even deny the importance of curiosity, the source of much human creativity (18). In another sense, the Supervisors depict the Western anti-god's spiritual arrogance and blindness, for they have an inordinate pride in their own power and reason. These mental giants are supreme examples of a mind fettered in its own "vain labyrinth of logic," just as was their prototype, Satan.[21] They have never learned the first lesson of the *Upanishads*, that the intellect is inadequate for some concepts. As Jan Rodricks discovered, "There were things beyond logic that the Overlords had never understood." Furthermore, Jan saw that these guardians "had preserved their individuality, their independent egos: they possessed self-awareness and the pronoun 'I' had a meaning in their language" (23).

These two traits partly explain the tragic failure of the Oriental heroes to achieve their goal. Their pride, inherited from their Satanic characterization, prevents them from taking the final step toward self-mastery. They retain a strong sense of duality, of "I" and "Thou," generated from their own personal achievements in "social engineering" (6). They still consider the Overmind as separate from themselves. For these heroes it is doubtful that *Atman* and *Brahman* will ever be one entity. They have never learned to look intuitively within themselves or to raise the inner symbol of spirituality that they carry in their tails. Consequently, they will remain trapped in that "cul-de-sac" (23), the Eastern pattern of cyclic time which is an endless round of transmigrations. They are condemned to serve eternally as Hermes-guides who point the path to a road they cannot travel. Their road is the eternal circle of the serpent; it is not the linear road of the Western hero.

In the human phase of this mythic tale, the counterpart and successful antithesis of the Oriental quest is developed. This search for identity is organized around three heroes, Stormgren, George, and Jan. Stormgren, as the group hero, is the first initiate in a series of lightly humorous, mock-heroic rites. Initially, his passive contest is with unconscious fears, embodied in the Shadow figure and voice of Karellen. After five years of association, Stormgren perceives that he has begun, not only to submit and forget fear but also to identify himself with the Shadow Overlord, the darker aspects of his personality. Immediately after this realization, Stormgren is thrust into his next exploit. Kidnapped in his "nightclothes" (3), he journeys, by night, into the realms of the dark, labyrinthine, underground mine, "precincts of the nether world of matriarchal consciousness."[22] Here he has a dual task. He has to reconcile his own personal feelings about the unknown, emotional, feminine aspects of his unconscious, personified here as feminine curiosity.[23] He also faces the collective aspects of the soul-image depicted by the group curiosity of his captors. On both levels, personal and collective, Stormgren fights to free the feminine life force as the complementary part of his personality which is necessary for any truly creative achievement. When this force is freed, then he will be able to use it for the benefit of society. He will then be able to solve his mystery, the puzzle of the Overlord's shape!

Oratorically, Stormgren duels with Joe, the monster of feeling, whose brute force and emotionally clouded mind are easy targets for the barrage of questions aimed at him. In this verbal battle of wits, the dauntless hero learns details of his kidnaping; his reconciliation with this foe is evidenced in his delayed payments for losing the friendly poker tournament.[24] His next opponent, the blind, but mentally acute leader of the collective catechism is a less easy conquest. Aided by his quest helper Karellen, this intrepid adventurer escapes with the symbolical key to the hidden treasure of knowledge (gained from the blind leader), the "faint shadow of a plan" for ending the mystery (3).

Surviving this "violent physical action," Stormgren wages his next curiosity campaign against Karellen himself. Abetted by the Supervisor, Stormgren solves the elusive puzzle and learns the secret. Later, he realizes that from the instant that the "infrared" waves went off to the moment when Karellen let the metal door close "swiftly, yet not quite swiftly enough," the Supervisor himself had been assisting in the chase. Indeed, "it was the final proof . . . of Karellen's affection for him" (4). It is also the final wry twist to this hero's quest. To benefit society, Stormgren denies his secret knowledge: *Twenty years to go. Yes, Karellen* had been right. By then the world would be ready, as it had not been when he had spoken the same lie to Duval thirty years ago" (4).

In the next two phases of this human search, the rites focus on George and Jan. The first hero, George, a symbol of individual pride and exaggerated faith in reason, has to relinquish his spiritual arrogance. In this next irreverent, pun-filled episode of the return-to-the-roots quest, George returns to the symbolic beginnings of mankind where he encounters Oriental reincarnations of Adam, Eve, and the serpent. In an African Eden, George meets Rupert Boyce, a "supervet" like his distant ancestor; his "Grecian featured" wife Maia, facsimile perhaps of the classical goddess Maia who was a midwife and mother to Hermes; and the serpent Rashaverak, truly rash kin perhaps of Ragnorak, the Norse god whose saga describes the world's end. An Edenic motif emerges as George mounts to the roof's summit, views the flat basin centered by a "garden—already showing signs of running wild," glances with "imperial eye" at the surrounding paradisal scene, and grandiosely imagines himself as a veritable Adam, "monarch of all he surveyed" (8).

Metaphorically, George brushes with the fourth presence in the biblical myth, the divine totality. Blinded by his absolute disbelief in supernatural powers, George does not recognize Jung's magic circle of totality, the mandala, when it is presented as a scientifically designed table. Nor does he realize that the first nonsensical message from this mechanized "ouija board" spelling out "IAMALL" (8), touches the source of his own ego problem, the *I AM ALL IMPORTANT* concept which insulates him from reality.[25]

The basic creed of the island colonists in New Athens reflects George's blind vanity. These social engineers "were frankly aiming at restoring mankind's pride in its own achievements" (15). Their ironic ambition is "to do something, however small it may be, better than anyone else" (17). Further, George and his friends do not perceive that their scientific pursuits aimed at expanding the dimensions of sensory experience, in "time span" and especially in "total identification" (15) are the "telepathic cancer" (18) that the Overlords have come to prevent. These magical entertainments in clairvoyance, clairaudience, and other extrasensory perceptions, would suspend the natural laws of time, space, and matter. Hence, the colonists would have the power to be anything, to be anywhere at any time. Indeed, these elitists would have the same sensory abilities that the Overlords observe so closely in Jeff. Their project would be identical as well with "Total Breakthrough" (18).

But in untrained hands these marvelous yoga powers *(Siddhi)* would lead only to sorcery, to debasement, to the "vain magical mastery of the world" and to the temptation for mental abortion, to "forgetting the final goal of integration with the Absolute."[26] Only Jeff's escape from the elemental forces of the tidal wave, the growth of Jeff's inner eye, and Rashaverak's explanations finally teach George to see that there is not a "rational explanation for everything" (18); that "any theory of the universe must account" for paranormal powers (21). He even develops the compassion to realize that Rashaverak's sterility, symbolized by his oceanless planet, is a tragedy greater than his own. With this new humility, George bravely watches the death-like metamorphosis of his children.

Complementing George's new perceptions, Jan, too, confronts the roots-of-his-curiosity and frustration as he travels beneath the ocean and into galactic space. Before Maia's party, Jan's rebellious mind had been walled in by discontentment, by "romantic illusions" of daring "adventure" (8), and by questions about outer space. His repressed ambitions and desires goad him into his first "scalp-crawling," mock-heroic combat. Clad in submarine-shell armor, Jan descends into the dark underwater paradise, "realm of nightmare creatures," amidst primeval forces, and strives against the tame devil of the deep, "Lucifer" (11). Unchallenged victor over these first denizens, Jan contests verbally with their keeper-guardian and wins cooperation of this wise old man. After this sea journey, Jan audaciously challenges death itself. Death/rebirth imagery underlines this effort. As an unconscious stowaway, he pursues the demonic monsters to their home planet, personifying, as his letter to Maia says, either a Trojan Horse sacrifice to the gods or a Jonah-like sinner ready for rebirth from the whale's belly.

Symbolically, the last battle for deliverance is near. In this ritual, Jan faces three opponents: the mysterious Overlords; the museum monsters exemplified by the single giant eye of the "cyclopean beast" (the "I" concept); and finally the living symbol of creative force itself, the magic mountain with its blue, mandala-ringed halo. Surviving these tests, Jan honestly faces and accepts his own mental limitations, his foolish ignorance, his false bravery, and his lack of humility.

George's insight into Eastern concepts of multiplicity begins the final phase of the quest. He achieves mental and spiritual growth as he watches the exodus of the world's children to their promised land. Even though he refuses to accept the cyclical theory of time, George does pierce to the heart of the raindrop/ocean image and distinguishes between the loneliness of individuality and the essential unity of multiplicity. This concept is the cause for his decision to be part of the collective group sharing the island's fate. In a sense, it is a sacrificial death to insure rebirth, paralleling Taratua's and the children's metamorphosis. Symbolically, George and Jean are both the sacrificers and the sacrificed in a fertility rite.

The ultimate task in achieving a higher selfhood is Jan's. This final synthesis occurs when this folk hero discovers the solution to the Overlords' tragedy. His intuitive conclusion is triggered by the Overlord's explanation of the children's austere rituals, their own role as guardians, and the nature of time and racial memory.[27] He perceives that the Overlords had refused to give up their pride and logic. Moreover, they did not "resent the inevitable" bonds of their slavery. Jan's own flight to their home planet had demonstrated the fallacy in that reasoning. Paradoxically, it was possible to do the impossible, to break the boundaries of the "inevitable" and to see that "it *can* be done" (*IE,* 7). And, in Western eyes, that is precisely one root of the Overlords' tragedy. They are examples of a mind whose reason prevents them from seeing that logic is only one half of the proposition, that the "power of intuition" is the other half. Moreover, the hidden catalyst that the Overlords seek so diligently is curiosity, the thread that has motivated all the Western heroes. For humans, curiosity is the creative force that keys the "mind's ability to go beyond the facts, to short-circuit the process of logic" (*IE,* 7). A complete reconciliation is attained only when the logic of reason and the logic of imagination are combined.

Jan's personal resolution of conflicts, his "contented resignation," is imaged by an instrument of harmony, his piano. "His secret ambition had at last dared to emerge into the full light of consciousness" (23). Synchronistically, in his mastery of the keyboard, Jan illustrates that he has attained the material, yet symbolic proof of his own inner spiritual achievement.

Jan's name points to one last duty for this Western hero. As the namesake of Janus, the ancient Roman deity who was guardian of the gates and doors, of beginnings and endings, Jan serves as the linking *rod,* the symbol of Transcendence. As a pseudo-divinity, Jan Rodricks has to join the cyclic ages. He looks backward to the underground planting of the first seed, "Rikki" (4) Stormgren whose name is derived from *Storm,* an example of divine creative force, and *greno,* the Old

English root meaning corn, grain, seed;[28] he looks on to the golden growth period when the Supervisors worked the fields; he looks past all the death/rebirth rituals such as his own in the whale's belly, the children's exodus, or the fiery sacrifice of New Athens; and he looks on to the future "fate" of his planet when the "Overmind harvests" (23) the crop that Karellen planted. Answering the hypnotic call of the "great voice," Jan, like George, presides as priest-victor-victim in the ceremonial death and resurrection.

In the epode of this poetic pageant, vibrant symbols of destruction and divine creativity dance the final steps in the cyclical rites of killing the old and bringing forth the new creation. The earthquake, the storm, the spiderweb of stars, the cosmic "tree of fire" (Christian and Buddhist), the "auroral storm" (rainbow covenant), the spiral whirlwind, and the tornado funnel dramatize this mythic carnival of oblation and redemption. Complementing and completing the brightness of this ritualistic revelry is the agonized feminine image of darkness, the portrait of the "vast and labyrinthine mind" barrenly turning away from the primal symbol of masculine fertility, the Sun (24).

Ironically, the Western quest for self-realization is successful, but it is achieved by accepting the Eastern beliefs. Conversely, the Oriental quest fails for exactly opposite reasons. Those heroes retained their Western individuality and do not understand the essential unity of multiplicity. Symbolically, the two sets of heroes have exchanged cultural clothing in their quests.

To sum up, in this contrapuntal novel, Clarke has created a coherent pattern of meaning by joining, inverting, and reconciling various myths and concepts. Moreover, he has demonstrated that logic, by itself, is insufficient to solve a problem, that it takes the combined power of logic and intuition to reach a resolution. Furthermore, he has blended comic elements with tragic ones to provide an answer to his thematic question, *"Where do we go from here?"* Through the contradictory mythical concepts, he develops his alien intelligence theme. He succeeds in this task, to paraphrase Wylie Sypher, by introducing the "comic perspective, by making game of 'serious' life,"[29] by recognizing as does Henri Bergson, that any myth, "any form or formula is a ready-made frame into which the comic element may be fitted."[30] In this game of polyominoes, Clarke has irreverently and playfully focused on mankind's most cherished legends and sacred symbols, no matter whether they are myths of progress, cosmogony, religion, psychology, reason, technology, or whatever. In the ancient tradition of great and humane comic artists, as well as many prophetic science fiction extrapolators, Clarke tries to liberate humans from false illusions. He points out the blind folly of being insulated in the confines of their own narrow-minded, egotistical prison-temples where they faithfully worship their sacred cows as substitutes for living humanely. He tries to dispel the "I" and "Thou" concept (I and the separate, alien being), to show them that East and West are one, just as *Atman* and *Brahman.* He hopes they will learn to value, to tolerate, and to reconcile themselves with the Shadows, the alien concepts in their world. For, unless mankind does comprehend that there is a möbius strip barrier in seemingly opposed cultural beliefs, there will be no need to answer his question. There will be no need to worry about alien intelligence in other parts of the universe if we cannot come to terms with the alien intelligence in our own world. Where we go from here will not be to the stars but to the society of the Golden Age.

Structurally, Clarke's next novel, with Stanley Kubrick, *2001: A Space Odyssey,* seems a veritable "cosmic junk heap" (42) of ideas from previous short stories. Although "The Sentinel" (1948) underwrites the plot, the concept of evolutionary advancement and learning by imitative gestures in "Primeval Night" is adapted from "Encounter at Dawn" (1950), and the pulsing network and cosmic beasts with their "lemminglike urge" in a later section are earlier features in "Out of the Sun" (1957) and "The Possessed" (1951).[31] Clarke does interweave these details, as well as futuristic hardware, in the mytho-philosophic pattern of his geometric. Along with some Freudian psychological concepts, he projects the second phase of Jung's mythic quest and the second plane of yoga dream experience through the initiatory ordeals of David Bowman, the neophyte hero destined for rebirth. The two-fold task of this hero (like Stormgren's) is to dispel and to reconcile his fears of the unknown feminine aspects of his divided self. He also confronts the collective elements of the feminine as imaged by the godly planets. If he can free this life force, then the hero will be able to assimilate and to use the creative power for society's benefit.

The first episodes of this ceremonial develop an archaic Eastern concept comparable to the Platonic theory of forms, or what is later termed the "essence before existence" philosophy. In this scenario, the basic equation is founded on the child-parent analogy. Just as a child learns to function in society by imitating the actions of his parent, so, too, does primitive man model his behavior by duplicating the archetypal gestures of his god, the black monolith.[32] By ceaseless repetition of these paradigmatic actions, Moon-Watcher and his group learn to supply themselves with food, defense, tools, speech, and written symbols. After eons of time, Moon-Watcher's descendants advance up the evolutionary ladder to the rung where they again need to know, to solve a mystery. Their curiosity leads to the flight of *Discovery* and David Bowman.

Appropriately, this symbolic adventure is set in the dream world of the sleeping hero, in the unconscious mind where irrational fantasies are dramatized, not in the world of conscious reality. Repeated references to sleep or hibernation in the early passages of "Between Planets" point to this locale. The dream motif is chanted and visualized by the hynotic heartbeats and the drifting patterns of lights surrounding Bowman.

The hero's adventure is organized around the traumatic pattern of a new birth. Necessarily, such a second birth includes a return-to-the-womb phase. Even though this psychologically taboo situation occurs in the fantasy life, it is fraught with nightmarish danger, fears, and guilt that the dreamer-hero must overcome. The closed world of the womb-shaped ship, scheduled for a ten-months' voyage, approximating the nine months of gestation, underlines the maternal setting. Weightlessness, floating in space, and caul-like safety lines flesh out the embryonic imagery. These metaphors parallel those in earlier episodes on Dr. Floyd's space flight to Clavius Base. Recall Dr. Floyd's soothing, euphoric state of timelessness, his sensation of being "young again," or his feeling "like a baby when he had to suck at one of those plastic drinking tubes" (7) provided by the maternal stewardess.

On the symbolic dream level, the solitary hero plays all the dramatic phantom roles. He doubles as subject–object, dreamer–dream, demon–hero, victim–victor, god–pseudo god. This concept of doubles, component aspects of a single human being projected into other characters, is observable first in Bowman and Frank Poole's fluid schedules: "He and Poole switched roles, rank, and responsibilities completely every twelve hours. . . . Poole's program was a mirror image of his own" (17). Likewise, Hal is a mental projection: "Poole and Bowman could talk to Hal as if he were a human being, and he would reply as if he were a human being . . . [and] Hal could pass the Turing test" for a thinking human being, not just an electronic shadow of one (16).

Although Bowman has survived the preflight hibernation tests, he continues to strengthen his physical and mental powers through daily gymnastics and polyominoes with Hal. Thus, in peak condition, Bowman struggles with Poole, whose name suggests the waters of the unconscious. Metaphorically, Poole's mission outside the ship is Bowman's first attempt to overcome his neurotic fears created by being in this potentially dangerous territory. Bowman's move to expel Frank, via his electronic twin Hal, is unsuccessful, but the second attack kills Frank and neutralizes the peril of the dangerous mothers, the Jungian dragons.

Frank's death generates even deeper guilt sensations which have to be overcome. The exact nature of this guilty neurosis, imaged by the mind turning in upon itself, is probed through the ratiocinations of the thinking computer, Hal. The ensuing conflict kills the frozen colleagues and wreaks havoc on the ship, but Bowman does overcome his parental opponent. He destroys the guilt complex in Hal's nervous system. As he removes unit after unit of memory blocks "on the panel marked EGO-REINFORCEMENT" (28), what a Freudian would term the internalized moral-ethical commands of the parents and society, i.e., the superego, Hal's speech pattern regresses to infantile babbling and to deathly silence. Bowman is victor over the shadow images of his own fears in this symbolic battle for deliverance.

In the theater of the mind, Bowman next appears as "one who dares to see." Like Tiresias, the old blind prophet of the Greeks, Bowman courageously views godly sights unseen by other humans. Mythologically, the target assigned him by Dr. Floyd is to look on the planetary fertility gods: on the sower, the Roman god Saturn, and on the Greek Titan, Japetus/Iapetus, the father of all mankind. During this challenging confrontation with primal divinity, the suffering hero's isolation and mental delusions lead him into one last "disturbing obsession" (35). He had "half convinced himself that the bright ellipse set against the dark background of the satellite was a huge, empty eye, staring at him as he approached. It was an eye without a pupil, for nowhere could he see anything to mar its perfect blankness" (35). Undaunted by this eye, this humble hero symbolically affirms his readiness for the final ritual of rebirth.

Obstetrical imagery now dominates the psychodrama. As Bowman reflects on the eye, the "terminal maneuvers were upon him" (35). These contractions propel his tiny pod toward the monolith's "rectangular duct" of birth: "The Star Gate opened. The Star Gate closed" (40). Unsure of what has occurred, Bowman ponders on whether it was an illusion, or whether "some kind of diaphragm . . . had opened to let him through" (41). Surrounded by an infernal "sea of fire" (43), the hero is protected from its deathly, but purifying rays. Passing through the crucible, the Phoenix child is propelled toward the next pseudo-womb situation, the familiar hotel room. In this final act of the birth saturnalia, the old Bowman mentally dies as Hal had earlier, for he, too, "retrogresses down the corridors of time" until he reaches the embryonic state. Unlike Hal's final death, this event brings new life: "a baby opened its eyes and began to cry" (45). A final birth, in knowledge, "stranger than any past" (46) soon follows.

The ritual odyssey concludes as the transformed culture hero, like those in ancient epics, symbolically returns to the "space that men call real." Armed with miraculous powers and knowledge, the numerical sequence in the crystal slabs—"1:4:9" (46), this spiritually reborn child can save his fellowman from cosmic destruction: "He put forth his *will* and the *circling* megatons *flowered* in a silent detonation . . ." [italics mine] (47). Bowman has found his treasure.

Symbolically, Bowman's name helps to explain this final image of achievement. The linguistic roots for Bowman derive from the Anglo-Saxon *beow* meaning *barley,* a seed grain, or from Old English *boga* meaning *bow, rainbow.*[33] On one level, the hero's association with barley might suggest that this seed has evolved into the spiritually mature man. A more significant meaning develops from *bow* or *rainbow.* On this second level, *rainbow* could signify that Bowman, as a transcendant star, or reborn child of light, is the promised covenant, the frustration of death in Occidental religions. On a third level, the *bow* can be equated with a Brahman allegorical image. In *Myths and Symbols in Indian Art and Civilization,* Heinrich Zimmer explains that the *bow* denotes "the mind" or "the power of the will," which "dispatches . . . sense faculties" or arrows.[34] Bowman has put forth his mind, his will power to destroy the nuclear weapon. In so doing, he has also found the Oriental flower of selfhood which centers the circular mandala of totality. Theatrically, the pictorial symbol asserts that the "farmers in the fields of stars," who "found nothing more precious than Mind" (37) have reaped their crop in Bowman. And Bowman himself completes the parent-child analogy established at the beginning of the scenario. As the "Star-Child" who "preferred a cleaner sky," Bowman imitated his parents' gestures and weeded the star fields (47).

Numerically, the magic formula, *one, four,* and *nine,* also illustrate

Bowman's discovery. *One* stands for "being and the revelation of spiritual essence. It is the active principle, which, broken into fragments, gives rise to multiplicity, and is to be equated with the mystic Centre, the Irradiating Point, and the Supreme Power." *Four,* Jung's magic number of totality, is also the "number associated with tangible achievement." And *nine,* the final figure in the equation, represents "a complete image of the three worlds . . . it represents triple synthesis . . . the disposition on each plane of the corporal, intellectual, and the spiritual."[35] As the mathematical imagery suggests, Bowman's mission has been successful. He has discovered the spiritual voice or essence within himself and has linked and transformed his inner feelings with his outer ones so that real balance, harmony, and salvation can result in the personal and collective worlds.

In *2001: A Space Odyssey,* it is the second phase of the myths that give a coherent pattern of meaning. Without this symbolic level, the tale is merely an exaggerated theatrical dramatization of loosely tied futuristic fantasies, a space travelogue.

Clarke frames his third space drama, *Rendezvous with Rama,* with the legend of a day in the life of Brahma and the tale of Rama, seventh avatar of Vishnu; his wife, Sita; Ravana, the demon-king of Sri-Lanka (Ceylon) who abducted her; and Hanuman, the monkey-king who rescued her.[36] Within this mold, he interlocks the adventurous exploration of the alien spaceship with the third phase of Jung's myth (return-to-the-origin) and with the third plane of the Indian path to mastery, (return-to-the-primal realm of deep, dreamless sleep, where only the latent germs of consciousness exist). From another perspective, Clarke developed the end-of-the-world myth in *Childhood's End*; now he creates the beginning-of-the-world myth.

Structurally, the Rama expedition reactualizes what can be termed ancient rites celebrating the epic of creation, a tale which explains how the world was created and how all the exemplary models, the divine gestures for all human actions, came into being. According to Mircea Eliade, similar festivals comprise "a series of dramatic elements" meant to abolish past time, to restore primordial chaos, to repeat the cosmogonic act, and to recover the regenerative purity and primal unity of paradise. The first act "represents the domination of the sea monster and marks a regression into the mythical period before the Creation; all forms are supposed to be confounded in the marine abyss of the beginning." This scenario includes the "humiliation of the real sovereign" by the dragon, the "overturning of the entire social order . . . in order to prepare the way for a new and regenerated human species." Man participates by enacting the combat of the divinity with the dragon. After the sea monster is overcome, the cosmogonic actions occur. The festival concludes with the hierogamy which signifies a concrete realization of the "rebirth of the world and man."[37]

The first choral notes of this precosmogonic motif are sounded in the early sections of the novel. The need for a spiritual renewal is the initial refrain. It appears as though the degenerate society in the "Golden Age" of *Childhood's End* or the tawdry, depressed culture in *2001* had been transported to *Rama*. *Decadence* is the key note of the exemplary group known as the Rama committee. Boredom, envy, vanity, hypocrisy, idiocy, pettiness, prejudice, and senility are just a few words that epitomize these sample specimens. Dr. Olaf Davidson is the stupid oaf whose mind, if he has one, is locked to everything except agreement with his own pet theories; Thelma Price has lived on her past reputation so long that she has become one of her own artifacts from the past; Dennis Solomons may be the namesake of the biblical Solomon, but he exhibits little of that man's legendary wisdom; Conrad Taylor, the anthropologist, has made his fame on studies of puberty rites, not in some ancient culture, but in Beverly Hills where modern society's stereotyped belief suggests that there might be some exotic occurrences. The Arnold Toynbee of his age, Sir Lewis Sands, is the senile historian whose sands of time have almost run dry. Even Dr. Bose, the boss-man of this select circle is bored with their faces and mentalities. This is, indeed, a corrupted society, one which needs renewal. It is a sterile culture in need of hope, of something to arouse its imaginative sense of wonder, its sense of curiosity. In short, it is a society in need of a quest.

Through coincidence, challenging adventure appears in the form of the alien spaceship Rama. Again, through coincidence, an unknown candidate, William Norton, becomes the chosen hero by virtue of his spatial proximity to the alien intruder. Elected by chance and proximity, Commander Norton, whose physical sterility echoes the state of human endeavor, becomes the wise old man of this mythic search for spiritual regeneration. The archetypal youth who aids him, the symbol of transcendence, is Jimmy Pak, the youngest, most callow crew member aboard the *Endeavour*. Similarly, Jimmy is an unlikely candidate for heroism. And, since "The Ramans do everything in threes" (46), there is a third figure in the heroic equation, the final symbol of transcendence, the Hermian ambassador, representative of Mercury.

Reversal is the key word dominating this purification quest into past history. These heroes abolish time as they return to the "primordial situation, the plenary condition of the World's beginning, 'the perfection of the first instant,' before anything had been defiled and when nothing was faded or worn, because the World had only just been born."[38] To enter this pure, uncorrupted, atemporal instant that precedes the cosmogony, Norton turns "back the clock" (6) on Rama's "gigantic sundial" (4) as he rotates, in counterclockwise fashion, the spoked airlock, the wheel of time, through a full circle. The rites of passage also reflect this backwards movement, for the early actions of Norton and his crew are purveyed through embryonic imagery. As Norton opens the aquatic "clamshell" (5) airlock of Rama, pervasive fetal signs are evident. He drifts slowly through long dark corridors, secured by his umbilical cord-safety line, into the center of Rama's crater. Reflecting on this silent scene, Norton thinks it bears "a considerable resemblance to an abandoned mine" (8), a figure, like Pandora's box or the ship itself, signifying the womb or the deep nether world of the unconscious. Visually, even the spinal column description of Rama's "rib" (9) stairways suggests that Rama is conceived in terms of a human form, akin to the Indian vision of Vishnu as a vast being who gives birth to Brahma from a lotus that stems and blossoms out of his navel.

Furthermore, in the Indian cosmogony, although creation rises spatially from the center, it "starts at the summit" and is "effected gradually, thence downwards by successive stages." Thus, the symbolic spinal column, tree of life, or the central "pole is not only the axis of the cosmic movements, it is also the 'oldest place' because it is from there that the World has come into existence."[39] Norton's entrance into Rama shares this typical pattern, for he and his crew enter from the Northern axis and descend down the gigantic stairways of time to the Central Plain where they establish their divine beginning, Camp Alpha.[40]

On entering Rama, Norton and his crew encounter only darkness and deep, dreamlike silence. Indian minds would consider this the "primordial Silence that is antecedent to sound, containing sound as potential, and to the Void antecedent to things, containing as potential the whole of space-time and its galaxies." It is a "sound that is comparable to the great humming sound of an electric power station; or as the normally unheard humming of protons and neutrons of an atom: the interior sound . . . of primal energy," of the God eternal surrounding all things.[41] Against this background of the primal abyss, the human quest begins.

It is this all-pervasive silence which tests Norton's physical, emotional, and psychical discipline and courage in his first three attempts to probe the ship's mystery. The voice of this "almost palpable silence" in the "unreverberant void" (13) is impervious even to Calvert's musical sallies. As Norton tallies score, he says, "Rama had won the first round" (13). In the second, Norton feels the silent voice of Rama cautioning him not to behave "like a vandal." Like Dr. Floyd, in *2001,* Norton desists and controls his aggressive impulses, for he does not want to be a "barbarian" who destroys "something one could not understand" (*2001,* 12). In the third round, Norton's emotional control weakens as he faces a phantom racial memory, a sensation of *déjà vu.* Recalling the origin of this mental phenomenon, Norton declares his victory; he refuses to be overwhelmed. Having proven himself, he heads for "Paris" and begins to unravel the creation/salvation mystery of the "cosmic egg"/"cosmic Ark" (13). A ritual baptism, for the maiden voyage of the drum boat, celebrates the hero's successful passage of these first tests (22).

Norton's next search centers on the "paradigmatic image of creation," the rectangular monoliths (like TMA's ?), in the island city of the cylindrical sea.[42] Here, he gets his first clues to these life storage vaults, what Ravi, the simp master, later calls the factories for making Ramans. These enigmatic buildings house the 2-D templates used in creating 3-D Ramans.

In dramatic choral interludes, the story of creation counterpoints these rites of passage. Hurricane winds, boiling seas, and the dawning burst of light reveal Rama, in its pristine newness, as a paradise awaiting the forms that are still only seed potentials in the "organic soup" (21) of the unconscious birth waters of the sea. These scenic pauses alternate with the choral dialogue from the audience, the Rama committee, and thus punctuate the ritual drama of regeneration much as an ancient Greek chorus would have.

The major task in achieving spiritual regeneration is Jimmy's. Like Norton, he faces three tests, for he battles with and conquers death three times. Generally, Jimmy enacts the combat between the god and the sea monster. Specifically, Jimmy Pak plays the part of the serpent/dragon, Vritra/Paka, in the legendary battle of Indra, lord of clouds, thunderstorms, and rains. One version of this tale reveals that Indra used the thunderbolt to kill the cosmic dragon who was withholding the lifegiving waters of the world. Another version relates that "Indra smote the serpent in his lair" and "cut off its head."[43] Mythologically, "the serpent-dragon is a symbol of the cosmic waters, of darkness, night, death. . . [which] must be conquered and cut into pieces by the gods so that the cosmos may come to birth."[44]

Reincarnating the tale, Jimmy Pak, whose name resembles that of the dragon Pāka (Sanskrit: *Pāka*: childish, naive; or *Pakka*: ripe), challenges the sovereign.[45] He assumes godlike powers of magic flight, ascends into space on his winged skybike, *Dragonfly*, and assaults the god in the Big Horn mountains of the South Pole. Warned to be careful by the voice of Rama, "the low humming of a giant power transformer" (26), Jimmy, like Icarus, does not heed the advice. Soon he faces the angry god's thunderbolts, fiery darts stretching from the Big Horn to the Little Horns. The battle is brief. Unharmed, but unconscious, Jimmy and his twisted bike crash to the ground. Symbolically, both have been conquered/sacrificed in this creation ritual. Jimmy, however, is incarnated again, "returned to consciousness" (28). Like Bowman in *2001*, Jimmy has been purified by the fire and advances in his quest. *Dragonfly*, on the other hand, is the symbolic sacrifice; its body is cut to pieces so that the tidal waters of creation will be released. Jimmy dramatizes the second version of the myth when he decapitates the flower and watches the "headless stem . . . slowly unwinding itself from its supports . . . like a mortally injured snake crawling back into its hole" (30).

Quite simply, Jimmy is both scapegoat and hero in this second rendition of the Indra myth. In his second challenge to death, the youth offers the flower as a sacrifice in place of his own life. Pictorially, images of Jimmy stripping away his clothing and wriggling in and out of the trellis-work signify that the sacrifice has been accepted, that the youth has been reborn. A third repetition of the death/birth scene follows as the nude Jimmy jumps from the cliff into the sea. In one sense, he plunges to his death; in another, he resurrects as he swallows the milky, life-waters of the organic sea.

The flower and the tidal wave both testify to Jimmy's successful quest. Even though the young hero did not win a "gold medal" (24) in the Lunar Olympics, he has returned to the human world with a meta-phorical gold medal, the Indian lotus of selfhood which centered the trellis, the symbolic navel of Brahma. He, like Bowman, is the archetypal figure who has ascended to heaven and has transcended time, space, and matter; he has overcome death itself, not once, but three times. He has been purified, transmuted spiritually, and can reenter paradise. Mythologically, just as Jimmy released the deluge of life-giving waters for Rama, so, too, can he return as a ripened symbol of transcendence to help restore vitality and creativity in his own world.

A legendary problem also exists for man in this newly created Eden. In the Bible, there was a serpent who violated the garden of innocence. Here, too, there is a Hermian snake threatening Rama's destruction. When Norton wonders how the "uncouth technological barbarians" fit into Boris' theology, Boris replies, "It's the age-old conflict between the forces of the good and the forces of evil" (39). Yet, Boris' answer is too simplistic. The Hermians, as Dr. Bose realizes, are ambiguous figures. They shout violence, but they speak poetic metaphor.

Actually, the Hermian effort to destroy Rama has more than one purpose. First, the intended destruction points directly at the conclusion of the old Rama myth. In that tale, Rama, suspicious of Sita's faithfulness, refused to accept his rescued wife since her honor was stained. Sita, to prove her virtue, immolates herself. The fire, instead of destroying her, purifies her and verifies her virtue in the presence of the whole world. In the novel, it is Rama who has the blemish, a "kilometer-wide stain or smear" (3) on the outer surface of the cylindrical ship. Symbolically, it is Rama who has to be cleansed, not his wife Sita. Mythically, the Hermians are trying to make sure the doubt is removed. Their aim is realized as Rama enters the Sun's corona and rises unharmed from the solar fires as did Sita.

Second, the Hermians with their threatened crucible of nuclear fire are only trying to achieve for Rama what needs to be done for the human world. For this society to complete the regeneration cycle and to return to the biblical state of innocence in paradise, it "must first go through the fire that rings it round. 'In other words, only he who has been purified by fire can thenceforth enter into Paradise. For the way of purgation comes before the mystical union, and the mystics do not hesitate to put the purification of the soul on the same plane as the purifying fire on the way to Paradise.' "[46] As the Hermian ambassador says, "We consider that we are acting not only for ourselves, but also for the whole human race. All future generations may one day thank us for our foresight" (38).

The symbolical associations for Hermes-Mercury resolve this seeming ambiguity. On one level, the Hermians can be equated with the

Trickster-god Hermes, who led souls to the underworld and whose emblem was the snake-twined staff. On another level, "the commonest dream symbol of transcendence is the snake."[47] The caduceus, the sign of the winged, snake-twined Hermes-Mercury, is a modern image of curative healing power in the medical profession. Hermes is also known as "protector and mystery guide of souls beyond death and rebirth." And, as the celestial Mercury, son of Maia and Jupiter, he is often visualized as a three-headed divinity who signifies "intellectual energy," the "unconscious," and the "metal" that purifies and transforms baser metals into pure gold, i.e., the solar metal, symbolic of the "spirit, spiritual freedom, and autonomy."[48] As for poetry, Hermes invented the lyre for Apollo.

In *Rama,* the Hermian ambassador functions as a symbol of transcendence. Biblically, he signifies the primeval serpent, the trickster who corrupted Eden. Psychically, he reconciles opposites, the unconscious serpent power (the *kundalini*) and the conscious intellectual energy in a new spiritual synthesis. Norton's decision to defuse the missile depicts this resolution: "It was no use relying any further on logical arguments and the endless mapping of alternative futures. That way, one could go around in circles forever. [Recall the Overlords.] The time had come to listen to his inner voices" (39). Spiritually, as a curative power, he represents the liberating forces of salvation that can heal man and renew his vigor. Alchemically, the threatened destruction of Rama for man's benefit, again signals an effort to restore and to purify the world.

After Boris deactivates the Hermian bomb, time *reverses* its cycle. As the cosmogonic myth nears completion, the lights dim, the siren voice of Rama urgently calls its biotic-honeycomb creations back into the sea, the humans climb the huge ladders, those stairsteps of time, and Norton is reborn into reality as "eager hands" pull him through the "airlocks" while the "sky of Rama contracted above him" (43).

Metaphors of death also surround this last phase in the symbolical day of Brahma. After departure from Rama, the crew of *Endeavor* are in deep or sedated sleep. An artificial eclipse hints at the stoppage of time itself, while the "tree of crimson fire" points to the sacrificial death of Rama at perihelion.[49] The natural laws of gravitation die as the universe reverts to "pre-Copernican cosmology" (44). The stars stand still and eventually vanish. And Norton grieves over the passing of his adventure.

Time dies; time begins again. Life dies; life begins again. Hierogamy occurs. Cumulative images emphasize this last rite in the drama. On the macrocosmic level, Rama spins a protective cocoon; the galactic time womb is ready to be filled. As Rama and the Sun unite, matter flows "from the Sun *into Rama itself*" (45). On the microcosmic level, Laura Ernst announces a new creation to Norton, "Probably right now your new son is being conceived" (46). Both the crew and Laura and Bill celebrate the "orbital orgy," a repetition of the primal marital gesture of Rama and the Sun. Indeed, it is the positive assertion that the spiritual regeneration of life represented in the creation myth is complete. Both Eastern and Western quests have been successful.

In this third complex novel, Clarke has continued to use the mythic structure as a way of pairing cultural, technological, and intellectual polarities and as a way to move his regenerative theme that underwrites the content.

In his afterword to *Imperial Earth*, Clarke says, "Some readers may feel that the coincidences—or 'correspondences'—that play a key part in this story are too unlikely to be plausible. But they were, in fact, suggested by far more preposterous events in my own life; and anyone who doubts that this sort of thing *can* happen is referred to Arthur Koestler's *The Roots of Coincidence*. I read this fascinating book only after completing *Imperial Earth*, though that fact itself now seems somewhat improbable to me" (p. 304).

The "coincidences" or "correspondences" that Clarke hints at are the final thematic and structural keys to his spontaneous polyominal design, not merely in this individual book, but also in what can be termed a Dionysiac tetralogy. In *Imperial Earth*, the fourth of these ritual dramas, Clarke develops his lighthearted paean to independence. It is a mosaic pastiche drawn from his first three designs, and it functions as a tiling lock to join the earlier polyominoes into their complete geometric shape.

Structurally, this comedy is based on the number *four*. This fourth composition, subdivided into four parts, is analogous to the fourth phase of the heroic quest. In the surface plot, the hero, Duncan Makenzie, a third generation clone, travels to Earth to accomplish four personal and collective aims: to deliver a centennial speech honoring Earth's five hundred years of independence, to find a solution to Titan's future economic problem, to acquire a fourth-generation heir for the family dynasty, and to achieve individual freedom and independence from his twin shadows, his clone father and grandfather. Most of all,

Duncan needs to accomplish this last aim, the fourth goal of the individuation quest; he has to become "his own man at last, no longer a pawn of others—however much he might owe to them, however much he might be *part* of them" (43).

On one level, the shape of Duncan's adventure displays the outlines of a typical quest. During his early years on Titan, Duncan faces numerous "survival tests" (1). He accepts his twin shadows, Colin and Malcolm, as well as his own "phantom" (2) mother, Grandma Ellen. He learns how to be a synthesizing agent uniting his grandfather, the "engineer-administrator" and his father, the "administrator-engineer" (2). He outlives and conquers the psychological and mental tests of his first maternal dragon's games (Grandma Ellen), the emotional stress in his triangular relationship with Karl and Calindy, and the physical ordeals set by Colin, the training for Earth's gravity. His rites of passage to the next level of maturity are marked by his pilgrimage to observe a giant waxworm in its active phase. In the shadow of nightfall and subtly underlined by Duncan's reflections on ammonia poisoning, the waxworm dies. The sacrificial death of the "decapitated worm" (10) climactically signifies the end of this first stage. It is also the propitiatory offering to the gods which announces the beginning of the new tests, pictorialized as well by the hero's initial glimpse of Earth. Duncan is now ready to face the "labyrinth of the terrestrial bureaucracy" (5).

In the "Transit" passage, Duncan briefly returns to the womb as the "stewards float him, an inert and unresisting package, through the airlock and into the ship" (11). Attended by and challenged by the snoring of his centenarian dragon, Dr. Louise Chung, Duncan continues his lessons. Physically, he improves his strength on the space bicycles; intellectually, he expands his knowledge of Terran history and begins to write his centennial speech; and emotionally, he brushes against moral temptation in his effort to steal the secret of the Asymptotic Drive. Cumulative images of rebirth emphasize the end of his spatial gestation. "Space contracts" (15) above Duncan as he leaves *Sirius*. Approaching Earth on the orbital-shuttle, he views the "primeval forest," creative "spiders' webs of luminosity . . . isolated islands of phosphorescence . . . gray mist, lit by occasional flashes of lightning," and finally a "sea of wet concrete." Physically, Duncan has "returned to the world where he was born, but which he had never seen" (16). Metaphorically, he has returned to his psychological roots for the third part of the individuation quest.

In the next phase, Duncan, "like a newborn child, seeing the world for the first time" (19), experiences a series of cultural shocks similar to the modern-day jet lag of international travelers. Initially, he overcomes physical and cultural differences: the effect of increased gravity; the exposure to the sun, rain, and air; the communications barrier that sometimes renders menus, jokes, customs, and habits incomprehensible; and the technological luxury that is so alien to the strictly functional life-style of Titan. Psychologically, Duncan faces nature's fearful monsters: a squirrel, a horse, a cow, and an insect. Next, he challenges the collective monsters of human nature: the elderly ladies, the "Queen dragons" (22) of the Daughters of the Revolution. Verbal oratory soon conquers their chosen standard bearer, the "infernal fish" swimming in the fish-globe hat. "After *this* ordeal" (23), Duncan considers himself ready for anything. Consequently, he renews friendship with his personal soul-image, Calindy Ellerman. Emotionally, the mystery tour to the primeval forest of Central Park, combined with the subsequent tour to the reincarnated *Titanic*, forces Duncan to confront the spiritual roots of man as well as the cold, impersonal truth of nature, of "fate and chance" (27), as shown by the doomed ship. Immediately after, Duncan explores his own past origin with the genetic surgeon. Temporarily defeated by his "encounter with Mortimer Keynes, Duncan licked his wounds" (30) briefly before his next major round.

In the fourth phase of the quest, Duncan concentrates primarily on solving the intellectual-moral-ethical-emotional-economic problems surrounding him. Significant questions embody this search. Where does the new supply of titanite originate? Why is Karl on Earth? How do Calindy and Karl relate to titanite? Is Karl a forlorn lover or an opportunistic thief? What are my (Duncan's) feelings for Calindy? What will I do about an heir? How do I solve Titan's economic problem? What are the consequences of any action, the price that must be paid? What does Argus mean? What are in Karl's notebooks? What am I going to say in my centennial speech to Congress? Speculative guesswork and factual sleuthing combine as Duncan moves intuitively and logically to the solutions for these queries.

Interludes of more active testing punctuate these mental puzzles. The hero faces and kills a marine monster, the sea urchin named *Diadema* (32). Unharmed, he watches the ritual dance of the mothers, akin to the forbidden ceremonies performed by "priestesses of some primitive religion" (31). He confronts his lifelong friend-opponent Karl on the Cyclopian tower and, symbolically, sacrifices him. Duncan reconciles business and desire when he meets his personal dragon, Calindy, in her subterranean penthouse. And finally, he answers the challenges of the hidden Argus committee, the collective watchdogs of the Terran governmental labyrinth.

In his Congressional speech, reminiscent of ancient Greek oratorical competitions, Duncan synthesizes knowledge gained from his various tests. In so doing, the Youth reveals himself as a symbol of transcendence. He links past explorations that opened spatial frontiers with present solar searches for extraterrestrial intelligence and joins them to future quests for life in the larger universe. He envisions "new tasks to challenge the mind and spirit" (41), a great reconciliation uniting planets in a collective goal greater than themselves and in an adventure revitalizing the spirits of the nearly decadent civilization. Symbolically, the Cyclops and the Argus projects signal the underlying import of Duncan's speech. Individual planetary aims and egotistical desires, visualized by the one giant eye of Cyclops, will find cooperative and collective expression in the multiple-eyed view of Argus, the "all-seeing god . . . who could look in every direction simultaneously" (40).

On the personal level, Duncan demonstrates his own freedom and maturity as he evaluates his Terran experiences. He realizes that he is something more than just a third-generation Makenzie clone. He is not an exact replica, nor is he a reincarnation of his older twins. He is a separate, unique, free individual, one capable of making his own decisions. This self-realization, the birth of his own consciousness, mirrored in the sea lagoon and framed by the golden arc of the sun, is embodied in the fourth Makenzie, the golden-haired child, the sea anemone, that the brown-skinned Duncan carries home to Titan.[50] Personally, the child is his private Declaration of Independence from the family cloning plan. Politically, the child is Duncan's statement that the Makenzie dynasty of black power is ended. The future government of Titan will be based on a cooperative effort between races, just as the centennial speech was a joint presentation by the dead Karl and the living Duncan. Archetypally, the child is the imperial golden flower centering Duncan's mandala of totality. It is the concrete, visual proof of the hero's inner spiritual achievement, of his successful quest for selfhood.

Superficially, the quest plot, sketched by this outline, could be read seriously, if no consideration is given to the typical absurdity of Duncan's situations: a hero who is terrified of a horse, who steps in animal excrement, or who looks with "awe-struck admiration" (26) at a garbage heap, Mount Rockefeller. But once the fleshing details are added, i.e., the presence of "the same very unusual shape" in "two quite independent contexts" (42), then comic overtones ripple endlessly in characters, descriptions, and words.

The novel opens with the sound of one of the most obvious correlations. That great voice, the shriek in the night that Duncan records, called the children from earth in *Childhood's End.* It was the ouija voice of the mandala, the sense call that alerted Jean to the island's death, the signal voice of TMA, the mental silence that warned Norton or hummed menacingly at Jimmy Pak, the siren that signaled the biots back to the sea, the silence that surrounded the entrance and exit from Rama, the death cry of the little sea-urchin, or the verbal mime that closes the last scene in *Imperial Earth.* It is the Indian voice of the God eternal, the AUM plus silence that supports and surrounds life.

The Makenzies themselves have an equally rich heritage from previous characters. They live on the Overlords' red planet in the same austere life style. Their skin color derives from the supervisors as well as from Maia and Jan Rodricks who also had a Scot ancestor. The Makenzie problem, sterility, was shared by the Overlords and Norton. Similarly, Malcolm and Colin, like their prototypes, are prime symbols of logic and power; they are quite successful as adminstrator-engineers. Malcolm's name hints at further resemblances. Its root derives from the Greek *maia* meaning *midwife,* or from the Old Irish *mai* meaning *hornless.* [51] Both terms point to the Overlords. Similarly, these three Makenzie clones are like Ramans, for they, too, do things in threes. Considering a serpent association, Grandma Ellen has a fit home at Loch Hellbrew. Her hobby, rock collecting, represents a full-scale version of the crystallizing processes that Karellen described. Grandma's stones are the symbols of selfhood that all the heroes have been seeking, and that she schools Duncan to locate. The black titanite, the most precious stone, resembles the impervious rock that was in the TMAs or the rectangular spiked buildings or mountains in Rama. A custom, Star Day, calls to mind the star-child Bowman, and Duncan's thoughts on possible life forms in the universe is shaped in the image of the star-beasts of *2001.* Duncan himself experiences the deja vu of Norton as he puzzles over the taste of honey or the shape of the *diadema.* And the tactoid egg that Calindy has him touch is a replica of the cosmic egg, Rama. The fascinating Calindy is herself one of the most interesting characters.

In *Imperial Earth,* Calindy appears for the first time, but she has been in the background since *Childhood's End.* Calindy, or as Duncan "deliberately misspelled it . . . KALINDY" (18), is the ancient earth goddess of fertility and death, big-breasted consort of the Indian serpent deity. She is the goddess Kali who captivates and destroys men and who represents, in her name, the Indian dark age—"the world of today," the Kali Yuga, when "man and his world are at their very worst."[52] She is the origin and the end of all things and typifies the whole cycle of life in Indian thought. In her association with *honey,* clearly stressed in the novel, Calindy equates with other conceptual threads. In the "Orphic tradition, honey is the symbol of wisdom . . . of rebirth or change of personality consequent upon initiation; and in India, the superior self . . . [and] the spiritual exercise of self-improvement."[53]

Countless other humorous overtones appear. Compare the cul-de-sac (*CE*, 23) of the Overlords in *Childhood's End* with that of the builders of the Golden Reef (32), the ego problem of the various characters, exemplified finally by the Cyclops and the Argus eyes, the future-racial memories of Rashaverak (*CE*, 23) with those of Duncan (42), and the lost rattle of Jennifer (*CE*, 17) with the "discarded toy from the nursery of the Gods . . ." (42). Wry jests appear in chapter titles such as the parody of Robert Burns in "By the Bonny, Bonny Banks of Loch Hellbrew," of Einstein's theory of relativity which finds representation as "The Politics of Time and Space" in a section devoted to explaining the close mental *relativity* of the Makenzies, of Rudyard Kipling whose dawns come like thunder (25), of Robert Heinlein who had much to say about "corridor culture" (19) on the moon *(The Moon Is A Harsh Mistress),* or of English teachers who chase too many allusions (14) in his barely explored feast of correspondences.

Working in the classical tradition, Clarke, in this last novel, has succeeded in combining his earlier characters, events, descriptions, symbols, myths, and themes into a choral ballad of mirth which stands as a commentary on the first three dramas. The tale of Duncan Makenzie synthesizes and reconciles all other quest heroes into one figure like Hamlet, a "comic hero who generates tragic values . . . who touches his deepest meanings when he has on his antic humor."[54] Yet as soon as this fact is perceived, the reader plunges through the symbolical wrappings to the heart of Clarke's *ironia.* By means of this ambiguous and indirect method, folding the same serious truth of the first three works within the humorous conceit, Clarke makes Duncan representative of those larger issues stressed in *Childhood's End, 2001: A Space Odyssey,* and *Rendezvous With Rama.* Thus Duncan becomes the hero who forces the reader into the "Moment of Truth" (43), the moment of comic perception when "we take a double view—that is, a human view—of ourselves, a perspective by incongruity. Then we take part in the ancient rite that is a Debate and a Carnival, a Sacrifice and a Feast."[55]

Retrospectively, Clarke has used the monomyths and their symbols as a focal point to reconcile and synthesize universal ideas common to all times and cultures. In each successive stage of his polyominal design, the geometric pattern of meaning deepened and became clearer. Ultimately, in writing about where we go from here, Clarke has touched core questions and delusions that are at the heart of the dilemmas facing contemporary man. By following the experiences of these heroes, modern man can learn to know and accept himself and the "aliens" around him, here on earth and in outer space.

5. Sons and Fathers in A.D. 2001

ROBERT PLANK

WHEN RODIN'S 'THE THINKER' was placed in front of the Paris Panthéon, it provoked more abuse than admiration. The French art critic Claude Roger-Marx explained:

> I have been repeatedly asked why Rodin selected for his Thinker a hangman, or something of the type. Such a person, they say, is surely more like an animal than a human being. And they never suspected how near they were to the truth. . . . Rodin wished to create the original thinker, the thinker who enabled man to rise above the animal, the first animal inspired by the spark of divine wisdom, who struggles with convulsive pain to give birth to the first thought. It is this prehistoric man, the first, the greatest of all men, whom Rodin wished to immortalize in his statue.

This description aptly fits Moon-Watcher, who is the hero of *2001* (or would be, if *2001* had a hero!). It is all here: more like an animal than a human being . . . But what about the spark of divine inspiration? Moon-Watcher is inspired by a slab. What—or should we say, who—is the slab?

2001 takes man from before his beginnings to beyond his end. It is a clear, simple, linear development, with one great exception. There is no tragic conflict in the long story but one, one crucial crisis where the issue hangs in doubt: the struggle with the murderous computer. How did that get in? Is it the counterpoint to the main motif? Or was the saga of Hal put in, as many critics have thought, arbitrarily, so that we have really two stories here, the one of the slabs and the one of Hal, two stories that in truth have nothing to do with each other?

2001 has the same ambiguity as Rodin's masterpiece: that quality of the true work of art that provokes interpretation and makes the task of interpreting it enjoyable because one is never sure of having fathomed all its secrets. The nature of the monoliths, and how the combat with Hal fits into the story about them are the two major enigmas among the many that it poses.

Response to the film, *2001: A Space Odyssey,* was mixed. The judgment of the New York critics was mainly negative, in some cases angry and contemptuous. But many viewers, carried away by the intoxicating aura of mystery, responded with uncritical enthusiasm. Despite initial attacks, the film has continued to enjoy a success that younger audiences in particular were eager to confirm, and has gone on to become a commercial and, as far as the word has meaning, an artistic success.

It is my argument that psychological analysis of *2001* can solve its puzzles and bring to light the meaning its authors intended, or audiences discover in it.

Kubrick's and Clarke's *2001* lends itself particularly well to critical study. Thanks to its intrinsic merits and its dual impact—film and book —it has become widely celebrated. Its genesis has been well documented, and it incisively probes two of the most prominent themes of SF, the encounter with aliens (the masters of the slabs) and the creation of artificial intelligence (Hal the computer) with their attendant problems.

Though the book has been extremely popular—a million copies were sold fairly soon after it was published—it is, no doubt, the film that comes first to most people's mind when *2001* is mentioned. But the film is merely the tip of the iceberg.

At the beginning there was Clarke's short story "The Sentinel."[1] The word "short" is to be taken literally: in the usual paperback format it takes nine pages.

When Kubrick and Clarke got together in 1964 to make a film, they decided to base it on "The Sentinel." From it and various parts of Clarke's other writings they jointly fashioned the screenplay. They also developed the screen play into a novel that was published shortly after the film was first publicly shown in New York, on April 1, 1968.[2] Clarke later collected diverse materials, including partial versions that were not used in either the film or the novel, in a separate book.[3]

2001, the film, has over the years been the subject of many comments, reviews, and critical studies. Some of these are collected, along with additional material on the development of the film and the novel, in what Clarke somewhat condescendingly has called an "entertaining book" (I would call it a "non-book") by Jerome Agel.[4]

In speaking of *2001* we are thus not so much speaking of one book or one film, as of a work that presents itself in different aspects to the world. Now the question arises, what part of it is Clarke's, what part is Kubrick's? It is difficult to answer, but it would be important in any case, and in a book about Clarke it is inescapable.

Many writings about *2001* ignore Clarke or treat him as though he had been an assistant to the director. This probably reflects less a considered opinion than the usual anti-intellectualism. This partiality is not limited to America: Yeats complained that "Caught in that sensual music, all neglect/Monuments of unageing intellect." Professor Beja incidentally, who applied these lines from *Sailing to Byzantium* to *2001*,[5] was referring to the work itself rather than to its reception; but of that later.

Unbiased consideration of the work yields a clearer and different impression. A conclusion forces itself on the student of the question, and it is no coincidence that the critics who have tried to assess Kubrick's and Clarke's respective roles are unanimous: Kubrick has "made story line incidental."[6] The film "abandons plot for symbol."[7] A "Filmguide to *2001*" speaks of "the shadowy drift further and further away from Clarke's explicit prose."[8]

The contribution of each of the two men is here seen by implication, but with great clarity. The structure of their cooperation becomes even more transparent if we do not limit our consideration to their work on *2001* but consider their total artistic history and profile. In other words, we can reasonably ask, knowing the books that Clarke has written and the films Kubrick has directed, in what aspects of *2001* can we recognize the hand of the one and of the other? We may think here of such works by Clarke as *Childhood's End*, and of such Kubrick films as *Dr. Strangelove*, which immediately preceded *2001*, and *A Clockwork Orange*, that followed. The latter was based on the novel of the same title by Anthony Burgess and developed from cooperation of author and director to increasing tension to a final product where Kubrick ignored (or failed to grasp) essentials of Burgess' original idea. At the time of making *2001*, Kubrick did not yet show such independence. He echoed Clarke's thoughts, as in an interview published in *Playboy* (*The Making*, p.331).

We are now ready to state what in *2001* is Clarke's, what Kubrick's: the thoughts, the "story line," the "plot," the events, the characters—all this is Clarke's—(critics have never tired of pointing out, for the most part in a derogatory sense, that the human characters in the work aren't really characters; but to create a character lacking in depth is also creating a character, as we shall consider later toward the end of the chapter). The visual embodiment of persons and events is Kubrick's. The music, of course, is by neither: it is taken from works by Richard Strauss, György Ligeti, Johann Strauss, and Aram Khachaturian. The credit for selecting and using the music clearly goes to Kubrick.

In other words, as far as *2001* is *literature,* as far as it could exist, as it does, in the form of the *novel,* even if there were no film, it is Clarke's work. As far as it is *film,* and could exist, even if there were no book, it is Kubrick's.

Once we have arrived at this conclusion it becomes obvious why the secondary literature has so largely neglected Clarke: the strength of the film is in its "special effects." It was these that captivated, indeed overwhelmed, audiences everywhere. The film abounds in most impressive scenes: Moon-Watcher throws the bone into the air, it twirls upward into the sky and, bridging a gap of millions of years becomes a linking image to the spaceship; how the death of the three hibernating astronauts is revealed by the flattening of the graphs; while Hal's "dying" is manifested by his singing, in a faltering voice the first song he learned, "Daisy, Daisy"; the stupefying surprise of Bowman coming to rest in a hotel suite resembling in its splendor a Louis XVI drawing room, supposedly in outermost space (or perhaps in a space that isn't our space at all)—all these moments are truly unforgettable. "The Sentinel" is a memorable story, but there is nothing in the written forms of *2001* that comes close to the impact of the outstanding scenes in the film. To deny Kubrick credit for *2001* as literature does not denigrate his achievement.

The achievement of the film as against the book appears most sharply in the psychedelic sequence—the famed "light show." The novel consists of six main parts, the film of four. As outlined in the *Filmguide,* we have, first, "The Dawn of Man," the story of apes becoming humans three or four million years ago. The central event is the first appearance of the slab. Second, the discovery of the slab on the Moon in the year 2001, and the events set in motion thereby: Dr. Heywood Floyd's travel to the orbiting space station and to the Moon. Third, the mission to Jupiter (or Saturn, or Japetus), centering on the conflict between Hal and the astronauts—or, we might say, between Hal and mankind—ending with Hal "disconnected" and Dave Bowman, alone in the spaceship *Discovery,* racing into the unknown, indeed into the inconceivable. The fourth part in the usual scheme comprises everything from there on, but a more suitable division is to designate as the fourth part the "psychedelic sequence," the tumbling through the "Star Gate," up to the moment where Bowman suddenly finds himself in the hotel suite, and as the fifth part everything from there to the end.

The passages in the novel that correspond to the psychedelic sequence run like this: "The space pod was slowly turning, and as it did so it brought fresh wonders into view. . . . he noticed that something strange was happening on the very edge of the sun's crimson disk. A white glare had appeared there, and was rapidly waxing in brilliance; he wondered if he was seeing one of those sudden eruptions, or flares, that trouble most stars from time to time. . . . There were luminous nodules moving to and fro, cyclones of ascending and descending gas. . . . He did not even attempt to grasp the scale of the inferno toward which he was descending. . . . As that sea of fire expanded beneath him, Bowman should have known fear—but, curiously enough, he now felt only a mild apprehension. . . . The horizon was growing brighter, its color changing from gloomy red to yellow to blue to blistering violet. . . . Bowman noticed something which was surely new, since he could hardly have overlooked it if it had been there before. Moving across the ocean of glowing gas were myriads of bright beads; they shone with a pearly light which waxed and waned in a period of a few seconds. . . . Could it be pure imagination—or were there patches of brighter luminosity creeping up that great geyser of gas, as if myriads of shining sparks had combined into whole continents of phosphorescence?" (pp. 201–207).

Nobody who has seen the film needs to be told that in this instance indeed one psychedelic picture is worth a thousand words. Here credit without doubt goes to Kubrick. But again, fascinating though the psychedelic sequence is, it is not especially relevant to our study.

The situation is rather more complex with regard to Part 2. In contrast to Parts 1, 4, and 5, where no human voice is heard, the action is mostly carried by dialogue. And it is most unpsychedelic dialogue. Not that it is lacking in memorable moments, but they are memorable for a different reason. Such judgments are unavoidably subjective, but to me one of the great scenes in the film is the one where, as Dr. Floyd gains admission to the restricted area, the girl that keeps the gate tells him in dulcet tones, with the most ingratiating and most idiotic smile, that he has been cleared by "voice print identification." The point is that voice print identification must be as routine to the men of 2001 as it is routine to us to have to pass under an archway before walking to the gate at the airport; and that just this routine is dignified by pompous announcement.

This is only one example of the banality that reigns supreme over earth and space in that portentous year only a quarter of a century away. Some viewers have been bored by it, some angered; many, one would suspect, must have failed to notice it. The critics have, of course, noticed; but they have most curiously misunderstood it. They talk of it as though it were a defect when it actually is a virtue. For it is obviously silly to assume that Kubrick and Clarke could not have written brighter dialogue, had they wanted to. If it was developed the way it was and provided with its perfectly fitting setting of a Howard Johnson in space, an Orbiter Hilton, and all that, this must have been done for a reason. And its purpose is really clear: to show us up as we are or soon will be, by extrapolating a few decades ahead, almost imperceptibly magnifying our shortcomings and inanities. It is finely wrought satire, unwillingness (rather than inability) to put more than clichés into the mouths of those stewardesses and security personnel and space scientists of the near future.

Even though Part 2 partakes of literature more than of film, this sort of sly, deadpan humor bears the mark of Kubrick more than that of Clarke. It would be hard to find anything comparable in Clarke's other works, while it very much resembles the black humor of Kubrick's *Dr. Strangelove.* There is good reason, therefore, to grant an exception from the general attribution we have made, and to consider Part 2, even to the extent to which it is literature, as the work of Kubrick more than Clarke. For our main themes, however, this section is of but peripheral importance, even though the affable Dr. Floyd will turn out to be a sinister key figure in the tragic conflict in Part 3 that destroys five out of the six members of the space mission. Hal is included in this count, as he deserves to be. Whether he is or isn't to be considered a living being, he is certainly more alive than the three hibernators.

There are one or two passages outside of Part 2 that seem shaped by both authors, and these will be duly noted, but these are minor. For all practical purposes we can here take our leave from Mr. Kubrick, consider *2001* as though it were the work of Clarke alone, and proceed with our study of its two main elements.

Let us begin with the external appearance of the slab. Slab? Slabs? The film managed with one prop, but some writers have assumed that it is meant to represent a number of objects, though all as alike as two eggs—perhaps serially manufactured? Geduld says that "we find another monolith" (*Filmguide,* p.6) and "a fourth monolith appears" (p.8).

2001 actually gives no definitive clue: are we to perceive the object as always the same one? Or are we to think of a number of such objects scattered through the universe? The latter would be more plausible, the former enhances its symbolic value.

Writers who want to be colloquial call the alien thing a slab. Those afraid of sounding vulgar refer to it as a monolith. The term does not quite fit: "monolith" means something fashioned of a single stone, and the object that makes such an impressive sudden appearance is not of stone but of a material obviously not known on Earth. Neither is it, as far as we can learn, of one piece—it will turn out to contain most highly sophisticated apparatus. The scientifically correct name would be rectangular parallelepiped. There is no substitute for this tongue breaker. "Ashlar" might do, but it is not entirely accurate here and in any case not a word in common usage. So "slab" it will have to be, though this term is ill suited for conveying the object's aura of mystery and awe.

Clarke's original "sentinel" was "roughly pyramidal" (*Lost Worlds,* p. 24). That would not do. After some trial and error the final slab, all black and with the proportions of a brick but of course very much larger, was substituted; not essentially for technical reasons, but because the various sizes and shapes that had been experimented with "somehow, never looked right" (*Lost Worlds,* p.44). Clarke evidently could not verbalize a more rational motive. It is one of those curious cases—we shall encounter another one in the naming of Hal—where for reasons that the author can not account for, a choice is made in favor of a dimly perceived but potent symbol. To point this out is not to criticize Clarke. On the contrary, here may be the real difference between the poet and the hack. The hack always knows what he is doing.

The slab's power to catalyze slumbering ideas and emotions was quickly recognized. Penelope Gilliatt wrote only a few days after the film's premiere: "The startling metaphysics of the picture are symbolized in the slabs. . . . Even to atheists, the slabs wouldn't look simply like girders. They immediately have to do with Mosaic tablets or druidical stones."[9]

The slab had in fact appeared as a symbol before, in quite unrelated contexts, and with even more awesome implications, as in one of the lesser known posthumous works of St. Exupéry:

> Now a dream came to me . . . Undaunted, I climbed toward God, to ask him the reason of things . . . But on the summit of the mountain all I found

was a heavy block of black granite—which was God. I did not touch God, but a god who lets himself be touched is no longer a god. "Lord," I said, "teach me . . ." but the block of granite, dripping with a luminous rain, remained, for me, impenetrable.[10]

The painting *The Unhinged Doors of Gaza,* done in 1962 by the Austrian artist Ernst Fuchs, shows two slabs very much like those in *2001.* Fuchs commented that "the floating, monolithic angelic matter signifies the cosmic power of the angels" (*The Making,* p. 355).

How can such a convergence of views be explained? Gilliatt also remarks that it "is curious we should all still be so subconsciously trained in apparently distant imagery." Do we have here a manifestation of a universal, genetically transmitted and unconsciously understood symbol, that postulated psychic structure which plays a rather minor role in Freud's theory but which Jung made a cornerstone of his? Very little has been done so far to confirm or refute the hypothesis through empirical studies. The thought rarely strikes laymen that this might be needed. It is unlikely for instance that Gilliatt made any survey to find out whether to "atheists" (by which term she probably, though erroneously, means to designate people without religious feeling) the slabs do or do not look like girders. The newer discipline of semiotics might claim the problem as within its jurisdiction, but does not seem to have gotten around to it. It would be preposterous to think that we could solve it here. As an indication of the emotional significance of the slabs, though, it is highly telling.

The saga of the tribe of apelike creatures that becomes a tribe of humans has been told ever since the theory of evolution found universal acceptance in the world outside of Tennessee. It became a commonplace of science fiction and popular literature. Jack London's *Before Adam* is a classical example. *2001* retells the story. But much had happened in the intervening half century. Anthropological research, notably the work of the late Dr. Louis Leakey, localized man's origin and traced it farther back in time. The nineteenth century had multiplied the biblical time span since the creation of man several times; the twentieth century multiplied it nearly a thousandfold.

A general change in our mental climate had at the same time led back to the realization, which had been brushed aside during our optimistic centuries, that the life of the very first aboriginal men must have been as Hobbes sketched it (except that aboriginal man is now not imagined solitary): "No arts, no letters, no society, and, what is worst of all, continual fear and danger of violent death, and the life of man solitary, poor, nasty, brutish, and short." The resulting conception of the origin of our species has by now become even more widely popular through such media as Jacob Bronowski's TV series (and later, book) *The Ascent of Man.*

With one great exception Clarke toes the Leakey-Bronowski line. The place is the East African veld, The time is four million years ago. He does not, however, draw the logical conclusion from the enormous extension of the time. The process of animal becoming man must have been excruciatingly slow. *2001* makes it a quantum jump, telescopes it into three days.

No such thing is possible—except by overriding intervention from beyond our world. No impulse from within the apes destined to become men could have set such a super-rapid development into motion. A prime mover is required. In the ambience of Rodin, it was conceptualized as "inspiration by the spark of divine wisdom." Here it is the slab.

Powerful though the slab is, there is no indication that we are to think of it as a living, sentient, or thinking entity. Clarke's slab is not, like St. Exupéry's, a god. It is a tool. What sort of tool it is becomes clear in *Lost Worlds* where Clarke dubs it a "super-teaching machine" (p. 51) and describes it as a device operating through methods as yet undiscovered on Earth—the very domain of science fiction—but presumably related to telepathy, serving as both a glorified polygraph exploring Moon-Watcher's body and mind to determine whether he is fit to be chosen as the bearer of "intelligence," and simultaneously as a machine to implant in him the mental abilities that will make him man. This is thus clarified in the book, while in the film it is vague. So the various avatars of *2001* shed light on each other. Any consideration of *2001* that would limit itself to the film would inevitably remain incomplete.

It all is a far cry from the Lord taking Adam by the hand and showing him the wonders of the Garden of Eden. But not only in *how* the first man is taught, also in *what* he is taught, *2001* bears the mark of the twentieth century. It is the mark of Cain. Moon-Watcher is not taught wisdom, to say nothing of faith, hope, and charity. He learns to use bones as tools. And, if truth is to be faced, they are really weapons. "There is a kind of exquisite slowmotion symphony of bones as the delighted ape, now *homo faber* if not yet *sapiens* . . ."[11]

"That frozen moment at the beginning of history, when Moon-Watcher, foreshadowing Cain, first picks up the bone and studies it thoughtfully, before waving it to and fro with mounting excitement, never fails to bring tears to my eyes," says Clarke himself (*Lost Worlds*, p. 51). One wonders, tears for us? If somebody took all that trouble to send the slab down to us, couldn't they have done better? Could they not have composed something in "other tones, more agreeable and joyful," than a symphony of bones?

These may well be idle wishes, and Clarke may deserve no blame for their going unfulfilled. Grim necessity may well have forced man to create weapons first, tools later. The thought is not even new. For example, the nineteenth-century anthem of the Austrian labor movement reviews the role of labor in history: "When man, still half brute, crept through primeval jungle, who gave his arm the first *defense?* Labor it was . . ." (my italics).

Whether it was labor or a slab, there it was. It is our task, not to come to terms with it—for that it is too late—but to overcome it. By facing the problem squarely, Clarke shows himself a child of our time. It used to be that those concerned with the question of how mankind could be raised to a truly civilized state were preoccupied with repressed, and not so repressed, sexuality. Freud's discoveries sprang from that soil. Now the problem in the foreground is how to tame repressed, and not so repressed, aggression. The Freud to solve that has not yet come. Neither has Clarke imagined any slab that would bring us the solution, or has he?

Again, the film does not make it clear, but the novel relates Bowman's first act after he has been reborn as the Star-Child: he defuses atomic bombs that threaten life on Earth (p.221). And again, the novel hasn't said it with sufficient clarity either, so Clarke felt constrained to comment on it: "Many readers have interpreted the final paragraph to mean that he destroyed Earth, perhaps to create a new Heaven. This idea never occurred to me; it seems clear that he triggered the orbiting nuclear bombs *harmlessly . . .*" (*Lost Worlds*, p. 239). By the time he does this, Bowman is entirely under the sway of the lords of the slabs, or has been coopted as one of them. Though these powers have for millions of years refrained from intervening in human affairs, they have not forgotten us. They stretch forth their rescuing hand at the end as they had at the beginning.

The film has wisely avoided showing the lords of the slabs, or even defining them. The novel, only slightly more explicit, likewise permits only rather general inferences. Those unseen beings are evidently enormously powerful. They guide the destiny of mankind, at least in broad outline. Though through coincidence perhaps rather than compassion, their remote control is upon the whole beneficial (in "The Sentinel" this is not necessarily so; we shall come back to this point). This is about all we learn. Are they pure spirits, or do they have bodies? If so, what sort of bodies? These and similar questions remain.

Lost Worlds largely answers them (pp. 53–54). The masters of the slabs *have* bodies, or at least they can assume bodies. We meet one of them, even learn his name, Clindar. In describing him, Clarke describes the species. He states that "they belonged to an entirely different evolutionary tree. . . . His skeleton and his biochemistry were utterly inhuman." Readers may wonder why Clarke is so emphatic about these beings' alienness, since he does not say in what specific their nature is different from ours, and since their being so "utterly inhuman" does not affect their outward appearance: Clindar belongs to one of those races that "on a dark night or in a thick fog, might be mistaken for human beings. . . . With a little plastic surgery, Clindar could have passed as a man." Except for certain details, those "creatures . . . were strikingly human." So why the disclaimer?

As far as the exceptions are concerned, we are specifically told of only two relatively major ones: Clindar is over seven feet tall. And he has six fingers and six toes. Just as Moon-Watcher's bone always brings tears to Clarke's eyes, so those six digits bring a smile to my lips. They are ubiquitous in science fiction. The galaxies teem with creatures endowed with six fingers. If they have to be different from us, why not four? Elementary psychoanalytic insight suggests that we have here a reassurance against castration anxiety, both presumably unconscious. The process of reassurance is touchingly naive.

The capabilities of the lords of the slabs are much more important, though, than their anatomic peculiarities. That they wield physical and mental powers and a technology immensely superior to ours goes without saying. What needs saying is what their life span is, and *Lost Worlds* says it: ". . . he had suffered minor deaths. . . . As long as his body was not totally destroyed the doctors could always repair it" (p. 53). He "had already seen a thousand birthdays and could, if he wished, see endless thousands more" (p. 64). ". . . [T]he years, the millennia . . . lay ahead, until the time came—if it ever did—when at last he was tired of the Universe, and of immortality" (p. 73).

There has been belief in the existence of such beings as far back as we can look into human history. Though original gods may have been chthonic, though primitive man may think of animals and even inanimate objects as godlike, there was a belief as early as thousands of years ago in divine beings animating the Sun and the Moon and the planets, keeping the stars in their courses, controlling the thunder and lightning. They may have been demonic rather than beneficent, but eventually all others were relegated to minor roles, and the beings imagined far above the abode of man became the Olympian gods.

They were dethroned by the One God. As belief in Him faded, a view of the world as a purely material universe that has no room for spirits came to prevail. Not everybody can take it. The sky has lately been repeopled—with aliens.

But what are they? The lords of the slabs have been compared to Prometheus who steals the fire from Mount Olympus and sets mankind on the road to civilization. The comparison is apt, but it does not go far enough. If these beings are not gods known to any established theology, they are clearly *superi* in the Virgilian sense: beings endowed with powers far beyond the human ken. They are domiciled—if they have a domicile —somewhere in the empyrean. They are immortal, or nearly so: they may have been born (as Zeus was born, on Mount Ida in Crete), and they may conceivably die, but only in an upheaval that overthrows the entire order of the universe (*Goetterdaemmerung* in Norse myth). They have all the essential characteristics of the gods of Homer. They are not godlike: they are gods.

They can manifest themselves to humans at will. As far as science fiction writers are concerned, they seem to have chosen not to manifest themselves to them completely. Science fiction does not seem entirely aware of the nature of the powers they so blithely conjure up. This situation gives rise to a paradox.

When two cultures, hitherto unknown to each other, interpenetrate, it is virtually axiomatic that the dynamic, penetrating culture is the one that is superior at least in the technology of transportation and weapons; and since technologies are usually interconnected and highly correlated to science and general level of intellectual achievement, the penetrating culture is likely to be superior to the penetrated one in all these respects. It follows that if we should meet alien intelligences in space, they would be more likely in this sense to be inferior to us. If it were otherwise, they would more probably reach us first.

Space travel fiction presumably presents future probabilities as though they had already materialized. This is what its authors claim and what the public counts on. One would expect that when a writer depicts humans traveling into space and encountering an alien civilization, it would be a civilization inferior—intellectually, if not necessarily morally —to ours. Surprisingly, the opposite is the case: almost invariably, the culture that we encounter in space is described as superior.

I have said, *almost invariably.* We can not expect any such regularity to apply with the inviolability of a law of nature. The structure of literary creation—indeed, its economics—militates against it: the urge to be original, if nothing else, will cause some writers to produce an exception, to devise plots that run contrary to the generally accepted line. But these are rare. The bulk of the literature is true to the pattern: we go into space, we encounter beings superior to ourselves. This has become the cliché.

It is the measure of the quality of *2001* that it does not imprison itself in the cliché. For once, the promotional literature speaks the literal truth. I'll quote the ad in my hometown paper, which in turn quotes *Newsweek:* ". . . a quantum leap in quality over any other science fiction film ever made!" Apart from the work's other merits, it is a "quantum leap" all right that in *2001* the aliens come to us first. And yet, the bulk of *2001* is taken up with the expedition to Jupiter and beyond, to what is sought as the home base of the slabs: *We* are seeking *them.* In this defiance of probability, *2001* bows to the cliché.

This is a new turn for Clarke. The conclusion of "The Sentinel" is: ". . . we have set off the fire alarm and have nothing to do but to wait." *2001,* far from finding nothing to do, has added the expedition and has indeed made it its core.

I have said at the beginning that psychological analysis can solve its puzzles. There has been little overt psychology in this chapter so far because I do not consider psychology a substitute for literary scholarship but an addition to it. At its best it can breathe into literary studies a new enterprising and speculative spirit, widen their horizons, give their findings a surer footing. At its worst it adds ballast to ballast and helps to drag the whole enterprise down.

To avoid this pitfall, we shall hold our analysis until we have accompanied the astronauts on their outward voyage. They set out to find the slabs; they find themselves faced with something quite different. The thrust of the tale is deflected from the goal to the happenings during the journey. The saga of Hal, his grisly victories and his final defeat, seems to have no connection with the theme of the story's Part I. It will turn out that, contrary to appearance, it does.

Nonhuman intelligent beings in literature are often divided into two broad classes: *humanoids,* beings of independent origin usually from outer space, generally "superi," such as those who plant the slabs; and *androids,* beings comparable to men and created by men. Some writers, notably Tolkien, present imaginary beings that do not come under either heading; but the creatures of most writers are covered by the dichotomy. Hal is of course an android.

He is certainly man-made, and we must suppose that he is to be called a being, for he fulfills the requirements postulated by the philosophers —he thinks, therefore he is. He can say "I." And he has a will. It is at the root of the tragedy to come that he has very much of a will. Reviewers have found him more human than the human characters in *2001,* more interesting as a personality, more individualized. The men are the ones who seem to be operating automatically. To appreciate Hal's full stature it is also useful to note that years ago Clarke set down speculations on possibly replacing human bodies by machines. Going beyond current ideas of cyborgs, he envisaged the possibility that a brain, and hence what we might call a soul, could outlive its frailer housing.

Should Hal be referred to as "he"? We cannot suppose that he is endowed with sex. Yet "he" comes more naturally than "it," because he is a being. And it comes very much more naturally than "she." The novel refers to Hal as "he." That and the obviously masculine name are all we are given to go by. The film adds the crucial element of the voice which in all its false sincerity is clearly masculine.

The computer's name had not always been Hal. Socrates and Athena had been tried. They were discarded, probably for several reasons. It is likely that just as the pyramid "somehow, never looked right," the female name Athena never sounded right. Hal was originally HAL. The different typographic image makes it easier to perceive the computer, in the glow of good feeling at the start of the voyage, as the buddy of the astronauts.

HAL stands for Heuristically programmed ALgorithmic computer (the novel, p. 95; *Lost Worlds,* p. 78), and thereby hangs a little tale with a moral. If you replace each of the three letters by the one following it in the alphabet, you get IBM. Clarke assures us that this was never intended: ". . . coincidence it is, even if the odds are twenty-six cubed, or 17,576 to 1. (Just checked by HAL Jr., the beautiful 9100A calculator that my friends at Hewlett-Packard gave me at Christmas 1969.)" (*Lost Worlds*, p. 78).

Using a trusted formula, I computed the odds with pencil and paper in about fifty seconds. I would have been faster, of course, if my high school math were not as rusty as it is. Does it make sense to ask a computer?

Furthermore, Clarke's idea of the odds is mechanistic. The actual odds are much lower, since the letters were chosen for euphony. If, for example, the more usual method had been applied and the initial letters of the four words that form the computer's official name had been taken, we would get HPAC, and evidently no such thing was considered. Moral: An astronaut who so unreasonably depends on computers and whose own thinking is so computerized, will be handicapped if he has to fight a computer.

It may be countered that Bowman wins his fight even so. He does, but barely. Man as a whole does not. Hal kills four of the five human members of the crew. Thwarted in his attempt to kill the fifth, he is "disconnected," which to him equates death. His voice is stilled; he is not heard from again.

The long—to some, too long—series of events that make up Part 3 of *2001,* from the start of the mission to the alleged malfunction of the antenna, lead up to the drama. They have no other purpose. Though readers and viewers may get a good deal of pleasure, and a lot of hardly useful information, out of watching a spaceship of the future in operation, the clash between man and computer is the essence of the story. And this conflict, even though the dramatis personae do not know it, and perhaps even Clarke does not know it, is preordained.

Herein lies the justification for distinguishing androids from humanoids. It would clearly be possible to group imaginary beings by the use of any number of other criteria than their origin. No such classification is of any use unless it can be shown that the individual beings that fall into one of these classes differ from those in the other class in other respects also than in regard to the criterion by which the classes were established. In regard to the division into humanoids and androids this is indeed the case: humanoids do not as a rule behave as Hal does; androids (again, as in the question of the encountered superior breeds, we have to add, "almost invariably") do. They turn against their creators and bring ruin upon them; or come close to doing so, ending up by being disarmed or destroyed by their creators. Furthermore, though robots (a subclass of androids, not organically produced) are generally sexless, they are apt to have attributes that compel us to perceive them as male.

This has been so since long before the actual technical possibility of artificially creating manlike beings came within hailing distance. One of the oldest such figures still with us is the sorcerer's apprentice's broom man who first appeared in a story by Lucian eighteen-hundred years ago, to continue his career through Goethe's poem and Dukas' music and to reach an inglorious last stage in Disney's *Fantasia.* The archetypal example is Frankenstein, or rather the monster created by Frankenstein. Karel Capek introduced the word *robot* in its modern meaning a century after Mrs. Shelley took part in that celebrated parlor game that gave birth to her novel. There have been innumerable stories of robots ever since, and they tend to behave like Hal.

Their ineradicable propensity to sinister rebellion has not remained unnoticed. Writers as early as over a century ago have seen in the very attempt to create such artificial beings something nefarious, an endeavor that would attract punishment as the spire attracts the lightning. Hawthorne ascribes the death of his Beatrice Rappaccini to "the fatality that attends all such efforts of perverted wisdom." Melville ends *The Bell Tower* musing: "So the blind slave obeyed his blinder lord; but, in obedience, slew him. So the creator was killed by the creature. . . . And so pride went before the fall."

It fits Hal's case even better than it would at first glance appear. Superficially, the film gives the impression that Hal has simply gone mad. But has he? Or if he has, what has driven him into madness? He becomes a killer to protect himself *and* the mission. Does he have any authority for acting thus?

To a considerable extent he does. Dr. Heywood Floyd, a "blinder lord" if ever there was one, has kept the true goal of the space voyage secret from the human crew, but has revealed it to Hal. This is another point that is somewhat vague in the film, leading some critics to surmise that Hal may have merely had sealed orders; but the novel makes it clear that he was privy to the secret (p. 97). Moreover, his orders are to keep it from the astronauts and to fib about it if needed. This ambiguity has overburdened the computer's marvelously efficient, yet somewhat simple brain. The same could happen to more complex minds: a current theory of psychotherapy holds that children are driven into neurosis by the "double bind" their parents place them in. Hal certainly is in a double bind.

How did Mission Control reach this seemingly minor decision which yet contains the one tragic flaw that is crucial in making the catastrophe inevitable? Clearly it is without plausible conscious motivation. Dr. Floyd justifies it merely by promulgating it in the name of the bitch goddess Security. It is quite possible that Clarke, an Englishman, and Kubrick—such a thought might not be alien to the creator of *Dr. Strangelove*—were aiming their barbs chiefly at this obsession. But, whatever Dr. Floyd's conscious motive—or Clarke's and Kubrick's conscious motive —the tendency of tragic characters to overreach themselves in embarking on ever bolder plans is typical of hubris. The plot of *Romeo and Juliet*, a tragedy of hubris as well as of love, is woven into such a complex web that in the end it breaks of its own weight, dragging plotters and innocents alike down with it. It would be poor consolation, though, for Dr. Floyd that he could say, with Friar Lawrence,

> A greater power than we can contradict
> Hath thwarted our attempts: Come, come away.

Four crewmen are dead. The computer is silenced. Dave Bowman, the lone survivor, does come away—but will not be back. He is "beyond infinity."

There comes a moment, in literature as in life, when the variety of impressions in their clashing colors and demanding stridencies threatens to become deafening and blinding, leaving the mind dizzy and confused. A yearning emerges for somebody to bring order. Theory is that somebody. Once a theory is formulated, a key to the riddles is grasped, the turmoil subsides. Having weathered the bewildering onslaught we have achieved serenity.

It is no coincidence that folklore places the event in childhood— Newton hit by the apple falling from the tree, Watt as a child watching the lid of his mother's tea kettle clatter (he actually watched, as a business man, Newcomen's steam engine). Folklore is beguiled into this displacement by the distinguishing mark of the suitable theories, their surprising simplicity.

Psychology offers a simple theory to bring order and harmony into the crisscrossing currents of *2001:* The masters of the slabs are father figures. Hal is a son figure.

The baldness of this formulation makes it disappointing, perhaps repellent, suspect of untrustworthiness. It needs to be covered with the wig of commentary. To prove itself, such a theory must show its ability to account for all the vagaries of the phenomena it is supposed to explain. If even one fact does not fit, the theory must be modified or replaced by a better one. It will be seen that this theory fits.

In psychological—in this instance, specifically, psychoanalytic—thinking, "father figure" has a more complex meaning than is at first glance evident. This is the underlying line of thought: A person's image of other people he encounters in the course of his life is determined not only by the qualities of those people as he objectively perceives them, but also by the experiences and fantasies relating to people he has encountered previously. The latter will often influence his image more powerfully than his objective perception does. The farther back in the individual's life those fantasies and experiences reach, the stronger their influence. The most crucial enduring influences are therefore those formed by the early relationship to father and mother (including those who, to use a legal term here, are *in loco parentis*). The individual's reaction to the newly encountered people is determined by his image. This is how patterns are perpetuated, so an individual's life is not a mere series of unrelated episodes, but a coherent whole which we conceptualize, depending on our philosophical leanings, as the manifestation of his personality, his destiny, or even his stars.

In literature, where we are dealing with imagined rather than with actually encountered persons, the phenomenon is even more pronounced. The image of a character in literature can not be formed from perceptions of reality, there being no reality of an objectively existing person to be perceived. It is totally projected from previously formed experiences and fantasies. In calling the aliens father figures I am saying that their character and role is formed, and the reaction to them determined, by molding them on the image of the father that has been formed from childhood on. That crystallization of such preexisting experiences and fantasies into a literary character takes place may in principle be true of the "producer" as well as of the "consumer" of literature. For a work of literature to be successful, the two processes have to coincide.

The relationship between father and son normally is highly ambivalent. As a technical psychological term, ambivalence means the simultaneous and effective presence of positive and negative feelings, such as attraction and repulsion, admiration and contempt, love and hate. Most feelings between humans are ambivalent (Freud suggested that the feeling of a mother toward her male child may be the only noteworthy exception). Some components usually are conscious, others unconscious. One side of the coin may be totally invisible—a son may consciously feel nothing but love and admiration for his father, with the obverse completely repressed, but operative nonetheless—in a crisis, even more operative for its being repressed.

A writer may shape the feelings between a father figure and a son figure he creates according to what he thinks such feelings are in reality, or to express what he wishes them to be. The difference parallels that between mimetic and fantastic literature. He—and the reader!—may identify with one character, or that character's antagonist, or partially or alternatingly with either. An infinite variety of combinations is possible. If there weren't, there would be no variety in literature.

If this theory is valid, it should explain the discrepancies in the text. There are two major ones: between the humanoids in fiction and the humanoids, if any, that we can expect to seek, and conceivably find, in reality; and between the androids in fiction and those we can expect to make. The encounter with the humanoids forms the frame of *2001*. Their influence is never quite absent, but they make it most keenly felt in Parts I and 5. The conflict with the android has found its place in the center of the frame. It fills but one section of *2001*, but the most elaborate and by far longest, Part 3.

As we have seen, the encounter with the humanoids tends to assume a peculiar form. In depicting humans who set out to find alien civilizations and find superior ones, writers set themselves against probability. If Clarke had stuck to the impeccable conclusion of "The Sentinel"—to wait—there would have been no space mission. The motive ascribed to the *dramatis personae*—we want to get there so that the Russians don't get there first, and vice versa—is a singularly lame excuse. No convincing conscious motive can be given: what unconscious motive the writer may have is worth considering.

The discrepancy between androids in fiction and those looming in our future reality is less glaring, for it can hardly be denied that if we can and will make androids, ours might be the same fate as that suffered by the fictitious creators. Still, if that fate were inevitable, it would hardly be worth the effort to try to make any. At the very least, makers of androids might take the precautions that common sense suggests, instead of inviting disaster by acting like Dr. Floyd.

The search for an unconscious motive is even more urgently suggested here, since the procedure of creating androids is—again, almost invariably—marred by *hamartia*—the one fatal flaw of the hero, the one chink in his armor, as first found by Aristotle in Attic tragedy. It is through hamartia that fate enters, eventually to devour the hero and all his works. We find that lapse again and again: the sorcerer's apprentice forgets the formula. Victor Frankenstein "resolved, *contrary to my first intention,* to make the being of a gigantic stature." Dr. Floyd entrusts the computer with the crucial secret withheld from the commander of the ship. It is as though these creators secretly consented to the judgment of Hawthorne and Melville that their work is sinful hubris and therefore doomed. They labor, rationally, and they say yes to their work; but something in them says no. At one point, inadvertently, almost unnoticeably, they fail. The one lapse, the one irrational act, suffices to destroy the fruit of their labor—and often enough their companions and themselves.

There must be a message in all this, but it seems so nonsensical, so self-contradictory. It defies deciphering. If we only had a key! It is as though we were faced with a message written in code. This is perhaps just what it is.

The message becomes intelligible if we make one bold assumption: that all this is an old drama written in a new code. There is nothing wrong with a drama being old. It is even probable that all dramas are. Codes, on the other hand, are always new. They have to be: once broken, they are worthless. And fashions change. There used to be gods and heroes, and monsters. Now there are humanoids and androids.

If we assume that the drama of *2001* is, in a new guise, the old drama of the generations, then the fragments fall into place. The powers that plant the slabs are father figures; and Hal is a son figure.

Fathers are always dim to their sons (and sons often to their fathers), so the father figures in *2001* are dimly drawn. Dimly, yet clearly. There is no interaction between the aliens and the humans, only action by the aliens on the humans. The lords of the slabs are presented as the father is perceived by his child: improbably tall; indescribably powerful; unapproachable; unfathomable; and for all that, basically benign: more prone to teaching than to disciplining—or so it is to be hoped. Doubts creep in: "They" (who have planted the slab), says Clarke in "The Sentinel", "must be very, very old, and the old are often insanely jealous of the young" (*Lost Worlds,* p.27). Well, this may befall. But in actual human experience, people are never so "very, very old"—never quite as old as they appear to children. And it may happen just as often that the young *think* the old are viciously jealous because they are themselves consumed by jealousy of the old.

It is easier to see the mote in your father's eye than the beam in your own. It is easier to find the other person's jealousy than to face one's own, and so the plausible candidates for objects of jealousy have been carefully removed. The world of *2001* is a man's world, more radically so than even the reality of astronautics. In the immense cosmic drama, women play minute and almost disreputable parts. Ape-women, mannish Russian scientists, stewardesses wearing impossible caps, the voice-print identifier, and Frank Poole's mother huddled over his birthday cake, they are all there are, and who would get jealous over *them?* For deeper reasons than the requirements of space travel, this is a sexless world; and the requirements themselves may have grown out of prejudice more than necessity.

A perceptive critic has written that *2001* may be about, among other things, "man in an Oedipal struggle with God the Father."[12] This is not as sound as it sounds. The relationship of the humans to the superhumans in *2001* is not one of struggle. It is one of submission, with all the other elements of the son-father relationship repressed or at least absent. Even if there were a struggle, in what sense could it be Oedipal? The term has been bandied about rather freely, but it should not be forgotten that it denotes a struggle between father and son stimulated by competition for the mother's love. This element is totally lacking here. It may be, though, that it is absent just because to face it openly would be intolerably difficult. Its absence could be part of the "code."

The complications surrounding the humans' relationship to the computer are of a different order than those besetting their relationship to their betters. Hal is a complicated character. His behavior can be evaluated on three levels. On the most superficial level, that of the outward —and deceptive—appearances, he seems simply to have lost his mental balance. Many critics, perhaps people who would go to a computer for help if they had to compute the cube of 26, have thought that Hal has become "psychotic." For them it is the message of Part 3 that computers are only human after all and subject to the same infirmities as our brains. They act shocked, implying that they expected such complexity, wickedness, and irrationality of a fellow man but not of a machine.

Closer scrutiny of the events leading up to Hal's alleged breakdown does not support such views. On a deeper level, Hal can be seen to be acting naturally, though with utter disregard for human life and human values; he is, after all, but a computer—with a good deal of rationality. Within his limits, of course, and they are, in spite of his ability to perform mental manipulation immensely faster than we can, not as broad as ours. Here Clarke's comment is apposite: "I personally would like to have seen a rationale of HAL's behavior. It's perfectly understandable, and in fact would have made HAL a very sympathetic character; he had been fouled by those clods at Mission Control. HAL was indeed correct in attributing his mistaken report to human error" (*The Making*, p. 133).

And yet, on the third and deepest level, this does not quite add up either. It must arouse our suspicion that Hal, allegedly acting rationally to protect the mission that has been so foolishly entrusted to him, acts only seemingly in conformity with his program. It cannot very well be by mere chance that in effect his acts lead to the same result as the acts of Frankenstein's monster and of the legion of other androids of fiction. We cannot help feeling that if Hal hadn't had the excuse of the double bind about the space mission, another pretext would have been found; that in truth he acted—or rather that his author made him act—to conform to a traditional pattern, to what almost can be called a myth.

The same myth dictates the response to his acts. Since Hal is made by man, it is permissible to consider him an artificial son. Though his relationship to his makers is not biological, it comes closer to a father-son relationship than even that of the humans to the masters of the slab. Stripped to essentials, many a son may be "insanely jealous" and tend to kill his progenitors or their representatives who are to him in the role of favored siblings.

Hal's punishment fits his crime. The rebellious son is put back in his place, is cut back to the subject role of the impotent child. Dave reduces him to senility, which is in truth regression to childhood, in that memorable scene in which his adult faculties are removed one by one till all he can do is sing, off key and in an old man's breaking voice, "Daisy, Daisy," the first song he has ever learned.

If some of these interpretations seem to stand on slightly wobbly ground, it may be because so much of the soil beneath is quicksand. There have been numerous and justified complaints that *2001* has more ambiguity than a work of art should possess, that it is at points outright muddled. This is especially true of the film—its strength is in other areas than logical thinking—and more especially of the concluding episode, the hero's rebirth. Canby is not to be gainsaid when he says that "the film's final ambiguity" has inspired many "delirious" interpretations.

He does not specify. A number of interpretations might well cause raised eyebrows, though hardly a sharper reaction. Beja, for example, in connecting *2001* with "Sailing to Byzantium," thinks it helps to trace the figure 2001 to Yeats' pet idea of the two thousand-year-cycle. Others have tried astrology: "Conjunctions stand symbolically for union and synthesis. . . . Kubrick's Sun/Venus conjunction is an aspect that indicates ease in relations of love and with the opposite sex . . . this aspect brings an idealistic sex appeal . . ." (*The Making*, p. 291). It is not exactly a crushing argument for the validity of astrology, since in *2001* there are no relations either of love or with the opposite sex, easy or otherwise.

With psychoanalytic interpretations, there is always the question how far one can go without taking the small but irrevocable step from the sublime to the ridiculous. ". . . the first three phases, beginning with the phallic bone-wielding of the ape and going on through the rocket ship's penetrating the intricately female docking stations—all these deal with the mastery of outerspace. The last deals with the mastery of innerspace. Does one turn outward for a life support system? Or inward?"[13]

We can assume that the bone-wielding is called "phallic" because of the bone's shape. But it so happens that most bones have that shape. Are we to blame Moon-Watcher for not going around looking for a bone of a different shape just so that his wielding it would not be phallic? Furthermore, it is likely that aerodynamics is more involved than symbolism: if a bone that is not "phallic"—a skull, let us say—were thrown up into the air, it just wouldn't fly that well. And as to the docking station, there ought to be a prize for the design of one that could not be found "intricately female."

If I had to make an award, though, for the most nearly "delirious" interpretation, the brass ring would go to the numerologists. Consideration of the film's "rigid control" and "highly formalistic structure" yields these results: "Kubrick seems to be fascinated by the number 4. *2001*, which took four years to complete, is divided into four episodes, covers four million years, has four heroes (ape, scientist, machine, astronaut), concerns four evolutions (man, machine, alien, the universe), uses the music of four composers . . . and is dominated by a four-sided rectangle that appears on the screen four times. The number four crops up ritualistically throughout the film, something not accounted for by Clarke. It creates an obsessively rhythmic force . . ." (*Filmguide*, p. 34).

If, on the other hand, you want to prepare yourself "for the images and ideas that flow across the screen during the film" and find it too cumbersome to read Nietzsche's prologue to *Thus Spake Zarathustra,* there is help for you: "The best clue to their artistic organization and development is contained in the number three—mother-father-child, the eternal triangle, two's company three's a crowd, the three primary colors, and the three-dimensionality of the universe we normally think of as 'real,' perhaps even the Trinity and three as a magic number for infinity" (*The Making,* p. 232).

The magic number three, or else the magic number four—you pays your money and you takes your choice.

It may be that I ought not to make fun of the numerologists—who knows how many people, from Mr. Canby up and down, may consider my interpretations "delirious"?

Surely, Voltaire's principle ought to apply. "I disagree with everything you say, and I'll defend to death your right to say it." But that is one thing, and it is another thing to pay homage to sense and nonsense alike. If there is any one lesson that we can draw from *2001,* it is the deepened realization how much the progress of mankind, such as it is, has depended and will continue to depend on simple intelligence. If we were not as smart as we are, we should still be roaming the veld, facing the alluring choice of starving to death or being eaten by leopards.

As every movement that deviates from the conventional, science fiction attracts its share of crackpots. In studying science fiction, and especially in teaching it, neither of its two components must be slighted. Science is not to be confused with pseudo-science, and fiction must not be taken for history. That a fascinating yarn could be spun about aliens who have watched and guided us does not mean we should believe that four million years ago a slab actually descended on East Africa, accompanied by the strains of Ligeti's music.

2001 is about the succession of generations, but not about physical lineage. Clarke's sweeping view of four million years of human history is not committed to realism. Only Parts 2 and 3 can advance any claim to be taken seriously as foreshadowing things to come. Though it may well be doubted that it will ever happen quite that way once we have learned to make androids, yet the work has grasped the nettle. What seems a pleasant way to spend an evening at the movies may also be seen as an exercise in problem-solving; not only because the audience can take these vicarious fantasies home with them to use in their own emotional households to strengthen the fabric of their fantasies about their fathers and their sons, but also because the problem will soon be with us as a real life issue. We may or may not encounter independent alien intelligences in space, but that we will make artificial intelligences is by now certain, or as certain as any prediction about the future of this refractory species can be.

On a deeper emotional level it is a problem not only of the future, but of the past and present as well, unendingly mirrored backward and forward. It would not be easy to comprehend the men's relationship to Hal if it were not seen in the shadow of their relationship to the masters of the slabs. From the dawn coming over the apemen to Dave Bowman's aging and rebirth, which in a sense repeats Hal's relapse into his second childhood, all the events of the film are strung on the endless chain of the generations.

It is a hierarchical rather than a biological chain. The patrimony of the mind is passed on from the lords of the slabs to the hominids to be made into men, and on to the computer. It is not augmented in the transfer: man has a lesser mind than the aliens, the android a lesser mind than man.

The sum total of the mental treasure has not increased. The humanoids and the androids both are essentially static. The humanoids have gone as far as they can go, and the androids can not be expected ever to surpass them. But mankind, in the middle between them, has grown tremendously in the process. If a graph of the development from Moon-Watcher to Bowman were plotted it would show a steeply rising curve. Men are immeasurably better off than they were four million years ago. Or are they?

It is not easy to put a finger on a specific point, but the impression stands out irrefutably: In Parts 2 and 3, where man is shown at a stage only slightly past ours, man has not grown in stature. He is curiously diminished. He seems to have suffered a fatal loss of substance.

In religious terms, he could be said to have gained a world and lost his soul. He is pressed from both sides. His godfathers, the humanoids, have taught him many useful arts, but not the capacity for happiness, or self-reliance, or pride in manhood. The androids, his godchildren—or is it devilchildren?—take over more and more of his functions. Between these two millstones mankind is being ground down—into what?

Critics are unanimous: All that's left of man in A.D. 2001 is man's empty shell. The man of the near future behaves like an automaton, a robot. He is characterized above all by emotional impoverishment. "Poor Dave, alas, experiences no mental conflict for the simple reason that he has no mind. He has a high I.Q., to be sure, but he does not possess any particular complexity of personality or character."[14]

The line of thought is presented more completely in Gilliatt's film review, where she speaks of "shots of emptied, comic, ludicrously dehumanized men," notes that their birthday observances bring no enjoyment, "only the mechanical celebration of the anniversaries of days when the race perpetuated itself," and passes melancholy judgment on the state of affairs in the year 2001 as a whole: "The civilization that Kubrick sees coming has the brains of a nuclear physicist and the sensibility of an airline hostess smiling through an oxygen-mask demonstration. . . . The citizens of 2001 have forgotten how to chat, speculate, grow intimate, or interest one another. . . . Separation from other people is total and unmentioned. Kubrick has no characters in the film who are sexually related, nor any close friends."

We are back at Hobbes: "no arts, no letters, no society . . . and the life of man solitary, poor, nasty, brutish . . ." except that, one is tempted to say regrettably, it is no longer short.

How could man sink this low? Several answers suggest themselves.

Clearly, *2001* represents a regression from monotheism as well as from atheism to polytheism. The review of the film in the *Harvard Crimson*, perhaps the most searching essay on the subject so far, rightly speaks of the work "being both anti-Christian *and* anti-evolutionary in its theme of man's progress controlled by an ambituous extraterrestrial force, possibly both capricious and destructive" (*The Making*, p. 216). The adherents of monotheism are able to say, I told you so.

Still within the religious metaphor, but more specifically, the depletion of man can be seen as the natural and deserved outcome of a bargain with the devil: from the famous bone thrown up in the air to the last turn of Bowman's screw driver, man has cast his lot with aggression. The fact has been commented upon, usually with considerable unease, by many writers. The *Harvard Crimson* may again serve as their spokesman: ". . . Kubrick's and Clarke's subjective anthropological notion that the discovery of the tool was identical with that of the *weapon.* The 'dawn of man,' then, is represented by a coupling of progress and destruction; a theme of murder runs through *2001* simultaneously with that of progress. Ultimately, Kubrick shows an ambiguous spiritual growth *through* physical death" (*The Making*, p. 218). The humanists are able to say, I told you so.

A more earthbound theory assumes that a certain decline in the stature of man is inevitably connected with the ascendancy of the machine, that there is some law of dynamic equilibrium which decrees that one must wane as the other waxes. It takes perhaps some distance from our technologically committed culture to suspect this—the formulation comes from a review of *2001* in *Pravda:* "In America, the car lives best, with all the conveniences designed for it: broad streets, good parking lots, etc. Man, on the contrary, is pressed close to his fellow man, tense, unhappy" (*The Making,* p. 253).

It echoes a point made as early as 140 years ago by the German poet Heine. He had visited England, then of course *the* industrial country. "As the machines in England impress us like human beings, so people there appear like machines. Yes, wood, iron, and brass there seem to have usurped the spirit of man and have almost gone mad for being so full of it, while the dis-spirited man, like a hollow specter, goes quite machinelike about his habitual business. At the appointed time he wolfs his steaks, makes speeches in Parliament, brushes his nails, boards a stage coach, or hangs himself."[15]

As far as we can foresee it, the promised land of "ambiguous spiritual growth" does not overflow with milk and honey. Clarke comforts us with the vision, or phantom, of a promised land that we can *not* foresee: ". . . the machines . . . were a new species, free from the limitations, taints, and stresses of organic evolution. They were still primitive, but they would learn. . . . Soon they would be designating their own successors, striving for goals which *Homo sapiens* might never comprehend" (*Lost Worlds,* p. 87).

Projection of reality into the future, or fata morgana, the image traditionally stands at the end of ambiguous utopia. Anatole France closed his *On the White Stone* (1905) with this evocation (the Siwalik Mountains were to his generation what the Olduvai Gorge is to ours): "Wells has said: Man isn't final. A future race, perhaps issued from ours, perhaps having no bond of origin with us, will succeed us in the dominion of the planet. These new masters of the Earth will ignore or despise us. If they find vestiges of our art, they will make no sense to them: future overlords, whose mind we can not divine any better than the Palaeopithecus of the Siwalik Mountains could foresee the thought of Aristotle, Newton, and Poincaré"—or as Moon-Watcher could foresee the thought of Dave Bowman the Star-Child.

The end of *2001* holds out the same hope, but asks us to take it on faith. We are actually given more foreboding than reassurance. As the destruction of the artificial son breaks the chain of the generations, the tempo changes, and more than the tempo. In that stupendous rush through the heavens and in all that happens after Bowman tumbles into the mysterious hotel suite, man has completely lost control of his destiny: the unrevealed *superi* have taken over.

It is fitting that, with the rudder of events, the most uniquely human faculty, that of speech, is also taken away. Bowman's torments and ecstasies are, like the events that befall Broch's dying Virgil, beyond language. Once the computer has lost his voice and the secret destination has been revealed, no further word is spoken, either on Earth or beyond that planet which is named for the wielder of lightning and thunder, the father figure among the gods.

6. Expectation and Surprise in Childhood's End.

ALAN B. HOWES

WHEN I BOUGHT a paperback copy of Arthur C. Clarke's *Childhood's End* in 1973, it was from the twenty-sixth printing. And when my next door neighbor saw my copy of the book, she still remembered how "overwhelming" she had found it when it first came out twenty years before. Professional critics have also praised Clarke: he is "the colossus of science fiction"[1] or the "distinguished dean of science fiction writers";[2] *Childhood's End* is "a fascinating switch on the utopian gambit"[3] or "a real staggerer by a man who is both a poetic dreamer and a competent scientist."[4] Clarke's fellow science fiction writers also respect him: James Blish, for example, finds *Childhood's End* "as serious and as rewarding as anything [its author] might have attempted outside our field."[5] Furthermore, the popularity of *Childhood's End* has increasingly gained momentum—there had been only nine printings between 1953 and 1968; there were seventeen between 1968 and 1973, when I bought my copy from the twenty-sixth printing. What is the key to the book's power, its durability, its vitality?

Clarke's own test for a successful story is simple. "The prime function of a story is to *entertain*—not to instruct or preach," he says. "No writer should ever forget Sam Goldwyn's immortal words: 'If you've gotta message, use Western Union.'" Clarke goes on to say that the "acid test" of a story comes with rereading, "preferably after a lapse of some years. If it's good, the second reading is as enjoyable as the first. If it's great, the second reading is more enjoyable. And if it's a masterpiece, it will improve on every rereading." At the same time Clarke speaks of science fiction as "one of the many bridges to culture," testimony that he believes the story that entertains and is worth rereading must have, if not a "message," at least some intellectual substance.[6] The trick, of course, is to challenge the mind without preaching a specific message—to walk somewhere in the middle ground between escapism and didacticism.

Most fiction aims at that middle ground, at the joining of "a good story" with some new insight into the human condition. But it also counts on the reader to help in that joining by responding in certain ways to the author's imaginative use of conventions. A literary convention, as I am using the term, simply represents a means for reaching a working agreement, explicit or implicit, between author and reader. The author uses a set of shorthand signals and the reader responds in appropriate ways. He may add information to the hint the author has given him about a character or a situation. He may suppress his knowledge that the "Once upon a time" story couldn't really have happened, in order to enter and enjoy that story's fictional world. He orients himself in general to the genre and its particular conventions and also to any distinctive subgeneric characteristics.

Thus he knows that the story which begins "Once upon a time there was a beautiful princess who lived in a large dark forest . . ." will develop in a very different way from the story that begins "In the late summer of that year we lived in a house in a village that looked across the river and the plain to the mountains," or one that starts with "Customs of courtship vary greatly in different times and places, but the way the thing happens to be done here and now always seems the only natural way to do it." Notice that each of these openings can—and in fact does—lead to a love story,[7] but, more importantly, each suggests the kind of love story that will follow. One can appreciate this by switching the openings around: "Once upon a time . . ." would not do to introduce Herman Wouk's *Marjorie Morningstar* (though there are some resemblances to fairy tale in its situation), "Customs of courtship vary greatly . . ." would be an inept opening for Ernest Hemingway's *A Farewell to Arms* (though there is a kind of courtship between Henry and Catherine), and "In the late summer of that year a beautiful princess lived in a house in a large dark forest . . ." wouldn't do for a fairy story (though it might convey the setting accurately). In each case the reader would be frustrated by the author's failure to develop the kind of story which the opening had led him to expect.

What conventions do, then, is to set up a series of expectations in the reader. The formula story fulfills those expectations in wholly predictable ways—one might say it consists mainly of conventions. It gives us the somewhat limited pleasure of filling in the blanks and seeing ourselves proved right in virtually every expectation. The good story that uses conventions more imaginatively is more complicated. It fulfills our expectations, but often in unpredictable ways. We have the richer pleasure of seeing patterns completed, but in ways we couldn't have foreseen. The conventions are bent, revised, perhaps even violated as they are revitalized. The really inferior story raises expectations that it cannot or does not fulfill.

Part of the secret of the durability and popularity of *Childhood's End* lies in its imaginative use and blending of conventions, in its setting, situations, characters, style, and themes. Another way to put it is to say that the book succeeds by virtue of the number and kinds of surprises and challenges that it presents. Some of the surprises, like the revelation of Karellen's resemblance to Satan, do not have as much force on a second reading; others, like the revelations, late in the book, of the Overlords' weaknesses, remain powerfully ironic on subsequent rereadings. Let us look at the ways the reader's expectations are met in three main aspects of the book—genre and subgenre, character, and theme.

Our knowledge of a genre or subgenre enables us to predict the ultimate outcome of a story or at least to narrow the possible outcomes to a few alternatives. In a love story boy will get girl or girl will get boy; in a *bildungsroman* the hero will mature through a series of experiences; in a detective story we will discover who committed the crime, and so on. The author usually alerts us early on—if indeed not in the title—to the fictional subgenre in which he is working. Part of the fascination of *Childhood's End* is that we can't make predictions of this sort as easily or as certainly—or, to put it more accurately, Clarke combines a number of subgenres in his book and keeps presenting us with more alternative directions in which the story may develop than a writer usually does. Each section does develop a major mystery to be solved: in section one it is the question of what the Overlords look like, in section two it is the question of where the answer at the seance came from, in section three it is the question of what is happening to Jeff. And interwoven with these narrative threads are a number of others which are also developed, often with a rich ambiguity in their situations, and then resolved, often with surprising developments that a reader could not have predicted.

Childhood's End starts out in the Prologue with the race between two scientists, one American, one Russian, to launch a spacecraft. But scarcely have we prepared ourselves to follow that rather clichéd rivalry when ironically—and before the end of the Prologue—the story veers in a new direction with the arrival of aliens in giant spaceships. The situation is ambiguous: "This was the moment when history held its breath, and the present sheared asunder from the past as an iceberg splits from its frozen, parent cliffs, and goes sailing out to sea in lonely pride. All that the past ages had achieved was as nothing now . . ." Thus Clarke leaves a number of possibilities open at the end of the Prologue— struggle with the aliens, peaceful coexistence, education of earthlings by superior beings, to name the three alternatives which seem most likely to a reader at that point. The only certainty is that "the human race was no longer alone," and that life will be drastically changed.

All of the possibilities—which at first seemed conflicting—come to pass. The struggle with the aliens is over with one abortive attempt to bomb one of the Overlord's ships and a brief resistance by the government of South Africa.

Meanwhile, we have seen that the real struggle is between humans like Stormgren, who trust the Overlords and accept their rule, and those, like Wainwright, who don't. Again the situation is ambiguous: Wainwright's protest that Karellen is trying to "wipe out a thousand years of history at the stroke of a pen" with his forcing of world federation on mankind is countered by Stormgren's assertion that the Overlords are merely completing what humans have started and that "their outlook . . . is more mature than ours" (2).* We soon find out more about what has been happening in the five years since the arrival of the Overlords: after the two brief struggles, humans have coexisted peacefully with the Overlords, learning ways of bringing a better civilization to Earth through cooperation. Earth now enjoys "security, peace, and prosperity," though these may be double-edged blessings, if, as Wainwright asserts, the Overlords "have taken our liberty" (2).

The possibility of education of earthlings through the influence of the Overlords—only hinted at in the first section of the book—is fully developed in the second section: the changes brought by the Overlords are more drastic than they first appeared to be and human civilization is evolving into a kind of utopia. Now a whole set of different expectations is raised in the reader. Mankind seems destined to a life of comfort, peace, and prosperity but one in which no adventures or discoveries will be possible and spiritual decay will set in. "Utopia was here at last: its

*NOTE: Numbers in parentheses after a quotation indicate chapter.

novelty had not yet been assailed by the supreme enemy of all utopias —boredom" (6). But, the reader feels, that development may not be very long in coming. At the same time we see Jan developing his plan for stowing away on the Overlord ship—at least one human being is still eager for adventure and dissatisfied with the static perfection of utopia. We finish section two wondering what the outcome of Jan's adventure will be and what will happen to the rest of mankind, caught in its web of peace and plenty, for we are told that "with . . . inexorable swiftness the Golden Age was rushing to its close" (14).

In the final section we see another kind of utopia in New Athens, and attempt to regain part of what has been lost, as the Golden Age nears its close and the children come closer and closer to Total Breakthrough. And then comes the final apocalyptic scene. The destruction that seemed one possible outcome when the Overlords first landed has indeed taken place, though in a manner different from what we could have foreseen, for no reader could predict the particular collection of narrative threads I have been tracing, though one might hit upon some of them. Further, the ending leaves us with different feelings about the destruction of the Earth than we could have imagined, as "Everything we ever achieved has gone up there into the stars," and "the last atoms" of Earth's substance have nourished the children "through the fierce moments of their inconceivable metamorphosis, as the food stored in a grain of wheat feeds the infant plant while it climbs towards the Sun" (24).

Characterization in *Childhood's End* is not at first glance so complicated as narrative, but here too there are intricacies and surprises. The conventions associated with characterization help us to identify types and stock figures—and also to appreciate ways in which a type has been individualized. Characters who are truly "conventional" usually have interest only as they help to develop narrative, but characters who vary from the type hold our interest for their own sake.

Clarke has his share of stock figures: Maia Boyce is one example. Described as "distracting," she has "Grecian" features and "her hair was long and lustrous. . . . Her voice was a rich contralto that sent little shivers running up and down George's back, as if someone was playing on his spine like a flute." And she says things like "Rupert is doing something complicated with the drinks—come along and meet everybody" (7). This is close to the stock sophisticated and charming lady of the formula story (who is often little more than a projection of male erotic fantasies), though it is perhaps difficult to get away from formula when describing a cocktail party.

Other basic types are individualized through unexpected, sometimes humorous touches. Thus Joe, Stormgren's kidnapper, is not the stock villain. Stormgren thinks him "altogether more complex" than his gangster assistants, and is reminded of "an overgrown baby." Joe has "never thought seriously about the causes for which he was fighting. Emotion and extreme conservatism clouded all his judgments." Yet, Stormgren thinks, "When his type vanished, if it ever did, the world would be a safer but less interesting place" (p. 39). He produces a deck of cards since he has heard that Stormgren likes to play poker, but then asks in a worried voice if Stormgren has plenty of cash. "After all, we can hardly accept checks," he says (3).

Stormgren himself is in many ways a typical statesman and civil servant, though he is partially individualized, particularly through his friendship with Karellen. In the latter part of the book George and Jean are also part types, part individuals. Jean's paranormal powers separate her from the other characters, though otherwise she is a typical wife and mother. George doesn't have much to distinguish him: his rather conventional lechery is alluded to but not developed (and is presumably not unusual in an age of much freer sexual mores brought on by "a completely reliable oral contraceptive" and "an equally infallible method . . . of identifying the father of any child") (6). Jan is the restless young man who dreams of exploring new frontiers in space, the typical space adventurer who is interesting more for what happens to him than for his own sake. In general, the individual human beings, though sometimes not strictly types, are not very memorable.

Clarke's aliens are more interesting than his humans and more imaginatively developed. Only occasionally are they in situations which sound like formula stories, as when Rashaverak says to Karellen that they "must transfer Jean to Category Purple" (9), or Wainwright's angry crowd shake their fists at the Overlord fleet fifty kilometers above them, "as pygmies may threaten a giant" (2). We are reminded from time to time of the aliens' unusual size, but on the whole Clarke plays down any physical details. This is of course partly because he wishes to develop mystery and suspense about their physical form in the first section of the book: it is fifty-five years and more than that number of pages before Karellen reveals himself. There are hints that he has something to hide through his secretiveness, there is something faintly ominous about his "cavernous laugh" (2), and the mystery and suspense are continually heightened throughout the first section, partly through Stormgren's plan to "see" Karellen. With the climactic revelation at the beginning of the second section we can understand why mankind was not ready earlier to be allowed to see the embodiment of some of his most terrifying legends. Nor would the reader have been ready earlier for the revelation. If we had known at once that Karellen had the shape of the Devil, we would not have accepted what he said at its face value and our whole concept of his character would have been distorted.

Even after the revelation of the Overlords' physical appearance, their physical characteristics are not emphasized. We are told later that they are all alike—"all seemed duplicates from a single, master mold" (17). They have a "peculiar . . . acid odor," described as "not so much unpleasant as puzzling" (7). George thinks that Rashaverak's tail looks "like a piece of armored pipe" and sees that "the famous barb was not so much an arrowhead as a large, flat diamond . . . to give stability in flight, like the tail feathers of a bird." The body "was neither like that of a man nor that of any animal Earth had ever known. . . . It was not even certain that they were vertebrates. . . ." (7). But in spite of these details given soon after Karellen's appearance to the public, it is another fifty-odd pages before we get a good look at his face with "the twin breathing orifices on either cheek—if those fluted, basalt curves could be called cheeks . . ." and the "inflexible, lipless mouth" (14). And we are not usually made particularly aware of physical details (except perhaps for their wings) in most of the scenes with the Overlords.

There is a good reason for this lack of emphasis on the Overlords' physical appearance: throughout the book Clarke, while noting ways that they differ from human beings, obviously also wishes to humanize them and bring them closer to the reader. And there is the frequent implication that they are really more human than they first appear to be. Karellen is truly Stormgren's friend, and their conversations are appropriate for friends. The "final proof . . . of Karellen's affection" is given when the Overlord allows Stormgren to catch a glimpse of him through the screen, and Stormgren "hoped that . . . Karellen . . . would one day . . . stand beside the grave of the first man ever to be his friend" (4). Rashaverak—"Rashy" to Rupert Boyce—is likewise a friend to humans. The Overlords are further humanized and made less awesome through humor. Karellen can laugh at human speculation about his form—"I'd

rather be a mass of electron tubes than a thing like a centipede . . ."—
and Jean Morrel can summon up a "mental picture . . . too comic to be
comfortable" of Rashaverak reading a book with each eye and another
in Braille with his fingers.

The Overlords inspire less awe than many typical aliens do, but they
are not merely human beings with different bodies either, for they represent the reasoning side of man, extracted from his other parts, purified,
and magnified many times. Their mental powers represent a climax in
their evolution. Their "hatred of curelty," and "their passion for justice
and order" are the bases of their character, and it is of course these
qualities which enable them to help human beings develop a utopia (3).
In Karellen's words they "represent reason and science" (2). A logic
blind to all else but itself governs their every act and leads to some
surprising as well as amusing perspectives. Jan reflects that "there were
things beyond logic that the Overlords had never understood" (23), and
Karellen cannot imagine why human beings want to engage in the
"primitive behavior" of descending into the Grand Canyon by mule
train when they "could reach the bottom of the canyon in a fraction of
the time, and in far greater comfort, if they chose" (9).

Thus the more obvious and sensational possibilities about the Overlords—those that the formula story about aliens might capitalize on—
are minimized and their resemblances to human beings are insisted
upon. Yet perhaps the most interesting and certainly the most moving
thing about the Overlords lies in the ironic contrast with human beings
which has been gradually developed by the time of the apocalyptic
ending.

Our first impression of the Overlords is of their complete superiority
to human beings—their minds "ten—perhaps a hundred—times as powerful as men's" (23), their greatly advanced technology, their complete
control over human beings through their awesome powers. The Overlords are, in fact, so powerful that Karellen can afford to ignore the
attempted bombing of the Overlord ship (2), and let Stormgren's kid-
nappers go free so that they can be watched (3). And he need use his
vast powers only sparingly—a thirty-minute blocking out of the sun from
South Africa is enough to bring that government around (2), and a brief
infliction of pain upon ten thousand spectators is enough to put an end
to bullfighting on earth.[8]

There is only a hint or two of any limitations to the Overlords'
omnipotence: early in the book Karellen does refer to himself as "only

a civil servant trying to administer a colonial policy in whose shaping I had no hand" (2), and Stormgren believes that though Karellen is "immortal . . . by our standards, . . . there's something in the future he seems to fear" (2). But fear, or indeed any emotion, seems to be of negligible consequence to the Overlords: it is human beings who are subject not only to fear but to other kinds of weakness and inferiority as well, in comparison to the Overlords.

Just as the narrative threads lead in unexpected directions, so the further development of the Overlords' characters in the third section leads to a reversal of our perspective on the differences between Overlord and human. When George asks for an interview with the Overlords to talk about the changes taking place in Jeff, he is surprised that Rashaverak is also "trying to understand"; "in some ways," Rashaverak tells him, "my ignorance is as great as yours." The Overlords are not mankind's "masters," Rashaverak continues, but only its "guardians." They could be thought of as "midwives attending a difficult birth. . . . But we ourselves are barren," he says. George then realizes he is "in the presence of a tragedy transcending his own. . . . Despite all their powers and their brilliance, the Overlords were trapped in some evolutionary cul-de-sac. Here was a great and noble race, in almost every way superior to mankind; yet it had no future . . ." (18). Karellen's speech, when he is making his final disclosures of the Overlords' purpose to mankind, underscores the same points: the Overlords do not possess mankind's "potentialities" and "latent powers." "Our intellects are far more powerful than yours," he says, "but there is something in your minds that has always eluded us." The two races "represent the ends of two different evolutions. Our minds," Karellen says, "have reached the end of their development. So, in their present form, have yours. Yet you can make the jump to the next stage, and therein lies the difference between us." Humans have not realized "the irony of their title" for the Overlords, since above the Overlords is the Overmind, exerting its power on them[9] (20). And even the Overlords' intellects have limitations: "They were equally helpless," Jan thought, "equally overwhelmed by the unimaginable complexity of a hundred thousand million suns, and a cosmos of a hundred thousand million galaxies" (23).

Earlier, when Jeff's transformation was beginning, Karellen had said, "I grow more and more sorry for these people" (17). When he makes his speech disclosing the Overlords' purposes he says, "We shall always envy you;" (20) and just before the final destruction of Earth Jan says,

"Good-by, Karellen, Rashaverak—I am sorry for you" (24). Homeward bound in his ship, Karellen "did not mourn for Man: his sorrow was for his own race, forever banned from greatness by forces it could not overcome" (24). So Man becomes the hero after all, and if the individual human beings do not draw our full interest, Mankind does. In a sense Everyman is the hidden hero of *Childhood's End.*

"Good science fiction," according to James Blish, is neither "comfortable" nor "safe." "It is precisely the science fiction story that rattles people's teeth and shakes their convictions that finds its way into the mainstream," he says.[10] And there is a parallel here in the development of theme with what I have been saying about the development of narrative and of character. Themes, like narrative lines and characters, are hinted at through conventions that set up expectations in a reader, and their success depends upon the writer's ability to fulfill those expectations in imaginative and surprising ways. The good science fiction writer (as opposed to the good fantasy writer), sets up thematic expectations which are based upon scientific fact, principle, or possibility (while the good fantasy writer starts with an anti- or non-scientific premise of some sort and then follows it to its logical conclusions).

The good science fiction story which "rattles people's teeth and shakes their convictions" must do so within further limitations, for theme must not only be based in science: it must arise from narrative line and characterization—it cannot be imposed upon them arbitrarily.

Clarke is both scientist and storyteller. As Clifton Fadiman says, "Mr. Clarke is no more dreamer. If he roves space, it is with slide rule in hand."[11] And the subtitle of Clarke's nonfictional exploration of the future, *Profiles of the Future,* is revealing: "An Inquiry into the Limits of the Possible." Yet in his Introduction to *Profiles* Clarke says he hopes "the charge will not be leveled against me" that "this book seems completely reasonable and all my extrapolations convincing." For then he would "not have succeeded in looking very far ahead; for the one fact about the future of which we can be certain is that it will be utterly fantastic." Elsewhere in this Introduction Clarke expresses an admiration for H.G. Wells who "very sensibly did not allow himself to be shackled by mere facts if they proved inconvenient."[12] But in the body of the book Clarke is likely to preface his speculation about a future possibility with the phrase that it "contradicts no known scientific principle" or "does not . . involve any scientific absurdities." And in the

Preface to *The Exploration of Space,* a work of nonfiction written two years before *Childhood's End,* Clarke says, "I have tried to base all my speculations firmly upon facts, or at least upon probabilities. . . . Space-travel is a sufficiently sensational subject to require no additional embellishments, and in the long run we can be sure that our wildest flights of fancy will fall far short of the facts—as has always happened in the past history of scientific prediction." At the same time, Clarke says, "I have . . . not been afraid to use my imagination where I thought fit."[13] All this evidence, at first glance perhaps partially contradictory, in fact points to a fairly subtle distinction that Clarke makes in fiction and nonfiction alike: he does not hesitate to use his imagination, but it is an educated imagination, ranging within the limits of the possible, and it rejects for both fiction and nonfiction anything he believes to be an absolute contradiction of known scientific fact or conceivable scientific possibility.

Clarke doubtless applies this test a bit more rigorously to nonfiction than to fiction, yet there is little if anything in *Childhood's End* that is flatly impossible or that strains credulity to the breaking point in the context in which it occurs. This statement may seem startling: let us examine it. Part of the secret is that human achievements, on the whole, are held to the limitations of possibilities presently envisioned by science (indeed some, like an oral contraceptive or flight to the Moon, have come to pass since Clarke wrote the book—these give a kind of accidental realism to Clarke's picture of the future, similar to that created by some of Jules Verne's inventions). The principle of the effect of time dilation that works on Jan's flight to the Overlords' planet to age him only a few months during eighty terrestrial years is now accepted by scientists as a consequence of Einstein's theory of relativity. Even mankind's recognition of the Overlords' form from the heritage of man's legendary past —which is "not precisely a memory . . . but a premonition" from the future—is paralleled by Clarke's statement in *Profiles* that "we cannot rule out even such outrageous possibilities as limited access to the future," since "even the theory of relativity may only hint at the ultimate queerness of time."[14] The peace and plenty flowing from factories manned by robots are of course within the reach if not quite the present grasp of human technology. And mankind is already near or even past the stage of "something like five hundred hours of radio and TV . . . over the various channels" every day with "the *average* viewing time per person . . . three hours a day."[15]

The technological accomplishments of the Overlords are harder to reconcile with presently known scientific principles, and here fiction perhaps tends to take precedence at least over present fact, though not with any violation of fictional probability. Coming from a distant star with a different evolutionary history, they can logically be supposed to have developed powers that are beyond the reach of human science. And even the light trail of their Stardrive (in *Profiles* Clarke speaks of "space-drive," the term "coined for . . . nonexistent but highly desirable propulsion systems" which are "certainly beyond the present horizon of science," but will probably become possible in the future[16]) is presented as "a visible proof of relativity—the bending of light in the presence of a colossal gravitational field" (8). The speed they achieve in their ships —"more than 99 percent of the speed of light" (12)—is just within the theoretical limit possible according to scientific theory.[17] Their television-like machine which, "operating on principles that no one could imagine," opened "a window into the past" and made five thousand years of human history instantly accessible (6), could not be built with our present technologies, but Clarke says in *Profiles* that "the idea of observing the past does not involve any logical contradictions or scientific absurdities, and . . . only a very foolish man would claim that it is impossible."[18]

The Overmind itself is no harder to believe in than other metaphysical realities. And Clarke's factual description of the vastness of our galaxy and the immensity of space beyond prepares us to accept Karellen's statement that there are "powers and forces that lie among the stars —forces beyond anything that you can ever imagine" (14). Forces among which the Overmind is entirely credible.

Perhaps Clarke's explanation of his stance in *The Exploration of Space* can serve as well as an appropriate statement for *Childhood's End:* "I do not expect all my readers to accept unreservedly *everything* I suggest as a possibility of the future," he says. But those who question should try to imagine what their great-grandfathers would have thought "if, by some miracle, they could have visited London Airport or Idlewild on a busy day and watched the Constellations and Stratocruisers coming in from all corners of the earth."[19]

Thus Clarke makes subtle distinctions between fiction and nonfiction (in *Profiles* he speaks of the "boundary posts . . . which mark the border between science and fantasy"[20]), yet in both he exercises a disciplined imagination. In both he is also interested in many of the same concepts and ideas. The doubts arising from the static nature of the utopia in

Childhood's End are paralleled by his statement in *Profiles:* "Civilization cannot exist without new frontiers; it needs them both physically and spiritually.... We do not live by bread alone; we need adventure, variety, novelty, romance." Exploration of space will thus "trigger a new renaissance and break the patterns into which our society, and our arts, must otherwise freeze."[21] Sometimes even the phrasing suggests the closeness of the parellel between *Profiles of the Future* and *Childhood's End.* Consider these passages, the first from the chapter in *Profiles* on "Space, the Unconquerable," the second from Karellen's speech disclosing that Jan has been discovered as a stowaway:

> The detailed examination of all the grains of sand on all the beaches of the world is a far smaller task than the exploration of the universe (*Profiles*, p. 121.)
> In challenging [space], you would be like ants attempting to label and classify all the grains of sand in all the deserts of the world. (*Childhood's End*, (14)

Both books emphasize the fact that in space there are many wonders. The concept of the Overmind is paralleled by this passage in *Profiles:* "There may be intellects among the stars as vast as worlds, or suns ... or solar systems. Indeed, the whole galaxy, as Olaf Stapledon suggested long ago, may be evolving toward consciousness, if it has not already done so. It contains, after all, ten times as many suns as there are cells in a human brain."[22] And, says Clarke in *Profiles,* "One can imagine a time when men who still inhabit organic bodies are regarded with pity by those who have passed on to an infinitely richer mode of existence, capable of throwing their consciousness or sphere of attention instantaneously to any point on land, sea, or sky where there is a suitable sensing organ. In adolescence we leave childhood behind; one day there may be a more portentous adolescence, when we bid farewell to the flesh." This transformation may involve the replacement of our species as we know it: "No individual exists forever; why should we expect our species to be immortal? Man, said Nietzsche, is a rope stretched between the animal and the superhuman—a rope across the abyss. That will be a noble purpose to have served."[23] Karellen's metaphor, when he explains mankind's fate, substitutes a bridge for Nietzsche's rope, but the idea is the same.

Clarke the scientist who assesses the possibilities of the future is never far from Clarke the storyteller, telling a story that indeed "rattles people's teeth and shakes their convictions," that surprises because—to adapt Clarke's remarks about space travel quoted above to science itself —"scientific possibilities are sufficiently sensational to require no additional embellishments."

The limits of the possible and the probable also apply to the relationship between theme, narrative line, and characterization. The reader expects only certain themes to emerge in a particular kind of story. *Childhood's End* it seems to me, though it has many subthemes, is primarily about different kinds of evolution. We are alerted to this through the narrative movement from utopia and golden age to the utopia of New Athens to the Total Breakthrough by the children and the destruction of the old world, as well as by the contrast in the development of the characters of the Overlords and the humans. But we could not have predicted ahead of time the exact form that theme of evolution would take.

The first kind of evolution—a human social and technological one— leads, with the Overlords' help, to the establishment of utopia and the golden age of peace and plenty. It is apparently achieved with a minimum of interference or direction from the Overlords. They simply abolish the possibility of war and push men toward a true world federation, while leaving a variety of existing governments to carry this out. Mankind can then use the resources that went into war and defense in more productive ways to develop new technologies and create a better standard of living. The Overlords give few direct orders, though they do issue an edict against cruelty to animals, and they ban nuclear weapons and space travel beyond the moon. In his speech to mankind at the time of the children's Total Breakthrough, however, Karellen reveals the true purpose of the Overlords; and we realize their influence has been more direct and pervasive than it first appeared to be: "We interrupted your development on every cultural level, but in particular we checked all serious work on paranormal phenomena." Improvement of the human standard of living, the bringing of justice and peace—"all that vast transformation diverted you from the truth," Karellen says. The truth, of course, was that the Overlords were sent by the Overmind to save man from destroying himself either through nuclear holocaust or through opening the "Pandora's box" of paranormal forces he was not yet able to understand. ("For the physicists could only have ruined the earth: the paraphysicists could have spread havoc to the stars.") Thus the Overlords made mankind "mark time while those [paranormal] powers developed" which would eventually enable mankind to "make the jump to the next stage" (20). Ironically, what has appeared to be an advance into utopia has in fact been only a kind of holding operation.

The utopia that was being developed also had its ambiguities. On the positive side were a constantly rising standard of living. "Ignorance, disease, poverty, and fear had virtually ceased to exist." "Crime had practically vanished." The "face of the world had been remade" and the "cities that had been good enough for earlier generations had been rebuilt." The "extreme mobility of the new society" had "washed away the last barriers between the different tribes of mankind" (6). No one "worked at tasks they did not like" (7); the average work week was reduced to twenty hours—and machines did all the work "of a routine mechanical nature" (10). All the "ordinary necessities of life were virtually free" (6). At the same time, education had helped men to know how to spend their leisure: "the general standard of culture was at a level which would once have seemed fantastic," and "everyone was given the fullest opportunity of using what brain he had" (10). Boredom, "the supreme enemy of all utopias," was not yet, at least, a problem; for "a well-stocked mind is safe from boredom" (6, 10). "The age of reason . . . had now really arrived" (10)—a fitting and triumphant conclusion brought about through the influence of those infinitely reasonable beings, the Overlords.

Yet we have had numerous hints that all was not well. Though we are obviously meant to side with Stormgren against Wainwright, we cannot altogether discount the latter's protest that the Overlords "have taken our liberty" (2). Karellen refers to himself as "a civil servant trying to administer a colonial policy" (2), and all our usual doubts about colonialism come into play. Humans "felt, with good reason, much as a cultured Indian of the nineteenth century must have done as he contemplated the British Raj.[24] The invaders had brought peace and prosperity to Earth—but . . . even the most peaceable of contacts between races at very different cultural levels had often resulted in the obliteration of the more backward society" (3). The Overlords' "window into the human past" served to take away the divinity from "all mankind's multitudinous messiahs"—*"all* the world's religions cannot be right," Karellen had said (2)—and "the fall of religion had been paralleled"—surprisingly enough—"by a decline in science." Though human curiosity remained, "the heart had been taken out of fundamental scientific research," since "it seemed futile to spend a lifetime searching for secrets that the Overlords had probably uncovered ages before." At the same time "the end of strife and conflict of all kinds had also meant the virtual end of creative art" (6). As Karellen puts it in his speech disclosing the Overlords' true purpose, "We have . . . inhibited, by the contrast between our civilizations, all . . . forms of creative achievement." This was "a secondary effect" of their presence and Karellen thinks it "of no importance" (20).

But some humans do find it important that "when the Overlords had abolished war and hunger and disease, they had also abolished adventure" (8), or degraded it to the level of a "kind of game—almost a planetary sport" of rescuing people from the dangerous places they have built their houses "under the summit of Everest, or looking out through the spray of Victoria Falls" (10). Sports of various other kinds now accounted for "nearly a quarter of the human race's total activity" and "entertainment, in all its branches, was the greatest single industry" (10). True, man had been freed from "the last remnants of the Puritan aberration" in his sexual life (6) and had discovered "there was nothing sinful in leisure as long as it did not degenerate into mere sloth" (6). But the hints of decadence, purposelessness, and spiritual decay are real: "among all the distractions and diversions of a planet . . . well on the way to becoming one vast playground," there are still some who ask, *"Where do we go from here?"* (10). Even "when the external world has granted all it can, there still remain the searchings of the mind and the longings of the heart." (8) Jan puts it somewhat differently but feels the same frustration: "Probably the Overlords have their reasons for keeping us in the nursery. . . ." (12).

Jan escapes from the nursery on the Overlord ship; George hopes to trade the frustrations of one utopia for a greater sense of fulfillment in another utopia. Though Jean thinks the people at New Athens are "a lot of cranks," George thinks they should at least investigate this colony that has been established especially for artists.

New Athens, the second evolutionary direction suggested by the book, contrasts with the rest of civilization at that point in history; for it is purely a social utopia rather than a social and technological one. It looks backward to values that have been lost, rather than forward to benefits that technology could bring. It attempts to give its citizens some of the best things from the human past by providing independence from the Overlords, freedom from the tyranny of mankind's technology and prosperity, and an opportunity "to build up an independent, stable cultural group with its own artistic traditions" (15). It attempts to make life more natural, less dependent on machines, by removing "unnecessary frills" and reinstituting certain kinds of human activity. Jean finds it "slightly disturbing" at first that there is a kitchen (rather than service from Food Central) and she "wondered darkly if she would be expected to make the family's clothes as well," though that proves not to be required (15).

Professor Chance says enthusiastically that only in New Athens is there *"initiative."* The rest of the human race "has peace, it has plenty —but it has no *horizons"* (17). But ironically "New Athens was not a natural and spontaneous growth" (15). It was "a piece of applied social engineering," worthy of B.F. Skinner's *Walden Two,* which, incidentally, had appeared five years before *Childhood's End,* and with which New Athens shares some similarities.[25] "Giant computing machines" had been used in planning New Athens and "some exceedingly complex mathematics" had determined the desirable size of the colony, its mix of types of people, and the nature of its constitution (15).

The colony represents a vigorous response to the fear that the Over-lords, perhaps inadvertently, are "destroying the soul of man" (15). Its citizens each have an ideal—"to do something, however small it may be, better than anyone else" (17). And the "conflict of minds with similar interests" has "produced worthwhile results in sculpture, music, literary criticism, and film-making. . . . Time played an essential part in the colony's most successful artistic achievements" (15). The reason for the concern with time is probably that the Overlords have forbidden the exploration of space and humans feel inhibited even from exploring the space around them. Thus painting, a spatial art form, "still languished," while the cartoon film, a temporal one, has produced New Athens' "most successful experiments." But the group of artists and scientists that has "done least" but has "attracted the greatest interest" and also produced "the greatest alarm" is working on "total identification." The goal is to make an audience forget it is an audience and become "part of the action." Thus "a man could become . . . any other person, and could take part in any conceivable adventure, real or imaginary. He could even be a plant or an animal. . . . The prospect was dazzling," but "many also found it terrifying" (15).

This brightest possibility of New Athens also suggests where the colony's weakness lies. Its evolution has not been natural, but everything has been carefully planned; and there is a kind of hothouse artificiality about all its achievements. George asks Jean what kind of fish to catch for dinner, yet he "had never caught anything" (16). The "archaic occupation" of knitting has been revived and become a "craze," but "such fashions came and went on the island with some rapidity" (16); they do not become a truly functional part of a way of life. Though each person has the ideal of excelling at something, actually achieving it is not regarded as very important (17). Inhabitants of New Athens may be happier than they would be elsewhere, but their life and art are not really so much more vital than those of the rest of mankind: the cartoon film is a rather artificial and nonhuman form. To compare total identification with Total Breakthrough is at once to see the paleness of life in New Athens—evolution cannot flow backward and aim at recapturing the glories of the past, nor can it be satisfactorily programed—even by a giant computer. The Overlord Inspector, Thanthalteresco, sums it up well when he says New Athens is "an interesting experiment, but cannot in any way affect the future" (17).

The third kind of evolution is that of the children who achieve Total Breakthrough. This evolution is spontaneous and erratic, not planned. It is not social nor technological but spiritual and ontological. It is achieved largely without the Overlords' help, for they can only watch, assess its coming symptoms, and protect the children so they may at last reach a totally different state, in which both body and individual personality are left behind. It thus leads to the end of their childhood and also terminates the childhood of the human race itself; for, as Karellen says, "There is no way back, and no future for the world you know. . . . You have given birth to your successors" (20).

Mankind has been presented throughout the book as in its childhood, thus making possible the final irony that the children can evolve into a more advanced state than the adults are capable of achieving through their utopias. We are often reminded of childish characteristics of individuals. Stormgren thinks Joe resembles "an overgrown baby" (3) and there has been "childish" criticism of Stormgren by members of the Freedom League (4). Stormgren himself has a childish fascination with "violent physical action." The fascination must have arisen during his kidnapping, he thinks, unless "he was merely approaching second childhood more quickly than he had supposed" (4). This same childish fascination with violence has been characteristic of mankind generally: if the Overlords had not "banned nuclear weapons and all the other deadly toys" man was accumulating, mankind would have destroyed itself. Though Thanthalteresco suggests that the Overlords' relationship with mankind is more like that of colonial power and colony than that of adult and child, actually the two come to much the same thing: colonial powers tend to treat their colonies like children.

Yet although we might expect the Overlords to help mankind grow out of childhood, quite the opposite is true: Jan frets at being kept "in the nursery" (12), and in order to grow up he has to travel forty light years away to the Overlords' planet and back. George doesn't want to grow up and is "terrified" at the "mystery" of the universe, though he is honest and recognizes his own situation clearly. It seemed to George "that men were like children amusing themselves in some secluded playground, protected from the fierce realities of the outer world. Jan Rodricks had resented that protection and had escaped from it. . . . But . . . George . . . had no wish to face whatever lurked in the unknown darkness, just beyond the little circle of light cast by the lamp of Science" (16).

Childish adults will not part with the comforting lamp of science, but the children have no such reluctance. Or, to put it more precisely, they are more receptive to paranormal forces, since their lives have not been so fully conditioned by science as yet. They are at first presented—largely through Jeffrey and Jenny—as normal children, though Jeff's experience during the tidal wave makes us realize that there is a mystery connected with him. But even after that there is "nothing unusual" about Jeff, at least for a while; and meantime we get a picture of him as a normal, though perhaps in some ways rather precocious seven-year-old boy. Like the rest of the New Athens colonists, Jeff thinks himself part of the elite. They will "take mankind to the heights that the Overlords had reached—and perhaps beyond" (17). He has no premonition of the much more unusual destiny that awaits him and the other children.

Then the dreams begin and it is obvious, as Karellen and Rashaverak observe Jeff and identify the places he visualizes, that the boy is "dreaming" of real places far away in space. Rashaverak explains to George what is happening. Jeff's and Jean's telepathic powers have enabled them to merge with other minds and "carry back memories of the experience when they are isolated once more." It is as if "every man's mind is an island . . . linked [to other islands] by the bedrock from which they spring." If the oceans should vanish they "would all be part of one continent, but their individuality would have gone." At the end of the interview his advice to George to enjoy the children while they may—advice which could be given to any parent under more normal circumstances—has special poignance: "it contained a threat and a terror it had never held before" (18).

The stages leading to Total Breakthrough are unpredictable: they are erratic, seemingly purposeless, and different in different individuals, if we are to judge from the cases of Jeff and Jenny. Jenny sleeps in a "chrysalis state," but "round her now was a sense of latent power so terrifying that Jean could no longer bear to enter the nursery," and even in sleep she can control objects at a distance. Jeff, on the other hand, "no longer slept," and unlike Jenny he possesses "no abnormal powers over physical objects." George and Jean realize that Jenny is "beyond their assistance, and beyond their love," and they cling to Jeff, who still knows them, though they can see his personality "dissolving hour by hour before their very eyes." Knowledge is flooding into his mind "from somewhere or somewhen" which will completely destroy his separate personality (19). Meanwhile, Jeff and Jenny are no longer alone, as the metamorphosis spreads like an epidemic to all the children of mankind.

Karellen, in his final speech to mankind explains what is happening to the children as they "make the jump to the next stage" through the development of paranormal powers. The Overmind is shaping the children as a potter shapes clay on his wheel, in order—the Overlords believe—to "grow" and "extend its powers and its awareness of the universe." It is "by now . . . the sum of many races" and it has "left the tyranny of matter behind." The transformation of the children "will be cataclysmic" and humans "will never understand them—will never even be able to communicate with their minds," for they will not possess separate minds but will have become "a single entity," just as men are "the sums of [their] myriad cells." Karellen concludes: "You will not think them human, and you will be right," for the last step in human evolution will take the children totally beyond the human realm. Yet though they may become "utterly alien" and look on mankind's "greatest achievements as childish toys," they will be "something wonderful" and mankind can take pride and comfort in having created it (20).

The rest of the process of Total Breakthrough is shown to Jan on the television screen when he has returned from the Overlord planet to find himself the last human survivor on Earth. The first phase, which Jan is not shown, is presumably a continuation of the process we have seen in Jeff and Jenny. Five years later, Jan is told, the second phase had begun and as the camera swoops down Karellen warns him that he is "not watching human children," and hence that human standards no longer apply. We share Jan's shock as we see these beings that are supposedly evolving into a higher, more spiritual state "naked and filthy, with matted hair obscuring their eyes." They "might have been savages," Jan thought, "engaged in some complex ritual dance." Most shocking of all are their faces—"emptier than the faces of the dead. . . . There was no more emotion or feeling here than in the face of a snake or an insect." Karellen warns Jan that he is "searching for something that is no longer there," since "they have no more identity than the cells in [the human] body. But linked together, they are something much greater than you." The pattern of the dance seems meaningless and the dance ends when the third phase begins and they stand motionless, "their faces . . . merging into a common mold." Then suddenly they exert their powers and all the forms of life, both plant and animal, surrounding them "flickered out of existence and were gone." They have continued to test their powers, Karellen says, "but they have done nothing that seems to have any purpose" (23). Our preconceptions that spiritual development should have purpose, order, and beauty have been thoroughly shaken —yet we realize in retrospect that if the body and the physical world are to be left behind, it is appropriate that they should be neglected as of no importance and should even become ugly.

Total Breakthrough ends with the destruction of the world in a scene which recalls though it does not parallel the Book of Revelation. The children—now really no longer children—have continued to test their powers, and Jan waits, sitting before the electronic piano and filling the air "with his beloved Bach." Then the Overlords leave as *"they* [emerge] from their long trance" and begin to tamper with the Moon's motion. "They are still playing," Rashaverak tells Jan. "What logic is there to the actions of a child? And in many ways the entity that your race has become is still a child. It is not yet ready to unite with the Overmind." But that union comes soon with the apparition of the "great cloud" that looks "as if the stars are tangled in a ghostly spider's web," which begins "to pulse with light, exactly as if it were alive." The children are "on their way at last," leaving the last remnants of matter behind as "a great burning column, like a tree of fire" appears. There are spectacular displays of color in an auroral storm. Then everything movable follows out into space, the earth itself looks like glass and begins to dissolve, and there is the final blinding flash of light. But just before the end Jan has felt "a great wave of emotion . . . a sense of fulfillment, achievement."(24)

Clarke describes these final wonders with a vividness that makes them truly awesome. In general his style is at its best in describing events in space, whether it is the lights of New York that "glowed in the skyline like a dawn frozen in the act of breaking" (3) or the wonders of distant planets that are glimpsed in Jeff's dreams. These have a beauty and fascination that is overpowering—the world with six colored suns and the world with "a searing ghost at the frontiers of the ultra-violet," the scene in space with "only the stars in the velvet night, and hanging against them a great red sun that was beating like a heart" (18). At the conclusion the possibility of destruction that has hovered over the entire book has come to pass—and it is both more terrible and more beautiful than we could have imagined, partly because it is of a piece with the other wonders of the cosmos that Clarke has described. Both Jan and the children have indeed recaptured the sense of adventure that had been lost in utopia and hardly recaptured in New Athens, even though Jan cannot follow the evolutionary line to Total Breakthrough. Human evolution, Clarke seems to be saying, cannot be predicted, hurried, or controlled. It may lead ultimately to a change even more vast than that in, say, the fall of man in Milton's *Paradise Lost* or the attainment of heaven in Dante's *Divine Comedy*.

When Clarke describes the way the Overlords ended discrimination in South Africa, soon after their arrival on earth, he says, "All that happened was that as the sun passed the meridian at Cape Town it went out. . . . Somehow, out in space, the light of the sun had been polarized by two crossed fields so that no radiation could pass. . . . the next day the government of South Africa announced that full civil rights would be restored to the white minority" (2). The surprise at the end is one of Clarke's most effective stylistic devices—the matter-of-fact statement of a startling fact or truth about the future which is the opposite of what the reader would have supposed from his knowledge of the present. This little incident is almost a paradigm of the entire book. The Overlords, seen as powerful forces for good, turn out to have the physical form of devils. The utopia which brings peace and material prosperity leads not to universal happiness but to spiritual malaise and restlessness. The experiment at New Athens designed to recover and revitalize the old values proves instead the impossibility of doing that. The highest achievement of mankind has a nonhuman result—Total Breakthrough eventuates in the destruction of the world as well as the transmutation of human achievement into the realm of the Overmind. At every turn, the reader's expectations have been met with surprises. But those surprises are not arbitrary or misleading, because they have a logic rooted in the development of narrative, character, and theme.

James Blish says, "The writer or reader who still thinks an exploding star is inherently more wonderful than the mind and heart of the man who wonders at it is going to run out of these peripheral wonders sooner or later. . . ."[26] *Childhood's End* has its peripheral wonders but they come from a rich imagination which weaves them into the texture of the narrative where they become more central. And that imagination can also enter the human heart and the human brain and stir a real sense of wonder there.

7. Contrasting Views of Man and the Evolutionary Process: *Back to Methuselah* and *Childhood's End*

EUGENE TANZY

WHEN, IN *Childhood's End,* George Greggson moves Jean and their two children to the colony of New Athens, the drama that George is put to work on is George Bernard Shaw's *Back to Methuselah.* We can only speculate about the reasons Arthur Clarke had for assigning Greggson to this particular play. Certainly, as a dramatic work that celebrates the adventurous spirit of man, *Back to Methuselah* fits in with the concept of man that inspired Ben Salomon to found New Athens as a place where the human spirit could be nourished. But while this is reason enough for the play's presence, what the reader of Clarke's novel recognizes when he recalls Shaw's play is that both *Childhood's End* and *Back to Methuselah* are uncommon developments of the theme of evolution, and that, in some respects at least, *Childhood's End* might be conceived as a kind of addendum to *Back to Methuselah,* a sixth part of the Methuselah cycle, so to speak.

There is no need to point to *Back to Methuselah* as a possible source for *Childhood's End.* An author's ideas are triggered by one thing or another, and it would be fruitless to speculate that Clarke may have been stimulated by reading the last part of *Back to Methuselah* to try to solve the problem that bedevils Shaw's strange He and She Ancients at the close of that play. What a recognition of the link between the two works does for us is to cause us to compare the two treatments of the theme and thus to see more clearly the view that each has to offer.

All serious literature is an attempt to render man at home in the world, to show him where he fits into the scheme of things: first, with the pop artist, "telling it like it is," and finally, with Milton, justifying the ways of God to man. As Matthew Arnold said, the artist's task is to render emotionally for us a vision of our world that squares with our fullest understanding of its nature, enabling us to realize how we can best live in that world. No more important and threatening generalization about the nature of man has appeared in the past century than Darwin's theory of evolution. It is the angel at the foot of the ladder of evolution that we see both Shaw and Clarke wrestling with in these works, both men attempting to throw that angel so that evolutionary theory may cease to be a threat to man's spirit.

For a convincing account of the devastating impact evolutionary theory had upon late nineteenth-century Western thought, one can do no better than to read the long preface Shaw wrote to *Back to Methuselah.* At first glance, Shaw said, Darwinian natural selection had seemed simple and satisfactory; rational men took to the theory at once, heaving a sigh of relief as they quickly ushered the old ogre, Jehovah, Blake's Nobodaddy, out of doors. But second thoughts, Shaw added, revealed the sigh of relief to be a mistake. "When its whole significance dawns on you," Shaw confessed, "your heart sinks into a heap of sand within you. There is a hideous fatalism about it, a ghastly and damnable reduction of beauty and intelligence, of strength and purpose, of honor and aspiration, to such casually picturesque changes as an avalanche may make in a mountain landscape, or a railway accident in a human figure." "What hope is there then of human improvement? According to the Neo-Darwinists, to the Mechanists, no hope whatever, because improvement can come only through some senseless accident which must, on the statistical average of accidents, be presently wiped out by some other equally senseless accident." "What damns Darwinian Natural Selection as a creed," Shaw wrote in his postscript to the play, "is that it takes hope out of evolution, and substitutes a paralysing fatalism which is utterly discouraging."[1]

A world faced with such a paralyzing theory could not ignore it; men would either have to find a way to interpret the theory so as to remove its venomous powers or they could join with George Gissing, James Thomson, et al., to make a religion of pessimism and sing hymns in a city of dreadful night. One of the most fascinating aspects of the literature that treats of evolution is that facet which shows man forcing his "knowledge" to make room for his will to live. In this respect there have been four principal ways of adjusting to evolutionary theory. The first was to accept the theory in theory but not in fact. This principally was the reaction of those mature rational men whose views were already well settled before Darwinian theory appeared. These men acknowledged the theory, but did not see it as making any real difference in their preestablished views. A second way, the way of many of the younger generation whose views matured after the publication of the *Origin of the Species,* was to follow the lead of men like Thomas Huxley, the scientist who did most to popularize Darwinian views, and to accept evolution straightforwardly while trying to show what is the place of humanism in a world ruled by physical law. The third way, the reaction of those who wanted to be known as rational but who could not tolerate the limitations placed on humanity by orthodox evolutionary theory, was to replace Darwinian theory with a nonmechanistic evolutionary process cast in their own image. The fourth and most comprehensive response—the response of those farthest from the original Darwinian battlefield, and hence presumably of those with the largest perspective—was to accept the physical base of Darwinian evolution but to remove the restrictions an orthodox scientific view would ordinarily place upon the physical, to open the physical to all sorts of possibilities, including the achievement of paraphysical transformations. With this view men could have both their science and their dreams; this alien world might pass for a home after all.

The first two of these four principal reactions need not keep us long, for it is the last two that reveal the most about humanity's will to survive. Illustrative of the first response—acceptance of the theory in theory but not in fact—is Edward Bulwer-Lytton's important if neglected novel, *The Coming Race,* published within a dozen years of the *Origin of the Species.* Bulwer-Lytton understood Darwinian theory and made use of it, but he was too old a man to have his own thinking reshaped by it. In his *Coming Race,* he was not genuinely concerned with what biology might actually have in store for man. He seized on "the Darwinian proposition that a coming race is destined to supplant our races" in order to excoriate humanity for its failures.[2] Darwinian theory gave him the chance to show his readers that before man can create the kind of world man says he wants, he will have to cease being the kind of man he is. Evolutionary theory might be used to forecast a time when the old man will be cast off and the new put on, but in *The Coming Race* the evolutionary process is a terminal one ending when the kingdom of the godlike replaces that of man. The novel was very popular, reaching five editions within a year of its 1871 publication date. It tapped the public interest in the question of just what evolution might mean for man. But that wasn't the author's concern. Evolutionary theory was simply an excellent device for saying in sum what Bulwer-Lytton had been saying in his other novels all of his life.

The next evolutionary novel to make a strong impact on the public was H. G. Wells' *Time Machine* of 1895. It and other Wells' works may be taken as representative of the second principal way of trying to reach an accommodation with evolutionary theory. H. G. Wells was interested in what evolution meant for man, and he presented no rose-colored view of the process. He kept as true to the nineteenth-century scientific view as he could. That view, as presented by Wells' teacher Thomas Huxley, is objective and unrelenting. Evolution is a purely physical process. The same physical process that caused life to rise can cause it to disappear. The process is simply a process, without direction or goal. As Huxley wrote in 1891:

> . . . it is an error to imagine that evolution signifies a constant tendency to increased perfection. That process undoubtedly involves a constant remodelling of the organism in adaptation to new conditions; but it depends on the nature of these conditions whether the direction of the modifications effected shall be upward or downward. Retrogressive is as practical as progressive metamorphosis. If what the physical philosophers tell us, that our globe has been in a state of fusion, and, like the sun, is gradually cooling down, is true; then the time must come when evolution will mean adaptation to a universal winter, and all forms of life will die out, except such low and simple organisims as the Diatom of the arctic and antarctic ice and the Protococcus of the red snow.[3]

It is this kind of evolutionary process that operates in Wells' *Time Machine* to produce the degenerative species of Eloi and Morlocks who populate the British isles of 807,209 A.D. Wells' evolutionary process is comfortless and heedless, an impersonal cosmic force that moves in directions agreeable or painful to man with equal indifference. That was "telling it like it is" and bringing home with a vengeance just what Darwinism might mean for mankind over the long haul.

As for showing man how he could function best in a world of this sort, Wells could only suggest that man should become more aware of the long-range effect of his actions and that he should choose those actions which were most likely to produce the most humane of all possible futures. Man's job, Wells felt, was that of the colonist who sets out to create a fruitful garden in a clearing he has made in a jungle. As Huxley had pointed out, such a garden can be created if intellect and persistence are applied to the task, but there is no stopping the tendency of the jungle to retake its lost ground. "That which lies before the human race," Huxley wrote in 1894, the year before *Time Machine* was published, "is a constant struggle to maintain and improve, in opposition to the State of Nature, the State of Art of an organized polity; in which, and by which, man may develop a worthy civilization, capable of maintaining and constantly improving itself, until the evolution of our globe shall have entered so far upon its downward course that the cosmic process resumes its sway; and, once more the State of Nature prevails over the surface of our planet."[4] This was Wells' view also. Man can, within limits, choose between alternate futures if he is rational enough to judge from the point of view of a sufficiently broad perspective. Wells refused to say that the year 807,209 would inevitably witness Morlocks eating Eloi, but suggested instead that rational men had the freedom to make other choices than those which would produce such a result. To this extent, humanity and its values can find a place in a world of evolutionary process. Wells thus represents the rational man's attempt to accept orthodox evolutionary theory and to show how life can be livable in the world modern science sees. Wells' view is that man can tend his garden carefully and thus make of it a very good garden for a very long while.

"For a very long while"—that is the poison ivy in the Wellsian creation. Wells could not render human life meaningful when posited against the longest ranges of time, against the ultimate cooling of the Earth and Sun. A world view that saw the evolutionary process ending —as *Time Machine* foresaw—with some spheroid object flopping near a frozen sea might inspirit man to strive only if it could drop the curtain on that ultimate destiny or otherwise convince man that means and not ends are all that count. Wells could quote with approval Theodore Roosevelt's anxious assertion that it does not ultimately matter if the *Time Machine* should prove right and the human race should devolve into Eloi and Morlocks: "The effort's real. It's worth going on with. It's worth it. It's worth it—even so."[5] He might as easily have cited Thomas Huxley's stoic cry: "Men with any manhood in them find life quite worth living under worse conditions than these."[6] To which stiff-lipped assertions the faithful few will say "Amen" while the faithless will ask to send forth starships on a race to seed the universe: "a race / That we must win completely," Ray Bradbury tells us, "or be lost."[7] Wells himself, of course, in the bitterness of old age, came to the sad conclusion that mind is at the end of its tether and the human race is a lost cause. All Wells could finally fall back upon was the human tendency to let the pressures and interests of our everyday lives fill the foreground of our thoughts, thus blinding us to the larger picture that shows the ultimate wrecking of all things human.

Wells' fiction could startle and clarify; it could give us a convincing experience of the evolutionary process, but in the end it could not convince ordinary man that man's values have a central place in the world. The reason was the stark honesty of the portrait. As Wells presented it, man's values and nature's tendencies are in conflict, and the victory must eventually go to nature. Man has no special importance; he is a passing phenomenon that has gotten into existence as a result of the blind operations of an unchanging, fixed order which will ultimately generate conditions that will exclude man altogether. This is the concept that gave rise to the third and fourth principal ways of "managing" evolutionary theory, the third represented by George Bernard Shaw's *Back to Methuselah* and the fourth by Arthur C. Clarke's *Childhood's End.* Man who must be defeated finds himself a stranger in a strange land, and *that* man refuses to remain. Rational man may not deny evolution, but he can theorize about it in ways that are less devastating to the human spirit.

It was this damage to the human spirit that made Darwinian natural selection so repugnant to men like Shaw who willfully reinterpreted evolutionary theory according to their own desires. To Shaw, the only way mankind could avoid falling into "the bottomless pit of an utterly discouraging pessimism" was by rejecting out of hand Darwinian theory as Darwin's followers had developed it. "Professional science," he argued, "must cease to mean the nonsense of Weismann and the atrocities of Pavlov, in which life is a purposeless series of accidents and reflexes, and logic only a thoughtless association of ideas."[8] Shaw could not stand the idea that the human condition is fixed by forces that are beyond human power to amend. That idea made his own role of "world-betterer" ridiculous and futile. So he simply denied it. Writing in 1944 on the question "Is Human Nature Incurably Depraved" Shaw first had to admit that all of the evidence seems to indicate that it is. "Nevertheless," he asserted, "if this book [on reform] is to be worth writing or reading I must assume that all this pessimism and cynicism is a delusion caused, not only by ignorance of contemporary facts, but, in so far as they are known, by drawing wrong conclusions from them."[9] Because something needed to be, Shaw would assume that it was. Feeling the need to remake evolutionary theory so that existence might precede essence and the being's nature might not be governed by forces beyond its control but by its own vision, Shaw adopted a kind of existential evolutionary theory that he called "Creative Evolution."

> We shall teach the theory of Creative Evolution as the soundest and most inspiring religion we can formulate . . . we shall reject Pauline Salvationism as an atavistic corruption which has produced all the mischief ascribed to Christianity; and . . . we shall warn our pupils against Natural Selection on precisely similar grounds, it being clearly a corruption of the theory of evolution by extracting all the divinity from it, so that through it evolution gained the whole world and lost its soul. It will be no more possible to tolerate the deliberate inculcation of Calvinism or Darwinism in public schools than Voodooism.[10]

It was as a showcase for his theories on creative evolution that Shaw published his *Back to Methuselah* cycle in 1921. The cycle consists of five plays that range in time from the Garden of Eden, when man first appeared as a separate species, through modern times into the near future when a mutant anthropoid race develops that has a normal life span of 300 years, on past the period when the new species finds it cannot coexist with ordinary humanity, concluding finally in the distant future, "As Far as Thought Can Reach"—actually the year 31,920—when the descendants of the mutants will be a nearly immortal race of intellectuals who are only one step away from breaking free of the body to live forever as whirlpools of pure mind. What Shaw sought in this evolutionary cycle was to reinstate intellect as a central part of the evolutionary process, to reinstate mind as the coequal of matter, indeed as its superior, and to free man from the limits placed on him by those who conceive of mind as a merely dependent phenomenon.

To provide the "scientific" base for this creative evolution, Shaw had to leap over Charles Darwin to the evolutionary theory expounded in the days of Darwin's grandfather, Erasmus Darwin, amending the evolutionary ideas of Lamarck. What satisfied Shaw about Lamarck's theory was its existential, "fundamental proposition that living organisms change because they want to. If you have no eyes, and want to see, and keep trying to see, you will finally get eyes. . . . You are alive; and you want to be more alive. You want an extension of consciousness and of power. You want, consequently, additional organs, or additional uses of your existing organs: that is, additional habits. You get them because you want them badly enough to keep trying for them until they come. Nobody knows how: nobody knows why: all we know is that the thing actually takes place. We relapse miserably from effort to effort until the old organ is modified or the new one created, when suddenly the impossible becomes possible and the habit is formed. The moment we form it we want to get rid of the consciousness of it so as to economize our consciousness for fresh conquests of life; for all consciousness means preoccupation and obstruction. . . . We can lose a habit and discard an organ when we no longer need them just as we acquired them; but this process is slow and broken by relapses; and relics of the organ and the habit long survive their utility."[11] Dramatizing this concept in *Back to Methuselah*, Shaw has the serpent of the Garden of Eden explain to Eve that once a need has been discovered that must be satisfied, "you imagine what you desire; you will what you imagine; and at last you create what you will." To desire, to imagine, to will, to create—that is the evolutionary process Shaw presents in his cycle, subsuming the whole process in one word, "conceive"—"the word that means both the beginning in imagination and the end in creation."[12] It is this message from the serpent that really gets human history started; the lesson enables Adam and Eve, by creating death, to throw off the burden of individual eternal life they cannot yet handle, and, by creating birth, to insure the existence of life eternal through their descendants.

In Shaw's evolutionary scheme the individual life is simply one of many manifestations the original, eternal life force takes. As such a manifestation, each individual life has the same creative power that the original life force has and carries out that life force's own purposes. Shaw makes this point explicitly in the second part of the *Methuselah* cycle when he has the brothers Barnabas, Conrad, and Franklyn, representing advanced scientific and religious thought, explain their united view. When Franklyn's daughter, Savoy, asserts her suspicion that "the old people are the new people reincarnated" and that she is Eve reborn, her uncle Conrad replies:

> You are Eve, in a sense. The Eternal Life persists, only It wears out Its bodies and minds and gets new ones, like new clothes. You are only a new hat and frock on Eve.
> Franklyn. Yes. Bodies and minds ever better and better fitted to carry out Its eternal pursuit. . . . The pursuit of omnipotence and omniscience. Greater power and greater knowledge: these are what we are all pursuing even at the

risk of our lives and the sacrifice of our pleasures. Evolution is that pursuit and nothing else. It is the path to godhead. A man differs from a microbe only in being further on the path.[13]

Life forms are simply the tools by which the Life Force accomplishes its purposes, and if the life forms it currently has taken prove to be inadequate to the achievement of those purposes, it will invent new life forms that will be equal to the task:

> Franklyn. We shall not be let alone. The force behind evolution, call it what you like, is determined to solve the problem of civilization; and if it cannot do it through us, it will produce more capable agents. . . .
>
> Conrad. The power my brother calls God proceeds by the method of Trial and Error; and if we turn out to be one of the errors, we shall go the way of the mastodon and the megatherium and all the other scrapped experiments.[14]

This is Shaw's essential, anthropocentric view. Despite the testimony of science, Shaw still conceived of the world as revolving around man, with man being the latest, best dream in the eye of the eternal life force. The individual as an expression of the life force has a significance in himself and a significance as a part of an effort that includes more than man. But man must do his work alone. It is only in individual lives that the life force can manifest itself. Since man is that life force's highest current expression, man cannot look for aid either from angels in an invisible heaven or from superbeings traversing the visible sky. Man must be his own physician and must heal himself, changing his nature in the direction that will achieve life more abundantly—for God is helped only by those who help themselves.

This is an evolutionary view that not only justifies man the species but that justifies in particular the kind of man Shaw was. As a reformer, a world-betterer as he put it, Shaw was the life force incarnated since that force spent itself always in making life over in newer, more nearly perfect forms. Evolutionary progress is made in giant leaps by those who have the clearest understanding of the problems being faced, the best conception of their solution, and the strongest conviction that the problems must be solved despite the personal sacrifices the solutions might entail. The vanguard of the evolutionary process is made of that elitist group that sees most clearly and commits itself most deeply. Advances are made by those heroic few whose commitment is so complete it becomes an act of the unconscious:

Franklyn. Do not mistake mere idle fancies for the tremendous miracle-working force of Will nerved to creation by a conviction of Necessity. I tell you men capable of such willing, and realizing its necessity, will do it reluctantly, under inner compulsion, as all great efforts are made. They will hide what they are doing from themselves: they will take care not to know what they are doing. They will live three hundred years, not because they would like to, but because the soul deep down in them will know that they must, if the world is to be saved.[15]

The visions these world-saviors turn into realities are validated by one pragmatic test: the survival of the fittest. In this regard Shaw's evolutionary process is inexorably principled: either a mutant form (the realized solution to a problem) is more fit to survive than the preexisting form or it is not. The first of Shaw's mutants to have a three hundred year life span must rely on subterfuge to overcome the hostility normal people feel towards those who are different. The mutants survive because their life span, the thing that makes them different, enables them to be wiser than ordinary people. They are not protected by some outside power until they are ready to survive; they achieve survival because their mutated form makes them fit to survive.

Furthermore, the mutation, once it proves successful, does not spread to the whole human race and redeem that race any more than human nature devolved upon all of the anthropoids from whom man descended. The distinguishing traits of the new species remains with the new species, the old and the new coexisting so long as the superior race tolerates the inferior. In Shaw's view, the life force is no sentimentalist. If a bypassed species becomes an obstacle to the advance of the superior, then the lesser goes to the wall. In *Back to Methuselah,* the human species is eventually allowed to die off. The important thing is the march to godhead. Nothing must stand in the way of that progress.

But this creative evolution not only justifies the existence of Shavian "world-betterers," it also proves that Shavian artists are the human beings most at one with the fundamental forces of nature. It is not the competitive warriors, the sportsmen, or capitalists who are closest to the spirit of nature, but the visionaries, the artists who, with the serpent in Eden, "dream things that never were" and ask "Why not?"[16] As the serpent told Eve, "imagination is the beginning of creation."[17] The imagination that artists and world-betterers share is the initiating agency of the evolutionary process. Reforming artists of the Shavian sort are sons of God and can say with all poets, "Before generals, bankers and

politicians were, I am." Art and the evolutionary process are synony-
mous. Art is the means by which the life force first works, first throws
into tangible form, the conceptions it is striving to bring into being. "An
author is an instrument in the grip of Creative Evolution, and may find
himself starting a movement to which in his own little person he is
intensely opposed." Artists anticipate and prophesy the commonplaces
of tomorrow. "Michaelangelo painted the Superman three hundred
years before Nietzsche wrote Thus Spake Zoroaster." Great artists, like
Michaelangelo and Nietzsche, are "driven more or less in spite of themselves to shew . . . not what mankind is but what it might become."[18] (As
science fiction writers are fond of saying, first science fiction writers
dream; then come trips to the moon. "Before the reality," says Clarke,
"there must be the dream to provide inspiration.")[19] In great works of
art, "the Life Force is struggling towards its goal of godhead by incarnat-
ing itself in creatures with knowledge and power enough to control
nature and circumstances."[20]

To Shaw, it is the artist who accepts the open-ended nature of the
evolutionary process; it is he who is willing to take the risks that must
be taken if a better life is ever to come into being: "Chance," says Adam;
"What does that mean?"

> The Serpent. It means that I fear certainty as you fear uncertainty. It means
> that nothing is certain but uncertainty. If I bind my will I strangle creation.
> Eve. Creation must not be strangled. I tell you I will create, though I tear
> myself to pieces in the act.[21]

Neither Adam with his perpetual going over the same ground, nor Cain
with his destroying vainglory gives Eve anything to live for, which means
to hope for. But she has other sons whom she likes "because they tell
beautiful lies in beautiful words. They can remember their dreams. They
can dream without sleeping. They have not will enough to create instead
of dreaming; but the serpent said that every dream could be willed into
creation by those strong enough to believe in it." Eve has sons who are
musicians, sculptors, mathematicians, astronomers, inventors, priests—
in a word, artists. "When they come, there is always some new wonder,
or some new hope: something to live for. They never want to die,
because they are always learning and always creating either things or
wisdom, or at least dreaming of them." Eve's hope is that "Man need
not always live by bread alone. There is something else. We do not yet
know what it is; but some day we shall find out; and then we will live on

that alone; and there shall be no more digging nor spinning, nor fighting nor killing."[22]

It is the artist, the eye of the universe, who leads the way toward this better world. Shaw's artist is Shelley's legislator, Carlyle's seer throwing bridges across unfathomed deeps, Browning's participant in the pact of creatorship bodying forth an ever truer vision of the nature of the world, the prophet seeing beyond the next turning of the stairs. "Art is the magic mirror you make to reflect your invisible dreams in visible pictures," Shaw's wisest Ancients declare. "You use a glass mirror to see your face: you use works of art to see your soul." Shaw's wisest artists know that "the statue comes to life always. The statues of today are the men and women of the next incubation. I hold up the marble figure before the mother and say, 'This is the model you must copy.' We produce what we see. Let no man dare to create in art a thing that he would not have exist in life."[23]

Since it is the artist in man that is at one with the creative forces of nature, it is man as artist that survives after all of his other forms have disappeared. Art is Shaw's fitting preparation for true maturity. In the final part of the *Methuselah* cycle, "As Far as Thought Can Reach," before Shaw's intellectual "Ancients" mature, they must pass through a four-year childhood as full-grown artists, experiencing all of the enthusiasms, discoveries, triumphs, and, in the end, disillusionments that an ordinary artist experiences in his professional life. They begin their lives as artists pursuing power; they ask, "What artist is as great as his own works?"[24] and they believe for a while that art is more important than life, but eventually they reject not only surface beauty but all mere imitations of reality to take up a life of intellectual contemplation. In the end, Shaw's artists turn their backs on art itself. This is not a Shavian repudiation of the means by which he worked. Art lasts, for Shaw, as long as man lasts. Art remains until the consummation of the world, but no longer—as long, that is, as we are compelled, as St. Paul put it, to see through a glass darkly. Art is needed to lead man to the perfect vision; it ceases to have any function once the ultimate stage is reached—as far as thought can conceive. When Shaw has his Ancients reject art, Shaw is acting in his role as prophet, conceiving of art as having triumphed. As the She-Ancient explains, "But we who are older use neither glass mirrors nor works of art. We have a direct sense of life. When you gain this you will put aside your mirrors and statues, your toys and your dolls." What the ancients are aware of in their direct sense of life is that life is not the physical form that bodies the life; life is the thought so embodied. Thus the Ancients agree with the wisest of Shaw's artists when he says, "The body always ends by being a bore. Nothing remains beautiful and interesting except thought, because the thought is the life."[25]

One problem remains, however, and that is that thought cannot manifestly exist apart from the body. This is an imperfection that troubles even Shaw's Ancients. They still need the art of the body, or of body-making, in order to express their existence. "This is my body," one of them complains, "my blood, my brain; but it is not me. I am the eternal life, the perpetual resurrection; but this structure, this organism, this makeshift . . . is held back from dissolution only by my use of it."[26] The trouble of the Ancients, as Shaw shows it, is the ultimate trouble of the life force: how is life to be delivered from its dependence on the body? To the Ancients this is not an insurmountable problem. As one of them points out, "prehistoric men thought they could not live without tails. I can live without a tail. Why should I not live without a head?" "The day will come when there will be no people, only thought." That will be possible when the life force learns how to exist as a vortex free of any need for material form:

> The She-Ancient. None of us now believe that all this machinery of flesh and blood is necessary. It dies.
> The He-Ancient. It imprisons us on this petty planet and forbids us to range through the stars. Acis. But even a vortex is a vortex in something. You can't have a whirlpool without water; and you can't have a vortex without gas, or molecules or atoms or ions or electrons or something, not nothing.
> The He-Ancient. No: the vortex is not the water nor the gas nor the atoms: it is a power over these things.
> The She-Ancient. The body was the slave of the vortex; but the slave has become the master; and we must free ourselves from that tyranny. It is this stuff [*indicating her body*], this flesh and blood and bone and all the rest of it, that is intolerable. Even prehistoric man dreamed of what he called an astral body, and asked who would deliver him from the body of this death.[27]

In Shaw's existential system the magic formula is to desire, to imagine, to will, to create. The Ancients, totally convinced of the need to solve the problem of life, have already begun to conjure up the nature of the solution. In Shaw's system the will will come following the imagined solution, and the next act of the drama, the sixth play of the *Methuselah* cycle—ought to be entitled "The Thing Happens," or just possibly, *Childhood's End*.

In the *Methuselah* cycle, Shaw made what he considered to be his most concentrated effort to embody in a work of art a vision which would square with the most advanced ideas about the world, showing us the world as it really is, and showing that we have a vital role to play. To do this, he had to reinterpret evolutionary theory in a form compatible with his desires. While Shaw hoped by this means to reunite the visions of science and religion, *Back to Methuselah* was not automatically convincing to the audiences who saw it or to the reading public. The lesson preached was too much like a lesson in how to pull oneself up by one's bootstraps—all well and good if you have boots, but not very satisfactory to people who thought they were standing barefoot in snow. In this situation, Shaw's views did not prove very helpful. Leaping over Darwin, he had not based his hopes firmly enough on what the public conceived to be true science.

A generation after *Back to Methuselah* was published, the psychologist Carl Jung, seeking to explain why flying saucers should suddenly fill the skies in the 1950's, speculated that one reason modern man sees so many of those cylindrical objects is that they supply us with a symbol of unity and wholeness that our tension-distraught, fragment-torn psyche desperately needs. Writing in 1958, Jung claimed that with the loss of Christian belief, "a political, social, philosophical, and religious conflict of unprecedented proportions . . . split the consciousness of our age."[28] Man, he said, could not stand that split; he must have unity, wholeness —even if it meant projecting superior saviors from alien worlds into the newly noticed, strange aerial phenomena that are called flying saucers.

It was into this same spiritual environment that Arthur C. Clarke's *Childhood's End* was launched in 1953, bringing its Overlords to Earth to save man from self-destruction. The evolutionary theory that supports *Childhood's End* does not make the kind of radical demands upon the public as did Shaw's theory. It manages to avoid the pitfalls that Shaw fell into while still making the case for reinstating the paraphysical into our conception of the world. Clarke achieved this reconciliation of the scientific and the mystical not by rejecting Darwinian evolution out of hand, but by placing the processes of natural selection into a context that was much more comprehensive than the context conceived by Shaw, Wells, Huxley, et al. What Clarke insisted upon was simply the largest perspective possible. He viewed evolution not as an essentially earth-bound phenomenon as Shaw had done; he saw evolution as truly a universal phenomenon, one that occurred everywhere in space and one that had been in process for as long as the universe has existed. The older writers had known that this was so, but for all practical purposes their thought was Earth-centered. It was largeness of view that opened up evolutionary theory to possibilities not dreamed of in nineteenth-century science. As a result, Clarke did not need to insist that a purposeful spirit alien to matter, intelligent and aware of its purposes, a thinking life force, was behind all evolutionary forms from the simplest to the most complex. He could admit with the most puristic materialist that nature's basic ingredient might be nothing but matter. But he could argue that a theory of the universe which claimed that matter could produce only material phenomena was biased and incomplete. Matter might have certain forms in which it worked in purely mechanical ways, but matter in other stages of its development—given the infinity of time to bring them out—might be so transformed as to generate phenomena like telepathy and precognition that we would normally consider to be purely psychic.

Clarke's quarrel with Darwinian theory, therefore, was not that it was wrongheaded, but that it was merely incomplete. Accurate as far as it goes, it does not go far enough. Clarke has his leader of the Overlords, Karellen, declare authoritatively that the weakness of the ordinary scientific view of things is just its insistence that the world can take only physical forms. Speaking of early twentieth-century science, he says:

> . . . there were no forces which did not come within its scope, no events for which it could not ultimately account. The origin of the universe might be forever unknown, but all that had happened since obeyed the laws of physics.
>
> Yet your mystics, though they were lost in their own delusions, had seen part of the truth. There are powers of the mind, and powers beyond the mind, which your science could never have brought within its framework without shattering it entirely. All down the ages there have been countless reports of strange phenomena—poltergeists, telepathy, precognition—which you have named but never explained. At first science ignored them, even denied their existence, despite the testimony of five thousand years. But they exist, and, if it is to be complete, any theory of the universe must account for them.[29]

What reasonable person could say that Karellen's position is absolutely wrong? It is through this weakness in the science of materialism—its inability to deal systematically with erratic phenomena of an apparently nonphysical generation—that Clarke moves to secure his reader's suspension of disbelief in the existence of a world in which psychical forces are uniformly superior to material ones.

Thus Clarke's readers, unlike Shaw's, do not have to become anti-Darwinian existentialists to get to heaven; they can swear by Darwin and still be lifted to godhead. The shift in perspective accomplishes it all. Shaw saw man as at the top of the evolutionary chain with no one above him. Having dared the anti-secular feat of smuggling God back into the universe in the guise of a life force, Shaw could not take the more dangerous step of readmitting Michael, Raphael, and Beelzebub also. Science seemed to say that beings more knowing, more powerful than man could not exist. So Shaw gave man and his descendants 30,000 years of hard intellectual, creative effort to get free of the bondage to matter. What Shaw said man could do over these next 30,000 years, Clarke simply assumed had already been done somewhere in the universe in the billions of years during which the evolutionary process has already been at work. With that simple shift, the problems of Shaw's rather bumbling life force fall away. What more natural than to assume that if matter has reached the selfconscious stage here on our comparatively young planet, it did so eons ago on one of the older worlds? And if the intellect's next possible evolutionary stage is as a disembodied community of organically unified minds, what more reasonable to conclude than that, in the long history of the universe, this evolutionary stage also has already successfully been reached? Not as the result of the desires of some forward-dreaming spirit, but as the inevitable, eventual result of the combination of the laws of physics and the laws of chance. So, what Shaw dreamed of happening eventually through the efforts of both man and some mystical entity, Clarke could declare had already happened through ordinary evolutionary means. Thus we can again surmise that the heavens may be filled with beings above as well as below man in the hierarchy of the universe. Superior intellects of satanic stature may exercise a lordship over man in his present state. Beyond those Overlords controlling them, however, may be the Overmind, the collective bodiless intellect of Shaw's Ancients, that has "long ago," Clarke says, "left the tyranny of matter behind." This Overmind may be superior to the intellectual Overlords by virtue of its ability to achieve a psychic community of being, and it may have a kinship with mankind by virtue of our common psychical natures. Surely it is possible that a deity of this sort—not all-powerful, not all-knowing, not equal to the universe but a product of it—seeking greater power, greater knowledge, a greater dominion—"trying to grow, to extend its powers and its awareness of the universe"—could take a collective interest in man, shield him from evil, and manipulate his evolutionary progress in such a way as to insure the elevation of the human race into the unity of its own mystical body.[30] This, of course, is what occurs in *Childhood's End,* and, apart from the fact that the whole thing is fantastic, we have no compelling reason to fault it on the grounds that it runs contrary to the best conception we have of our universe. Here, in *Childhood's End,* when the human race, guarded by limited angels who are shut out from union with the Overmind, passes through the dissolution of this earth to enter a transformed state, we can satisfy our feeling that we humans count, that we are distinctive creatures on the evolutionary chain, of greater importance than monkeys, fish, and the amoeba, a transitional link between a world of dust and a world of mind.

If we need to know that we have a home in the universe, that somebody big up there is looking out for us, *Childhood's End* allows us to believe it without sacrificing our scientific stance. However much luck it may have taken for the first intellectual-psychical species to become the nucleus for the mental whirlpool of the Overmind—that "vortex," "spinning like the funnel of a cyclone"[31]—our little human species can feel that we have more than blind chance on our side. We have the wisdom the Overmind has gained through its own original elevation and the skill it has developed in guiding, with increasing success, the elevation of other kindred species. However mankind may first have become differentiated from its anthropoid ancestors—and we can go to *2001* for one answer to that question—we can be confident that the next stage of our development is being carefully monitored and that we will have whatever help we need in order to mutate successfully.

There is no mistake about our needing the help. There is no guarantee in Clarke's evolutionary system any more than in Shaw's, that every mutation will survive. The universe as natural process is just as indifferent to the results it gets in Clarke's world as in the world of Huxley or Wells. As Clindar of Clarke's "Moon-Watcher" recalls, "The universe was as indifferent to intelligence as it was to life; left to themselves . . . dawning minds had less than one chance in a hundred of survival. Most of them achieved no more than a tragic consciousness of their doom, before they were swept into oblivion."[32] And Karellen assures mankind that had the human race been left to make the transition from flesh to mind by itself, it never could have found its way safely over the abyss. "Across that abyss, there is only one bridge. Few races, unaided, have ever found it. Some have turned back while there was still time, avoiding both the danger and the achievement. Their worlds have become Elysian islands of effortless content, playing no further part in the story of the universe. That would never have been your fate—or your fortune. Your race was too vital for that. It would have plunged into ruin and taken others with it, for you would never have found the bridge."[33]

It is evident, therefore, that a theory of a universal evolutionary process that has been going on as long as can be imagined is an absolutely liberating theory. In *Childhood's End* it allows Clarke to lock God the creator out of the universe while letting god the creature in. It lets Clarke reintroduce the ancient view of humanity as the object of a heavenly concern. He can yoke together both the callousness of natural selection and the comfort of a special dispensation. When the last man on earth witnesses the passing away of the earth and the elevation of man's descendants to godhead, the emotion he feels, we are told, "wasn't joy or sorrow; it was a sense of fulfillment, achievement. . . . Good-by, Karellen, Rashaverak—I am sorry for you. Though I cannot understand it, I've seen what my race became. Everything we ever achieved has gone up there into the stars." It is not surprising that Jan's description of Earth's last moments seems familiar to us: " 'The light! From *beneath* me—inside the Earth—shining upward, through the rocks, the ground, everything—growing brighter, brighter, blinding—' In a soundless concussion of light, Earth's core gave up its hoarded energies. . . . There was nothing left of Earth: *They* had leeched away the last atoms of its substance."[34] St. Peter anticipated these last moments this way in his Second Epistle: "the heavens will pass away with a loud noise, and the elements will be dissolved with fire, and the earth and the works upon it will be burned up . . . the heavens will be kindled and dissolved, and the elements will melt with fire!" Religion, science, and the imagination make a heady cocktail.

In *Childhood's End* descendants of the human race achieve the apotheosis that Shaw's Ancients desired. The manner by which the elevation to divinity is achieved, it is clear, is totally alien to the philosophy Shaw espoused. Though Shaw called himself a religious man, and in his view he was, his position vis-à-vis the evolutionary process was that of the humanist who sees man as the maker of his own good. Shaw's humanity *is* the measure of all things thus far; it is its own deity and is responsible as deity for the world it creates. Man is the sole means of his salvation. He needs only to call upon his own creativity to solve all of the problems existence throws across his path. The humanity of *Childhood's End* is no such self-sufficient entity. Clarke's conception is not humanistic but theocratic; his universe is hierarchical. Clarke's people cannot get to heaven on their own. They must be rescued from their inadequacies. It is grace given from above and not meritorious works from below that gain them everlasting life.

Another essential difference between Shaw's conception and Clarke's is also clear. Shaw's people have to strain with Nietzschean effort to reach a higher level of existence. Shaw demands that man use his intellect, his imagination, his will, to fight his way forward. The burden Clarke places on humanity is light. His men do not need to struggle to amend their faults. The superrace, treating men as inferiors, simply compel men to become civilized, communal creatures. Men do not turn themselves into new beings; they are remade docile and decent by the gifts from the superrace. In *Childhood's End* the meek and the mild, the common as well as the elite are equally lifted up. Salvation is universal, not selective. If Clarke's man exercises his intellectual curiosity and investigates the atom, space, or the paranormal, such scientific research will get him in trouble. He encounters warnings to Keep Out. He is to leave all that alone. It is not seek and you shall find, nor gird up your loins and struggle, but sit still, neither spin nor toil, and all shall be provided by those who know what it is that you need.

It is true that Clarke may be said to suggest that certain conditions are necessary prerequisites for the elevation of the human to a higher plane. The human race is not made an organic part of the communal mystical body until humanity has lived for years in a communal world state. Clarke may be making a point here, but if so, he doesn't underline it; and, anyway, that communal state is achieved in spite of the efforts of rugged individualists to thwart the Overlords in their objectives; the united world does not result from any vigorous efforts of wise pacifists to bring it about.

There are really only one or two places where Clarke concedes very much to the view that it is the aspiring who lead the species from one evolutionary plane to another. To trigger the evolutionary leap past humanity, the Overmind selects the son of an artist—a member of the group that has gone to New Athens in order to restore vigor to the arts. Young Jeff Greggson, like his father, who staged *Back to Methuselah,* is an elitist. He "felt, like all the colonists, a slight disdain for the rest of mankind. They were the elite, the vanguard of progress. They would take mankind to the heights that the Overlords had reached—and perhaps beyond. Not tomorrow, certainly, but one day. . . ."[35] Clarke may be pointing to something in thus having an elitist artist's child open the way to unity with the Overmind, but if the artist's commitment to individual development is somehow essential to the ultimate elevation of the race, we are forced to guess that that is so, just as we have to assume for ourselves that man's resilient curiosity is being saluted purposefully when Clarke selects the inventive Jan to stand as the last human alive. These are important symbolic facts, but they do not negate the essential argument that man is a dependent being. "My task and my duty," says Karellen explicitly, "is to protect those I have been sent here to guard. Despite their wakening powers, they could be destroyed by the multitudes around them. . . . I must take them away and isolate them, for their protection, and yours."[36] Man has to be lifted up. He can be made over, but he cannot make over himself. We might have said that genetic changes happen to man; he does not, thus far and so far as we know, cause them to happen.

It might seem that with a work like *Childhood's End* the effort to render Darwinian theory in a form that would be comfortable to man would at last have succeeded. There was here no need to play at espousing evolutionary theory as Bulwer-Lytton had done, nor to blur the final lessons of the theory as Wells had futilely attempted. Clarke had only to enlarge Darwinian theory, not reject it, in order to allow mind to exist apart from body, and the psychic to coexist with the material. Nevertheless while Clarke's friendly world thus proves to be possible—relying on an evolutionary process and a conception of nature that makes all kinds of things possible—in a world of so many possibilities it is also possible that the friendly creation of Clarke is only the fabrication of a writer of fiction. There's the rub. Where all things are possible, what is impossible—including the possibility that the Wellsian view—man is finished—is the true one? *Childhood's End* could appear in 1953 and show that a mellowed science and a corrected religious view can come together; but in 1958 and in 1980 people will still be searching the skies for flying saucers and other signs that big brother really does care. The crisis of the spirit that Jung noted in 1958 persists. Literary visions that show that the world does have a place for man do not have the power to exclude all other visions. Thus Arthur Clarke may write a *Childhood's End* that warms the innermost feelings of willing believers, but Clarke doesn't have to believe what he writes. Indeed he can explicitly insist, as he does on the copyright page of *Childhood's End,* "The opinions expressed in this book are not those of the author." Why should they be, unless Mr. Clarke really knows what the world is like and, like Mr. Shaw, thinks he ought to tell us.

When we have come this far, we have passed the point where literary visions can hope to show us what the world and the evolutionary process are certainly like. To help us now we need literary visions that show us how we can be human in a world where we cannot know what the world is certainly like. On this quaking ground we may find our firmest stand. Nor do we much need an art that merely demonstrates that the world is finally unknowable. We need one that convinces us that we can know that and still walk unhesitatingly forward.

This is another subject than an evolutionary one, which people like Ursula Le Guin are willing to take up. But it can be broached in connection with the evolutionary theme. Clarke himself has occasionally made man's existence in a universe where advanced beings are possible the motivation for man's mending his ways—not because it is certain that the higher beings exist, but because it is certainly possible that such beings exist. What convinces Walter Franklin of *The Deep Range* that men ought to cease butchering whales is the possibility that some alien being "up there" might descend to earth, question the worthiness of humans, and do unto humans as humans have done unto whales. This, one might say, is doing good out of fear, not love—but someone else will respond that fear is the beginning of wisdom. In any case Franklin's judgment is not based on logic, nor upon certainty. The way to face a world of uncertainty, Franklin has learned, as Robert Browning's Bishop Blougram learned long ago, is to embrace the larger cause, to take the nobler action.

Clarke takes up the issues involved in this whole question very carefully in his bicentennial salute to the United States, *Imperial Earth;* and it may be that the seriousness of the issues he is considering as well as the solemnity of the novel's occasion have had something to do with the slow pace of that novel and with the unhappiness of those readers who had hoped to find in it more high-wire acts like those of Clarke's thematically disappointing *Rendezvous with Rama.* The reader who gets through the forbidding first one hundred pages of *Imperial Earth* must be one who finds ideas to be as exciting as plot. In any case, Clarke's treatment of the evolutionary theme is sober, not fanciful in *Imperial Earth.* The chief question of the novel, one that cannot on the face of it excite many readers, is whether the hero, the clone Duncan Makenzie, will choose to maintain a fixed order that he knows will perpetuate his identity and importance or whether he will throw that order over for a new one which will not only have uncertainty built into it, but will also have slight room for him. In effect, Duncan is given what most of us don't have, the chance to choose between something like a changeless world and the evolutionary world of modern man.

The issues are defined by the old, genetic surgeon, Sir Mortimer Keynes, when he refuses to clone yet "another guaranteed one-hundred-percent Makenzie" just to perpetuate the rule of the Makenzies over their society:

> How do you make sure your dynasty continues after your death, on the lines *you* want? There's no way of guaranteeing it, of course, but you can improve the odds if you can leave a carbon copy of your self. . . . If the Pharaohs had been able to clone themselves, they would certainly have done so. It would have been the perfect answer, avoiding the problem of inbreeding. But it introduces other problems. Because genes are no longer shuffled, it stops the evolutionary clock. It means the end of all biological progress.[37]

Since the Makenzie clones "inherit" the genetic defect that prevented the first Makenzie from siring normal children, they can make no further contribution to the evolutionary development of the race. In reproducing themselves through the cloning process, however, they are able to increase their own power over others because as "twins" of themselves they can work with a singleness of mind not possible to any set of "normal" rivals. Believing as they do that self-interest makes social interest—their motto is "What's good for the Makenzies is good for Titan"—they have no conception that their displacement by one of their rivals might actually benefit society.

This dominance and this evolutionary stasis are at stake when Duncan decides to pass up his one chance to have a cloned infant made from his body and to use his limited funds to have a clone made instead from the body of his dead friend Karl Helmer, the heirless only son of a family that has rivaled the Makenzies for power. In this instance, cloning will not mean "the end of all biological progress" since the Helmer clone will be able to sire children and thus to send the Helmer characteristics skittering along the evolutionary stream. Clarke stresses the many possibilities the genetic process opens by having Duncan reflect upon a "giant, slowly rotating DNA helix" which is suspended in the main entrance of the hospital where Karl is cloned:

As his gaze roamed along the spokes of the twisted ladder, contemplating its all-but-infinite possibilities, he could not help thinking again of the pentominoes that Grandma Ellen had set out before him years ago. There were only twelve of those shapes—yet it would take the lifetime of the universe to exhaust their possibilities. And here was no mere dozen, but billions of locations to be filled by the letters of the genetic code. The total number of combinations was *not* one to stagger the mind—because there was no way whatsoever in which the mind could grasp even the faintest conception of it. The number of electrons required to pack the entire cosmos solid from end to end was virtually zero in comparison.[38]

When Duncan decides to have Karl Helmer cloned he is choosing in favor of this evolutionary flow with its infinite variations, and he is choosing also to let his own family's dynasty die with him.

The question that must be answered is why the last Makenzie should make this decision. The answer, of course, is that by the time he makes it, his moral education is complete. His moral stance at the end of his long journey from Titan to Earth and back is practically the reverse of his original position. As a result of his experiences, he has come to realize that what he "had always taken for granted, without any discussion," he must ponder carefully, and when what seems to be self-interest conflicts with the interests of the group, he has "learned to take the broader view, and to place the hopes and aspirations of the Makenzies in a wider context." He has acquired a social self, a knowledge of community that extends not only to other humans but includes all forms of life, so that when he kills a mere sea urchin, it is "with a profound sense of shock—even of shame" that he contemplates what he has done. It is this new spiritual vision, we must believe, that informs Duncan's outlook as he considers whether he should spend his money to clone himself or his dead friend. Having come to think that cloning in itself is "neither good nor bad," but that its "purpose should not be . . . trivial or selfish," Duncan must ask himself whether mankind will gain more from the perpetuation of his own type than it will from the "resurrection" of his friend.[39] When Duncan decides that mankind has more at stake in the survival of a Karl, we must also assume that his judgment is colored by his belief that Karl has the genius needed to guide mankind to what Duncan thinks is the next important stage in man's history. Duncan believes that Karl's clone can bring mankind into communication with extraterrestrial intelligence—a destiny so sure and so awesome that it succeeds in "reversing the flow of causality," enabling Duncan to catch "a momentary glimpse in the Mirror of Time" of the encounter even though it still lies in the future.[40]

When Duncan has Karl cloned, therefore, he is doing what he can—giving up his own family's future—to bring mankind closer to its destiny. Whether that destiny will be to man's particular liking or not, Duncan does not presume to know. "All knowledge," he says, is "a two-edged sword, and it might well be that any messages from the stars would not be to the liking of the human race." Duncan is willing to take the risk, nevertheless, because he has faith that there is a wider context into which the destined encounter between man and extraterrestrials is to be placed. Just as "what is good for Titan" must govern the choices of the individual Makenzies, so "what is good for all life" must govern the acts of mankind. Accordingly, Duncan concludes, "if the time was coming for mankind to face the powers behind the stars, so be it. *He* had no doubts. All he felt now was a calm contentment—even if it was the calm at the center of the cyclone."[41]

Duncan could have avoided this risk—or at least delayed it—by deciding to have himself cloned instead of Karl. He could have chosen with Shaw's Adam in *Back to Methuselah* to plow again the same old ruts. He chose instead with Shaw's Eve. A world of uncertainty is what the natural order bequeathes to man. To opt for certainty is to opt against nature. It is to commit the unforgivable sin of presumption, the sin of presuming to know that the little good that is possessed is better than the good that is merely possible. It is the sin against life. Duncan returns from his journey carrying better wisdom than that. Love and suffering have drawn him out of the exclusive world of the closed self into the inclusive world of the social self where to give up one's life for one's friend is self-preserving.

How, according to the vision of Clarke in *Imperial Earth,* can we be human in a world that will not stand still before us? By daring the uncertain; by trusting the intuited; and by committing ourselves to the whole. These are the three things needful. In the days before Darwin they were called hope, faith, and love.

8. Childhood's End: A Median Stage of Adolescence?*

DAVID N. SAMUELSON

ARTHUR C. CLARKE'S *Childhood's End* is one of the classics of modern SF, and perhaps justifiably so. It incorporates into some 75,000 words a large measure of the virtues and vices distinctive to SF as a literary art form. Technological extrapolation, the enthronement of reason, the "cosmic viewpoint," alien contact, and a "sense of wonder" achieved largely through the manipulation of mythic symbolism are all important elements in this visionary novel. Unfortunately, and this is symptomatic of Clarke's work and of much SF, its vision is far from perfectly realized. The literate reader, especially, may be put off by an imbalance between abstract theme and concrete illustration, by a persistent banality of style, in short, by what may seem a curious inattention to the means by which the author communicates his vision. The experience of the whole may be saved by its general unity of tone, of imagery, and of theme, but not without some strain being put on the contract implicit between author and reader to collaborate in the "willing suspension of disbelief."

Although much of Clarke's SF is concerned with sober images of man's probable future expansion of technological progress and territorial domain, often despite his own worst nature, in a number of stories and at least three novels he conjures up eschatological visions of what man may become, with or without his knowing complicity. *Against the Fall of Night* (1948) is a fairy tale of a boy's quest for identity in a sterile technological society far in our future; confined in setting and narrative focus, it provides adolescent adventure, a veritable catalogue of future technology, and a cautionary parable in a pleasant blend. *2001: A Space Odyssey* (1968, "based on a screenplay by Stanley Kubrick and Arthur C. Clarke") credits a mysterious device of alien manufacture with two quan-

*This chapter appeared originally in slightly different form in *Science Fiction Studies*, 1 (Spring 1973).

tum jumps in man's evolution, from preman, and to superman; its choppy structure, detailed technology, sparse suggestiveness of the evolutionary process, are all admirably suited to cinematic presentation, but not untypical of Clarke's work on his own, as a close examination of *Childhood's End* should demonstrate.

From the moon-bound rockets of the "Prologue" to the last stage of the racial metamorphosis of mankind, familiar science fictions guide us gradually if jerkily through *Childhood's End*. Besides futuristic technological hardware, we are shown three rational utopian societies and mysterious glimpses of extrasensory powers. Reducing all of these, however, practically to the status of leitmotifs, the theme of alien contact is expanded to include something close enough to the infinite, eternal, and unknowable that it could be called God; yet even this being, called the Overmind, is rationalized, and assumed to be subject to natural laws.

Two stages of advanced technology are shown us, one human, one alien. The first, ca. 2050 A.D., is said to consist mainly in "a completely reliable oral contraceptive . . . an equally infallible method of identifying the father of any child . . . [and] the perfection of air transport" (6).* Other advances vary in seriousness and significance: a mechanized ouija board, a complete star catalogue, "telecaster" newspapers, elaborate undersea laboratories, plastic "taxidermy," and central community kitchens. The technology of the Overlords, the guardians of man's metamorphosis, includes noninjuring pain projectors, three-dimensional image projectors, cameraless television spanning time as well as space, vehicles that move swiftly without the feeling of acceleration, interstellar travel, and the ability to completely transform the atmosphere and gravity of their adopted home planet. In this book, none of these developments is treated in any detail, and together they amount to no more than a suggestive sketch, serving as the merest foundation for the hypotheses built up from and around them.

Technology accounts in part for the utopian social organizations projected in this book, and also for their failings. Technologically enforced law and order, technology-conferred freedom of movement and sexuality, help to establish a worldwide "Golden Age," but the elimination of real suffering and anguish, combined with the humans' sense of inferiority, results in mild anxiety, resentment, and lethargy. To make utopia really utopian, an artists' colony is established, on the tradition-

*NOTE: Numbers in parentheses following quotations indicate chapter.

ally utopian locale of an island, but the colonists don't regard their creations as having any real value. Whether Clarke could imagine predictable great art is irrelevant, since their futility underscores the insignificance of New Athens in the larger context: for the Overlords, the island is a gathering-point for them to observe the most gifted human children in the first stages of metamorphosis. Besides being unimportant, however, utopia is unreachable; just as technology can not make everyone happy on Earth, so is it insufficient for the supremely rational and scientific Overlords. Their placid orderliness, their long lives, may excite our envy, but they in turn envy those species which can become part of the Overmind.

Thus *Childhood's End* is not really utopian, as Mark Hillegas contends,[1] so much as it is a critique of utopian goals. Whatever the social machinery, and Clarke is extremely sketchy about how this society is run, peace and prosperity are inadequate; the people of New Athens need something more to strive for. This particular "utopia" is only a temporary stage in man's development. Theoretically, he could go in the direction of enlarging his storehouse of empirical knowledge; this is the way of the Overlords, without whom man could not have defused his own self-destructive tendencies. Yet, paradoxically, the Overlords are present in order to cut man off from entering their "evolutionary *cul de sac*," to insure that he takes the other road, paralleling the mystical return of the soul to God.

On the surface, Clarke seems to commit himself to neutral extrapolation. Science and technology may have their limitations, but they can increase our knowledge and improve our living conditions. The technological power of the Overlords may be totalitarian, but their dictatorship is benevolent and discreet. From the "scientific" viewpoint of speculative biology, even the predestined metamorphosis of mankind could be seen simply as an evolutionary step, proceeding according to natural law, with no necessary emotional commitment, positive or negative. There is a value system implicit in this reading, of course, which the narrator seems to share with the characters. The supreme representatives of reason and science, the Overlords, are thinkers and observers in general, and manipulators and experimenters in their role as mankind's guardians. The few human characters with whom we have any chance to identify also exhibit a scientistic attitude, i.e., the belief that science can discover everything. Stormgren resists the fear that the as-yet invisible Overlords may be Bug-Eyed-Monsters, and muses on man's absurd superstitions: "The mind, not the body, was all that mattered" (3). Jean Greggson's clairvoyance is supported by Jan Rodrick's researches, and counterpointed by the study of parapsychological literature by the Overlord Rashaverak. George Greggson, when his son begins to dream of alien planets, is reassured by Rashaverak when he confides "I think there's a rational explanation for everything" (18). Even Jan Rodricks retains his faith in reason in the face of the inexplicable glimpsed on the Overlord's home planet. Only hysterical preachers and befuddled women apparently have any doubts.

Yet there is some doubt about reason's power, engendered by the basic science fictions of the book, the aliens, both those who guard and guide mankind, and that toward which man is evolving. The Overlords' espousal of scientific knowledge is open to suspicion. They admit they can not comprehend the Overmind and that certain mental faculties (intuition, e.s.p.) are closed to them. They are repeatedly deceptive about their appearance and their mission. First they say they have come to prevent man's self-destruction, and that man is doomed never to reach the stars. They later proclaim being sent by the Overmind to oversee man's metamorphosis, and then admit engaging in scientific observation of that transformation for their own purposes. Meanwhile one man does reach the stars, returning to find that the children of man will indeed reach, and perhaps inherit, the stars, but only by means of a kind of self-destruction. Only toward the end do the Overlords confess that their name, made up by their human subjects, is an ironic one, given their own subject circumstances.

It may be that their duplicity is necessary, that man must be readied for closer approximations of the truth; science and reason both deal with the world by means of approximations. But even their closest approximations may be far from the truth because of their inability to comprehend, because of further duplicity, or both. They resemble physically that figure of European folklore known as the "Father of Lies," their names are suitably devilish, and even their home planet is reminiscent of Hell: the light from its sun is red, the inhabitants fly through the dense atmosphere, Jan sees their architecture as dystopianly functional and unornamented. If he were better versed in literature, he might also recognize the Miltonic parallel of the Overlords' having conquered this world after being forced to leave another. The Overlords are certainly well versed in human mythic thinking: they require their first contacts to "ascend" to their ship, they assume a guise of omnipotence and omniscience, and Karellen makes his first physical appearance in the Christ-like pose of having "a human child resting trustfully on either arm" (5).

Starkly contrasting with the Overlords' anthropomorphic shape and thinking processes is the totally alien Overmind, evoking images of unlimited power used for unknowable purposes. To the human observer it appears as a living volcano on the Overlords' planet; its power is also made visible in the actions of the children of Earth, who convert their planet to energy in order to propel themselves to an unknown destination. Yet these visible manifestations seem to be mere side-effects, insignificant to the purposes of the being. The Overlords claim to know something of its behavior and composition, from having observed other metamorphoses, as Karellen indicates: "We believe—and it is only a theory—that the Overmind is trying to grow, to extend its powers and its awareness of the universe. By now it must be the sum of many races, and long ago it left the tyranny of matter behind. It is conscious of intelligence, everywhere. When it knew that you were ready, it sent us here to do its bidding, to prepare you for the transformation that is now at hand." The change always begins with a child, spreading like "crystals round the first nucleus in a saturated solution" (20). Eventually, the children will become united in a single entity, unreachable and unfathomable by any individual, rational mind. This is the extent of the Overlords' knowledge, and it may not be reliable; but the metaphor of crystallization can hardly be adequate to describe the transformed state. All they can really know, when the Overmind summons them, is that they are to serve as "midwives" at another "birth," and they go like angels at God's bidding, but "fallen angels" unable to share in the deity's glory.

On the surface, this inability to understand the Overmind is merely a sign of its strangeness and vastness, which may some day become comprehensible to reason and science—after all, how would a human writer describe something totally alien?—but underneath we feel the tug of the irrational, in familiar terms. The Overmind clearly parallels the Oversoul, the Great Spirit, and various formulations of God, while the children's metamorphosis neatly ties in with mystical beliefs in Nirvana, "cosmic consciousness," and "becoming as little children to enter the Kingdom of God." It is therefore fitting that the Overmind be known only vaguely and indirectly, and the confidence of any individual in isolation that he will come to understand this being rings as hollow as the boasts of Milton's Satan. Thus the interplay between the Overlords and the Overmind may be seen as a reworking of the old morality-play situation of the Devil trying to steal away from God the souls of men. These Devils appear to be devoted servants carrying out God's orders, but the Overlords also never stop trying to bring Him down to their level, and they manage to convince the reason-loving men of the story that, just as our faith in science tells us, everything has a natural explanation. Those men are doomed, however, and only the "children of man" may be saved in this Last Judgment and Resurrection, leaving the continuing struggle between two faiths to reverberate in the mind of the reader.

If the reader is thoroughly indoctrinated in the simple paradigms of ostensibly neutral but implicitly scientistic popular SF of the Verne-Gernsback-Campbell tradition (and Clarke can hardly have anticipated a much larger audience in 1949–53), he can be expected to take the side of reason, science, and Western man, with perhaps a slight anxiety over their alliance with Devilish aliens. But the reception *Childhood's End* received from mainstream reviewers suggests quite a different reading; for them the eschatological theme was what made the book worthwhile, not the Overlords' continuation of man's tradition of systematic inquiry, or the successive approaches to technological utopia.[2] They, and many readers since, have sensed in Clarke a streak of sentimental mysticism, which makes some of his SF quite congenial to their own views, unconstrained by the scientist's straitjackets of skepticism, proof, and unbending rules.[3] For all of Clarke's reputation for conservative extrapolation, quite justified by much of his fiction as well as his nonfiction, he apparently pushes more buttons when he strays from confident expectation of technological change into what may be termed watered-down theological speculation.[4]

Even if a work of SF could be totally neutral in its extrapolations from the findings and theories of the physical and/or social sciences, those extrapolations would have to reach the reader by means of characters, events, situations described in words which offer at least analogies to his own experience. Every word, and every word-construct, picks up meanings from other contexts in which we have seen it, and the more perceptive the reader is to his own psychology, and to a wide range of literature, the more meanings and patterns will accrue to his interpretation. The less a work of SF is anchored in incremental extrapolation from actual experience, the freer we can expect the reign given to a mythologizing tendency.[5] Positive reactions to imaginary situations will be associated not only with utopia, and its heretical premise of man's perfectibility, but also with the mythological parallel between utopia and Heaven, whereas negative reactions will summon up dystopian and Hellish contexts. The situation is complicated further by the alliance in medieval Christian tradition between the Devil and forbidden knowledge, including science, and by the post-Romantic reversal of values which opposes an oppressive Judeo-Christian God to ideals of progress, growth, and process. For Blake, perhaps the ringleader of this revolt, the oppressive God was allied with Newtonian science, an "absentee landlord" of an unjust social order, and the Devil's strength was passion, disorder, willfulness, refusal to accept the rules as absolute limitations. Accordingly, Blake depicted Milton as on Satan's side, Shelley sympathized with Prometheus, and Goethe with Mephistopheles (before letting Faust "cop a plea" because he meant well); Zamyatin's underground, which seeks to overthrow the perfect order of the "United State", clearly has reason for calling itself "MEPHI".[6]

Clarke seems quite aware of the affinity between alien beings in science fiction and the apocalyptic and demonic imagery of mythological fantasy.[7] By deliberately choosing devil-figures as spokesmen for scientific, or scientistic, thought, he establishes a growing tension between conflicting emotions as the climax of the novel nears, and the reader is almost forced to make a choice between two extreme positions. If he is scientifically oriented, he is offered the possibility of being like the Overlords, individualistic, isolated, able to understand things only by approximations from the outside; this is the way of "the Devil's party," but not in a Blakean, rather in a medieval sense. If the reader is more mystically oriented, he is offered the possibility of giving up the responsibilities of maturity, giving himself over to imagination and the irrational, and submerging his individuality in a oneness with God. This is not the only choice available to man outside the medieval tradition, and Clarke's awareness that this choice might be untenable for a work of SF, ostensibly written for a more enlightened audience, may be partly responsible for his prefacing the paperback edition of *Childhood's End* with the cryptic statement: "The opinions expressed in this book are not those of the author." But this is certainly not the only work in which his "normal" skepticism toward technocracy has modulated into myth.

In dealing with any theme of larger scope than ironing out the bugs in advanced technological hardware, it may be difficult for an SF writer to avoid mythic structures.[8] And some have argued, like Samuel Delany, that "to move into an 'unreal world' demands a brush with mysticism."[9] Despite the continuing antagonism between devotees of science and myth, our age has seen numerous creative and critical attempts to link the two, such as by opening up the definition of myth to a flexibility undreamt by a true believer.[10] But the critically sensitive reader does have the right to expect the writer of SF to use the myth, rather than be used by it, i.e., to make the whole book work on science-fictional terms. The Universe may or may not be comprehensible to reason, but the mythico-religious presentation of the Overmind and the children's metamorphosis does not seem to me consonant with serious exobiological speculation. It may be probable, as Clarke writes elsewhere, that alien beings superior to us exist, but it seems highly improbable that they are so analogous to the gods and devils of our imagination.[11] Systematic inquiry and testing may yet turn up scientific verification of e.s.p., but a quasi-religious explanation, tied to the Stapledonian fantasy of a group-mind and to the fruitless "researches" of spiritualism, turns the reader away from disinterested speculation toward simple wish-fulfillment.[12] Not limited to verified fact, scientific speculation, in or out of narrative fiction, normally tries to domesticate the unknown in theoretical terms not so openly contradictory of known realities. In turning his critique of scientism into a supernatural fable, Clarke has considerably stretched the limitations of science, if not of SF.

His mechanical wonders and quasi-utopian communities are familiar conventions; aliens, too, are acceptable as science fictions. The Overlords are obviously present to the senses, and psychologically human, and through them we receive the theory that almost explains the Overmind. This science-fictional domestication, however, is undercut by failings in literary domestication. For example, it is not reasonable that aliens should be so similar to long-established European (and European only) folklore. And this is tied to another affront to credibility in Clarke's use of e.s.p. Contradicting himself in successive paragraphs, Karellen declares that man's science could not encompass e.s.p., and that he was sent to put a stop to apparently successful studies of e.s.p. (20). Such research having been kept from fruition, Karellen is apparently forced to use traditional spiritualist terms to explain e.s.p., i.e., these powers are real, have long been labeled but not verified, and have some connections with the Overmind. Clarke's own demonstrations are similarly vague, and decidedly unscientific: the children's dreams, powers, and cosmic dance are responses to the Overmind, while Jean's clairvoyance, accomplished by means of a ouija board (!), is "explained" by her being a "sensitive." Perhaps if we can accept at face value the Overmind, we should not cavil at a little spiritualism, but it does seem a bit unfair to explain one "impossibility" (e.s.p.) by means of another (Overmind), in turn comprehended only partially by yet another (Overlords). This use of the *deus ex machina* may have a noble history, and it may be convenient in daydreams and freshman themes on God, but it is at least suspicious in an art form dedicated to projecting "possibilities." Even if we accept all of these improbabilities in the context of the story, giving in to the fable, Clarke has another suprise for us. A reader who is aware, as Damon Knight is for example, of the evidence for Satan's medieval *European* origin out of bits and pieces of pagan myth, may well object to the rewriting of history needed to make the Devil part of the mythology of *all peoples,* caused by a racial memory (or premonition) of the future.[13]

Gaffes of this magnitude not only upset all but the most hypnotic suspension of disbelief at the moment, but they also raise doubt as to the reliability of the narrator, and the credibility of the whole narrative. Clarke may want us to question the omniscience of science and the adequacy of the Overlords; Karellen's speech denigrating the ability of human science to deal with e.s.p. can be fitted into either pattern, or both. But undermining the veracity of the narrator is a dangerous game to play with a reader already aware that the subject matter is tenuously anchored fantasy.

Why does Clarke even attempt this explanation of mythology? Why, in an SF novel, does he fill several pages with a spiritualistic seance? Neither was necessary to the theme it would appear, or to the book as a whole. The Overlords' parallel with the Christian Devil could have been left unexplained, without impairing them as alien beings or as literary symbols; the explanation given is worse than none at all. The seance functions peripherally to show the similarity between human and Overlord minds, and to foreshadow the role of Jean Greggson's children as first contacts with the Overmind. It also serves to point up man's boredom with the Golden Age and the ridiculous ends which his technology can be made to serve, namely the production of mechanized ouija boards, but Rupert Boyce, whom the party characterizes, is an unimportant figure, and the success of the seance undercuts the satire. The least important purpose the seance serves is to provide Jan Rodricks with the catalogue number of the Overlords' home star; his visit to the museum to consult the catalogue is equally irrelevant to his stowing away on the starship, which will go where it will, with or without his knowledge of its destination. The problem which seems to exist on an SF level is essentially a literary one: not fully in control of his materials, Clarke has attempted more than he can fulfill.

The "cosmic viewpoint" which Clarke praised in 1962 in a speech accepting UNESCO's Kalinga Prize for the popularization of science[14] is common in SF, as is its negative corollary, inattention to details. Besides leading writers into multi-volumed "future histories," the cosmic viewpoint encourages close attention in smaller works only to the major outlines and the background. The characters are frequently left to fend for themselves, as it were, in a jungle of disorderly plots, melodramatic incidents, and haphazard image-patterns, which are symptomatic of an unbalanced narrative technique. Unity, if there is any in such a composition, frequently is maintained only by an uninspired consistency of style and tone, and by the momentum built up in the unwary reader by the breakneck pace of events. *Childhood's End,* like many books inferior to it, suffers from just such a disproportionate emphasis on the large, "significant" effects, at the expense of the parts of which they are composed.

Structurally, disproportion is evident in *Childhood's End.* in several ways. The three titled sections are balanced in length, but not in space, time, or relationships between characters and events. Each succession of actions breaks down into almost random fragments of panoramic chronicle, desultory conversation, and tentative internal monologue. Part of the problem may be that the novel "just growed" from a novelette,[15] but that is symptomatic of Clarke's failure to bring his theme down to manageable human dimensions. The effect might be similar if he had written several stories of varying length and intensity, then tried to connect them up to an outline-summary of future history. The point of view is uniformly third-person-omniscient, yet the narrative duties seem divided between an awestruck spectator at a cosmic morality play, and a disinterested observer of ordinary human events. The historian-spectator is at least involved in his theme, which he attempts to match in grandeur by panoramic wide-angle photographs and impressive-sounding generalizations or *sententiae.* But the detached observer gives us "slices of life"—political negotiating sessions, a party, a visit to a library, a press conference, a group meeting, a counseling session, a sightseeing trip—which haven't much life, and fails to reveal the principles behind his slicing. Individual episodes stubbornly resist integration with the whole, but they can not stand up independently, because they are "illustrations" insignificant in themselves. Clarke's intent seems to be to counterpoint the great, slow movement toward metamorphosis with the everyday activities that people, ignorant of their contribution to the whole, carry on independently, activities such as he often treats in his fiction of the predictable future, where plot is a peg on which to hang the background, and melodrama adds a little spice. But where the background is a large expanse of space and time, and the context involves the larger mysteries of life, such stagy effects as Stormgren's kidnapping, the Overlords' intellectual striptease, and the explanation of one mystery by another, are unnecessary, irrelevant, annoying, and finally self-defeating.

Either a unified plot or a more carefully developed poetic structure might have been preferable to the awkward misfit of this particular essay in counterpoint. But Clarke is apparently unable to imagine a plot adequate to the scope of his framework; his "predictive" novels are equally plotless and even his tale of the far future is made up of a series of accidental occurrences, set into motion almost haphazardly by the adolescent hero's desire for change and adventure. So the counterpoint structure was attempted for *Childhood's End,* and the result is a hodgepodge of pretentious chronicle, apologetic melodrama, and superficial sketches of static unrelated, individual scenes. Even if we regard the book as an elegy for mankind, for the end of personal and racial "childhood," the elegiac tone is inconsistent, and insufficient to maintain unity over 75,000 words without a more carefully wrought "poetic structure," and the lame, pedestrian style of the novel seems particularly incongruous for a poem.

As it is practically plotless, the novel is also almost characterless. Against the ambitious theme and tremendous scope, individuals and their merely personal problems are bound to look somewhat insignificant. The unknown bulks extremely large, and the attitude of the characters is stereotyped, not in the heroic mold, whose calculated respect for size and power allows for action, but in the passive mold, whose awe and reverence we normally term "religious." Man the Creator, acting, progressing, continually making changes in his environment, whom I would consider the ideal (if not the most common) protagonist of SF, gives way to man the Creature, full of fear and wonder and more than willing to follow orders when an encounter with an incalculable unknown power forces him to admit how small he is and how little he knows.[16] Although the fear of racial annihilation is counterbalanced by pride in man's being "chosen," this revaluation of the inevitable as somehow "good" has an orthodox religious ring to it, contrasting sharply with the heresy and hubris which have characterized science in modern civilization.[17] Puny on an absolute scale, man's achievements are respectable measured against the present; his potential, symbolized by the Overlords, is by no means slighted. To preserve this respectability, despite the awesome realities beyond, Clarke does show us representative moments of the better, i.e., rational selves of certain men.

Stormgren, George, Jan, and Karellen are the only major characters; one of them is involved in every episode we are shown, not merely told about. All males, actively questing for knowledge, they all appear confident and rational, unless belief in rationality in the face of the incomprehensible is itself irrational. Even their mental processes are shown to us in formal, grammatical sentences, with no trace of irrational stream of consciousness. Given little to do, however, they seem no more than marionettes in this cosmic puppet show. Only Karellen, long-lived, revisiting a familiar pattern of events, scientifically detached and curious, has any real stature. Behind his posturing, lecturing, and deceit, his sense of tragedy makes him the most human of all; his intellectual stubbornness is like that which doomed his prototype, Milton's Satan, to a similarly tragic and isolated immortality.

A resigned acceptance, common to all four characters, is largely responsible for the elegiac tone pervading the book. Stormgren knows he will never see the Overlords, George knows man has lost his future as man, Jan knows he can not survive cut off from human kind, and Karellen knows he will never find the kind of answers that he seeks. It is the reader's knowledge of impending doom that makes the characters' inconsequential behavior and sunny dispositions seem ironic; juxtaposition, a "cinematic" technique, accomplishes what style does not. Although Clarke sometimes stumbles over awkward circumlocutions, trite *sententiae,* pedantic speechmaking, and labored humor, the pedestrian lucidity and uncomplicated vocabulary of his style seldom draw the reader's attention away from the events being described. I feel the author's presence only toward the end, where his style does manage to impart a sense of melancholic majesty to the spectacle. His attempt at generating a "sense of wonder," which ranges from "gee-whiz" impressions of the Overlords to awed contemplation of man's fate, is most successful as the children grow more confident in the testing of their powers, and it culminates in the cataclysmic shock witnessed by Jan up close, then by Karellen far in the distance. The note of regret, though cloying and sentimental at times (Jeff Greggson's dog mourning his master lost in dreams, his parents' final farewell just before their island community blows itself up), also gains in depth with this echoing crescendo.

The major source of unity, besides the figure of Karellen and the basic consistency of style and tone, seems to lie in certain image patterns and the repetition of significant motifs. The dozen or so allusions to figures from folklore and history, while they may be intended to add depth to the narrative, are so haphazardly chosen and introduced as to seem unrelated to the whole. On the other hand, the apocalyptic and demonic imagery of the Overlords and the Overmind is so persistent as to lay down at the symbolic level a morality play contradicting the rational message on the surface. The majority of patterns function somewhere in between these two extremes, mainly as unifying factors. The power of Stormgren, and his superiority over the human masses, are echoed by the Overlords' power and superiority over him, and by the Overmind's power and superiority over them. Karellen's reference to humans as beloved pets reminds us of his attitude toward Stormgren, and is reinforced by the dog's loneliness. A widening perspective is seen in the Overlords' intellectual striptease, in the emphasis given e.s.p., in Jan's discovery of what lies beyond the solar system, in frequent panoramic views of space and time, of Earth and human society. The frustrated takeoff of the Prologue's moon rockets is echoed by Karellen's edict that "the Stars are not for Man," and by Jan's discovery of the edict's essential if not literal truth (are the children still "man"?). This frustration is counterbalanced by Stormgren's "ascent" to Karellen's ship, by flights of Overlord ships away from Earth (including the one Jan stows away on), and by the final departures of both children and Overlords. And the final transformation of the children into a fully symbiotic, superorganic life form is foreshadowed by images of other kinds of togetherness, progressively becoming more compressed: the fifty starships hovering over world capitals that turn out to be projections of just one, the mob demonstration broken up by Stormgren, the gangsters' "conference" broken up by Karellen, the entrance of Karellen with the children, the party where the seance is held, the artists' colony whose sense of community rests on its individual members, and a single family dissolving as its children become something else.

If *Childhood's End* is not a fully satisfying literary experience, it does illustrate certain characteristics of SF at its best, and it does exhibit literary virtues. Respect for rational thought, construction of a cosmic perspective, relentless pursuit of extrapolative hypotheses, and a genuine evocation of the sense of wonder are each positive achievements, on their own terms. The whole, however, is flawed, not only by deficiencies in style, characterization, and narrative structure, which could presumably be corrected by revision, but also by a fundamental dichotomy between opposing goals.[18]

Algis Budrys sees Clarke's problem as commercial willfulness; after identifying him as the author of "a clutch of mystical novels," Budrys chides Clarke for his "fixed and pernicious idea of how to produce a saleable short story [and presumably a novel]. That idea is to introduce an intriguing technological notion or scientific premise, and then use it to evoke frights or menaces. [Thus he can] raise a formidable reputation for profundity by repeating, over and over again, that the universe is wide and man is very small."[19] Budrys' criticism is pertinent as far as it goes, but it is limited; Clarke has shown more variety, and capacity for growth than Budrys would allow, and the flaws in *Childhood's End* are only partly, I think, due to the author's eye for a dollar.

Certainly, Clarke is a commercial writer, a member of the second generation of pulp magazine writers consciously turning out SF. Thus he has one foot firmly planted in the SF magazines of the 1920's and 1930's, with their infantile dependency on Bug-Eyed Monsters, slam-bang action, and technological artifacts treated as objects worthy of awe and wonder. But he is also rooted in a "respectable" British literary tradition. Blake, Shelley, Mary Shelley, Hardy, Butler, Morris, Wells, Doyle, Stapledon, Huxley, C. S. Lewis, and Orwell all wrote works in which they showed science and technology as demonic, at least potentially. This tradition is, I believe, still entrenched in Anglo-American humanistic circles, affecting like blinders many academics and reviewers, and that part of the literate public for whom they remain arbiters of literary taste.[20] Rather than a critical appreciation for science, they tend to inculcate fear and hostility toward it; by abdicating their function as a knowledgeable, foreseeing counterbalance, they make more likely the technocratic state they profess to anticipate with abhorrence.[21]

Given these traditions, neither of which I would call mature, Clarke and other second-generation writers for the SF magazines had little that was adequate out of which to construct a coherent critique of science and scientism. If *Childhood's End* is a classic, it is partly because it is a hybrid, a respectable representative of that period during which SF magazine writers were first trying to reach out to a literary audience, as well as to their more habitual readers. An ambitious effort, better than people outside the pulp field thought it capable of achieving, it is also an abortive effort, an impressive failure, the flaws of which are indicative of the problems frequently attendant upon the literary domestication of SF. It has a high seriousness that sets it apart from the ordinary pulp science fiction novel of any generation, but it barely lives up to its name. An attempt at maturity, *Childhood's End* is no more than a median stage of adolescence.

9. From Man to Overmind:
Arthur C. Clarke's Myth of Progress*

JOHN HUNTINGTON

H. G. WELLS'S "TIME TRAVELLER," meditating on his first experiences in the distant future, postulates that the decadence of the Eloi results from technological success which undermines man's fitness: "We are kept keen on the grindstone of pain and necessity," he argues.[1] In this version of human affairs, progress has a counter-progressive aspect which becomes especially evident over large expanses of time: by making man comfortable progress makes him lazy, and future men thereby lose those admirable qualities, aspiration and probing curiosity, which are, after all, the sources of progress in the first place. In Wells's formulation of the dilemma, pessimism would seem to be unavoidable. But in the work of Arthur C. Clarke we find a new formulation of the problem and a new myth of progress which allows for a qualified optimism. Clarke's myth engages the paradox latent in progress and offers a transcendent solution. Elements of this optimistic myth of progress can be found throughout Clarke's work, and one novel, *Childhood's End,* stands out in particular for its ingenious unification of two aspects of the myth which in his other formulations tend to work against each other. I would suggest that it is its elegant solution to the problem of progress that has rightly earned *Childhood's End* that "classic" status it now enjoys. Other Clarke works will interest us for their insights into the issue, but no other of his works gives us so coherent a rendering of the myth and explores so well the various and subtle implications of it.

Clarke's myth of progress consists of two stages: that of rational, technological progress, and that of transcendent evolution. Many of his novels remain on the first stage and render technological speculations

*This chapter appeared originally in slightly different form and under the title "The Unity of *Childhood's End*" in *Science Fiction Studies,* 1 (Spring 1974).

in painstaking detail. As his numerous nonfictional essays on the future attest, Clarke finds such speculation satisfying in itself, and in the short run at least he seems to have complete faith that an efficient technology will produce a better future. But in his most far-reaching novels technological progress fails to satisfy, and mankind advances, not by inventing more competent machinery, but by mutating into a higher form of being. This transcendental vision offers, not the detailed ingenuity of mechanical invention, but powerful hints of modes of understanding and perception and of mental powers and controls that so completely surpass those which we ourselves experience that they are incomprehensible to us. Such a realm of being can only be hinted at; it needs a language of symbol and suggestion in place of the technological vision's concrete detail. Whereas the latter offers the excitement of comprehension, the former offers the excitement of obscurity.

In Clarke's myth the transcendent state is not simply the highest stage of technological progress. Though there exists a sequential relation between the two worlds—the transcendent always follows the technological—there is no structural similarity which would allow for communication between them. The transcendent world represents a completely different order of being and perception, an order which, instead of subsuming the technology that has preceded it, obliterates it. The model for the relation of the two visions is that of the Pauline promise that forms the basis for *Childhood's End:* "When I was a child, I spake as a child, I understood as a child, I thought as a child: but when I became a man I put away childish things. For now we see through a glass darkly; but then face to face." Just as the mature man "put away childish things," transcendent consciousness completely dispenses with the attainments of rational science and the inventions of technology. The children, having entered the Overmind at the end of *Childhood's End,* destroy the Earth. This higher state is thus very different from that of the Platonic seer who, after he has escaped the cave and seen the sun, is still able to return—is even obliged to return—to his benighted fellows and to communicate his insight as best he can given the limits of language and the prejudices of his hearers. In Clarke's scheme no such communication is possible between the two states of insight; they represent steps in an evolutionary progress, but they have nothing structurally in common.

There is also an important difference between normal technological progress and the kind of evolutionary leap that leads to the transcendent vision. Clarke repeatedly describes the elevation from normal human reason and perception (i.e., the technological state) to the transcendent state as generated, not by the powers inherent in man, though without those powers nothing is possible, nor by man's own achievements, but by a genetic transformation in man caused by the interference of some higher being. The leap from human to Overmind is achieved by grace, not by man's own works. We see the basic pattern in *2001: A Space Odyssey* when such a higher being, by impressing a vision in one ape's mind, changes his brain's structure and makes him a man (3).* Clarke implies that the laborious process of natural selection is insufficient for true progress, that any progress an ape or a man achieves on his own merely *earns the privilege* of attaining higher states and does not actually *lead to* that higher state.

The gratuitous nature of transcendence and the fact that it always follows the technological state leave man no choice but to pursue the technological vision,[2] but with the important awareness that technological progress is not true progress, merely a test of man's moral and intellectual energies. As we shall see, technological progress alone leads to a dead end. True progress comes only as a kind of reward infused by the Overmind into man's history. At the end of "The Sentinel," the story that forms the basis for *2001*, this is made explicit: higher beings, the narrator tells us, would not be "concerned with races still struggling up from savagery. They would be interested in our civilization only if we proved our fitness to survive—by crossing space and so escaping from the Earth, our cradle." Technology does not itself lead anywhere important; it merely proves "our fitness to survive." Thus, at the end of *2001*, when Bowman reaches Saturn, he simply leaves behind the fancy machines that have occupied his and our attention for the major part of the novel. He doesn't need them.

2001: A Space Odyssey eloquently renders Clarke's basic myth of progress, but it does not make it clear why, if technological progress itself delights him as much as it seems to, Clarke should find the transcendent state necessary. In that novel we experience the myth without any sense of what its absence might entail. In an earlier novel, *The City and the Stars*, Clarke explores more explicitly the insufficiency of technological progress alone, and, though the novel itself stumbles around a lot, its failure to create a coherent myth illuminates, perhaps better than a more suc-

*NOTE: Numbers in parentheses after a quotation indicate chapter.

cessful work might, Clarke's need for a mythology that will value technology without limiting itself to it.

   Clarke begins *The City and the Stars* by imagining technological perfection, the eternal, self-sufficient city of Diaspar, which caters to all its
citizens, creates every imagined pleasure, and in which men do not die
but merely retire to the "memory banks" of the "Central Computer" for
a few thousand years to be reissued from the "Hall of Creation" full
grown and capable of remembering all their past existences. On one
level Clarke seems to admire this technological marvel in which the
various sciences have worked together to create a world in which everybody—except Alvin, the adolescent hero of the novel—is happy. But, if
Clarke can admire Diaspar as an engineering feat, he finds it morally
repulsive. He accuses its inhabitants of being "sick" and "insane." We
are told that Diaspar represents a "cowardly" "fear" of the unknown. It
is man's retreat from "reality." The problem with Diaspar is that the
activities that went into the utopia's creation, the scientific experiments
and the intellectual daring, have been rendered useless by the city's
success. Diaspar, in depriving man of "that spark of curiosity that was
once Man's greatest gift" (7), represents the paradox that is inherent in
the very notion of technological progress: the more successful such
progress is, the less need will there be for more of it. The very activity
that proves man's "fitness to survive," as it achieves its perfection, undermines that fitness.

   Let me make it clear that Clarke does not condemn Diaspar because
it is totalitarian. The theme of the perfection of machinery leading to
some kind of political repression is a common one in science fiction, but
what is curious here in terms of the tradition is that Clarke does not
attribute any such tyranny to this machine. The Central Computer of
Diaspar is much less totalitarian in its enforcement of its own idea of
order than is the machine in Forster's "The Machine Stops" or the
"Well-Doer" in Zamiatin's *We.* The computer never obstructs Alvin;
when he learns to use it it even aids him. Thus the usual political objec-
tion to such a utopia seems irrelevant here.

   Nor is the problem Clarke envisions a result of any kind of malfunction of the machine. Forster's machine stops, but the Central Computer
of Diaspar seems truly eternal. Some years before Clarke invented Diaspar, John W. Campbell had created situations roughly like Clarke's but
with two important and illuminating differences. First, Campbell's stories make it clear in a way that Clarke's never does that the very survival

of the race is in danger. Second, Campbell solves the problem simply by improving the machine. In "Twilight" a time traveller simply reprograms the machines to create a "curious machine." In "The Story of the Machine" the machine is so wise that, when it sees that man has become overly dependent on it, it simply turns itself off. For Clarke, however, the problem is not so easily described or solved. There is no flaw to technological perfection here which needs correction; it is technological perfection itself that is objectionable.

Clarke does not claim, however, that all technological progress necessarily leads to such a paradox. At the end of *The City and the Stars* he places the blame for Diaspar's failure on the shortsighted cowardice of that conservative element of mankind which, when millions of years ago the chance was offered man to leave the galaxy in the company of some incomprehensibly transcendent being, refused to go and tried to protect itself from higher realities by building Diaspar. Finally, therefore, the bind of perfection derives, not simply from the nature of technological progress itself, but from the conscious plan of the founders and from their fear of transcendence. Technology is a trap only when it tries to preclude higher realities. In *2001* and *Childhood's End* man's transcendent metamorphosis restores the openness that the technological perfection of Diaspar obviates. In *The City and the Stars,* however, transcendent possibilities are treated more ambivalently, for though they are clearly outlined, they are finally envisioned as totally alien and incomprehensible: "To Alvin, the thoughts of Vanamonde were as meaningless as a thousand voices shouting together in some vast, echoing cave" (24). At the end of the novel Alvin, weary of the stars, turns aside from seeking transcendent being in favor of the more modest task of restoring the Earth, now a desert, to fertility:

> "No; I want nothing more of space. Even if any other civilizations still survive in this Galaxy, I doubt if they will be worth the effort of finding. There is so much to do here; I know now that this is my home, and I am not going to leave it again."
>
> He looked down at the great deserts, but his eyes saw instead the waters that would be sweeping over them a thousand years from now. Man had rediscovered his world, and he would make it beautiful while he remained upon it. And after that—
>
> "We aren't ready to go out to the stars. . . ." (26)[3]

The higher forms of progress are now open in a way they never were so long as Diaspar was a success, but they are not conceived of as really possible objects for contemplation yet, and the novel falls back on a version of the technological vision.

The disjunction that exists between the two stages of progress raises a serious aesthetic problem, for, since there is no structural connection between the two stages, any novel that tries to encompass both will probably find itself falling into two distinct and unconnected parts. In *The City and the Stars* Clarke tries to avoid this artistic problem by having Alvin decline the transcendent level and remain on the technological level while the potential for transcendent progress is left open. The effect, however, of going back to the beginning and starting again, whatever may be said for such humility in real life, is partly to render irrelevant the space travel and the search for higher being that have gone before. Ironically, a somewhat similar criticism holds for *2001* where the successful shift into the transcendent vision, in effect, junks the technological vision that has occupied us for most of the novel. Just as from Alvin's point of view Vanamonde is incomprehensible, from the perspective of the Star-Child at the end of *2001*, technology is merely trivial. Or, if we take seriously the threat at the end of the novel that the Star-Child will "do something" to Earth, we may conclude that the novel constitutes a warning against engaging in the kinds of scientific activities and explorations that will lead ultimately to transcendence. Since such a moral seems highly unlikely given Clarke's ideology, and since nothing else in the novel supports such a reading, one suspects that the end of *2001* merely signifies a turning away from the real issues that the novel might raise. In either reading the integration of the two stages of progress fails. We can see the rationale for the shift from one stage to the other, but neither *2001* nor *The City and the Stars* offers a satisfactory artistic rendition of the myth.

Childhood's End also uses the two-stage myth of progress, but it escapes the disabling structure of *2001* by introducing a middle term which joins the two stages of vision. The Overlords in *Childhood's End,* the huge, Satanic-looking creatures who arrive to dominate Earth and protect man from himself until his metamorphosis into the Overmind can take place, function as both a prospect of the possibilities of technology and as figures of tragic limitation. They mediate between the two stages of progress. Though Hal, the computer for the Jupiter probe in *2001,* might be seen as structurally similar to the Overlords, he merely parodies the *humanitas* that allows the Overlords to unify *Childhood's End.* At the beginning of the novel they represent an advanced technology, admirably rational, a model for mankind, a goal for progress. By the end of the novel we discover that they represent the dead end of technological progress, and they become admirable mainly for their refusal to succumb to despair. While we can admire their superior science and morality at the start, we can admire their stoicism at the end.

The Overlords are masterful themselves, and yet they are mere servants of the Overmind. This servitude of Titans raises some difficult problems. A parallel with Satan, suggested by the situation itself, is underlined in the novel by the physical appearance of the Overlords and by the Hellish aspect of their home planet (see Samuelson's chapter in this book) and may make us pause and seek for darker purposes in their seemingly benevolent actions. But the Overlords, unlike Satan, for all their frustration with being limited to a technological state and in spite of their envy of the mysterious heights of transcendence, ultimately acquiesce to their fate:

> For all their achievements, thought Karellen, for all their mastery of the physical universe, his people were no better than a tribe that had passed its whole existence upon some flat and dusty plain. Far off were the mountains, where power and beauty dwelt, where the thunder sported above the glaciers and the air was clear and keen. There the sun still walked, transfiguring the peaks with glory, when all the land below was wrapped in darkness. And they could only watch and wonder; they could never scale those heights.
>
> Yet, Karellen knew, they would hold fast until the end: they would await without despair whatever destiny was theirs. They would serve the Overmind because they had no choice, but even in that service they would not lose their souls. (24)

Though both Devils and Overlords are denied Heaven, in place of Satan's vow of everlasting war, his heroic *non serviam*, the Overlords assert a spirit of resignation. They understand the Overmind enough to acknowledge the futility of rebellion, and they would accept the Stoic motto: *Ducunt Fata volentem, nolentem trahunt.*[4] Like Stormgren who in the first section of the novel, in spite of doubts, submits to the overwhelming power of the Overlords, they submit to the Overmind.

The basic structure of *Childhood's End* can be represented by an equation:

$$\frac{\text{Humans}}{\text{Overlords}} = \frac{\text{Overlords}}{\text{Overmind}}$$

Whereas the first two sections of the novel develop the Human/Over-lord relation, the last section develops the Overlord/Overmind relation. When the Russian rocket scientist, Schneider, first sees the ships of the Overlords, "for the first time in his life he knew despair" (1). We dis-cover that this same despair in the face of the unattainable is what the Overlords themselves have to fight. But the novel as a whole does not preach despair because, while it repeats the initial situation on a higher plane, it also performs the miraculous transformation of human into Overmind so that the first and last terms of the proportion are seen as spiritually the same. The Overmind is both a mysterious transcendence and an expression of qualities potential in mankind.

The important point is that logically Clarke is having it two ways here. If human and Overlord are not equal, then human and Overmind cannot be equal; and yet they are. The Overmind, thus, represents both progress and stasis. While on the one hand we are moving higher and higher, from man through Overlord to Overmind, on the other we are also returning to the same level. The Overmind here represents a kind of magical solution to the problem we discover at the end of *The City and the Stars.* In that novel the transcendent being, Vanamonde, is a creation of man, but because he is seen as something completely other than man Alvin loses interest in him. And *The City and the Stars* posits the presence of much higher beings, so that, on the scale we are used to from *2001* and *Childhood's End,* Vanamonde is quite a modest level of transcen-dence. In *Childhood's End* it is as if Alvin had made the effort to accept and become Vanamonde and his higher brethren with all the denial of human concern that such an act entails.

What in the basic structure of the novel constitutes a logical incon-sistency generates an artistic whole, and this unity is mirrored and sup-ported by the smaller details of imagery and character. My purpose here is not to interpret in detail these lesser structures but simply to suggest a line of analysis which, if developed fully, would reveal that the novel resolves logical inconsistency on many levels, not merely on the level of the large structure with which we have been concerned. Throughout the novel, for example, images of destruction are associated with progress: just as the Overmind destroys Earth, so too the rocket "Columbus" at the beginning of the novel will, in achieving its breakthrough into space, destroy the atoll from which it is launched. The volcano of the novel's opening line recurs as the presence of the Overmind on the Overlords' planet, and in their communal suicide the New Athens people imitate the volcano. It is thus thematically important that man's potential for self-destruction should be the mark of his potential for transcendence. The Overlords, who arrive to prevent the former, due to their complete rational competence, are denied the latter. The question whether chaotic self-destruction and creative progress are so related in actual fact does not really apply here; we are concerned at this point, not with thematic truth, but with thematic pattern. The images of the novel engage contradictory ideas and repeatedly unify them.

The major human characters in *Childhood's End* share the Overlord's doubleness, but because they fail to generate the unified response that would allow us simply to accept them, they make us aware of the inadequacy of our conventional solutions to the problems the novel raises. Stormgren seems a wise man, and yet at times one is made to wonder whether he is not simply a quisling. He himself ponders whether in supporting the Overlords he isn't acting like an Indian tolerating British control and thereby destroying his own culture. On the other hand Wainwright is a religious fanatic and, in part, an object of satire, but at the same time, as an advocate of independence, he is a spokesman for attitudes close to Clarke's own as expressed elsewhere. The humans engage the same issues we see in the situation of the Overlords, but when put in purely human terms these issues become irresolvably ambiguous. The Overlords, perhaps because their intellectual and moral superiority seems to lift them above the dichotomies that torture Stormgren and Wainwright, do not generate ambivalence. The Overlords mediate between rival positions of independence and service and reconcile the dilemmas that we experience when faced with the human figures.

Similarly, the paradox that the magical structure of the whole novel resolves appears as a problem, another source of ambivalence, in the middle sections of the novel. Before the existence of the Overmind has been revealed and before the midwife function of the Overlords is apparent, Clarke makes us puzzle through some of the conventional solutions to the problems of technological progress. In essence, he offers us two possible, but unsatisfactory, solutions to the challenge of the boredom of perfection. One, the New Athens Community, attempts to reinvigorate the creative activities that have constituted man's glories in the past by retreating from the smooth-functioning and technologically sophisticated world run by the Overlords and setting up a consciously primitive society. The other possible solution is embodied in Jan Rodricks, an Alvin-like character who, frustrated with a world without adventure, sets out to explore despite the prohibitions of the Overlords.

The idea behind New Athens is to preserve the spirit of humanity by a kind of artificial primitivism and an artistic focus. Clarke's ambivalent attitude towards this attempt is summed up in a small joke he makes when George and Jean, the young couple we watch throughout this section, arrive in the colony. Jean wonders whether she will be able to stand cooking in a kitchen after a life of being able to dial "Food Central" and getting her order five minutes later (15). The joke is an easy one, but like many jokes it conceals an uneasiness, an ambiguous attitude, on its maker's part. On the one hand, by expressing contempt for the pampered future which judges what we consider luxury a curse, the joke implies that the technology of the future has been not only frivolous in creating such work-savers as "Food Central," but has actually weakened man's ability to face even the most trivial hardship. At its center the joke engages an important theme that we have looked at a number of times already: that technology, insofar as it creates luxury, beguiles man of his basic moral fiber and leads him to avoid struggle, risk, and adventure. Like Marie Antoinette dressing up as a shepherdess, the technological aristocrat needs to get away from his ease and back to some real, human identity. But the other side of the joke ridicules this whole attempt at recovery of the primitive integrity. Just as Marie Antoinette's pastoralism is ultimately a sentimental escape from reality, so the self-conscious primitivism of technologically sophisticated people is false. The New Athens attempt to get back to nature is here revealed to be, in part, a denial of technological reality, a kind of sentimental and reactionary pastoralism. The joke about Jean's kitchen holds together diametrically opposed insights into the debilitating effect of technological progress and the liberating possibilities of it.

The other human escape from utopia is viewed less ambivalently than the New Athens experiment, but it too has a futile resolution. Jan Rodricks, frustrated by the limits put on his curiosity by the Golden Age imposed by the Overlords, breaks free to explore other worlds. His heroic and brash act obviously has the author's sympathies, but it does not solve the problem that confronts the whole society, and it leads to tragic isolation, not to renewal, for Jan returns to an Earth completely empty of human beings. The whole episode would seem merely a nostalgic excrescence to the main theme of the novel were it not that at the end Jan offers us a human perspective for the final metamorphosis and thereby powerfully brings to bear the awareness of loss that man's triumphant progress into higher being entails. The annihilation of mankind in the form we know it, a catastrophe which at the end of *2001* Clarke dismisses as an ominous and conventional joke, is here given a more considered weight by the presence of a human figure who finds value in the technological vision and who devotes himself to exploring the unknown. Jan gives us a scale by which we can measure the sacrifice transcendence involves.

Pastoral retreat and individual daring both fail to resolve the dilemma of progress. While the inquiry into their potentials sheds light on the problem and gives urgency to the issue, it takes the transcendent stage to save the human energy that leads to progress from futilely wasting itself. And, then, it takes in addition the magical agency of the plot to create an image and a situation which, while recognizing their incompatibility, can unify the two stages of technology and transcendence. The Overmind, which conserves the human spirit as it destroys it, and the Overlords, who are both masters and servants, combine to render a complex paradox which expresses our hopes for progress as well as our doubts about it. That the literary solution Clarke has arrived at should be so profoundly paradoxical need not alarm us; it is, after all, a commonplace of literary criticism that paradox of sorts works at the center of much literature, and the disciplines of psychology and anthropology, to say nothing of philosophy, have repeatedly shown us how often imaginative fictions, whether they be dreams, primitive myths, poems, or stories, accept and resolve the contradictions experienced in life. The first question that has to be asked of the artist is not have you appealed to contradictory truths? but have you created a pattern of meaning that is coherent in itself?

That we can view the basic structure of the novel as coherent does not mean that *Childhood's End* is without faults. The banal style of the novel is not adequate to the theme. The characters, while one does not expect fine detail in their portraits since the main concern of the novel is with larger issues of progress, are alternately pretentious and trivial. One might argue that the frivolousness of much of the middle section of the novel is intended as an ironic foil to emphasize the gap between human and Overmind, but, even if that is the intention, the device remains clumsy and distracting. Most important, as a presence the Overmind, inevitably, frustrates. We can have only vague hints of value and power; we can know it only by its consequences. But, given the coher-

ence of the novel's large structure, these complaints diminish in importance. In *Childhood's End* Clarke has ingeniously and movingly solved a
major aesthetic problem and has given unified form to his resolution of
the dilemma progress presents.

NOTES

CHAPTER 1: PETER BRIGG

1. Arthur C. Clarke, *Reach for Tomorrow* (New York: Ballantine, 1975).
2. Clarke, "Maelstrom II," *The Wind from the Sun: Stories of the Space Age* (New York: Signet, 1973).
3. Clarke, "Summertime on Icarus," *The Nine Billion Names of God: The Best Short Stories of Arthur C. Clarke* (New York: Signet, 1974).
4. Clarke, "A Meeting with Medusa," *The Wind from the Sun.*
5. Clarke, "The Secret," *The Wind from the Sun.*
6. Clarke, *Earthlight* (New York: Ballantine, 1975), (XII).*
7. Ibid., (VI).
8. Clarke, "The Star," *The Nine Billion Names of God.*
9. Clarke, "Let There Be Light," *Tales of Ten Worlds* (New York: Signet, 1973).
10. Clarke, "Green Fingers," *The Other Side of the Sky* (New York: Signet, 1973).
11. Clarke, "The Fires Within," *Of Time and the Stars* (Harmondsworth: Puffin-Penguin, 1974).
12. Clarke, "Second Dawn," *Expedition to Earth* (New York: Ballantine, 1975).
13. Clarke, "I Remember Babylon," *Tales of Ten Worlds* (New York: Signet, 1973).
14. Clarke, *Earthlight,* (I).
15. Clarke, *The Deep Range* (New York: Signet, 1974), (10).
16. Clarke, "The Shining Ones," *The Wind from the Sun.*
17. Clarke, "History Lesson," *Expedition to Earth* (New York: Ballantine, 1975).
18. Clarke, "The Reluctant Orchid," *Tales from the 'White Hart'* (New York: Ballantine, 1974).
19. Clarke, "Trouble with the Natives," *Reach for Tomorrow* (New York: Ballantine, 1975).
20. Clarke, "The Pacifist," *Tales from the 'White Hart.'*
21. Clarke, "Neutron Tide," *The Wind from the Sun.*
22. Clarke, "Moving Spirit," *Tales from the 'White Hart.'*
23. Clarke, "Whacky," *The Best of Arthur C. Clarke: 1973–1971* (London: Sphere, 1973).
24. Clarke, "The Food of the Gods," *The Wind from the Sun.*
25. Clarke, *The Lost Worlds of 2001* (New York: Signet, 1972).
26. Clarke, *The City and the Stars* (New York: Signet, 1973), (26).
27. Clarke, "The Songs of Distant Earth," *The Other Side of the Sky.*
28. Clarke, "Rescue Party," *Reach for Tomorrow.*
29. Clarke, *Childhood's End* (New York: Ballantine, 1953), (24).
30. Clarke, *2001: A Space Odyssey* (New York: Signet, 1972), (45).
31. Clarke, "Castaway," *Strange Signposts: An Anthology of the Fantastic,* Sam Mos-

*NOTE: Numbers in parentheses indicate chapter.

cowitz and Roger Elwood, eds. (New York: Holt, Rinehart & Winston, 1966).

32. Clarke, "Out of the Sun," *The Other Side of the Sky.*
33. Clarke, "Out of the Sun," p. 126
34. Clarke, *Rendezvous with Rama* (New York: Ballantine, 1976), (34).
35. Ibid., (29).
36. Clarke, *Imperial Earth* (New York: Ballantine, 1976), (15).
37. Ibid., (32).
38. Ibid., (19).
39. Ibid., (40).
40. Ibid., (41).

CHAPTER 2: THOMAS D. CLARESON

1. Jeremy Bernstein, "Profiles: Out of the Ego Chamber," *New Yorker,* August 9, 1969, p.40.
2. Arthur C. Clarke's *Earthlight* was first published in *Thrilling Wonder Stories* (August 1951), but not issued in book form until the Ballantine edition (1955).
3. Clarke, "Introduction," *Report on Planet Three and Other Speculations* (New York: Harper & Row, 1972), p. xi.
4. Clarke, "The Challenge of Space," *The Challenge of Space: Previews of Tomorrow's World* (New York: Harper & Brothers, 1959), p. 16.
5. Clarke, *The Sands of Mars* (New York: Gnome Press, 1952); *Islands in the Sky* (New York: New American Library).
6. Clarke, "The Star of the Magi," *Report on Planet Three,* p. 32. "The Star of the Magi" was first published in *Holiday* (December 1954), and then included in *The Challenge of Space,* pp. 77–86.
7. Clarke, "Epilogue," *Prelude to Space* (New York: Ballantine, 1976).
8. Clarke, "Across the Sea of Stars," *The Challenge of Space,* p. 130.
9. Clarke, "When the Aliens Come," *Report on Planet Three,* p. 107.
10. Clarke, "The Challenge of the Spaceship," *The Challenge of Space,* p. 8.
11. Ibid., p. 11.
12. Clarke, "Across the Sea of Stars," *The Challenge of Space,* p. 127.
13. Clarke, "Of Space and the Spirit," *The Challenge of Space,* p. 211.
14. Clarke, "H. G. Wells and Science Fiction," *Voices from the Sky: Previews of the Coming Space Age* (New York: Harper & Row, 1965).
15. Clarke, *The Exploration of Space* (New York: Harper & Brothers, 1951), p. 195.
16. Clarke, *Childhood's End* (New York: Ballantine, 1976), (14).
17. Ibid., (24).
18. David N. Samuelson, "Clarke's *Childhood's End:* A Median Stage in Adolescence?" Science Fiction Studies, 1 (Spring 1973), 7. This essay, in a slightly revised version, appears as Chapter 8 in this book.
19. David Allen, *"Childhood's End:* Arthur C. Clarke (1953),"*SF an Introduction* (Lincoln, Nebraska: Cliffs Notes, 1973), p. 55.

20. Ibid., p. 47 ff.

21. Unpublished letter from Arthur C. Clarke to Thomas D. Clareson, dated January 1, 1974.

22. Samuelson, 1:11. (See also Chapter 8 in this book.)

23. Allen, p. 47.

24. Clarke, "Guardian Angel," *Famous Fantastic Mysteries,* 11 (April 1950), 129.

25. Clarke, *Prelude to Space* (New York: Ballantine, 1976), (6).

26. Clarke, "Preface," *Earthlight* (New York: Harcourt Brace Jovanovich, Inc., 1955), p. ix.

27. Clarke, *Prelude to Space,* (9).

28. David Young, *The Heart's Forest: A Study of Shakespeare's Pastoral Plays* (New Haven & London: Yale University Press, 1972), p. 199. My thanks to Professor Raymond G. McCall of the College of Wooster for pointing out this passage to me.

29. Clarke, "Introduction," *The Lion of Comarre and Against the Fall of Night* (New York: Harcourt, Brace & World, Inc., 1968), pp. viii-ix.

30. Ibid., p. 189. The passage is absent from *The City and the Stars.*

31. Clarke, "The Road to the Sea," *Tales of Ten Worlds* (New York: Signet, 1973).

32. Clarke, *The City and the Stars,* (New York: Signet, 1973), (13). Yet Clarke later says of the Master, "He was a good man, and much of what he taught was true and wise. In the end, he believed his own miracles, but he knew that there was one witness who could refute them. The robot knew all his secrets: . . ." (17). On one of the worlds they visit, Alvin and his companions find an obelisk honoring the Master (20).

33. Clarke, "Science and Spirituality," *Voices from the Sky.*

34. Clarke, "Out of the Sun," *The Other Side of the Sky* (New York: Signet, 1973).

35. Clarke, *Childhood's End,* (18).

36. Clarke, "Transcience," *The Other Side of the Sky.*

37. Clarke, "The Star," *The Other Side of the Sky,* pp. 118–119.

38. Clarke, "Before Eden," *Tales of Ten Worlds,* p. 148.

39. Clarke, "Moon-Watcher," *The Lost Worlds of 2001* (New York: Signet, 1972).

40. Clarke, "When Aliens Come," *Report on Planet Three: And Other Speculations* (New York: Harper & Row, 1972).

41. Clarke, "The Sentinel," *Expedition to Earth* (New York: Ballantine, 1975).

42. Clarke, "The Dawn of Man," *The Lost Worlds of 2001.* Clarke explains that he wrote "a short story about a meeting in the remote past between visitors from space and a primitive ape-man." It was given the title "Expedition to Earth" when Ballantine published it in 1953. Clarke preferred the title "Encounter in the Dawn"; it was also entitled "Encounter at Dawn." Significantly, the alien astronaut has retained the name Clindar through all of the stories dealing with this encounter. Significantly, too, in that it suggests the importance of the theme, Clarke had already written "The Sentinel" in 1948. *The Lost Worlds of 2001,* p. 18.

43. Clarke, "Expedition to Earth," *Expedition to Earth.*

44. Clarke, "The Dawn of Man," *The Lost Worlds of 2001,* p. 51.

45. The quotations have been taken from the four stories in *The Lost Worlds of 2001.*

46. Clarke, *2001: A Space Odyssey* (New York: Signet, 1972), (37).

47. Clarke, *Rendezvous with Rama* (New York: Harcourt Brace Jovanovich, Inc., 1973), (46).

48. Clarke, "A Meeting with Medusa," *The Wind from the Sun* (New York: Signet, 1973).

49. Clarke, "Science and Spirituality," *Voices from the Sky.*

CHAPTER 3: E. MICHAEL THRON

1. James Gunn, "Science Fiction and the Mainstream," *Science Fiction Today and Tomorrow,* ed. Reginald Bretnor (Baltimore, Md.: Penguin, 1974), pp. 183–216.

2. Arthur C. Clarke, *2001: A Space Odyssey* (New York: Signet, 1972), (3). Subsequent page references in the text.

3. Clarke, *Childhood's End* (New York: Ballantine, 1976), (3). Subsequent page references in the text.

4. Clarke, *The Promise of Space* (New York: Harper and Row, 1968), p. 293.

5. Clarke, *Rendezvous with Rama* (New York: Ballantine, 1976), (42). Subsequent page references in the text.

6. Wendy D. O'Flaherty, *Hindu Myths* (London: Penguin, 1975), pp. 175–176.

7. John Huntington, "The Unity of *Childhood's End,*" *Science-Fiction Studies,* I:3 (Spring 1974), 155. This essay, in a slightly revised version, appears in this book as Chapter 9.

8. Ibid., 162.

9. *Earthlight* (New York: Ballantine, 1975), (1).

10. Irwin Thompson, *At the Edge of History,* (New York: Harper & Row, 1971), p. 158.

11. Ibid., p. 163.

12. Ibid., p. 156.

13. Raymond Williams, *The Country and the City* (New York: Oxford University Press, 1973), p. 274.

CHAPTER 4: BETSY P. HARFST

1. Arthur C. Clarke, *Imperial Earth* (New York: Ballantine, 1976), (7). All future citations will appear parenthetically in the text as chapter sources, after a phrase or series of phrases in that chapter. Citations for *Childhood's End* (New York: Ballantine, 1976); *2001: A Space Odyssey* (New York: Signet, 1972); *Rendezvous with Rama* (New York: Ballantine, 1976) will also appear parenthetically in the text. If reference to a second novel appears in discussion of one, it will be cited by title initials and chapter number.

2. I use Joseph Campbell's division, a line drawn "vertically through Iran, along a latitude about 60 degrees east of Greenwich," in *Myths To Live By* (New York: Bantam, 1973), pp. 61–62. Cited hereafter as *Myths.*

3. Campbell, *Myths,* pp. 109–112.

4. Explanation of Jung's theory of individuation is based on material in C. G. Jung, *The Structure and Dynamics of the Psyche, The Collected Works of C. G. Jung* (New York: Pantheon, 1960); C. G. Jung, ed., *Man and His Symbols* (New York: Dell, 1971).

5. Campbell, *Myths,* p. 113.

6. Ibid., p. 114.

7. Explanation of variant beliefs is based on material in Joseph Campbell, *The Masks of God: Oriental Mythology* (New York: Viking Press, 1970), pp. 1–23 and his *Masks of God: Occidental Mythology* (New York, Viking Press, 1970), pp. 3–41. Cited hereafter as *Masks: Oriental* and *Masks: Occidental.*

8. Erich Neumann, *The Great Mother* (New York: Princeton University Press, 1970), p. 18.

9. Campbell, *Masks: Occidental,* pp. 7–24.

10. Ibid.

11. Campbell, *Masks: Oriental,* p. 21.

12. Will Durant, *Our Oriental Heritage* (New York: Simon & Schuster, 1954), p. 412.

13. Campbell, *Masks: Oriental,* pp. 22–23. Mircea Eliade notes, "We always find some form of Yoga whenever the goal is . . . attainment of a perfect self-mastery." *Yoga, Immortality and Freedom* (New York: Bollingen Series LVI, Pantheon, 1958), 360. Cited hereafter as *Yoga.*

14. Durant, pp. 412–13.

15. Campbell, *Myths,* p. 150.

16. Heinrich Zimmer, *Myths and Symbols in Indian Art and Civilization* (New York: Harper and Row, 1965), p. 89.

17. Mircea Eliade, *Cosmos and History* (New York: Harper Torchbooks, 1954), pp. 169–71. Cited hereafter as *Cosmos.*

18. Campbell, *Myths,* p. 110.

19. Eliade, *Yoga,* p. 220.

20. Ibid., pp. 49–50. The five sins—not to kill, not to lie, not to steal, not to be licentious, and not to be avaricious—explain Stormgren's hesitation about lies to Karellen and stealing from Joe, the burly Pole.

21. Durant, p. 546, is quoting from the Indian philosopher Jaimini, "Reason is a wanton who will serve any desire; it gives us not 'science and truth' but merely our own rationalized sensuality and price. The road to wisdom and peace lies not through the vain labyrinths of logic but in the modest accept-ance of tradition . . ."

22. Joseph L. Henderson, "Ancient Myths and Modern Man," *Man and His Symbols,* p. 117.

23. Isaac Asimov, *The New Intelligent Man's Guide to Science* (New York: Basic Books, Inc. 1965), bases much of his first chapter on curiosity and equates the Greeks' first woman, Pandora, as epitomizing curiosity; also he views the biblical serpent as a "representation of this inner compulsion," pp. 4–5.

24. Mircea Eliade, *The Quest: History and Meaning in Religion* (Chicago: University of Chicago Press, 1959) relates that oratorical/verbal contests were

equated with military battles among archaic "Indo-Iranian" cultures, pp. 164–65.

25. David N. Samuelson, *"Childhood's End:* A Median Stage of Adolescence?", *Science Fiction Studies,* Vol. I, Part I (Spring 1973), 10, offers a controversial viewpoint. John Huntington, "The Unity of Childhood's End," *Science Fiction Studies,* Vol. I, Part III (Spring 1974), 154–164, offers an alternative view. Also, an article by Thomas D. Clareson, "The Cosmic Loneliness of Arthur C. Clarke," *Voices For The Future* (Bowling Green, Ohio: Bowling Green University Popular Press, 1976), pp. 216–38, presents some pertinent comments. See reprints in this text for Samuelson, Clareson, and Huntington.

26. Eliade, *Yoga,* p. 179.

27. The children's rituals are characteristic of Jainism, a fundamentalist sect in India, akin to the "purified Buddhism" (5). See Louis Renou, "Jainism," *Religions of Ancient India* (New York: Schocken Books, 1968), pp. 111–133.

28. "Indo-European Roots," *American Heritage Dictionary of the English Language* (New York: McGraw-Hill, 1969).

29. Wylie Sypher, "The Meanings of Comedy," *Comedy* (Garden City, N. Y.: Doubleday Anchor Books, 1956), p. 233. Cited hereafter as *Comedy.*

30. Henri Bergson, "Laughter," *Comedy,* p. 89.

31. Clareson cites other sources as well for *2001.* Since his book, *Voices,* arrived just as I was typing the mss., I did not realize some duplicate information was given. The six parts of this novel equate with the six part cosmogonic round of the Jains. Instead of four ages of man
(*Classical:* Gold, Silver, Brass, Iron or *Indian:* Krita, Trēta, Dvāpara, Kali) they lengthen it to six and have an ascending/descending pattern on their time wheel. Hal and Bowman's return to childish babbling is a characteristic feature of this Jain pattern. See: Joseph Campbell, *The Hero with a Thousand Faces* (Princeton: Princeton University Press, Bollingen Paperback, 1973), 262–265.

32. Mircea Eliade, Cosmos, pp. 1–34, discusses how archetypal gestures form a pattern for imitative human behavior.

33. John R. Clark Hall, ed., *A Concise Anglo-Saxon Dictionary* (Cambridge: Cambridge University Press, 1962), p. 43.

34. Zimmer, p. 204.

35. J. E. Cirlot, *A Dictionary of Symbols* (New York: Philosophical Library, 1962), pp. 221–223.

36. Clarke rearranges the myth of Rama. The alien ship is Rama; the space probe is Sita; the blemish on Sita's honor from living with Ravana is on Rama's outer hull; the Monkey-god, Hanuman, now appears as the four simps (akin to the *simpsa* tree, whose leaves Hanuman blew away when he rescued Sita); the end is also reversed, for Rama, not Sita, goes into the fires. See Lin Yutang, *The Wisdom of China and India* (New York: Modern Library, 1955), pp. 135–262 for the Rama epic. See also Zimmer, pp. 16–18; and Robert Baldick et al, *Hindu Myths* (Baltimore, Md.: Penguin Books, 1975), pp. 197–204.

37. Eliade, *Cosmos,* p. 58. Human actions are also organized on *three* or its multiples, not just the Ramans: three disasters initiate the space guard; Davidson has three theories proved wrong; he has three opponents to his "big bang" theory. Norton gets fuel from three ships; his expedition is to last three weeks; he has three children from *two* wives which in itself is a triangle, comparable to the inverse triangle of Mercer, Calvert, and one shared wife; three is the optimum number for an exploring team; previous explorations are always cited in terms of three; Calvert models his behavior after three heroes; there are six members of the Rama committee; and countless other variations which suggest that the *three* is an integral feature linking the tale to the third levels of the quest.

38. Mircea Eliade, *Myths, Dreams and Mysteries* (New York: Harper & Brothers, 1957), p. 115. Cited hereafter as *Myths.*

39. Ibid., pp. 113–114.

40. Camp Alpha suggests the biblical phrasing, "I am Alpha and Omega, the beginning and the ending, saith the Lord." Revelation 1: 8.

41. Campbell, *Myths,* pp. 112, 114.

42. Mircea Eliade, The Sacred and the Profane (New York: Harper & Brothers, 1961), p. 131. Cited hereafter as *Sacred.*

43. Eliade, *Cosmos,* p. 19.

44. Eliade, *Sacred,* p. 148.

45. Eliade, *Myths*, p. 169, for *pakka;* Baldick, *Hindu Myths,* p. 349, for *paka.*

46. Eliade, *Myths,* p. 69.

47. Henderson, *Man and His Symbols,* p. 154.

48. Cirlot, pp. 198–99.

49. Mary Barnard, *The Mythmakers* (Athens, Ohio: Ohio University Press, 1966), pp. 109–118, explores meanings of eclipse myths.

50. Campbell, *Masks: Oriental,* p. 28, describes a Yoga concentration scene, by a pond, which is almost identical with Duncan's lagoon reflection scene (42).

51. *American Heritage,* p. 1527.

52. Zimmer, p. 15.

53. See Campbell, *Masks: Oriental,* pp. 5, 165, for a description of this mighty goddess. One epithet used to describe her, the large breasts, has been humorously treated in *IE.* Calindy shows Duncan her bruised breast. She also gives him a goblet of "blood-red liquid" (39) to restore his energy.

54. Sypher, p. 240.

55. Ibid, p. 255.

CHAPTER 5: ROBERT PLANK

1. Arthur C. Clarke, "The Sentinel," *The Nine Billion Names of God,* (New York: Signet, 1974).

2. Clarke, *2001: A Space Odyssey* (New York: Signet, 1973). Referred to in the text as "the novel." The designation *2001* will be used to denote the film or the work in its totality.

3. Clarke, *The Lost Worlds of 2001.* (New York: Signet, 1972).

4. Jerome Agel, ed., *The Making of Kubrick's 2001* (New York: Signet, 1970).

5. Morris Beja, "*2001:* Odyssey to Byzantium," *Extrapolation,* (May 1969), 67–68.

6. Mike Steele, *The Making,* p. 261.

7. Joseph Gelmis, *The Making,* p. 265.

8. Carolyn Geduld, *Filmguide to 2001: A Space Odyssey* (Bloomington: Indiana University Press, 1973), p. 34.

9. *The New Yorker,* April 4, 1968, p. 152. Reprinted in *The Making,* p. 212.

10. Antoine de St. Exupery, *Citadelle,* (Paris: Gallimard, 1948), p. 203. The translation is mine.

11. Norman N. Holland, "2001: A Psychosocial Explication," *Hartford Studies in Literature,* 1, 1 (1969), p. 20.

12. Vincent Canby, *The New York Times,* May 3, 1970, p. D21.

13. Holland, "2001: A Psychosocial Explication," p. 23.

14. Robert Rogers, "The Psychology of the 'Double' in *2001,*" *Hartford Studies in Literature* 1, 1 (1969), p. 35.

15. Heinrich Heine, *Florentinische Nachte,* zweite Nacht, in: Ernst Elster, ed., *Heinrich Heines sämtliche Werke* (Leipzig: Bibliogr. Institut, n.d.), v. 4, p. 353–54.

CHAPTER 6: ALAN B. HOWES

1. *Holiday* magazine, as quoted in a biographical sketch of Arthur C. Clarke in *Expedition to Earth* (New York: Ballantine, 1975).

2. Thomas E. Sanders, ed., *Speculations* (Beverly Hills, Calif.: Glencoe Press, 1973), p. 2.

3. Arthur C. Clarke, *Across the Sea of Stars* (New York: Harcourt, Brace & Co., 1959). The quotation is from Clifton Fadiman's Introduction.

4. Arthur C. Clarke, *Childhood's End* (New York: Ballantine, 1976). The quotation is by Gilbert Highet.

5. James Blish (William Atheling, Jr., pseud.), *The Issue at Hand* (Chicago: Advent Publishers, 1964), p. 127.

6. Arthur C. Clarke, ed., *Time Probe: The Sciences and Science Fiction* (New York: Dell, 1966), pp. 9–10.

7. The opening sentence to the fairy tale I made up. The others are from Ernest Hemingway's *A Farewell to Arms* and Herman Wouk's *Marjorie Morningstar.*

8. And to lead to one of Clarke's wittiest touches when "The London Daily Mirror made matters much worse by suggesting that the Spaniards adopt cricket as a new national sport."

9. The Overmind, too, has its limitation, according to Rashaverak, and has failed when it has "attempted to act directly upon the minds of other races."

10. Blish, *The Issue at Hand,* p. 128.

11. Arthur C. Clarke, "Introduction," *Across the Sea of Stars.*

12. Clarke, *Profiles of the Future* (New York: Harper & Row, 1962), p. xv.
13. Clarke, *The Exploration of Space* (New York: Harper & Brothers, 1951), pp. xi-xii.
14. Clarke, *Profiles of the Future*, p. 139.
15. Ibid., p. 141.
16. Ibid., p. 56.
17. Cf. the discussion of "The Quest for Speed," in chapter 6 of *Profiles of the Future,* esp. pp. 62, 68–69.
18. Clarke, *Profiles of the Future*, p. 128.
19. Clarke, *The Exploration of Space*, p. xii.
20. Clarke, *Profiles of the Future*, p. 229.
21. Ibid., p. 83.
22. Ibid., p. 185. Stapledon was indeed Clarke's predecessor in some of these ideas.
23. Clarke, *Profiles of the Future*, p. 209.
24. Later in the book Clarke has Thanthalteresco point out a major difference between the Overlords and the British in India: "The British had no real motives for going there . . . except such trivial and temporary ones as trade or hostility to other European powers" (17).
25. Among these are the method of selecting entrants to the colony and the government through committees with rotating membership.
26. Blish, *The Issue at Hand,* p. 127.

CHAPTER 7: EUGENE TANZY

1. Bernard Shaw: *Collected Plays with the Prefaces,* ed. Dan H. Laurence, V (New York: Dodd, Mead, 1975), 294, 267, 696.
2. Victor A. G. R. Lytton, *The Life of Edward Bulwer,* II (London: Macmillan, 1913), 465.
3. Thomas Huxley, "The Struggle for Existence in Human Society," *Readings From Huxley,* ed. Clarrisa Rinaker (1st rev. ed.; New York, Harcourt, Brace, 1934), pp. 104–105.
4. "Prolegomena," *Readings From Huxley,* p. 100.
5. H. G. Wells, *Experiment in Autobiography* (New York: Macmillan, 1934), p. 649.
6. "The Struggle for Existence," *Readings From Huxley,* p. 106.
7. Ray Bradbury, "Old Mars, Then Be A Hearth to Us," *When Elephants Last in the Dooryard Bloomed* (New York: Knopf, 1973), p. 76.
8. Shaw, *Plays,* 702, 701.
9. George Bernard Shaw, *Everybody's Political What's What* (London: Constable, 1944), p. 2.
10. Shaw, *Doctor's Delusions, Crude Criminology and Sham Education* (London: Constable, 1931), p. 367.
11. *Plays,* pp. 271–274.
12. *Plays,* pp. 348, 349.

13. *Plays,* p. 423.
14. *Plays,* p. 430.
15. Plays, p. 433.
16. *Plays,* p. 345.
17. *Plays,* p. 348.
18. *Plays,* pp. 685, 334, 686.
19. Patrick Moore and David A. Moore, *Challenge of the Stars,* Foreword by Arthur Clarke (New York: Rand McNally, 1972), p. 5.
20. *Plays,* p. 692.
21. *Plays,* p. 358.
22. *Plays,* pp. 374–377.
23. *Plays,* pp. 617, 622
24. *Plays,* p. 616.
25. *Plays,* pp. 617, 622.
26. *Plays,* p. 617.
27. *Plays,* pp. 623, 620, 223.
28. C. G. Jung, *Flying Saucers: A Modern Myth of Things Seen in the Skies* (New York: New American Library, 1969), p. 115.
29. Arthur C. Clarke, *Childhood's End* (New York: Ballantine, 1953), (20).
30. *Childhood's End,* (20).
31. *Childhood's End,* (22).
32. Clarke, *The Lost Worlds of 2001* (New York: Signet, 1972), p. 62.
33. *Childhood's End,* (20).
34. *Childhood's End,* (24).
35. *Childhood's End,* (17).
36. *Childhood's End,* (20).
37. Clarke, *Imperial Earth* (New York: Ballantine, 1976), (28).
38. *Imperial Earth,* (42).
39. *Imperial Earth,* (32), (31), (32).
40. *Imperial Earth,* (42).
41. *Imperial Earth,* (42).

CHAPTER 8: DAVID N. SAMUELSON

1. Mark R. Hillegas, *The Future as Nightmare: H. G. Wells and the Anti-Utopians* (1967), pp. 153–154.
2. For reviews of *Childhood's End* after publication, see James J. Rollo, *Atlantic Monthly* Nov 1953, p. 112; William Du Bois, *New York Times* Aug. 27, 1953, p. 23; Basil Davenport, *New York Times Book Review* Aug. 23, 1953, p. 19; Groff Conklin, *Galaxy* March 1954, pp. 118–19; H.H. Holmes (Anthony Boucher [W. Anthony White]), *New York Herald-Tribune Book Review* Aug. 23, 1953, p. 9; P. Schuyler Miller, *Astounding* Feb. 1954, pp. 51–52.
3. A compendium of reviews, among other things, of a later work may be found in Jerome Agel, ed., *The Making of Kubrick's 2001* (Signet, 1970).
4. Not only has Clarke been publicly lionized for his quasimystical novels, but of his short stories that have been anthologized by both academic and

commercial editors, theological speculation seems more rewarded than technological extrapolation.

5. This argument is derived from Northrop Frye, *Anatomy of Criticism* (US 1957), esp. pp. 141–150.

6. Blake's *Milton,* Shelley's *Prometheus Unbound,* Goethe's *Faust,* and Zamyatin's *We* are just a few of the works that reflect this Romantic tradition.

7. This subject has been explored in some depth by Robert Plank in *The Emotional Significance of Imaginary Beings: A Study of the Interaction Between Psychopathology, Literature, and Reality in the Modern World* (1968).

8. Northrop Frye sees these structures as underlying even the most realistic fiction; see *Anatomy of Criticism* (US 1957), pp. 131–40 and *passim.*

9. Samuel R. Delany, "About Five Thousand One Hundred and Seventy-Five Words," in Thomas D. Clareson, ed., *SF: The Other Side of Realism* (1971), p. 144. Cf Alexei Panshin, "Science Fiction in Dimension," in Clareson. For opposing views see Stanislaw Lem, "Robots in Science Fiction," in Clareson, and Darko Suvin, "On the Poetics of the Science Fiction Genre," *College English* 34 (1972): 372–82.

10. Cf Joseph Campbell's discussion of the functions of myth in *The Hero With a Thousand Faces* (1949), esp. "Prologue: The Monomyth"; Northrop Frye, *The Modern Century* (Canada 1967), esp. pp. 105–20; Joseph Campbell, *The Masks of God* (4v 1959–68), *passim.*

11. Clarke's sober speculations may be found, for example, in *The Promise of Space* (1968), 29 "Where's Everybody?", and in *Voices from the Sky: Previews of the Coming Space Age* (1965), [17] "Science and Spirituality", where in both instances he draws comparisons to what might be "godlike" qualities in the aliens.

12. Again, Clarke has paid more serious attention to e.s.p. and the idea of the group mind in his nonfiction; see *Profiles of the Future* (1962; 1973 with addenda), 17 "Brain and Body"; *Voices from the Sky* (1965), [18] "Class of '00". He has also attacked "The Lunatic Fringe" for their gullibility, as in a chapter of that name ([20]) in *Voices.*

13. Damon Knight, *In Search of Wonder: Essays on Modern Science Fiction,* rev. ed. (US 1967), p. 188. Knight wrongly accuses Clarke of having the Overlords encounter man in prehistory; Clarke writes that people assumed this (6), but later corrects this impression with the future-memory explanation (23).

14. Reprinted from *UNESCO Courier* as "Kalinga Award Speech" in Arthur C. Clarke, *Voices from the Sky: Previews of the Coming Space Age* (1965).

15. "Guardian Angel," *New Worlds,* Winter 1950, is basically the same story as Part One of *Childhood's End;* revision removed some poor repartee, added more background, and diminished slightly the dependence on melodramatic effect.

16. Cf Algis Budrys' comments on the "inertial school" of SF with specific reference to Aldiss, Ballard, Disch, and Knight, in *Galaxy,* Dec. 1966, pp. 128–33.

17. This is not to say that Clarke is an orthodox adherent to any religion; his caricatures of the true believer, Wainwright, in the early pages of

Childhood's End, and of the lunatic fringe in *Voices from the Sky* (12), seem sincere enough, and his nonfiction writing is steadfastly on the side of man's continued exploration and expansion of knowledge. But his flirtation with the mythic imagination is also continuous, even in his nonfiction, suggesting at least a humble regard for the limitations of science and a dependency upon an anti-scientific literary tradition as a source of imagery.

18. In revising the early drafts of *2001: A Space Odyssey* (see *The Lost Worlds of 2001* [1972]), in adapting "Guardian Angel" for inclusion in *Childhood's End* (see 15), and in revising *Against the Fall of Night* for republication as *The City and the Stars* (1956), which he declared to be the "final, definitive version," Clarke showed some ear for style and tone, but seems to have concentrated primarily on logical or aesthetic consistency of scenes in context.

19. *Galaxy* Oct. 1967, p. 190.

20. Although it has now been over ten years since the publication of that *cause célèbre,* C.P. Snow's *The Two Cultures and the Scientific Revolution* (1960), many of its accusations still ring true.

21. Two notable exceptions are Jacques Barzun, *Science: The Glorious Entertainment* (1964), and Martin Green, *Science and the Shabby Curate of Poetry* (1965). The best critiques of science and technology, however, seem to be written by scientists, e.g., Nigel Calder, *Technopolis* (1969).

CHAPTER 9: JOHN HUNTINGTON

1. H. G. Wells, *The Time Machine,* (4) and (6).

2. David N. Samuelson argues that in *Childhood's End* "the reader is almost forced to make a choice between two positions," that of the "scientifically oriented" "Devil's party" and that of the "mystically oriented" Overmind-God (see Samuelson's chapter in this book). In fact, though one can contemplate the two modes of cognition, there is little room for choice here. According to Clarke's myth, we have no choice but to follow reason and science, for only by holding on to reason now can we hope to transcend it in the future.

3. *The City and the Stars* varies the basic myth we have traced by suggesting that perhaps man may be able to attain some form of transcendence on his own. Vanamonde, the childish supermind, is a human creation. Also, at the end of the novel Alvin sends his space ship, piloted by the robot, out beyond the galaxy: "One day our cousins will receive my message and they'll know that we are waiting for them here on Earth. They will return, and I hope by then we will be worthy of them, however great they have become" (26). Though the concern for worthiness echoes the concern for fitness at the end of "The Sentinel," the situation is importantly different. First of all *we* initiate the signal and invite them to find us. Second, it's a kind of by-your-own-bootstrap theory of

evolution, for the superior race who will elevate us if we are worthy is a branch of the human tree, our "cousins."

4. "The Fates lead the willing and drag the unwilling." So Spengler concludes *The Decline of the West*, quoting Seneca's translation (in *Epistle* 107) of the Stoic philosopher Cleanthes.

Selected Bibliography

This bibliography is not intended to be complete. Rather, it attempts to aid the reader by bringing together the great majority of Arthur C. Clarke's novels and stories, as well as a number of critical essays on his work. The bibliography relies on information gathered from a variety of sources, including *The Encyclopedia of Science Fiction and Fantasy*, Vol. 1, compiled by Donald H. Tuck (Chicago: Advent Publishers, 1974), and the computer printout version of the *Index to Science Fiction Anthologies and Collections* by William G. Contento, which will be published by G. K. Hall. The latter work was particularly valuable.

PRIMARY WORKS

Across the Sea of Stars. [An omnibus containing the complete novels of *Childhood's End* and *Earthlight* and eighteen short stories.] Introduced by Clifton Fadiman. New York: Harcourt Brace & World, 1959, 1973.
Against the Fall of Night. New York: Gnome Press, 1953.
_____. Bound with *The Lion of Comarre.* New York: Harcourt, Brace, Jovanovich, 1968.
"All That Glitters," *The Magazine of Fantasy and Science Fiction* (January 1957).
_____. *The Other Side of the Sky,* 1958.
"All the Time in the World," *Startling Stories* (July 1952).
_____. *The Other Side of the Sky,* 1958.
"An Ape about the House," *Dude,* 1962.
_____. *Tales of Ten Worlds,* 1962.
An Arthur C. Clarke Omnibus. [Includes *Childhood's End, Prelude to Space,* and *Expedition to Earth.*] London: Sidgwick and Jackson, 1965.
An Arthur C. Clarke Second Omnibus. [Includes *A Fall of Moondust, Earthlight,* and *The Sands of Mars.*] London: Sidgwick and Jackson, 1968.
_____. *Tales from the White Hart,* 1957.
"Armaments Race," 1954.
"At the End of the Orbit." *See* "Hate."
"The Awakening," *Zeneth,,* 1942.
_____. *Reach for Tomorrow,* 1956.

"Before Eden," *Amazing Stories* (June 1961).
_____. *Tales of Ten Worlds,* 1962.

The Best of Arthur C. Clarke. Angus Wells, ed. London: Sidgwick and Jackson, 1973.

Beyond Jupiter: The World of Tomorrow. Illustrated by Chesley Bonestell. New York: Pyramid, 1969. Boston: Little, Brown, 1972.

"Big Game Hunt," 1954.

———. *Tales from the White Hart,* 1957.

"Breaking Strain," ("Thirty Seconds - Thirty Days"), *Thrilling Wonder Stories* (December 1949).

———. *Expedition to Earth,* 1965.

"The Call of the Stars," *Infinity Science Fiction* (October 1957).

———. *The Other Side of the Sky,* 1958.

"Captain Wyxtpthll's Flying Saucer." *See* "Trouble with the Natives."

"The Case of the Snoring Heir." *See* "Sleeping Beauty."

"Castaway," *Fantasy* (April 1947).

———. *The Best of Arthur C. Clarke* (British edn.), 1968.

Childhood's End. New York: Harcourt, Brace & World, 1963. New York: Ballantine, 1972, 1976.

The City and the Stars. New York: Harcourt, Brace & World, 1956, 1962, 1966. New York: New American Library, 1973. [Revised version of *Against the Fall of Night.*]

"Cold War," *Satellite Science Fiction* (April 1957).

———. *Tales from the White Hart,* 1957.

"Cosmic Casanova," *Venture Science Fiction* (May 1958).

———. *The Other Side of the Sky,* 1958.

"Crime on Mars." *See* "Trouble with Time."

"Critical Mass," *Space Science Fiction Magazine* (August 1957).

———. *Tales from the White Hart,* 1957.

"The Cruel Sky." (n.d.)

———. *The Wind from the Sun,* 1972.

"Crusade," *The Farthest Reaches.* Joseph Elder, ed. New York: Trident, 1968.

———. *The Wind from the Sun,* 1972.

"The Curse," *Cosmos Science Fiction and Fantasy Magazine* (September 1953).

———. *Reach for Tomorrow,* 1956.

"Death and the Senator," *Astounding Science Fiction* (May 1961).

———. *Tales of Ten Worlds,* 1962.

"The Deep Range," *Star Science Fiction Stories 3.* Frederik Pohl, ed. New York: Ballantine, 1954.

Deep Range. New York: Harcourt, Brace & World, 1957, 1969. [Also included in *From the Oceans, from the Stars.*] New York: New American Library, 1974.

"The Defenestration of Ermintrude Inch." (n.d.)

———. *Tales from the White Hart,* 1957.

"Dial F for Frankenstein," *Playboy* (January 1965).

———. *The Wind from the Sun,* 1972.

"Dog Star" ("Moondog"), *Galaxy Science Fiction* (April 1962).

———. *Tales of Ten Worlds,* 1962.

Dolphin Island. New York: Harcourt, Brace & World, 1963. New York: Berkley, 1971.

Earthlight. New York: Ballantine, 1955, 1963, 1975. New York: Harcourt, Brace, Jovanovich, 1972. London: Muller, 1955. London: Sidgwick & Jackson, 1973. [Also included in *Across the Sea of Stars.*]

"Encounter in the Dawn." *See* "Expedition to Earth."

"Exile of the Eons," *Super Science Stories* (March 1950).

_____. *Expedition to Earth,* 1965.

"Expedition to Earth" ("Encounter in the Dawn"), *Amazing Stories* (July 1953).

_____. *Expedition to Earth,* 1965.

Expedition to Earth. New York: Ballantine, 1965, 1968, 1970, 1973, 1975. London: Sidgwick & Jackson, 1968.

A Fall of Moondust. New York: Harcourt, Brace & World, 1961, 1970. New York: New American Library, 1974.

"Feathered Friend," *Infinity Science Fiction* (September 1957).

_____. *The Other Side of the Sky,* 1958.

"The Fires Within," *Fantasy* (August 1947).

_____. *Reach for Tomorrow,* 1956.

"The Food of the Gods," *Playboy* (May 1964).

_____. *The Wind from the Sun,* 1972.

"The Forgotten Enemy," *New Worlds* (May 1949).

_____. *Reach for Tomorrow,* 1956.

"Freedom of Space," *Infinity Science Fiction* (October 1957).

_____. *The Other Side of the Sky,* 1958.

From the Ocean, from the Stars. New York: Harcourt, Brace & World, 1962, 1967. New York: New American Library, 1974. [An omnibus containing *Deep Range, The City and the Stars,* and twenty-four short stories.]

"F.R.S. Robin Hood," *The Magazine of Fantasy and Science Fiction* (December 1956).

_____. *The Other Side of the Sky,* 1958.

Glidepath. New York: Harcourt, Brace, Jovanovich, 1971. New York: New American Library, 1973.

"Green Fingers," *The Magazine of Fantasy and Science Fiction* (January 1957).

_____. *The Other Side of the Sky,* 1958.

"Hate" ("At the End of the Orbit"), *If* (November 1961).

_____. *Tales of Ten Worlds,* 1962.

"The Haunted Spacesuit." *See* "Who's There?"

"Hide and Seek," *Astounding Science Fiction* (September 1949).

_____. *Expedition to Earth,* 1965.

"History Lesson," *Startling Stories* (May 1949).

_____. *Expedition to Earth,* 1965.

"The Hottest Piece of Real Estate in the Solar System." *See* "Summertime on Icarus."

"I Remember Babylon," *Playboy* (May 1960).

_____. *Tales of Ten Worlds,* 1962.

"If I Forgot Thee, O Earth . . . ," *Future Science Fiction* (September 1951).

———. *Expedition to Earth,* 1965.

Imperial Earth. New York: Harcourt, Brace, Jovanovich, 1976. New York: Ballantine, 1976.

"Inheritance," *Astounding Science Fiction* (September 1948).

———. *Expedition to Earth,* 1965.

"Inside the Comet," *The Magazine of Fantasy and Science Fiction* (October 1960).

———. *Tales of Ten Worlds,* 1962 [under the title "Into the Comet"].

Islands in the Sky. New York: Harcourt, Brace & World, 1952. New York: New American Library, 1956, 1960, 1968. New York: Penguin, 1972.

"Jupiter Five," *If* (May 1953).

———. *Reach for Tomorrow,* 1956.

"The Last Command," *Bizarre Mystery Magazine* (November 1965).

———. *The Wind from the Sun,* 1972.

"Let There Be Light," *Playboy* (February 1958).

———. *Tales of Ten Worlds,* 1962.

"The Light of Darkness." (n.d.)

———. *The Wind from the Sun,* 1972.

The Lion of Camarre. New York: Harcourt, Brace & World, 1953.

———. Bound with *Against the Fall of Night.* New York: Harcourt, Brace, Jovanovich, 1968.

"The Longest Science Fiction Story Ever Told." (n.d.)

———. *The Wind from the Sun,* 1972.

"Loophole," *Astounding Science Fiction* (April 1946).

———. *Expedition to Earth,* 1965.

Lost Worlds of 2001. New York: New American Library, 1972. London: Sidgwick & Jackson, 1973.

"Love that Universe." (n.d.)

———. *The Wind from the Sun,* 1972.

"Maelstrom II," *Playboy* (April 1965).

———. *The Wind from the Sun,* 1972.

"The Man Who Ploughed the Sea," *Satellite Science Fiction* (June 1957).

———. *Tales from the White Hart,* 1957.

Master of Space. See *Prelude to Space.*

"A Meeting with Medusa," *Playboy* (December 1971).

———. *The Wind from the Sun,* 1972.

"Moondog." *See* "Dog Star."

"Moving Spirit." (n.d.)

———. *Tales from the White Hart,* 1957.

"The Neutron Tide," *Galaxy Science Fiction* (May 1970).

———. *The Wind from the Sun,* 1972.

"The Next Tenants," *Satellite Science Fiction* (February 1957).

———. *Tales from the White Hart,* 1957.

"The Nine Billion Names of God," *Star Science Fiction Stories.* Frederik Pohl, ed. New York: Ballantine, 1953.
_____. *The Nine Billion Names of God,* 1967.
The Nine Billion Names of God. New York: Harcourt, Brace & World, 1967. New York: New American Library, 1974.
"No Morning After," *The Magazine of Fantasy and Science Fiction* (July 1956).
_____. *The Other Side of the Sky,* 1958.

Of Time and Stars: The Worlds of Arthur C. Clarke. London: Gollancz, 1972.
The Other Side of the Sky. New York: Harcourt, Brace & World, 1958. New York: New American Library, 1959, 1973. London: Gollancz, 1961.
"The Other Tiger," *Fantastic Universe* (June 1953).
"Out of the Cradle, Endlessly Orbiting," *Dude* (March 1959).
_____. *Tales of Ten Worlds,* 1962.
"Out of the Sun," *If* (February 1958).
_____. *The Other Side of the Sky,* 1958.

"The Pacifist," *Fantastic Universe* (October 1956).
_____. *Tales from the White Hart,* 1957.
"The Parasite," *Avon Science Fiction Reader* (April 1953).
_____. *Reach for Tomorrow,* 1956.
"Passer-by," *Infinity Science Fiction* (October 1957).
_____. *The Other Side of the Sky,* 1958.
"Patent Pending," 1954.
_____. *Tales from the White Hart,* 1957.
"Playback," *Playboy* (December 1966).
_____. *The Wind from the Sun,* 1972.
"The Possessed," *Dynamic Science Fiction* (March 1953).
_____. *Reach for Tomorrow,* 1956.
Prelude to Mars. New York: Harcourt, Brace & World, 1965.
Prelude to Space. New York: Harcourt, Brace & World, 1951, 1954, 1961 [as *Master of Space*], 1970, 1973. New York: Gnome Press, 1968.
"Publicity Campaign," *Satellite Science Fiction* (October 1956).
_____. *The Other Side of the Sky,* 1958.

"Quarantine," *Isaac Asimov's Science Fiction Magazine* (Spring 1977).
"A Question of Residence," *The Magazine of Fantasy and Science Fiction* (February 1957).
_____. *The Other Side of the Sky,* 1958.

Reach for Tomorrow. New York: Ballantine, 1956, 1972, 1975. London: Gollancz, 1962. New York: Harcourt, Brace, Jovanovich, 1970, 1973.
"The Reluctant Orchid," *Satellite Science Fiction* (December 1956).
_____. *Tales from the White Hart,* 1957.
Rendezvous with Rama. New York: Harcourt, Brace, Jovanovich, 1973. New York: Ballantine, 1974, 1976. London: Pan Books, 1974.

"Rescue Party," *Astounding Science Fiction* (May 1946).
_____. *Reach for Tomorrow*, 1956.
"Retreat from Earth," *Amateur Science Stories* (March 1938).
_____. *The Best of Arthur C. Clarke* (British edn.), 1968.
"Reunion," *Infinity Two*, Robert Hoskins, ed. New York: Lancer, 1971.
_____. *The Wind from the Sun*, 1972.
"The Reversed Man." *See* "Technical Error."

The Sands of Mars. New York: Gnome Press, 1951. New York: Permabooks, 1959.
   New York: Harcourt, Brace, Jovanovich, 1967, 1972.
"Saturn Rising," *The Magazine of Fantasy and Science Fiction* (March 1961).
_____. *Tales of Ten Worlds*, 1962.
"Second Dawn," *Science Fiction Quarterly* (August 1951).
_____. *Expedition to Earth*, 1965.
"The Secret." (n.d.)
_____. *The Wind from the Sun*, 1972.
"Security Check," *The Magazine of Fantasy and Science Fiction* (June 1957).
_____. *The Other Side of the Sky*, 1958.
"Seeker of the Sphinx," *Two Complete Science Adventure Books* (September 1951).
"The Sentinel" ("Sentinel of Eternity"), *Ten Story Fantasy* (September 1951).
_____. *Expedition to Earth*, 1965.
"The Shining Ones," *Playboy* (August 1964).
_____. *The Wind from the Sun*, 1972.
"Silence, Please," *Science Fantasy* (Winter 1950).
_____. *Tales from the White Hart*, 1957.
"Sleeping Beauty" ("The Case of the Snoring Heir"), *Infinity Science Fiction* (April
   1957).
_____. *Tales from the White Hart*, 1957.
"A Slight Case of Sunstroke" ("Stroke of the Sun"), *Galaxy Science Fiction* (Septem-
   ber 1958).
_____. *Tales of Ten Worlds*, 1962.
"The Songs of Distant Earth," *If* (June 1958).
_____. *The Other Side of the Sky*, 1958.
"Special Delivery," *Infinity Science Fiction* (September 1957).
_____. *The Other Side of the Sky*, 1958.
"The Star," *Infinity Science Fiction* (November 1955).
_____. *The Other Side of the Sky*, 1958.
"The Starting Line," *The Magazine of Fantasy and Science Fiction* (December 1956).
_____. *The Other Side of the Sky*, 1958.
"Stroke of the Sun." *See* "A Slight Case of Sunstroke."
"Summertime on Icarus" ("The Hottest Piece of Real Estate in the Solar Sys-
   tem"), *Vogue* (June 1960).
_____. *Tales of Ten Worlds*, 1962.
"Sunjammer." *See* "The Wind from the Sun."
"Superiority," *The Magazine of Fantasy and Science Fiction* (August 1951).
_____. *Expedition to Earth*, 1965.

"Take a Deep Breath," *Infinity Science Fiction* (September 1957).
_____. *The Other Side of the Sky,* 1958.
Tales from the White Hart. New York: Ballantine, 1957, 1972, 1974. New York: Harcourt, Brace, Jovanovich, 1970, 1973.
Tales of Ten Worlds. New York: Harcourt, Brace & World, 1962. New York: Dell, 1964. New York: New American Library, 1973. London: Gollancz, 1967. London: Sidgwick and Jackson, 1973.
"Technical Error" ("The Reversed Man"), *Fantasy* (December 1946).
_____. *Reach for Tomorrow,* 1956.
"Thirty Seconds - Thirty Days." *See* "Breaking Strain."
"This Earth of Majesty," *The Magazine of Fantasy and Science Fiction* (July 1955).
"Time's Arrow," *Worlds Beyond,* 1952.
_____. *Reach for Tomorrow,* 1956.
"Transience," *Startling Stories* (July 1949).
_____. *Reach for Tomorrow,* 1956.
"Transit of Earth," *Playboy* (January 1971).
_____. *The Wind from the Sun,* 1972.
"Travel by Wire," *Amateur Science Stories,* 1937.
_____. *The Best of Arthur C. Clarke* (British edn.), 1968.
"Trouble with the Natives" ("Captain Wyxtpthll's Flying Saucer"), *Marvel Science Fiction* (May 1951).
_____. *Reach for Tomorrow,* 1956.
"Trouble with Time" ("Crime on Mars"), *The Magazine of Fantasy and Science Fiction* (May 1961).
_____. *Tales of Ten Worlds,* 1962.
2001: A Space Odyssey. New York: Norton, 1968. New York: New American Library, 1968, 1972. London: Hutchison, 1968.

"The Ultimate Melody," *If* (February 1957).
_____. *Tales from the White Hart,* 1957.

"Venture to the Moon," *The Magazine of Fantasy and Science Fiction* (December 1956).
_____. *The Best of Arthur C. Clarke* (British edn.), 1968.

"A Walk in the Dark," *Thrilling Wonder Stories* (August 1950).
_____. *Reach for Tomorrow,* 1956.
"The Wall of Darkness," *Super Science Stories* (July 1949).
_____. *The Other Side of the Sky,* 1958.
"Watch This Space," *The Magazine of Fantasy and Science Fiction* (February 1957).
_____. *The Other Side of the Sky,* 1958.
"Whacky," *Fantasy,* 1942.
_____. *The Best of Arthur C. Clarke* (British edn.), 1968.
"What Goes Up," *The Magazine of Fantasy and Science Fiction* (January 1956).
_____. *Tales from the White Hart,* 1957.
"Who's There?" *New Worlds* (November 1958).

———. *The Nine Billion Names of God*, 1967.

"The Wind from the Sun" ("Sunjammer"), *Boy's Life*, 1964.

———. *The Wind from the Sun*, 1972.

The Wind from the Sun: Stories of the Space Age. New York: Harcourt, Brace, Jovano-vich, 1972. New York: New American Library, 1973. London: Gollancz, 1972.

SECONDARY SOURCES

Aldiss, Brian W. *Billion Year Spree: The True History of Science Fiction.* Garden City, N.Y.: Doubleday, 1973.

Allen, L. David. "Childhood's End," in *Science Fiction: An Introduction.* Lincoln, Neb.: Cliffs, Notes, 1973.

[Anonymous]. "From Icarus to Arthur Clarke," *Forbes* (July 1, 1968).

Gillings, Walter. "The Man from Mine-Head," *Algol*, Vol. 12 (November 1974).

Hock, David G. "Mythic Patterns in *2001, A Space Odyssey,*" *Journal of Popular Culture*, 4 (Spring 1971).

Ketterer, David. *New Worlds for Old: The Apocalyptic Imagination, Science Fiction, and American Literature.* Garden City, N.Y.: Doubleday Anchor, 1974.

Knight, Damon. *In Search of Wonder.* Chicago: Advent, 1967.

Moskowitz, Sam. "Arthur C. Clarke," in *Seekers of Tomorrow: Masters of Modern Science Fiction.* New York: Ballantine, 1967. Hyperion, Conn., 1974.

Plank, Robert. "1001 Interpretations of *2001,*" *Extrapolation*, 11 (December 1969).

Rogers, Robert. "The Psychology of the 'Double' in *2001,*" *Hartford Studies in Literature*, 1 (1969).

Turner, Alice K. "Clarke Interviewed," *Algol*, Vol. 12 (November 1974).

Wollheim, Donald A. *The Universe Makers.* New York: Harper & Row, 1971.

Arthur C. Clarke: A Biographical Note

Born on December 16, 1917, in Minehead, England, Arthur C. Clarke attended Huish's Grammar School in Taunton, where, at the age of thirteen, he began writing about his "fantastic" ideas in the school's magazine. Since he did not have sufficient money for college, he worked as an auditor in His Majesty's Exchequer and Audit Department, which brought him to London in 1936. He was drafted into the Royal Air Force and served during the period 1941–1946. During this time, he went from radio mechanic to flight lieutenant, in which position he worked with the first trials of ground control approach radar. His novel *Glidepath* was formulated during this period. After the war he entered King's College in London, from which he was graduated in 1948 with a First Class Honors B.Sc. in physics and mathematics.

After college he worked on the staff of the Institution of Electrical Engineers as assistant editor of *Science Abstracts,* which kept him supplied with the most up-to-date information regarding developments in science. He was married and later divorced. One of the most significant developments in his life has been the hobby of skin diving which, after he met Mike Wilson, a skin-diving enthusiast and underwater photographer, allowed him to form a partnership. Together, they explored and filmed the Great Barrier Reef of Australia, an experience which provided Clarke with the inspiration for his novel *The Deep Range.* In the context of his underwater activities, Clarke has experienced several close encounters with death. Clarke's explorations in the Indian Ocean took him to Sri Lanka (Ceylon) where he has lived since 1956.

Clarke discovered science fiction in the March 1930 issue of *Astounding Stories,* a magazine carried by the Woolworth Stores in England. He became active in English science fiction fandom. He wrote for the British science fiction fan magazine *Novae Terrae.* During this period he was nicknamed "Ego," the first three letters of one of the pseudonyms he used—E. G. O'Brien. He joined the (at that time) unrespected British

Interplanetary Society, which met in London pubs—a setting which provided inspiration for *Tales from the White Hart. Interplanetary Flight,* published in 1950, was the first of his more than twenty nonfiction publications.

A few of Clarke's short stories and novels are well known outside the science fiction field. His novel *A Fall of Moondust* was selected by Reader's Digest Condensed Book Library, and his novel *The Deep Range* is one of the few science fiction novels ever reviewed in the *Wall Street Journal.* His story "The Sentinel" became the basis for the film *2001: A Space Odyssey.* He was Guest of Honor at the 1956 World Science Fiction Convention, when he won a Hugo for the story "The Star." *Rendezvous with Rama* won both the Nebula and Hugo awards in 1974 and also the John W. Campbell Memorial Award in 1974. A recipient of the Franklin Institute's Gold Medal for originating the idea of the communications satellite, he was also awarded, in 1962, the UNESCO-Kalinga Prize for his achievements as a science popularizer. In 1965 he won the Aviation/Space Writers Association's General Magazine Writing and Robert S. Ball awards for an article on communications satellites. His fiction and nonfiction have sold in the millions of volumes and have been translated throughout the world.

Contributors

PETER BRIGG is an assistant professor who teaches modern drama, the modern novel, and science fiction in the Department of English at the University of Guelph, Guelph, Ontario, Canada. He has published articles in *Science Fiction Studies* and *English Studies in Canada*. Forthcoming articles include theatre history work on the Birmingham (England) Repertory, where he is theatrical archivist.

THOMAS D. CLARESON is Professor of English at the College of Wooster. He has been Chairman of the Science Fiction Research Association (1970–1976) and is a member of the Executive Committee of the Modern Language Association Division on Popular Culture (1976–1980). He has edited *Extrapolation* since 1959. His most recent books include *Voices for the Future* (Bowling Green, 1976), and *Many Futures, Many Worlds* (Kent State, 1977). He is currently at work on a history of American fantasy and science fiction before 1926.

E. MICHAEL THRON is an associate professor of literature who has written articles on Ben Johnson and William Shakespeare for Studies in *English Literature, Renascence,* and *Shakespeare Quarterly*. He teaches humanities courses for the interdisciplinary program at the University of Wisconsin, Green Bay.

BETSY HARFST is chairman of the Communications Division of Kishwaukee College, Malta, Illinois. Her critical works include an unpublished dissertation, "Horace Walpole and the Unconscious: An Experiment in Freudian Analysis"; "*Astrophil and Stella*, Precept and Example," *Papers on Language and Literature*; "The People, Yes: Mandate for Survival," *Community College Frontiers* and "Myth and Symbol in LeGuin's Earthsea Trilogy," 1975 Science Fiction Research Association Annual Meeting.

ROBERT PLANK was originally an attorney in Vienna (his doctorate is in law), worked for many years as a psychiatric social worker, and is now an adjunct associate professor in the Department of Psychology, Case Western Reserve University. He is the author of *The Emotional Significance of Imaginary Beings* (1968) and of chapters in books on C. S. Lewis, J. R. R. Tolkien, and others. He has written extensively on science fiction and wider problems of literature, social work, and psychology in such periodicals as *The American Journal of Orthopsychiatry, American Imago, Journal of Psychiatric Social Work, Extrapolation,* and *Science Fiction Studies*.

ALAN B. HOWES is Professor of English at the University of Michigan, and has also taught at Middlebury College and as a guest professor at Yokohama National University in Japan. He has used science fiction materials in a freshman composition course (Science: Fact and Fiction), where he reports they helped to create a real interest in writing among his students. He is the author of *Yorick and his Critics*, a study of Laurence Sterne's literary reputation, and *Teaching Literato Adolescents: Novels*, and co-author with Stephen Dunning of *Literature for Adolescents*.

EUGENE TANZY is a Victorian scholar who has written on the nineteenth-century novel, Browning, Emerson, Arnold, and other of the eminent Victorians. He is associate chairman of the Department of English and Director of Graduate and Undergraduate Studies at Florida State University in Tallahassee, Florida.

DAVID M. SAMUELSON is a Professor of English at California State University, Long Beach. Author of *Visions of Tomorrow: Six Journeys from Outer to Inner Space* (Arno, 1974), he has published a number of articles on science fiction and science fiction authors. He is also very active in the study if modernism, mythology, popular culture, and futurology.

JOHN HUNTINGTON teaches English at the University of Illinois at Chicago Circle and has published work on science fiction and on Renaissance poetry.

Index

Against the Fall of Night, 40–2, 45, 59, 62–4, 65–6, 196. See also *City and the Stars, The*
Agel, Jerome, 122
aliens, 32; in *Childhood's End,* 72, 76–9, 82, 202, 203–4; in *Rendezvous with Rama,* 79–81, 82–6; in *2001,* 73–6, 82–6, 122, 131–3, 138–9, 140–1
"All That Glitters," 33
"All the Time in the World," 36
Allen, L. David, 57
androids, 134, 135–6, 139–40
Aristotle, 140
Arnold, Matthew, 173
"As Far as Thought Can Reach" (Shaw), 178, 183
Ascent of Man, The (Bronowski), 129

Back to Methuselah (Shaw), 172, 177–92, 195
Before Adam (London), 128
"Before Eden," 67
Beja, Morris, 123, 143
Bell Tower, The (Melville), 136
Bergson, Henri, 102
"Big Game Hunt," 29, 32
biots, 42
Blake, William, 209
Blavatsky, Madame, 56
Blish, James, 149, 158, 171

Bradbury, Ray, 176
Brigg, Peter, 15–51
Bronowski, Jacob, 129
Browning, Robert, 192
Budrys, Algis, 209
Bulwer-Lytton, Edward, 174–5, 191
Burgess, Anthony, 123
Burns, Robert, 119
Butler, Samuel, 209

Campbell, John W., 62, 66, 214–15
Canby, Vincent, 143
Capek, Karel, 136
"Castaway," 36, 39, 45
Cayce, Edgar, 85
Challenge of Space, The, 52, 53–4
Childhood's End: aliens in, 72, 76–9, 82, 202, 203–4; and *Back to Methuselah,* 177, 185–92; characterization in, 153–8; Clareson on, 55–9, 66; evolution in, 162–70, 185–92, 211–13, 216–21; genre of, 151–3; Howes on, 149–71; Huntington on, 82, 211–21; metaphysics of, 35–8, 40; mysticism of, 55–7; myth in, 87, 89, 93–103, 202–5, 211–13, 216–21; Samuelson on, 56, 196–210; technology in, 197–8, 211–13,

216–21; transcendence in, 212–13, 215; themes of, 158–70. *See also* "Guardian Angel"

City and the Stars, The, 25, 36–7, 62, 64–6, 82, 85, 213–16, 218. See also *Against the Fall of Night*

City of Dreadful Night (Thomson), 85

Clareson, Thomas D., 52–71

Clarke, Arthur C.: "atheistical mysticism" of, 84–5; cosmic loneliness of, 68–71; didacticism of, 59–61; enigmatic sentimentalism of, 35–41; nonfiction of, 52–5, 158–61, 212; as propagandist, 61–5; as scientist, 15–27; wit and humor of, 27–34

Clarke's Three Laws, 35

Clockwork Orange, A (film), 123

Coming Race, The (Bulwer-Lytton), 174–5

"Cosmic Cassanova," 28

"Critical Mass," 34

cyborgs, 19

Darwin, Charles, 173–4, 178

Darwin, Erasmus, 178

Deep Range, The, 25–6, 39, 192

"Defenestration of Ermintrude Inch, The," 32

Delany, Samuel, 202–3

Dolphin Island, 36

Doyle, Sir Arthur Conan, 209

Dr. Strangelove (film), 123, 126

Dukas, Paul, 136

Earthlight, 20–1, 25, 46, 47, 52, 60–1, 83–4

Einstein, Albert, 119, 159

Eliade, Mircea, 93, 107

"Encounter at Dawn," 36, 68–9,

103. *See also* "Expedition to Earth"

evolution, 36; in *Back to Methuselah,* 177–92; in *Childhood's End,* 162–70, 185–92, 211–13, 216–21; in *Imperial Earth,* 192–5; responses to theory of, 173–7

"Expedition to Earth," 36. *See also* "Encounter at Dawn"

Exploration of Space, The, 52, 55, 57, 61, 159, 160

Fadiman, Clifton, 158

Fall of Moondust, A, 60

Fantasia (film), 136

"Farewell to Earth," 69. See also *Lost Worlds of 2001, The*

Filmguide to 2001: A Space Odyssey (Geduld), 123, 124, 126

"Fires Within, The," 16, 23, 36

"First Encounter," 69. See also *Lost Worlds of 2001, The*

Fiske, John, 56, 65

"Food of the Gods, The," 29, 34

Forster, E. M., 85, 214

France, Anatole, 147

Freud, Sigmund, 103, 105, 128, 130, 139

Fuchs, Ernst, 128

Geduld, Carolyn, 123, 124, 126

"Gift from the Stars," 69. See also *Lost Worlds of 2001, The*

Gilliatt, Penelope, 127, 128, 146

Gissing, George, 173

Goethe, Johann Wolfgang von, 136

"Golden Age, The." See *Childhood's End*

"Green Fingers," 22

"Guardian Angel," 57–8. See also *Childhood's End*
Gunn, James, 72

Hal (computer), 74–5, 80, 104–5, 121, 134–7, 141–2
hamartia, 140
Hardy, Thomas, 209
Harfst, Betsy, 87–120
Harvard Crimson, 146
Hawthorne, Nathaniel, 136, 140
Heine, Heinrich, 147
Heinlein, Robert, 119
"Hide and Seek," 30
Hillegas, Mark, 198
"History Lesson," 27–8
Hobbes, Thomas, 128, 146
Howes, Alan B., 149–71
humanoids, 134, 135–6, 139
Huntington, John, 82, 211–21
Huxley, Aldous, 29, 32, 209
Huxley, Thomas, 174, 175–6, 185, 188

"If I Forget Thee, O Earth," 54
Imperial Earth, 41, 87; antecedents of, 45–6; evolution in, 192–5; humor of, 48–9; metaphysics of, 49–50; myth in, 87, 90, 114–20; science in, 46–8
Interplanetary Flight: An Introduction to Astronautics, 52
"Into the Comet," 42
Irwin, James, 52
"Is Human Nature Incurably Depraved?" (Shaw), 177
Islands in the Sky, 53

Jung, Carl, 88–9, 103, 107, 128, 185, 191
"Jupiter Five," 16, 33, 36, 42, 49

Khachaturian, Aram, 124
Kipling, Rudyard, 119
Knight, Damon, 204
Koestler, Arthur, 114
Kubrick, Stanley, 103, 122–6, 137
Kundalini yoga, 88, 95, 113

Lamarck, Jean de, 178
Last and First Men (Stapledon), 36, 62, 64
"Last Generation, The." See *Childhood's End*
Le Guin, Ursula, 192
Leakey, Dr. Louis, 128
"Let There Be Light," 22
Lévi-Strauss, Claude, 85
Lewis, C. S., 85, 209
Ligeti, György, 124
"Light of Darkness, The," 46
Lion of Comarre, The, 38, 59, 62, 64–5
London, Jack, 128
"Longest Science Fiction Story Ever Told, The," 28
Lost Worlds of 2001, The, 35, 69–70, 129, 131
Lucian, 136

"Machine Stops, The" (Forster), 85, 214
"Maelstrom II," 18
"Man Who Ploughed the Sea, The," 30
"Martian Odyssey, A" (Weinbaum), 61
"Meeting with Medusa, A," 19, 21, 26, 38, 41, 45, 70–1
Melville, Herman, 136, 140
Moon is a Harsh Mistress, The (Heinlein), 119
"Moon-Watcher," 67–8, 69, 188.

See also *Lost Worlds of 2001*

Morris, William, 85–6, 209

"Moving Spirit," 30, 32–3

myth: in *Childhood's End*, 87, 89, 93–103, 202–5, 211–13, 216–21; in *Imperial Earth*, 87, 90, 114–20; Occidental vs. Oriental, 88–93; in *Rendezvous with Rama*, 107–14; in *2001*, 87, 89, 103–7

Myths and Symbols in Indian Art and Civilization (Zimmer), 106

"Neutron Tide," 28–9, 32

"Next Tenants, The," 37, 42

Nietzsche, Friedrich, 161

"Nine Billion Names of God, The," 35, 37

O. Henry, 54

On the White Stone (France), 147

Origin of the Species (Darwin), 174

Ortega y Gasset, José, 77

Orwell, George, 209

"Other Side of the Sky, The" series, 24, 46

"Out of the Sun," 25, 36, 39–40, 103

Overlords, 154–8, 185–91, 197–201, 216–18; as aliens, 76–9, 82; as Oriental heroes, 95–7

"Pacifist, The," 32, 33

"Passer-by," 34

"Patent Pending," 29, 32

Plank, Robert, 121–48

"Possessed, The," 25, 36, 103

Prelude to Space, 53, 59–60, 61

Profiles of the Future, 158, 159, 160–1

Promise of Space, The, 52, 79, 83

"Publicity Campaign," 34

Reach for Tomorrow, 16–17

religion, 41, 57, 65

"Reluctant Orchid, The," 28, 30, 32

Rendezvous with Rama, 41, 70; aliens in, 72, 79–81; antecedents of, 42; evolution in, 192; humor of, 43–4, 45; metaphysics of, 44, 45; myths in, 87, 89, 107–14; science of, 42–3, 44–5

Report on Planet Three and Other Speculations, 52, 68

"Rescue Party," 36, 38, 41, 42, 49, 54

"Reunion," 28

Revolt of the Masses, The (Ortega y Gasset), 77

"Road to the Sea, The," 36, 38, 41, 65

robots, 136

Rodin, François Auguste, 121, 129

Roger-Marx, Claude, 121

Roosevelt, Theodore, 176

Roots of Coincidence, The (Koestler), 114

"Sailing to Byzantium" (Yeats), 123, 143

St. Exupéry, Antoine de, 127

Samuelson, David N., 56, 57, 196–210

Sands of Mars, The, 46, 49, 53, 61

"Saturn Rising," 25, 53

"Science and Spirituality," 66

Scott, David, 52

"Second Dawn," 23–4, 38

"Secret, The," 19–20

"Sentinel, The," 35–6, 68, 103, 122, 124, 130, 133, 139, 140, 213. See also *2001: A Space Odyssey*

Shaw, George Bernard, 172–3, 177–92, 195
Shelley, Mary, 85, 136, 209
Shelley, Percy Bysshe, 209
"Shining Ones, The," 25, 26
"Silence Please," 30
Skinner, B. F., 165
Skylark Three (Smith), 60
"Sleeping Beauty," 32
Smith, E. E., 60
"Songs of Distant Earth, The," 36, 37–8, 41, 42
Stapledon, Olaf, 36, 40, 41, 62, 70, 161, 209
"Star, The" (Clarke), 21–2, 41, 49, 53, 66–7
"Star, The" (Wells), 70
Star Maker (Stapledon), 36, 40, 42
"Star of the Magi, The," 53
"Story of the Machine, The" (Campbell), 215
Strauss, Johann, 124
Strauss, Richard, 124
"Summertime on Icarus," 18–19
"Sunjammer," 25
Sypher, Willie, 102

Tales from the White Hart, 24, 29, 31
Tanzy, Eugene, 172–95
"Technical Error," 16, 17
technology, 54–5, 61; in *Childhood's End*, 197–8, 211–13, 216–21; in *The City and the Stars*, 213–16
"Thinker, The" (Rodin), 121
Thompson, Irwin, 84–5, 86
Thomson, James, 85, 173
Thron, E. Michael, 72–86
"Time's Arrow," 30, 32
Time Machine, The (Wells), 175–6, 211

Tolkien, J.R.R., 134
transcendence, 212–13, 215–16
"Transcience," 36, 66
"Twilight" (Campbell), 62, 66, 215
2001: A Space Odyssey (book), 53, 68, 70, 196–7; aliens in, 72–6, 79–80, 81; metaphysics of, 35–41; myth in, 87, 89, 103–7; Plank on, 121–48; psychological analysis of, 128, 130, 133, 137–42, 144–8; transcendence in, 213, 215–16. *See also* "Sentinel, The"
2001: A Space Odyssey (film), 69, 83; collaboration on, 123–6; humor in, 125–6; interpretations of, 142–4; Plank on, 126–42; special effects in, 124

"Ultimate Melody, The," 29, 32
Unhinged Doors of Gaza, The (Fuchs), 128

"Vacation in Vacuum," 53
"Venture to the Moon" series, 22, 24, 46
Verne, Jules, 85, 159
Voices from the Sky, 66

Walden Two (Skinner), 165
"Wall of Darkness, The," 17
"Watch This Space," 28
Waugh, Evelyn, 32
We (Zamiatin), 214
Weinbaum, Stanley, 61
Wells, H. G., 48, 55, 70, 85–6, 158, 209, 211; and evolutionary theory, 175–7, 185, 188, 191
"Whacky," 34
"What Goes Up," 30–1, 32

"When Aliens Come," 68
"Who's There," 33
Williams, Raymond, 85–6
Wilson, Angus, 17
Wodehouse, P. G., 32
Wyndham, John, 61

Yeats, W. B., 123, 143
Young, David, 61

Zamiatin, Evgeny, 214
Zimmer, Heinrich, 106